OCTOBER FERRY TO GABRIOLA

by the same author

ULTRAMARINE

UNDER THE VOLCANO

HEAR US O LORD FROM HEAVEN THY DWELLING PLACE

SELECTED LETTERS OF MALCOLM LOWRY

LUNAR CAUSTIC

DARK AS THE GRAVE WHEREIN MY FRIEND IS LAID

October Ferry
to Gabriola

Malcolm Lowry

EDITED BY MARGERIE LOWRY

JONATHAN CAPE
THIRTY BEDFORD SQUARE LONDON

FIRST PUBLISHED IN GREAT BRITAIN 1971
© 1970 BY MARGERIE BONNER LOWRY

JONATHAN CAPE LTD,. 30 BEDFORD SQUARE, LONDON WC I

ISBN 0 224 00532 4

THE PUBLISHERS ARE GRATEFUL TO PETER OWEN LTD.
FOR PERMISSION TO QUOTE FROM *Demian* BY HERMAN HESSE,
TRANSLATED BY W. J. STRACHAN.

PRINTED IN GREAT BRITAIN
BY LOWE AND BRYDONE (PRINTERS) LTD, LONDON
BOUND BY G. AND J. KITCAT LTD, LONDON

CONTENTS

*I wish to express my thanks to William C. McConnell,
barrister, solicitor, and friend, for his help
in all the legal matters in this book.*

M.L.

It is an old story, that men sell themselves to the tempter, and sign a bond with their blood, because it is only to take effect at a distant day; then rush on to snatch the cup their souls thirst after with an impulse not the less savage because there is a dark shadow beside them for evermore. There is no short cut, no patent tram-road, to wisdom: after all the centuries of invention, the soul's path lies through the thorny wilderness which must be still trodden in solitude, with bleeding feet, with sobs for help, as it was trodden by them of old time.

GEORGE ELIOT: "The Lifted Veil"

Al stereless with-inne a boot
    am I
A-mid the see, by-twixen windes
    two,
That in contrarie standen
    ever-mo.

CHAUCER: Troilus and Cressida

OCTOBER FERRY TO GABRIOLA

CHAPTER 1   🍃   *The Greyhound*

Farewell, Farewell, Farewell, Eight Bells, Wywurk, The Wicket Gate. The little house looked all right. So we love forever, taking leave.

The October morning sunlight filled the swift bus, the Greyhound, sailing through the forest branches, singing straight out to sea, roaring toward the mountains, circling sudden precipices.

They followed the coastline. To the left was the forest; to the right, the sea, the Gulf.

And the light corruscated brilliantly from the windows in which the travelers saw themselves now on the right hand en-islanded in azure amid the scarlet and gold of mirrored maples, by these now strangely embowered upon the left hand among the islands of the Gulf of Georgia.

At times, when the Greyhound overtook and passed another car, where the road was narrow, the branches of the trees brushed the left-hand windows, and behind, or in the rearview mirror ahead reflecting the road endlessly enfilading in reverse, the foliage could be seen tossing for a while in a troubled gale at their passage. Again, in the distance, he would seem to see dogwood rocketing through the trees in a shower of white stars. And when they slowed down, the fallen leaves in the forest seemed to make even the ground glow and burn with light.

Downhill: and to the right hand beyond the blue sea, beneath the blue sky, the mountains on the British Columbian mainland traversed the horizon, and on that right side too, luminous, majestic, a snowy volcano of another country (it was Mount Baker over in America and ancient Ararat of the Squamish Indians) accompanied them, with a white distant persistence, and at a different speed, like a remote, unanchored Popocatepetl.

Name:	Mr. and Mrs. Ethan Llewelyn	Seat No. 17
Address:	c/o Mrs. Angela d'Arrivee	Northbound X
	Gabriola Island, B.C.	Southbound
	Date: October 7, 1949	

Important: to insure your return space on the Vancouver Island Limited register your ticket upon arrival at your destination.

| Victoria | Duncan | Nanaimo |

"Well, damn it," he said, "I don't think I'm going to."

"Not going to what, Ethan sweetheart?"

Ethan and Jacqueline sat, arm in arm, in the two back left-hand seats of the Greyhound and once when he saw their reflections in the window it struck him these were the reflections of some lucky strangers who looked too full of hope and excitement to talk.

"Register our tickets at the depot to insure return space. It seems to be tempting fate either way you look at it."

Jacqueline smiled at him with affection, absently, patting him on the knee, while Ethan regarded their ticket again.

Victoria . . . Duncan . . . *Nanaimo hath murdered sleep.*

And in Duncan too, the poor old English pensioners, bewhiskered, gaitered, standing motionless on street corners, dreaming of Mafeking or the fore-topgallant studding sail, or sitting motionless in the bankrupt rowing club, each one a Canute; golfing on the edge of the Gulf, riding to the fall of the pound; bereaved of their backwaters by rumors of boom. Evicted . . . But to be evicted out of exile: where then?

The bus changed gear, going up a hill: beginning: beginning: beginning again: beginning yet again: here we go, into the blue morning.

The vehicle was rounding a high curve and as it turned down toward the valley below, Jacqueline leaned forward for a better view from the right-hand windows: the sea swarmed with islands, and one of them was surely Gabriola.

Gabriola! Ah, if it should prove the right place, her eyes were saying, the dreamed-of place, and the old skipper's house Angela had written about still for sale, and, more important, within their means to buy! Of course, there was this other "lot" they could almost certainly get, but then they'd have to build a house, and that would take so long.

For the Llewelyns, like love and wisdom, had no home.

Jacqueline, he knew, already saw the skipper's house as theirs, as *their* home. Small, but with big sun-filled seaward windows it stood for her, facing the Pacific and the blue mountains of the mainland, while behind, it was guarded by a forest of huge knotted maples and firs and ancient cedars and, against the sky, tall slender alders, swaying . . .

She had a passion for gardening, so for her a garden was all-important. But also the wide verandahs, big cupboards, a stone fireplace: all these delightful (and to Ethan, after their life on the beach in Eridanus, by now almost irrelevant) possibilities, combined with other "conveniences" not long since all but forgotten, would be taking shape in her mind, just as they had no doubt many times taken shape in her mind this last unhappy month of loss and searching—only for her to be confronted by the reality of bare treeless grassless yards, soulless dessicated war-built bungalows, or older houses yet more moribund, for the awfulness of having to live in which no "conveniences" whatsoever would even compensate, homeless homes with stoves full of old bones, and subaqueous basements, neglected and run down during the last years, houses once well situated, but now viewless as Shakespeare's winds, cackling, who knows, with poltergeists.

B

Yet *this* time, she would be thinking, ah this time it would be different, for surely a skipper of all people would be one to have rendered his own house shipshape, even if a retired skipper. As if shipshapeness were the entire question with her either.

> **Gleaming white cedar siding home**
> **Clean as a pin from stem to stern.**
> **Living room, dining room, kitchen with**
> **Sun room off. And two bright bedrooms.**

It was an ironic little chant they had. At this point they would always pause and then add in unison, laughing:

"Only ten thousand dollars down!"

CHAPTER 2 🌀 *The Magician of the Toodoggone River*

*E*than Llewelyn was sharply reminded that he himself was "retired," and that his total income now amounted to not much more
than $10,000 in two years. He was in an income tax bracket more
compatible with the role of public defender he had so often, to his
credit and the detriment of his pocketbook (Ethan was really thinking in this peculiar manner), assumed in the past, and for which
he was still even nationally famous. A prosperous criminal lawyer,
despite this, he had, though still a fairly young man, given up
practice two years and four months ago, three summers and two
winters, after one of the most gruesome and complicated cases he
had ever defended. Well, it was not exactly retirement. Nor had he
made the move because he'd lost this particular case: in part it was
perhaps because, having for so long sincerely believed his client, a
deceitfully benign watchmaker, innocent (and such was Ethan's
genuine train of thought), it had only been to discover, after he'd
saved him from the scaffold, locally in this instance a disused prison
elevator shaft painted bright yellow, that he could not have been
more guilty.

With means, if more than a little diminished means, of his own
Ethan had done what his father before him, likewise a lawyer, had

done, and had once in days past counselled him to do before it was too late, before this might spell an irrevocable retirement. He made a "Retreat." (To be sure he had not been bidden so far afield as had his father, who'd spent the last year of peace before the First World War as a "legal adviser on international cotton law" in Czarist Russia, whence he brought back to his young son in Wales, or so he announced, lifting it whole out of a mysterious deep-Christmas-smelling wooden box, a beautiful toy model of Moscow; a city of tiny magical gold domes, pumpkin- or Christmas-bell-shaped, sparkling with Christmas tinsel-scented snow, bright as new silver half-crowns, and of minuscule Byzantine chimes; and at whose miniature frozen street corners waited minute sleighs, in which Ethan had imagined years later lilliputian Tchitchikovs brooding, or corners where lurked snow-bound Raskolnikovs, their hands stayed from murder evermore: much later still he was to become unsure whether the city, sprouting with snow-freaked onions after all, was intended to be Moscow or St. Petersburg, for part of it seemed in memory built on little piles in the "water," like Eridanus; the city coming out of the box he was certain was magic too—for he had never seen it again after that evening of his father's return, in a strange astrakhan-collared coat and Russian fur cap—the box that was always to be associated also with his mother's death, which had occurred shortly thereafter; the magic bulbar city going back into the magic scented box forever, and himself too afraid of his father to ask him about it later—though how beautiful for years to him was the *word* "city," the carilloning word "city" in the Christmas hymn, "Once in Royal David's City," and the tumultuous angel-winged city that was Bunyan's celestial city; beautiful, that was, until he "saw" a city—it was London—for the first time, sullen, in fog, and bloodshot as if with the fires of hell, and he had never to this day seen Moscow—so that while this remained in his memory as nearly the only kind action he could recall on the part of either of his parents, if not nearly the only happy memory of his entire childhood, he was constrained to believe the gift had actually been intended for someone else, probably for the son of one of his father's clients: no, to be sure he hadn't wandered as far afield as Moscow; nor had he, like his younger brother Gwyn, wanting to go to Newfoundland, set out, because he couldn't find another ship, recklessly for Archangel; he had not gone into the desert nor to sea himself again or entered a monastery, and moreover he'd taken his wife with him; but retreat it was just the same.)

"It is a course the wisdom of which should not be impugned because its objectives, briefly, may often be expressed only in clichés," his Scottish father-in-law, a not unexpected ally, had observed in his solemn oratorial burr. Ethan smiled to himself; the thought of Jacqueline's·father, when he could bring himself to believe in the existence of such a man on earth at all, afforded him keen pleasure. The British Isles beget bizarre sons: and examples of her most fabulous were to be found in Canada. And if Canadian policy (as once with the strategy of the Battle of Britain) was never, according to reliable report, formulated by its higher ministers without recourse by its highest to counsel from the angelic host, and if there were, and their friend the gamewarden in Eridanus swore there were, Englishmen in British Columbia who lived up trees, why not a Scotsman in the Dominion of whom it was said, like Virgil, that he was a white magician? Fantastic though it sounded, Angus McCandless was or had been a cabbalist, and one of high degree, even a sort of Parsifal: this once accepted, if you like *cum grano salis,* his interior life seemed, to a layman, of a transcendent, an almost unapproachable seriousness, though he could discuss aspects of it with anything but seriousness; the humor of the situation entered for Ethan via the fact that the old practitioner of ceremonial magic was also a hard-fisted and tough rancher, farmer, ex-soldier (precisely how he squared his magical activity with his conscience Ethan had never understood, for The McCandless, besides having been a Mason, was also a Catholic). "Before the amassing of money, and in Canada the law is a method of making it appallingly facile," The McCandless had gone on, "you may now consider your own, and my daughter's deeper needs. You may now place health and the pursuit of happiness first, it being a providential thing that your grandfather saw fit to provide in his will for your son's education. Aye. And I am profoundly glad that you are anxious to know yoursel', to discover, if possible, other, profounder capacities in yoursel'. Perhaps after all," he had added with unconscious sarcasm, "you are not essentially a lawyer, even if it is to be hoped you will never lose your affection for the paradoxes and absurdities of the law itself." (Indeed Ethan still lectured occasionally—or had until these last months—on Canadian law, to the changing of which, in certain horrendous items, he yet hoped to contribute.) Another peculiar thing about Jacqueline's father was that, a Scot of Scots, he had not been born in Scotland at all, but in Bordeaux, being directly descended from a Scottish laird who in the ancient days of Bordeaux greatness, was a knight-at-arms in the retinue of the Duke of Berwick, the son of James II and Marlborough's sister, who once held there what approximated to a court-in-exile. One branch of the family had never left the old seaport, and it was on his own parents' visit to these relatives that Angus McCandless had been born. Still half loyal in his heart to the victor of Almanza and the House of Stuart, The McCandless had emigrated to Canada after being informed that several original letters of Montesquieu, discovered in the family archives, were his property. These had been sold to the library of the Arsenal in Paris, though the proceeds didn't get him very far. "As for me," the old magician said, "my life has been full of retreats. In this country I started at eight dollars a month in 1905 on a stock farm working from daylight to dark. There was a retreat for you . . . The following year I got forty dollars a month breaking horses on a ranch in Saskatchewan. Then I rode herd on the Toodoggone River Ranch for twenty-five dollars a month and board. That's two more retreats. In 1908 I took up a homestead sixty miles from Dumble, Alberta. I sold that for twenty dollars an acre after three years homestead duties, which was worse, on the whole, than the Montesquieu Letters. I went overseas in 1914, more in pity than in anger still faithful to Old England—the most unusual bloody retreat of the lot . . . I was invalided home with a leg wound in November 1917 and in February 1919 I bought a poultry farm at Onion Lake, where I lost heavily on account of the low price of eggs."

Finally he'd bought another farm: "And I may say this was all bushland and took me nine years to pay for it working out, which was another retreat for you, and by then of course we had young Jacqueline to look after."

CHAPTER 3 🌀 *Outward Bound*

*E*than had met her one winter afternoon of thunder and snow in 1938 within the foyer of a suburban Toronto cinema, where they were showing Douglas Fairbanks, Jr., in *Outward Bound*. This was a merry euphemism; they had shamelessly picked each other up, a cause of much later laughter between them, since it was a movie house that showed "serious films for high-class audiences," and it had struck them both simultaneously that this of course sanctified such giddiness. Slim and supple, dark-eyed, dark-haired, and incredibly young and passionate-looking—Ethan was not capable of more detailed asseverations in regard to women, as he explained it to her afterwards, her legs were so beautiful he felt as if he had swallowed a bolt of lightning—and lounging by the velvet curtains of the entrance, smoking a cigarette, she greeted him gaily and almost as if they were lovers already. Rouging her lips, she told him she prided herself on her independence, went everywhere unescorted if she felt like it, was a chain smoker, liked to drink gin and orange juice, loved good movies and taught school in an Ontario village: music, French, botany, literature, everything, and had twenty-two pupils.

"It's a little school just outside Norway, about a mile off the main highway."

"—Norway's the town where we used to live part of each year, in Wales, on the Caernarvonshire coast."

"My Norway's just a little place east of Toronto."

Ethan suggested that perhaps she'd consider him as her twenty-third pupil, and added that talking of twos, he'd left Canada when he was two, having been born here in Ontario itself, and hadn't returned until he was twenty-two, which was six years before.

"And how do you find your native country after so long?"

"Big."

She said that her father came from "the old land," and Ethan, taking her cigarette and putting it out in the sand-filled trash stand, remarked that he'd returned largely because of the depression in order to help disentangle his father's affairs in Canada.

"I feel lonely," he said. "Everybody takes me for an Englishman and they seem to hate the English like the devil. Myself, I take pride in saying I'm English even though I'm half Welsh, even though strictly speaking I'm a Canadian."

"I'm Scottish."

"—but are we going to heaven, or hell?" the great voice of one of the characters in the show boomed through into the foyer . . . *"Ah,"* came back the answer, *"But they are the same place,* you see." Had the voice been that of the Inspector, who was supposed to be God, who had come aboard that ship of the dead to judge the passengers? Or was it Scrubby the barman speaking, the "halfway," destined because of his suicide to commute eternally on that spectral ferry between earth and the unbeholden land?

CHAPTER 4   ❧ *Isn't Life Wonderful*

*B*ut from the first Jacqueline and Ethan had been completely at home with one another. They joined a film society showing film classics on Saturday afternoons in an auditorium—it turned out—belonging to the tuberculo-therapic annex of the General Hospital, where they went to see, for a start, D. W. Griffith's *Isn't Life Wonderful*.

Life might be wonderful, or seem so at the moment, but it hadn't occurred to Ethan before that it could be provoked to actual mirth at the mere hint of death or dissolution . . . Yes, uncharitable as it was merely to entertain such a thought here, even in the absence, naturally, of the patients, Ethan and Jacqueline, seated almost alone in the stalls equipped with objects they at first mistook for ashtrays, every time they reflected on their environment vis-à-vis the title of the picture, found themselves, to their shame, beset by promptings to irreverence similar to those which sometimes tempt the kindliest folk to bizarre behavior at funerals. And for a few minutes they actually had a hard time stopping each other laughing out loud. Ethan soon discovered the film was impressing him deeply and in a new and strange manner in which he never remembered being impressed before. The scene was laid somewhere in the Balkans, and the film opened with two young lovers, newly married, being driven from their home, a hut on the edge of the forest, by looting soldiers who killed their parents and then set fire to their hut. Now the lovers were fleeing for their lives, dragging their sole remaining possession: a sack of potatoes. Behind them, distantly, their home burned. The day declined in the forest with a turbulent sky above the trees presaging storm, and the lovers, fearful of more soldiers, or bandits, did not know what path to take. Next, bandits ambushed them and robbed them of their sack of potatoes. Night fell. The defenseless lovers were lost in the forest. All was dark . . . The story thus far had the virtue of its own naïveté but also to their more modern eyes the film occasionally appeared so crude and jerky it was difficult not to laugh now for that reason. But quite suddenly Griffith's genius began to transmute all this, and in such a profoundly beautiful way, Ethan felt it almost beginning to change something in himself. The camera traveled slowly up to the treetops bending in the wind and now you saw the tempestuous sky brighten as the moon sailed out of the clouds. And instead of giving way to despair as the lovers had seemed about to do, they gazed up with a hungry supplication at this wild beauty of trees and stormy moonlight above them, then turned to each other with love, as to say, a supposition confirmed by the subtitle, *Isn't Life Wonderful*.

Ethan, who had his excuses, reflected he hadn't often felt life was very wonderful—certainly not in that way. Still, he must have sometimes gazed at the beauty of trees or the moon or the sea—undoubtedly the sea—in much this fashion, in youth at least, though such yearning was always short-lived with him, short-circuited by embarrassment at himself, the foolishness of the girl he was with, by some feeling of general frustration, more often sexual, or a humble, obscure and complicated sense of ignorance, as from some lack of ratification for what one saw, which perhaps was not what one was supposed to see, or which was not all a finer nature would see. And how many times had not misery or loneliness, or when he grew older, guilt, even complete hopelessness, got in the way? Anyhow, this scene on the screen with the transfigured faces of the lovers gazing up at the moonlight falling through the treetops struck him all of a sudden as so much more poignant than anything he had ever experienced in fact, and seeing it with Jacqueline affected him with so much the more uninhibited wonder, that what happened was extraordinary. It was like deducing the real from the unreal. It was as though the moonlight falling through the trees on the screen inside the theatre, by the transpiercing beauty of the manner in which it was perceived and photographed, gave the remembered moonlight of the world outside a loveliness it had never before possessed for him, nay, gave the earth, life itself, for him, another possible beauty, a new reality somehow undreamed-of theretofore.

But now here was all this, and here he was, aware of Jacqueline's moist hand in his, of both of them trying not to weep, but he could feel it happening by a perfect identity, they were the lovers themselves. Now they saw with the lovers' eyes. It was they who, having lost everything, had not given way to despair. It was they themselves, Ethan and Jacqueline, who were gazing up now at this wild beauty of trees and stormy moonlight above them in rapture, and thanking God for their love, because life was wonderful and they were in love themselves and this was what it was to exist!

The film ended with a similar scene of trees in sunlight with the lovers approaching down a long road, hand in hand, gazing up at the over-arching treetops overhead, then there was only the long road stretching into the future . . . while the next moment Jacqueline and he were standing outside the cinema on a similar deserted road, one of the quiet tree-lined avenues adjoining the hospital grounds; beyond to the right they found a small park, where a few convalescents were walking or being wheeled by nurses, and where now, excited by the film and uncertain where to go (Ethan was still afraid of her youth, didn't know where to take her, and perhaps was a little afraid of himself), they began to drift up and down, discussing the film. Ethan became so enthralled he scarcely knew after a time whether he was talking or simply thinking to himself. Not only was the film not sentimental, he decided, there was no irony in the title. It was, in a mysterious way, the truth, yes even in Keats' sense. (Latterly Ethan, then almost totally ignorant of literature, unless rhetoric be a branch of it, but anxious to prove himself indeed Jacqueline's twenty-third pupil, had taken to reading poetry, Jacqueline having started him off recklessly with Keats.) There was the beauty of truth within which was the truth of love, and the truth of beauty above, which love perceived through its own eyes, and to which it mysteriously corresponded. Something like that. So that if you had love, even if you'd lost all your worldly goods you simply spoke the truth when you said, "Isn't Life Wonderful?"

Suddenly death appeared an enemy, the world (so different from the earth), not less so: then you were a great deal stronger than death too, if you had love, and faith in that love. Ethan waxed impassioned, derivative, contradictory, philosophically profound, personally adolescent. He also felt himself being very entertaining, in the manner of a lover who arouses gaiety with all the ardor of one making love, a gaiety in which, especially when remembered in later marriage, sometimes sounds a note of sadness, as though such moments foreshadowed not only the lightheartedness and companionship of that married life, but its pitfalls, sorrows and bereavements too . . .

As he was saying, only the earth with all its beauty was your friend, and the outward correspondence of your inner nature, when you were blessed with love. And if you betrayed this by too much attachment to the things of the world, love could only revenge itself by appearing in material guise too and bring about your downfall. And it was scarcely Ethan's most logical or original argument for the defense, that that had started out on behalf of "life," nor involved any point of view or law—whether *jus civile, jus divinum, jus gentium,* not to mention *post liminium*—he had ever formerly maintained or thought of maintaining. But certainly it was his most eloquent and persuasive speech, which (while rendering yet more untrue that sentence we read in the novel on our grandmother's shelf: "Seldom can a proposal of marriage have veiled itself in terms calculated to seem less attractive to a beautiful young girl") was no doubt more illogical under the circumstances than anything in it, and, as it proved for him, certainly his most important.

"Ethan, are you saying you love me?"

"Am I—I—"

"Would you do that for me?"

". . . Would I do what—?"

"If we were driven out of our home into a forest with everything gang agley, and all our plans turned round in mid-air and thrown away in an old boot, and there we were with sweet damn all in the world, and everyone against us and nowhere to go, would you still look at the moon like that with me and say, 'Isn't Life Wonderful?'"

Ethan looked up at the moon through the trees which the ratepayers of this district had recently petitioned to have removed as a menace to life, and as old-fashioned eyesores not in keeping with the modern development of this fine section. It was the first time he had so passionately sided with the trees, even though he did not know what kind they were.

"Is that what you feel, Jacqueline?" Ethan, still looking up at the trees under a sky like an illuminated eiderdown, felt suddenly sorrowful and hopeless. "But I'm too old for you."

Jacqueline put her arms around his neck and kissed him. "Aye, you're a sad disappointment to me, with all your sorrow and gloom."

"It's because I'm so terribly in love with you."

"Huh. I've known that for ages."

They stood with their arms about one another. "Oh, I can see we're going to be a terrible comfort to each other," Jacqueline said wryly.

CHAPTER 5   🌀 *A Devilishe Pastime*

*I*t was spring and they walked down the sidestreets toward a field where a game of English rugger was in progress and where, along its edge by the pavilion, near which Ethan had parked his car, trees were already in bloom. Bluebells and crocus and little wildflowers were blowing in the grasses here, and above the sun was shining. Grim Toronto was still a little town called York in this place. Ethan asked what sort of trees these were but Jacqueline seemed still in a strange mood induced by the film they had just seen, *Wuthering Heights*.

"I asked you about the trees?"

"Ah yes, the trees," Jacqueline, who had been gazing, deeply abstracted, at the wildflowers, woke up again, and turning to him suddenly flung out her arm in a graceful dramatic gesture. "Cherry, peach, pear, my God, don't you know that? Don't you see *any*-thing? Except hildy-wildy films with me. And don't you *do* any-thing, besides defend people charged with horrible crimes? I mean. Belong to any clubs, or anything? Don't you *know* anyone?"

"Yes, I belong to a club, composed of other people who defend people charged with horrible crimes."

They were watching the rugger game, Jacqueline rather listlessly, Ethan intermittently, and with some sardonic relish passing such un-Canadian judgments as "Jolly well tackled, sir." Or "Drop a goal, why don't you?" Or "Heel it out of that scrum."

"If it matters, very few people outside my work. And if you want to know too," he glanced about him at the gently tremulous pink-and-white snow of blooms on the trees among which the ball, the consequence of a wildly aimed drop-kick, was bounding erratically, and now, fielded by one of the dozen or so spectators at their end was returned with a heavily expert air, "this is the first time I've ever really *seen* a spring, this time with you, in my whole goddam life. And if you want to know why, it's partly because I was blind, or almost blind, from the age of eight or nine to thirteen or thereabouts, so I never acquired the habit of looking at things, trees and flowers you see, or understanding what nature was about, and anyhow there was no one who cared to teach me . . . But perhaps you'd feel better if I told you I got sidetracked from an important brief last week reading those bits of Hardy and Burns you suggested . . . Wonderful. But it's almost all a revelation to me. Almost all new . . . Back we go into touch—another line out!"

"Ethan, my poor darling!"

"I only told you partly to explain why I still have difficulty in reading, and understanding certain things. I just didn't acquire the habit." Later, he said, at the University, he took to law enthusiastically, "I think I can say because a lot depends on memory," and he'd acquired an encyclopaedic memory of a narrow kind. Otherwise he'd also inherited from his childhood a capacity for concentration and wandering attention about equally extreme. "Anyhow, the way it's worked out—though I won't say I wasn't read *to,* even my father read to me when he felt in a mood to listen to his own voice—and though I must have crashed through heaven knows how many libraries of law books by now, and even have some philosophical training—I've only read about half a dozen serious novels right through without skipping. *Crime and Punishment* . . . I read all that, including the epilogue . . . And I know something about music, and can even pretend to tootle on the clarinet like Mr. Goodman." He said all this quite seriously, looking down at Jacqueline, who made sounds both soothing and admiring.

"But poetry, ancient and modern, was almost absolutely a dead issue with me till I met you, and art, in the sense of painting, is totally beyond my knowledge. I secretly believe the world is flat, and have such godawful difficulty working out my income tax it's come to be a standing joke with the income tax department . . . Well, I'm partly joking now . . . Take a breathah, you fellows! Or let that bloody ball out to the threes—" He turned back to her. "At least *this* isn't illegal any more, or considered a 'devilishe pastime which led to brawling, murther, homicide, and great effusion of blood.' Though can't you just see a Toronto Leet Roll ban after the pattern of the Manchester one three centuries ago 'because of great disorder and the inhabitants charged with makynge and amendynge of their glass windows broken by lewd and disordered persons playing with the foote-ball . . .' I have a lot of apparently useless knowledge like this. I find it invaluable in court."

Jacqueline was laughing. "But you seem to know a lot about this game."

". . . that bit was cheating, really. It sounds as if I'd been making esoteric legal researches but actually I got it out of the *Manchester Guardian*. Besides, it strictly pertains to soccer. I played rugger for three and a half years at an English public school and got to like it a lot, though I never was much good. I had plenty of time to transcend it all, but maybe the damage was done."

"You mean your eyes? But you recovered, didn't you?"

"No. I didn't. I mean from the cruelty. The bloody obscene cruelty of those fiendish little bastards of children when they had somebody helpless like me at their mercy. Pardon me." With suddenly trembling fingers he relit his pipe, then proffered her a crumpled Sweet Caporal from a flattened package. But Jacqueline shook her head abruptly and took out of her bag a small leather-

C

bound case in which lay tightly packed about seven yellowish-brown cigarettes; she selected one and Ethan shielded the match for her, his hands still trembling.

"Caucasian cigarettes," she said. "A gift from a Scottish admirer —they were sent him from Constantinople by a Russian exile." There was no one looking and she kissed him, looking long into his eyes. "But you don't wear glasses."

"It wasn't that kind of trouble. It was simply corneal ulceration, and it can be cured these days in a fortnight or less."

"My dear darling. Did you have such a wretched childhood?"

"Properly speaking I didn't have any childhood at all, though cheerfulness, as they say, would keep breaking in. I hope you'll admit I acquired a sense of humor at least. My father sent me away year after year to prep school—a boarding school in Stoke Newington of which he was one of the directors and which boasted, by the way, of being Edgar Allan Poe's alma mater. I like to think it was, even if most of the old buildings have been pulled down. But once there, divided in their mind, I daresay, as to how to treat such a valued, if useless pupil—they wouldn't let me do any work, or play any games, so I just wandered about the grounds in dark glasses, or a double eyeshade, or one eyeshade, according to the status of my affliction, and had a perfectly wonderful time looking after the headmaster's dog for four years or so. Meanwhile also keeping the head himself, who had a wife unsympathetic on that score, well supplied with whiskey. Well, there was no law in those days against a child going into a spirit merchants, or buying it at the chemists. His brand of usquebaugh was Golden Guinea, I recall . . . Altogether the ideal life."

Ethan also recalled for her that despite these special privileges he'd been kept in a state of semistarvation, was lucky if he saw an egg or a glass of milk in a month, and that the services of one school doctor were dispensed with for having tactlessly argued that gross malnutrition was at the root of the trouble. Following this, an occasional spoonful of malt was added to his diet, apart from which he never remembered receiving any treatment for his eyes beyond zinc ointment, castor oil, and a flogging, when he had a relapse, from a junior master (who had attributed his condition, Ethan did not mention, to "certain dirty schoolboy habits . . ." As had his father, who however, when Ethan was home for the holidays, preferred to beat him over his chilblains with a razor strop, at the same time insisting—which Ethan didn't mention either—how his filthy vice which had probably already led to complete impoverishment of his blood, would result in atrophy, complete idiocy and finally death at the age of nineteen.)

"As I was saying, the old man preferred the razor strop," Ethan went on, "I told you that sort of eye trouble could be cured in a short time today. But my father didn't condescend to take me to an eye specialist until I was thirteen . . . He'd lost Mother some years before all this started and of course I couldn't guess what he was going through at the time. Finally he took me up to London and a Queen Anne Street ophthalmologist put cocaine on my eyes and simply scraped the affliction away in half an hour, like a sailor scraping rust off a deck."

"Good God, Ethan," Jacqueline said, "I never in my life heard such an awful story. Good God, it must have hurt you!"

At the far end of the field a three-quarter broke away from the disbanding scrum, sold two dummies, cut in over the twenty-five, dodged the opposing fullback, changed his course and sprinted at the corner flag, knocking it down as he slithered in to score a try. Not satisfied with that, the captain of his side made the rare decision of selecting the same man to attempt its conversion into a goal. Taking his aim wonderfully, still panting, covered with dirt and blood, the exhausted three-quarter did so, kicking right from the corner of the twenty-five. Curving in from its great wide angle the ball hovered, dropped accurately over the cross bar.

"But if you ask me didn't I have any happiness at all in my youth, the answer is yes," Ethan said. "Bravissimo!" he joined in the renewed applause. "When I was seventeen I left my public school and signed on a sailing ship for five months and went to Ceylon and I was happy when I was aloft. In fact the higher aloft I got away from everyone on board the better I liked it. My best friend of all was the moonsail, which is the highest sail of all, which almost doesn't exist, and I became so fond of it the captain said when I left the ship I better take it home and go to bed with it or I wouldn't be able to sleep, just as the saying is among sailors they won't be able to sleep when they get home unless they hire someone to pour buckets of water on the roof all night. You'd have thought I'd have learned something too from that experience, which was a devilishe pastime in many ways, and you're quite right I did, though it hadn't occurred to me really what till this moment . . . I ran into the bosun in Birkenhead a year after I'd got back—he'd been quite a tyrant on board—and we had a beer together and he said to me: 'Ethan, I wouldn't say you were one of my star turns, but you were a good lad, and I never knew you shirk a dirty job, and now I suppose you're telling all your tiddley friends you had enough experience to last you a lifetime after all we went through on that packet, and you went through with your old bloody bosun hazing you and one thing and the other.' I told him I'd enjoyed a lot of it but on the bad side I thought I'd taken as much as anyone could expect to take on a first voyage, to which he replied: 'First voyage! If you want to be a real hard case like me you'll go back on another ship, worse than that one, with a bloody bosun ten times worse than I ever was, and *that*'ll be your first voyage!' 'You haven't *had* a first voyage yet, son,' he said."

Jacqueline appeared to find his laughter catching, for she laughed herself till she got out of breath, and even seemed to be half crying.

"But at least you *had* a father," she said finally, as the whistle blew prolongedly (the game, probably the last of the season, over, won—to judge from the catastrophic thwackings of approbation the three-quarter was receiving, that now nearly brought the fellow to his knees again—won at the last moment for his side by the last indefectible and indefeasible place-kick, and the players began to disperse toward the pavilion.

"Oh yes, had and have a father. He's living in Niagara-on-the-

Lake again, in the house where I was born, poor old chap. I've grown kind of fond of him, though I'm not much more popular with him now than I was then . . . Sure, I had a father all right all right."

"Well I'll tell you what," Jacqueline said gaily. "*I* didn't . . . That is, I did . . . But I'm a bastard . . . And now we're going to a beer parlour."

CHAPTER 6 🌀 *Niagara*

*I*n the Niagara, a pub from whose suddenly opened door crashed a hubbub like a tape-recording of black brandts in the mating season, sitting in a niche in the Ladies and Escorts, under the notice forbidding alcoholic beverages to minors and Indians, Jacqueline drank her beer and said:

"You've been holding out on me, you're a famous man, I saw your picture in the Sunday supplement last week."

"Quite possibly. I got into the news for breaking up a case based on prima facie evidence a couple of years ago and they've been writing me up ever since."

"You've known me all this time, we're even engaged, and you never once thought there was anything odd about me, you don't know anything about me either."

"No. I didn't. I don't."

"Maybe that's because you've lived so long in England. Well, I'll tell you—" Jacqueline laughed and took a long drink and blew out a flood of smoke from her yellow "Caucasian" cigarette. "It was very interesting. I was picked up on the doorstep as a baby. And just for the record, my father and mother were coming back from the movies . . . No, but what's *really* funny, it was a D. W. Griffith film, *Intolerance*—or maybe *Way Down East*."

Or perhaps (and ah, the eerie significance of cinemas in our life, Ethan thought, as if they related to the afterlife, as if we knew, after we are dead, we would be conducted to a movie house where, only half to our surprise, is playing a film named: *The Ordeal of Ethan Llewelyn,* with Jacqueline Llewelyn), or perhaps *The Ten Commandments,* he resisted a temptation to say. "Go ahead, it seems I wasn't taking you seriously after all."

"It was in Winnipeg, and I'm not joking. That was after I'd been abandoned by my real mother as a child about a week old."

Ethan buried his hands on his face on the table.

"No, please don't say 'Good God, how awful for you,' after all, I didn't know anything about it. Sit up, you fool. My adopted father, that is, he's my real father too—you'll probably like him a lot—well—" Jacqueline laughed again in a certain oblique smoke-wreathed way, and trying to fan off the smoke, that was to become so familiar. "That isn't quite the point either. What I want to make clear is—my *life.*" Like a little tree divesting itself of rain, she shook from herself a merry cascade of laughter. "My father is a magician."

"Oh? You mean he's an illusionist—in show business?"

"Heavens, how he'd like that—no I mean, like Werner Kraus in *The Student of Prague,* that we're going to see at the film society—only a *good* magician, a white one."

"I see," Ethan looked wildly, and said blankly. "—Um, you got as far as their finding you on a doorstep. The white magician, not played by Werner Kraus—"

"Yes, though *that* isn't the point at all. Anyhow they did, and not having any children of their own—my dad and mum, my father and my foster-mother that is—they took me home and in the end adopted me. And they've always been very good to me, and I really loved them. And still do."

With a pang Ethan saw the lonely child lying on the cold door-step under the moon. Assiniboine Street. The Wild Assiniboine! . . . The two figures, the magician, muffled in a dark cloak, and his wife, in coat of shabby karakul, emerge from the back exit, over which glows a single ruby bulb, of the Strand Cinema. Picking up the infant in swaddling clothes they move off down the dark alley under a maze of telegraph wires past the Bone Dry Fertilizer Company. The moonlight falls on their faces, revealing for a moment the pure cold face of the child, slides down the iron of fire escapes. "Fain would I, dear, find some shut plot of earth's wide wold for thee where not one tear, one qualm, would break the calm," Ethan thought, looking, deeply moved, though feeling a sense of complete unreality, around the roaring beer parlour: he caught sight of their waiter and held up four fingers for more beer.

"I thought you ought to know, but now I tell it it doesn't sound interesting at all."

It is bad enough to learn one's home life began by being plucked up as a baby on a January night from a freezing doorstep in Winnipeg without being informed that this sort of thing in England is considered a subject for loud laughter, Ethan was thinking, both the stock-in-trade of Victorian melodrama and a household joke, together with the drunken man embracing a lamp post, father compelled to play Jack-pick-up-sticks, the hysterical wife throwing a flatiron at him, and the deserted woman, also with her chee-ild, in a snowstorm, on Waterloo Bridge. In this category British humor also placed cripples and all those suffering from the pox, and Oscar Wilde, handcuffed, compelled to stand from eleven A.M. to two P.M. at Clapham Junction before being consigned to Reading Gaol. Truly those were right who said the British could take it. It was a pity there was often such a sneering curve to the otherwise stiff upper lip.

"By the way," Jacqueline was saying, "I mean—are you religious?"

"Religious? . . . I've seen so much suffering, heartbreak, so much, sometimes lying awake at night I want to bite trees—I want to travel the world, walk through all the thunderstorms, to put a stop to someone innocent being hurt—"

"I mean do you have any specific religion?"

Ethan shook his head slowly at the terrible beer parlour, shook his head very slowly without looking at her, much in the manner of a doctor at the wheel of the car trying, without taking his eyes off the road, to convey mutely to someone beside him that the injuries of the man in the back seat would not prove fatal. A Niagara of noise, he thought.

"My parents, when in Wales, attended the Church of England. Though my father had a Puritan streak, he had a romantic side too, once went off to Czarist Russia after a quarrel with my mother, when I was three or four. Nowadays there's nothing he believes in. My grandmother—my father's mother that is, actually despised my father, which wasn't surprising since it was her husband made the cash after all, made it in the Cariboo, while it was my father lost most of it—my grandmother was a fanatical Swedenborgian——"

"Anyhow, my father's a real live magician—how do you like that?" Jacqueline interrupted. "Many people think he's crazy as a hoot owl. Will you give me a cigarette?"

"You've got one burning in the ashtray."

Jacqueline smiled, peeling a fleck of yellow cigarette paper from her lower lip. "Father's in Toronto now, lecturing at the Cosmological—I think the Cosmological Society Temple is what it's called."

More beers arrived while she told him for the first time about The McCandless. Since she laughed frequently both at her own remarks and everything Ethan said, it was hard at first, amid this Saturday tumult of the beer parlour, to obtain any sort of clear or plausible picture. But after a while a pattern emerged, and the strangest thing about this pattern was that shortly one found one had taken it for granted, like those inhabitants of Vicksburg, Pennsylvania, he had read about, who, happening to observe one sunny afternoon of the eighteen-seventies an object shaped like a man pedaling solemnly across the sky at a height of three thousand feet, more or less, questioned finally neither their eyes nor their sanity, but watched with interested attention while the forever unexplained phenomenon passed overhead in the rough direction of Maryland.

A religious division had developed in Jacqueline's adopted family because Jacqueline's Scottish foster-mother was and had remained staunchly Presbyterian, whereas The McCandless, in the course of their marriage and his magical and agricultural and military career, had become a Catholic, and this not because he became "converted" to Catholicism—a procedure which would have dishallowed his magical oath—but because from a "magical" viewpoint he generously conceded the Catholic Church to be no less than what she claimed to be: "The Guardian of the Mysteries." For a similar reason, which was another massive thought, he'd once, previously, become a Mason. Jacqueline's foster-mother, who was still living on the prairies, having no children of her own, had latterly adopted other children. But Jacqueline's parents had come to live mostly apart, so she no longer had a "home"; meanwhile her father still made her a small allowance and she was always welcome to stay with either parent when she wished. At present Jacqueline shared an apartment with another teacher on the outskirts of the town, a small bus ride from her school, which until today, despite their declaration of love—their engagement!—and on this dull word what a miraculously bright and wistful transformation was wrought by that love, how it shone with a diamonded light!—was almost all Ethan knew about her.

Ethan smiled courteously, but discouragingly, at a bearded drunk of, now one thought about it, Satanic mien, who had risen at the next table and, detaching himself from a group of six other drinkers seated before at least twenty-six glasses of beer, seemed, standing there, nodding confidentially at Jacqueline and himself (who he perhaps imagined were discussing lacrosse or horse racing), threatening to come over and join them.

". . . But that doesn't mean one can really laugh at people like my father," Jacqueline was saying, through the din. "Oh, it's all holy enough in its way, all too holy. But it's colossally complicated too— oh, you nearly have to be a higher mathematician to understand most of the gibberish. Oh holy gibberish!" She sighed. "All I can say is that *he* thinks it's important, poor man, and maybe it is. Anyhow latterly—and what do you think of this?—Daddy's had the idea that people like him are needed to combat the evil side of it all, which he maintains is flourishing now more than it did in the Middle Ages. He's got a bee in his bonnet about Hitler, for example."

"*Ich auch*. Who wouldn't?"

"But he says that on this side too there're evil forces at work—and that there're some alchemists too among the scientists, like an old wizard friend of his in Cleveland—and that in a few years they'll have the power to blow the whole world to smithereens—it sounds crazy, doesn't it?"

"Yes, and dangerous too," said Ethan.

"Well," said Jacqueline, "I never caught on to the Catholic religion, or any religion particularly, and Father counselled me never to give over my will into the hands of another power—not even his. Will you order some more beer, the waiter's looking at you."

"To holy gibberish," Ethan raised his glass.

But Ethan felt his brain reeling, despite these noble sentiments on the side of latter-day earnestness and good behavior, the Middle Ages closing over him. God knows in his profession he'd had glimpses of some curious ways of existence . . . One's common or garden conception of betrothals, streets, houses, family life, was here suddenly overthrown. Jacqueline's story of her upbringing would have been frightening had she not been so funny about it. It was not only that The McCandless, as he was later to find out for himself, literally thought of nothing else but the great "Plan" of the universe (what was more extraordinary here was perhaps that the average person never reflected, unless solipsistically, about such matters at all), but thought of himself, if with a saving Highland cynicism, as a single factor whose conduct vitally affected it. If he so much as marked out a chicken run, it was the reciprocal path of the Hierophant that he was tracing, "which would always have an influence horizontically across the Abyss of the Tree below." The humblest piece of gardening—the laying out, say, of a walk between the strawberry beds and the loganberries, or the setting up of a scarecrow, would elicit from him, Jacqueline was saying, some such phrase as "This you see is the path of the Hanged Man which will always leave him suspended from the reciprocal path of the Star, or Aquarius, of the next 'Tree' while he is seen below Tiphereth—that's him over there—on his own Tree . . ."

"You can imagine these sort of conversations going on between him and Mother on the farm," Jacqueline said, "punctuated by other arguments about the price of harrows or thrashers or whether one should buy thirteen yards of well-rotted cow or what not, or how much alfalfa one should plant that year, and always Mother accusing him of inviting hellfire down on us all—you couldn't help liking him, though I doubt not in another age he'd have been burned at the stake, and I'm not sure he'll go free in this. But none of this was what I really wanted to tell you."

She gave him a long, dark, almost savage look, at the same time pleading and humorous, which was later also to become so familiar, then she said very quickly: "You see, my adopted father is my real father, I mean I'm his bastard, my own mother committed suicide. No, please don't say anything. Just let me tell you."

"Tell me."

"*She* made *sure*. They found her hanging in a gas-filled flat."

"She *hanged* herself?"

"She hanged herself."

CHAPTER 7 🌀 *A Grey Hair in God's Eyebrow*

*E*than took her hand across the table and held it for a moment, but she drew it away, gulped her beer, talking impetuously, almost incoherently now, it seemed to Ethan, and as Saturday afternoon resoundingly merged into Saturday night the pandemonium within the Niagara grew so demoniacal he could hear only part of what Jacqueline was saying. Furthermore there appeared to be two versions of the story, and Jacqueline jumped without warning back and forth from the first to the second; the one, based on the construction the coroner and the general public had put on the tragedy, the other, The McCandless' own.

He had gone overseas in the Great War, he and Jacqueline's foster-mother had been married only a short time, and when he returned, wounded, late in 1917, they had found it hopelessly difficult to take up their lives again. Apparently their physical incompatibility couldn't have been more complete, but not unrelated to this, there were spiritual divergences yet more sundering. Not strong enough to resume farm work immediately, The McCandless sought ever-increasing refuge in his occultist activities which, having now some cause to be jealous of them, his wife challenged him to give up altogether. This resulted in their separation for several months and during this period Jacqueline's father had a short-lived but violent affair with her real mother whose name (her middle name was also Jacqueline) was Flora McClintock, a beautiful and wild girl of Highland stock, an intellectual, and a Scottish patriot, but who had been born in Nova Scotia.

At the inquest, and apparently quite without consulting the finer points of the evidence, they had turned on the brokenhearted McCandless all the mountain howitzers, skoda guns, spavined horses and mules available to the moral forces of municipal Canadian nonjudicial opinion, shortly to become popular opinion, had blasted him up and down as a "moral leper," as one—a touch that would have pleased Von Stroheim—whose conduct had been unworthy of an "officer and a gentleman" (The McCandless having refused a commission had been a master-sergeant of cavalry in the Royal Caledonian Horse serving with which he had won the DSM), held his status as a Canadian itself in question, not so surprising since there was no such thing as a bona fide Canadian citizen in those days—in fact there was no such thing then in 1938—and even raised the possibility of his deportation (whether to France or bonny Scotland or the sixth dimension was another matter) and all this to his credit Angus McCandless mostly endured in silence.

It was assumed, as such things are so often publicly given the impression of being assumed, that he had ruined this "innocent and penniless girl," not merely in the accepted manner, but also by his "corrupt and immoral practices" and his "evil rites." (Ethan, who'd since defended a man who called himself a "practicing astral healer" from a charge of rape brought by one of the man's clients who'd patently attempted to seduce him—whereas she claimed he had, on the contrary, persuaded her against her will to undertake with him an astral journey to Venus, couldn't help wondering if the statistically large number of involvements in such ugly human scandals by "honest" practitioners of the occult were not part of the price they had to pay for being what they were, or what they thought they were, as if this might be, for their pretensions to the superhuman, their inevitable human penance.)

But the actual facts, as Ethan now began to perceive them, were far more sympathetic to his father-in-law-to-be, the more so since he'd clearly lost the only person he'd ever truly loved, and as far as Ethan was concerned, much more sympathetic to Jacqueline's real mother, who appeared as a unique person, and an interesting and astonishing one. About the only true thing to emerge from the inquest was that Flora McClintock was a magical pupil of Angus McCandless at that period, if scarcely a neophyte. (She had ably and with professional zeal come to his assistance in a feud he was currently waging with the Rosicrucians, a society he had not forgotten to bait, however, even in his days with the Royal Caledonian Horse.) The irony was that The McCandless not only had *not* "ruthlessly cast her adrift after making her his mistress," as the coroner's jury's verdict asserted, but had actually, and passionately, wanted to marry her, and this before ever she became pregnant, a knowledge, incidentally, that had not for some reason been imparted to him. Jacqueline's foster-mother would not consent to a divorce (Angus was not in his Catholic period then), and the second objection, which might have seemed to many more of a recommendation, was one affecting The McCandless pride. Far from being penniless, Flora McClintock had much more money than he had. She was a relatively wealthy woman who preferred to live in conditions nearly resembling poverty, at the same time being extremely generous and in the habit of giving large sums away. But the third and most potent reason was that this magical pupil, whom the hapless magician considered his intellectual superior, who combined an interest in ceremonial magic with anarchy, was besides one of the early Scottish nationalists and was distantly related to a Scottish lord of session, and did not believe in marriage at all.

Anything was better than to accept the social lie, or such was Flora McClintock's pose. Her sole concession to the human norm, it seemed, was to have fallen madly in love with The McCandless, and her influence on him was to be seen partly in Jacqueline's own upbringing. But she must have eventually come to hate Angus more, at least at one time, and this for reasons by no means apparent. To begin with she had not disclosed her pregnancy to Angus, and when at the fourth month she found it becoming impossible to conceal this much longer, she had with sudden and inexplicable felinity driven the poor McCandless away and refused thereafter, on hearing he had revisited Jacqueline's foster-mother on this first occasion, to see him again. Most perplexing of all was to discover any valid motive, other than the false one established at the inquest, seeing the sort of person she was, for the suicide itself. Here again, her father said, she had sometimes threatened it but (Ethan winced at Jacqueline's words) to do this simply out of curiosity. Certainly there had seemed a motive of revenge in her two related melodramatic actions. But it was all very unlike the most abnormal workings of ordinary jealousy. In a way, and such was Jacqueline's opinion, it had been more like a chastisement, an act of unbalanced yet total and final rebellion against what she considered The McCandless' own apostasy—though what choice he had had considering her treatment of him was not clear—in having "gone over to the enemy" by having returned meantime to live with his wife. In any case Ethan's little Hardyan fantasy about Assiniboine Street had not been quite accurate. Jacqueline had been left on The McCandless' own doorstep, with a note pinned to the blanket she was wrapped in leaving no doubt as to her identity. On the same day, and before Angus could reach her, Flora McClintock killed herself. The fact that she had been living with someone else in her deceitfully poverty-stricken flat shortly before Jacqueline was born never came out at the inquest. Nor that, with magnificent illogic, she had left all her money to the Rosicrucians.

At this point in Jacqueline's recital some people at the next table, unable to attract the waiter's attention, started banging their glasses on the table and Ethan lost track completely of what Jacqueline was saying.

". . . and so you see, through Mother, that makes me also one-eighth Indian," Jacqueline's voice emerged brightly out of the brouhaha into another lull as the drinkers' glasses were returned replenished, "and you are breaking the law in yet another way by bringing an Indian into a pub."

"An Indian——? I don't think . . . Anyhow, if it does I was breaking it eightfold the other afternoon in Oakville, where I dropped into a pub and fell in with the chief of the Mohawks. I don't believe anybody would have dared to refuse him a drink. He's a client of mine, in a way—he once called on me to help in the case of a fellow Mohawk in trouble. Are you a Mohawk?"

"Assiniboine. Like the street. Sioux. It was a coincidence, simply."

"Oakville—" he said and then was silent.

"?"

"Oh . . . I thought it might be a wonderful place for us to live, there right on the lake . . . and unspoilt as yet . . . Of course with this showdown with Hitler that seems to be coming they may start moving in Moxo—Alas my poor brother! Or some other indispensable war industries . . . Still, one can hope not. There's a judge's old wooded estate, on a rural route, that's being broken up into lots—you could get a lovely place with the lawn under the Judas trees going right down to the lake . . . There's the advantage of a school nearby."

"Oh, you're extending me the privilege of going on working after we're married." Jacqueline gave him a tender look.

"I didn't mean that . . . If you want to, of course . . . Maybe I was being a bit previous . . . I was thinking . . . The point is, the judge built five or six really beautiful little homes there, but quite widely separated. But his old edict stands that more houses can't be built on his property. And it's a huge estate. He had other more uncomfortable edicts, such as that no one even after his death can smoke on the property, but I don't think anyone's going to pay much attention to that. He was an eccentric old duck, with a terrible fear of fire . . . In effect, you have acres upon acres of elbow room." Suddenly he said passionately: "I can't stand the idea of all the heartbreak and homelessness you've been through!"

"Oh for God's sake, please don't feel tragic over me, because I don't."

"I love you."

"But the whole thing is, Ethan dear, it's made me a bit of a

D

snob . . . I'm proud of being part Indian and I'm even more snobbish about having a great-uncle who had a title. And The Mc-Candless too. After all, he *is* The McCandless, even though the McCandless clan are not so very large or important, and he left Scotland when he was a very young man, and it doesn't mean so much any more, this chieftain business. Still, I'm glad. Sometimes it's the only way I can reconcile myself to being a child of passion, of being a bastard. I don't like to think of myself being conceived in a place like this, even if I was. It somehow washes the footmarks off the pillowslips a little, if you see what I mean." She laughed.

"Great God, how your mother would not have approved of those sentiments!"

"So you don't see what I mean," Jacqueline immediately took him up. "You don't see at all—yet."

Ethan, eating from a bag of potato chips bought from a crippled vendor the waiters hadn't the heart to deny entrance, noticed that the tables on the "Ladies and Escorts" side of the "parlour," as a touching little tribute to the genteel, wherever they had survived the assaults of the table-bangers, were covered with tablecloths, observed after a while, a wide brass-railed companionway leading to a higher roped-in level with more tables to accommodate an overflow nearer closing time, the ceaseless murmuring and clattering and battering and monotonous ships-engine-like clamor, the whole place suggested a nightmare dining saloon of indeterminate class far below decks in a transatlantic liner (or, for a moment of stillness, one of those "trick" illustrations, apparently intended half to suggest such a liner's dining room, but with the subscription by the artist: What's wrong with this picture?), observed he was afraid she didn't get much support from his side of the family, though he *had* had an ancestor in Canada's first Parliament in Niagara-on-the-Lake— "It was he first built the house, though Grandfather renovated it—my father's living in it with a housekeeper who is a horror, a long-suffering Negro butler who was a Pullman porter, and a Yugo-slavian practical nurse, which house incidentally I may inherit with luck, so we can have one on *both* sides of the lake"—he passed her the bag of chips—"It's sometimes pretty hard to think of the old man as even a Canadian at all. I've occasionally put it down to the fact that he was such a British chauvinist at heart he'd begun by being ashamed he was originally Welsh or that we had miners at one time, and for that matter even coal-heavers, in the family—I remember one drunken wooden-legged uncle with a great sack on his back with affection—well, one has to be sympathetic. Grandfather really made the pile—the family'd fallen into the discard meantime—and Dad didn't have quite so adventurous a spirit, and no doubt his idea of the success story was to be a sort of Canadian in reverse, like Lord Beaverbrook, and to become Lord Barkerville of Norway. For my part I've never been allowed to think of either Norway or Niagara as home and so as a consequence I don't."

"Now you're looking all tragically at me again."

"I was thinking of your father and how much he must have suffered."

"He did. He suffered abominably. But he always had pretty harsh ideas on the subject of remorse. And after he became a Catholic they became harsher."

"But it's a terrible thing to feel you've been even partly responsible for somebody else's death."

"So far as his own guilt was concerned—and you'd have to know Father to know he wasn't being callous—he said that it was of less significance than as if a single hair had gone grey in God's eyebrow."

"As if . . ." Could one only believe it were true, that one's guilt meant so little. Or so much.

Ethan went out to buy some hamburgers (which, like the potato chips, it was illegal to bring into a beer parlour) and when he returned he found himself alone. And as a matter of fact this was illegal too in Canada. If Jacqueline were away too long he'd have to move out of the Ladies and Escorts over to the Men's side, though it was a ruling seldom enforced outside of reason in these days. What a country of fatuous prohibitions! When would they grow up? What would people like his grandfather have made of it? It wasn't as if they made use of what freedom they had—the Niagara, in common with a great many pubs in Ontario, was licensed to serve wine, but almost none of them did so, a supersession deplored by his father, a teetotaler all his life, and dying of cirrhosis of the liver, who was still president of the Vintner's Association, Niagara-on-the-Lake being a town that adjoined the vineyards on the peninsula. Quebec's liquor laws were more sensible.

Why on earth was Jacqueline so long? She'd gone to phone the friend she shared an apartment with that she'd be late. . . . Dear God, what a history was hers. And his! Suddenly, his sense of guilt increasing intolerably as he sat on alone, with his wretched hamburgers concealed on a chair, Ethan felt he simply had to tell Jacqueline about Peter Cordwainer. He tipped their waiter, asking him to keep their places with the beers still standing on the table, and asked to be paged when Jacqueline returned. Then, though he hadn't been asked to shift, he went next door to have a bottle of eastern ale and think how to approach the subject. How to tell about—Peter Cordwainer.

CHAPTER 8

🌀 *"Really, Serving Mother Gettle's Soup Is Lots Simpler"*

Seated by himself, half hidden in the Men's parlour, though warmed by the excellent bottle of ale, Ethan was possessed from head to foot by the sensation of his own loneliness without Jacqueline. He didn't want to eat his share of the hamburgers without her, though they were growing cold, and had that been his object in being seated so askance. From that small absence of hers had taken root, too, for the first time, the full consciousness of how lonely he'd been all his life. He hadn't wished to admit to himself that his whole life since the business of Peter Cordwainer had been in the nature of self-inflicted penance, just as what had happened to him in childhood had been a similar penance, only inflicted on him from outside. And that former was a penance which also, despite his career, that might have seemed to contradict this, had essentially cut him off from mankind. Though he'd never really got to know any of his clients, with the possible exception of old Henry Knight—and what had happened to him by the way?—he identified himself with them completely, and no guilt was too bad for him to be able to identify himself wholly with its subject even while passionately declaring that subject's innocence. Beyond any self-love involved, he knew there was latent a genuine and compassionate love of humanity somewhere in this, but it was not a love that had ever made him feel *part* of mankind. He stood apart, self-condemned, a kind of pariah, and imperceptibly his colleagues had come half to feel this too, without being able to give a reason for it, and no matter how they might personally like him, or admire his talents. Jacqueline was right—and he had been right too, that afternoon—he was also like an actor, but like an actor continually playing the part of one engaged in his own self-defense. His life had been less a life than a sort of movie, or series of movies. But now perhaps his penance would be over. He had taken enough punishment, had been punished, for one thing—and this was surely something of rare occurrence in a man of his age—by never having known what it was really to love before. But with Jacqueline, he need never be lonely and homeless. He would need no longer to feel himself so cut off. Now there would be someone else to think of who must, whatever she said, have often felt as lonely and homeless as himself. Gone, anyhow, was the savagery of this afternoon. His whole heart went out to Jacqueline as to some deep wound of homelessness he sensed in her and longed to assuage. Good heavens, the way in which she had told her story, detachedly, wryly, jesting, her tone mostly that of enthusiastic high-school gossip about beaux or jazz orchestras, the substance of her worlds not more strange and primordial than had they concerned some changeling brought up by the Demogorgon. It had given Ethan at one point a sudden awful feeling of being situated in a chaotic limbo at the very outermost fringes of the world, no, peripheral to it, beyond it, where one could not imagine that this beer parlour with its eternally recurrent ranged batteries of soapsuds-filled glasses on the bar was spinning on the same axis as he did, at the centre of the world, Piccadilly Circus and the Pantheon.

And meantime what a lonely home from home was the Men's

side of a beer parlour in a great Canadian city. Nowhere in the world perhaps were there similar places whose raison d'être is presumably social pleasure where this is made harder to obtain, nowhere else places of such gigantic size, horror and total viewlessness. And you wouldn't have thought at first you *could* be lonely, even by yourself, especially on Saturday night, for if they were the hugest and ugliest drinking places on earth they were probably among the most crowded and so with that much more possibility of invitation to the human fellowship that exists. And exist of course it does, in those rare cases where it can survive the evil-favoredness of the surroundings. But beer parlour! Yes, their final ghastly malevolence was summed up in that one genteel and funereal substantive, once and for all: in that too, within their gloomy, music-bereft and often subterranean portals, you were obliged to drink nothing but that drink which of all alcoholic drinks perhaps most powerfully suggests gardens, song, merriment . . .

It seems that man if alone cannot resist gazing at his reflection while drinking, however horrible the result, and a huge flawed mirror running down one side of the parlour produced the illusion from time to time that everyone was talking to himself. And perhaps essentially it was so. But now Ethan became aware of something very curious. Even in sombre places like this, and not because of the menace, he had always remained half-conscious of his isolation from his fellow man. He'd tended to *see* people in groups, integrated among themselves, excluding him—"See—that fellow sitting over there in the corner, I'm not sure I like the shifty look of him, he isn't one of *us*," he could feel people saying of him, with a suspicion that could quicken in his returned glance to enmity as easily as his heart could be touched by a look of warmth. But now he found himself looking at the faces about him with a quite new affection. He saw that these were just the same kind of tragic, isolated individuals as himself. Like himself; yes, but not like. For never before, despite all the material advantages of his life, had Ethan seen himself, as now, a creature of luck. And this newfound knowledge he accepted with humility; on account of it gazed around him with that much more sympathy and love. The two poor, shabby, half-starved lone old Englishmen seated under those fake ye olde coache and horses lanterns, in which burned sinister bulbs that had glowered all this spring afternoon, still fostered some crepuscular illusion that this was their favorite brew (and who dared say the English were not a great and tragic race when even their favorite drink was bitter?), what brokenhearted destiny had they to look forward to? What loveless, lonely, misbegotten haunt of collapsed illusions to which they hoped to crawl back, supposing them capable of reaching it—Yes, and what of that ancient, bearded and turbaned Hindu, wafted here by some freak of irreligion, and now on the point of being thrown out, and to whose rescue he wanted to go, though it was already too late—what lonesome, battered, dirty old squatter's shack down by the waterfront did he live in he would not see till after a night in gaol? And then, what voice of love would welcome him? And that Negro, perhaps a Barbadian, who seemed dancing even while sitting down, and glancing nervously about him, in a sort of paroxysm of laughing terror, who, though it was anything but a warm evening, had brought a lump of ice with him, and having first put it in his beer, was now pretending enthusiastically to suck at it? Or this poor fellow trying in grisly travesty to sell one of his front teeth that had just fallen out. Had these people got homes, or had they come here to escape from them? And having escaped from them, what was it they found here, or rather, alas, what was it that they would not find? Could never, or so rarely, or so pitifully find, and having found, what then? Roofs of a fallen sort over their heads they might have, but drink was the only tie-beam of their despair. And to transpose but a single letter of that word "home," what *hope* did they have? Or hope or love that could compare with his, Ethan Llewelyn's, the hope and love that was bestowed on him now mercifully through Jacqueline? And it was not merely of these obviously hapless mortals he had this feeling, but of everyone in the beer parlour.

What had that large prosperous Canadian, of benign demeanor, in tweed sports coat, smoking a pipe, and leaning back comfortably with folded legs on the opposite chair reading a book entitled *Devils in the Dust,* who seemed to be the only one reasonably happy and contented to be where he was—what had he of luck or romance in his destiny to compare with his own? And being sympathetic with him he felt all the fonder of this man too.

It was as though through his sudden overwhelming conviction of his own good fortune in loving and being loved by Jacqueline he possessed all at once a sublimated and all-embracing love of all mankind. He had forgotten about Peter Cordwainer altogether . . .

This mood of empathy and personal luck extended itself to positive bonhomie in the men's washroom, where two youths of wild appearance, standing up drinking from a bottle in the shoulder-high lavatory stall, offered him a snort of hard liquor. Gin. He handed the bottle back, wiping its mouth with his coat-sleeved elbow before replacing the cap, with exaggerated thanks for the generous, almost sublime gesture, it seemed to him in his exalted state of mind—considering how depleted the state of the bottle. Yes, his acceptance by the human family had already begun. All the more heartwarming it should first come from a younger generation!

But that sullen depressing monotone in here, that murderous sound of machinery, like a noise of death, that whirring crashing gruesome noise of weeping and gnashing of teeth, punctuated by those rushing gobblings at recurrent intervals when the idols of the urinal gushed forth and the antiseptic phosphorence swept weepingly down the drain, and his perception of all this in these hellish terms even as he was telling himself what a child of hope, and now of virtue and good resolution he was, might have forewarned him he was not altogether unwatched by destiny.

For it was every bit as if it had been waiting for him, planted there on purpose, or some malefic force had enticed him into the washroom, with the express object of showing it to him at this particular moment. On the floor lay a discarded page of a newspaper, in the middle of which was framed an advertisement that, for all its complete absurdity, could not have struck his eyes more violently had it been ringed with hellfire.

MOTHER GETTLE IS MOVING WESTWARD
For 75 years established in Quebec
Now following the traditional path of Progress
Opportunity and Freedom

SHE IS MOVING WEST
Soon to have established factories in
Ontario, Saskatchewan, Alberta,
And finally in British Columbia
Helping to build

A NEW CANADA
And bringing at these troubled times
Work to the Workless
Homes to the Homeless.

MOTHER GETTLE'S KETTLE-SIMMERED SOUP. M'MM. GOOD!
MOTHER GETTLE SERVES HUMANITY
(Sherbrooke, Quebec, Canada. Also London, England, Pontypridd, South Wales.)

CORDWAINER PRODUCTS

Ethan raised his eyes slowly to the mirror above the washbasin, lowered them once more to the newspaper on the floor.

If the offspring of one pair of flies lived to maturity the entire surface of the earth would be covered to a depth of 47 feet in one season.

He was informed . . . It was not a *Toronto Star* either, but part of a western paper. The *Vancouver Daily Messenger*. "And finally

British Columbia!" Ethan raised his eyes slowly to the mirror again. How many times lately had he discovered that Mother Gettle was haunting him? Very occasionally he'd seen a scattered hoarding, scarcely ever a newspaper advertisement. And not since the winter at least, not since, now he thought of it, he'd begun meeting Jacqueline regularly. Oh, he'd seen isolated advertisements commending or commemorating the product, mostly when glancing over the Quebec newspapers, but not so frequently it had given him that frightening feeling he'd had of old of being actually hag-ridden by the thing. It had seemed to him he'd been "getting rid of it," at least he'd never seen the hoarding with the picture of Peter himself as a boy on it, for years. He had practically allowed himself to assume the business must have failed, or as good as failed, in the depression, like so many others, and himself been given absolution in the process. He had all but forgotten Peter Cordwainer himself for whole months at a time. But now it seemed that by the very act of starting to think again about Peter, wanting to tell Jacqueline about him, he had conjured the family firm back to life again, given it such life as it had never possessed before, at least in Canada, caused it to start expanding, start moving west to Toronto, over the whole country, the whole world, so that in the end perhaps there would be no place on earth he could hide his head without being reminded every day, every hour, through the fatuous medium of Mother Gettle's Soups, of Peter Cordwainer himself and what he, Ethan, had done. *Llewelyn,* meaning unknown. Ah, that sorrowful, humorous, subtle, Protean, too honest, too innocent face you have, Ethan Llewelyn. Was that a human face anyway that regarded him from that mirror, or the face of a sort of devil, or of one who had once played the part of the devil . . . What mask had it assumed that night in Peter's rooms at Ixion, at the University of Ely! If only he had not gone out that night for that last bottle of gin. "Let the bugger die!" they had shouted that night in the Headless Woman just before closing time—And there was no question of the kind of expression his face wore now. It was one of mortal agony. And behind it despair suddenly seemed written in letters ten feet high.

CHAPTER 9   ✾ *Called to the Bar*

M_{r.} Ethan Llewelyn wanted in the next bar, please!"

He'd heard himself being paged over the loudspeaker (the ar-
rière-ban, the twice repeated call to arms, to action that must not
only transcend the past, but the claims of the devil himself—after
all, he hadn't quite sold his soul to the devil that night, had he?!
there were extenuating circumstances; maybe he hadn't sold it at all
—it was just that the devil, like a confidence man taking advantage
of a man blind drunk the night before, liked to insist he had made
the bargain), heard himself paged the second time as he came out
of the washroom, and Ethan felt his long elbowing walk, past the
countless tables of the Men's parlour from which all eyes seemed
turned on him rendering him outcast again, becoming an ordeal . . .
But his spirits rose when he caught sight of Jacqueline beckoning
from the other room, and they greeted each other with a rush of
love.

"Awfully sorry I was so long phoning," she was saying gaily as
the waiter, with a welcoming tray of beers, beamed above them like
a benevolent father, "I was just telling my girl friend that there's
nothing like having a cabbalist for a father to help you figure out an
income tax return for your future husband in nothing flat."

Income tax—or *die Recknung?* . . . Ethan, who was suddenly
much soberer than he'd thought, feeling a stab in his heart, wondered if, to the contrary, Jacqueline had not been worrying in a

girlish fashion lest anything she'd told him might make him less anxious to marry her, and she'd been seeking sisterly consolation or advice from her friend on the point. And the memory of Cordwainer struck its claws into him again.

"Jacqueline, I've got something damned serious," he began, but Jacqueline had already interrupted him:

"Listen, but I must tell you what really made me take so long," she was saying. "Angela just told me she's going to be married to a chap from British Columbia called d'Arrivee she's been going with. But what do you know, they plan to live in a remote island out there with only about two hundred inhabitants—one of the Gulf Islands, called Gabriola. Don't you think that sounds like fun? His business is in Nanaimo on Vancouver Island, they'll commute by ferry."

Into Ethan's mind came for a moment a clear vision of the ferry, but, for some inexplicable reason, sad, a glum Charon's boat, plying up and down between mountains, the sun gleaming in the saloon windows: above, black clouds shot with bars of sunlight . . . And eternally bound as between some ultima thule and a nethermost suburb.

"Wouldn't that be exciting," Jacqueline said.

"I don't know," Ethan said. "If you'd asked me that half an hour ago I'd probably have said yes. But I was thinking in the other bar . . . Well anyway; wouldn't that mean living too cut off from everybody and things . . ."

And it was somehow still not the right time to tell her about Peter Cordwainer. It would be outrageous enough to tell the story in the half-frivolous way which had become his normal manner of speaking. It certainly wasn't a subject suited to his own special brand of *Galgenhumor* with which he'd be bound to invest it after all he'd drunk. It was not conceivably a subject suited to any kind of humor, gallows humor least of all, be that from another standpoint the only humor appropriate. Yet that was the manner in which he would inevitably tell it, as he had told it in the past to so many others after a few drinks, and in telling it had nearly always found himself lying. And he did not want to lie to Jacqueline, if it would be no lie to say he did not know the whole truth. No, face it, and be honest with her he must. It was a bad enough thing to have to live with for the rest of one's life without his soul being further corroded, and it had been corroded, by his own half-falsehoods on the subject. And then again: she might not take it seriously. It would be no more than "a grey hair in God's eyebrow." Few people ever had taken it seriously, partly, no doubt, because of that very manner he had of telling it. And there was an extremely good argument against saying anything about it at all to her, but would he be able to do that? Remorse, yes, he still felt shattering remorse, but was it remorse that made him want to talk about it, embroidering the whole damned mess with senseless inventions, or rather that he felt in some sense proud of the appalling thing he had not prevented from coming to pass? Or secretly admired Cordwainer for what he had done . . . But this much was an advance. Not for very many years now, and until he'd come to fall in love with Jacqueline, had he even fully admitted to himself how appalling it really was; unless this last fact, considering how long ago it had all happened, were not more appalling still . . . He had just about made up his mind again to try to tell her when there was a sudden embarrassing hush in which he heard Jacqueline saying airily:

"Half the people in here look like criminals to me."

"Don't be a bloody snob, Jacky sweetheart," said Ethan, who had however been momentarily thinking nearly the same thing.

"I am . . . It's just as I said . . . I don't think people are my brothers at all. I'm positively regal at bottom. My ambition runs to Nubian slaves. Not seriously, you know. I have this bad side . . . But I daresay there's something in what you say," she went on. "If so, it certainly wasn't Father's fault. People were always finding out about me for the simple reason *he* thought I *shouldn't* be ashamed and my foster-mother was always telling everyone too. But that doesn't mean people didn't form their *own* opinions."

"Anyhow I'll bet there's no criminal in here so bad that he persuaded one of his oldest friends——" Ethan began, looking round.

But the noise had started again and she hadn't heard. Ethan again wanted desperately to tell her about Peter Cordwainer but did not, and they sat awhile without either speaking or looking at one another. The idea of having dinner in a restaurant, if that was what they'd do in the end, had become repulsive to both of them. Ah, how he longed to take her home to some pretty little house under the trees, a home whose windows and firelight would welcome them with kindness and warmth, as with the words: "I am yours, yours and hers . . ." Even on Gabriola Island; perhaps now particularly on Gabriola Island, that they were scarcely to mention again for over a decade, Jacqueline and Angela having somehow stopped writing one another during the war, and himself barely to remember after living in British Columbia itself for three and a half years. And, after all, what difficulties were in their path? Ethan had money. He was successful. The complications appeared few. It all seemed as normal and simple as did the desire. Little did Ethan suspect that one day they would find a place that said, not "I am yours," but "You are mine!"

Meantime the feeling of one's love here for a poignant moment was like the sound of ghostly sleighbells, that had been rain falling in the lake that day they sat beside it. But the next moment this feeling of one's love and destiny in this place where one could scarcely see or hear for the noise was like a roaring beneath it, ominous, like a massive growl of thunder in a blinding snowstorm.

CHAPTER 10 ❧ *The Hound of Heaven*

*T*he Greyhound bus swept on and their reflections with it . . .

Jacqueline was now thirty-one, Ethan still eight years older, and if they both looked ten years younger than they were, it was due in some measure, whatever Jacqueline sometimes said, to the character of the life they'd been living during the larger part of that "retreat"; certainly no habit of sun or sea or lake from earlier summers could have caused in both of them that glow of health and well-being which, however deceitful (like that glow of the Indian summer outside which promised neither good nor ill of October but whose veiled threat was frost and sudden death), still shone through in spite of all.

Well, we are what suns and winds and waters make us. And, Landor might have added, fires and sorrows and hangovers too.

The way they were travelling one tended to forget Vancouver Island itself was mountainous. The bus was really running along the base of high mountains, but through the window to the left you couldn't see the peaks for the forest. Or the higher peaks ahead, behind where Nanaimo would be. So, though the scenery the Greyhound traversed was in reality varied and exciting, the journey began to be monotonous, its points of interest more and more at a remove, its mountain beauties confined to those on the mainland, more and more as if being left behind. Not that Mount Baker over there, or its summit, was not still trying to keep up with them—old Squamish omnipotent and kind Mount Ararat (not to be confused with Mount Arafat, Ethan thought, on top of which, according to Moslem legend, Adam and Eve were supposed to have met after the eviction from Paradise); but the places had grown fewer where their road skirted the sea, of which they now had only occasional glimpses. And their Gulf Islands had disappeared altogether, and with them, in a subtle way, the envisaged future.

The Greyhound was going at a tremendous pace. Other motor-cars, Victoria-bound, crashed past with a sigh. A natty Royal Canadian Mounted Police car shrilled by with great red spotlights and gramophone horns on the roof. All was rush, quickness, the beauty of swiftness and light. But the omnipresence of the ever-cleaving, yet towering and all-obliterating forest, primeval forest, forest, mostly Douglas fir here with a few clearings where it had been logged, the autumn-flowering dogwood blossoms themselves gleaming through the foliage like stars, and always that backward-swooping carpet of gold interspersed with dusty goldenrod too, acres of dandelion, imposed on the senses finally, in spite of the sheer exhilaration of speed, an extremity of motion that was no motion, where past and future were held suspended, and one began thinking of treadmills, or walking down an upward-moving escalator in a department store. As Tommy once liked to do . . .

Ethan glanced sideways at his wife, who at the moment, in the window, seemed to be sitting in an orchard. The bus had been going so fast through the forest, with not so much as a farm to break the monotony, that it was difficult to realize it had a moment or two since stopped, and was now honking slowly through a long strag-gling village or country town. *My God Bay,* the general store, between two gnarled apple trees, announced. And outside, the head-lines from the *My God Bay Advertiser:* ACUTE HANGING SHORTAGE. What? ACUTE HOUSING SHORTAGE. RAPPED BY RATE-PAYERS . . . And where no bay was to be seen. My God, My God Bay, where art

E

thou? Probably the main road bypassed it. They'd paused to take on a group of schoolchildren.

Jacqueline was wearing her silver-grey squirrel coat he'd bought her in their Toronto days, a little grey hat like a Juliet cap rimmed with grey fur, a green silk scarf, gloves, emerald-green suede shoes, and she carried a bag of the same color he thought he remembered in Toronto too. She looked both lovely and elegant and for a second it was impossible to see her as the same woman of their beach life. Ethan saw her expression growing aghast; everybody in the bus suddenly turned and looked out of the window. The part of the orchard they were now passing had been badly burned. To the left they saw the house itself, set back from the road with the orchard behind, among trees, where the mischief had clearly started, probably the night before. But the house, small, of lovely lines, with a curious long narrow tin chimney giving it the air of some little English steamer of the 1840s, and a lean-to kitchen, with green asbestos shingles on its beautiful sweep of roof, making it like a little replica too of their own old house in Niagara, had been partially saved, a bit of the roof had fallen in, or been hacked through. All the rafters still held. The upper windows (above which, on the sill or a dormer, housed by it, still menacingly, or movingly, or heraldically, perched a fire-scarred stuffed owl) were all broken, not a pane remaining, and those rooms behind were gutted. But all the rooms on the bottom floor, thank God, seemed intact. No broken windows here. Only the porch was a chaos, giving evidence of panic, or the impression that some people had at one point been trying to loot the house, rather than save it. In the trampled garden disembowelled and blasted sofas, antique chairs and tables, damaged and undamaged, were set among smashed panes of ‚glass underfoot beneath the blackened apple trees; on the branch of one hung what looked an expensive chandelier, as if placed for an afternoon tea of friends. Worst of all, below the porch, perhaps dragged out at the frantic behest of the owners from a room that had been spared, but which, proving too heavy for its would-be salvagers, had been allowed to crash down the steps, was a broken baby grand piano, lying overturned with its legs in the air like a huge helpless insect. (*Aidons nous, merci!*) Had its owners given up? Who could say? At a little distance in a well-tended rose garden an old lady was calmly pruning her trees. Wandering in a lake of grass a little further on, a small child, clutching in one hand to her breast a bouquet of rusty goldenrod, was picking red leaves from a low vine-leafed maple tree. An official took notes in an official notebook. And from somewhere about the place Ethan heard, above the bus's motor—or could it be, and say it was not, demolition!—the hopeful sounds of hammering.

Ethan saw tears welling in Jacqueline's eyes: did those beloved dark eyes of hers see what he saw and was better forever forgotten? or simply beyond this more gentle golden decline of goldenrod and maple in the woods now again around them (though the town had not ended, the tattered woods gentle and exhausted save where in some ever verdant place the sun struck life with a sudden tremendous glittering of green!) see sumac and teazel, the blaze and sumptuous opulence of eastern autumns? He gripped her gloved hand tightly:

> **Gleaming white cedar siding home**
> **Clean as a pin from stem to stern**
> **Living room dining room kitchen with**
> **Sun room off and two bright bedrooms**

"Only ten thousand dollars down!"
"Aedes flammantes vidivit!"

The observation, breaking a silence that had fallen on them, came from one of the children, whom Jacqueline was regarding, no doubt remembering her own days as a schoolteacher, a boy of fifteen or sixteen who'd sat down in front of two slightly younger girls, not pretty, with imitation-Ginger-Rogers hair, and dressed in jackets, skirts, bobby socks, flat-heeled shoes. The boy had now turned round in his seat, leaning on the back, and proudly addressed the girls, and Jacqueline gave Ethan a sudden smile. The boy, tall for his age, thin, had a lean, alert, smart face at once young and rather mature, and about which also there was something faintly familiar.

Where had he seen that face before? observed that manner so completely self-assured, casual, and even cocksure, cruel but indifferent? To the girls, who murmured shrilly, piping their adoration, he was clearly a hero. Probably he was a "good enough lad." What would Tommy be like at that age? Acute Housing Shortage Rapped, he saw again outside another store. THE BOY CHAMBERS WILL KEEP HIS DATE WITH THE HANGMAN ON DEC. 22.

"I figure I got seventy-five—maybe seventy-four, no, I definitely got seventy-five out of a hundred and twenty-seven questions," the boy was saying. "Not good, but I'll pass Latin."

Ethan turned to Jacqueline and whispered: "I've not forgotten I was your twenty-third pupil but I learned *that* before I was ten," and then aloud to the boy, without quite knowing why he felt constrained to say this:

"You might have got seventy-six, youngster, if you'd said *vidit.*"

The group was silenced and turning round, a youth at the far end of the bus, not meaning, doubtless, to be overheard, said, "What did Old Somebody back there say?" and the boy, already turned toward the Llewelyns, stared and said, neither politely nor impolitely:

"Yeah. That's right too, isn't it? *Video—videre—vidi . . . Aedes flammantes vidit.* He saw the house blaze." The other schoolchildren laughed.

"Did anyone?"

"Naw, not us. We live the other end of town. But we heard the engines going in the night."

"No one hurt or killed?"

"Nope. But one of our teachers's head of the volunteer fire brigade—that's why we got off school early today. Been up half the night and has to make a report or something. What the heck . . . Just one of those old firetraps of houses like. Should have been pulled down years ago."

When the children got on the bus Ethan had been pleased with the Island Limited for not being as limited as all that. He was more often terrified of children, but these kids had seemed to add a note of lightheartedness to the trip, and besides he couldn't help thinking of his own son with tenderness. But he had not liked being called "Old Somebody" in front of Jacqueline, and now this bit of seeming callousness on the part of the boy, who in fact was probably just repeating what his father who lived in a house of stone (if not like Don Giovanni) had said at breakfast, both hurt him and made him angry, though it hurt more. So that when he heard the boy once more showing off to the girls with the words: *"Ad morte eunti obviam factus sum,"* Ethan again interpolated, and with more acerbity:

"You might have got seventy-seven if you said *ad mortem . . ."* And could not stop himself adding (really there was something wrong with him today) "Maybe you'll get a hundred next time if you can say correctly: 'After mounting his horse he galloped off to the camp.'"

"Gee up. Got on his old horse and rode off in all directions," put in one of the girls half impudently. "That's our famous Canadian author, Stephen Leacock, you know."

Jacqueline was beginning to look slightly embarrassed, yet Ethan somehow had to persist and tell the boy he must use *guum* with the pluperfect subjunctive. "It seems," he heard himself saying sardonically, "between us it's a case of *'vocabulis discrepamus.'"*

"Crap anyway——" put in the same youth who'd referred to him as Old Somebody, but instantly clapping his hand over his mouth, tittering.

Quite suddenly Ethan felt overwhelmed with humiliation. It was not that the boy he'd been addressing had meant to be rude. He was simply indifferent, and was already talking boastfully about something else to the two girls. But what on earth had prompted Ethan to get into this ridiculous conversation in the first place with the brat? And why should he, a grown man, have so much resented him, have, so to speak, and almost as an equal, set himself up in competition with him? It was preposterous. And worse . . . And worse still, why should he feel so crushed? Ethan, unable to look Jacqueline in the face, stared at the floor. That he was singularly equipped to speak about elementary Latin composition was a fact. As a boy himself, before his eye trouble, he'd always been good at parroting whole chunks from Latin grammar or composition books. The ability had often stood him in good stead during that very time of darkness and misery at prep school, exhibiting, in those early Stoke-Newington days, and long before he found he had a truly encyclopedic memory, his feats on every possible occasion, much as another boy, socially crippled by shyness, might use his skill on the ukulele, later to become a dominant principle, even, that touching and underrated little instrument, a kind of secondary sexual characteristic. But he was no longer still aged ten. Or twelve. Or, by God, was he? *Ad mortem eunti obviam factus sum.* I met him as he was going to death . . . Had stood him in good stead, yes, until—And then, gazing up at that obdurate, alert, too mature, callous, indifferent face of the boy still turned the Llewelyns' way talking to the girls (that cocksure, yet finally so unsure, finally so tragic face), he knew. Peter Cordwainer. The face was that of Peter himself, not Peter at nineteen as he last remembered him at the college of Ixion, at the University of Ely, had last seen him, nineteen years ago tonight, October seventh—that date which had wrapped itself round his memory like a cancer strangling the upper bowel—nor yet the Peter of the hoarding, a portrait of a slightly older boy than was this, a Peter that never was perhaps, save in an agonized parent's heart, forever preserved at seventeen in touching posthumous dignity, on the hoarding that thank God he hadn't seen now for a long time—indeed he'd been mercifully spared too much objective reminder in general of Mother Gettle, in turn that ridiculous and ghastly mnemonic, here so far in British Columbia, who if she'd carried out her threat to come west to this province, had not been too ubiquitous on the mainland, his eye having fallen rarely enough on an advertisement even in the *Vancouver Daily Messenger;* no, it was the face of Peter Cordwainer before he'd become his friend, when he was his worst enemy indeed, the Peter of Stoke-Newington days, the dreaded all-corrupting face seen dimly through dark glasses or from beneath a double eyeshade, when such scornful casual indifference, always presaging something far worse, had been one of the instruments of Ethan's own torture. The boy was now telling the girls how he'd spent his summer vacation; he had contrived some position as a waiter on one of the transcontinental railways apparently; Jacqueline was smiling to herself, and Ethan had to smile too, even while this also was not without its nightmarish side. It was all merely due to some psychological aberration—God, what if it were not?—but this was like a reincarnated Peter Cordwainer, who had done, in a measure, the only kind of thing that might have saved him. How often had not he, Ethan, and before the end, and yes, at the end too, until he gave up in desperation, tried in vain to persuade Peter Cordwainer completely to reorient himself, give up booze, to immerse himself for a time in some new reality, to take some job requiring physical labor, no matter how monotonous, go to sea as a common seaman, as Ethan himself had gone to sea, anything to get away from the viciousness that was leading him to destruction. But though Peter had admired Ethan's own spirit in this, he had, a Canadian in exile, self-corrupted in his own soul, lacked finally that very courageous native sense of adventure, rarer in the British of that period, which, "the greatest asset of North American youth," as they say, might have permitted him to do so. And yet, great God, how could he be said to have lacked it when he had not shrunk from the most terrifying journey of all?

"Yeah, I've traveled twelve thousand miles already," the boy was saying. "But some of the men, the old-timers, why they've traveled *billions* of miles. *Billions*. They've been on the railroad all their lives. Maybe forty years. They've traveled *billions* of miles. Isn't that great stuff? . . . No, you never know where you're going when you go down to the station. I've been across the country twice now."

"Do you know," one of the girls spoke up, "I've never been on a train in all my life. What's it like?"

"What's it like? Why, you're just on a train. It's swell! . . . Yeah, I had a six-hour layover in Calgary last time through. Calvary's all right, a swell place (had Ethan heard aright, Calvary?), but it was full of American sailors and they're terrible. They're a disgrace to their uniform. Most of the soldiers are bad enough but the sailors are terrible."

"What's *wrong* with them?" piped the girls.

"Well for one thing they were so drunk they were falling all over the streets, full of that cheap wine, bootleg stuff, I guess. The Canadian sailors are bad, but the Americans are terrible. Boy, the navy's a good place to stay out of! . . . In Calgary I went into a little beer joint with another guy who was working on the train with me. It was a lousy joint though, just full of drunken American sailors banging around . . . And there wasn't a single pretty girl in Calgary, yeah, I looked them all over and I can tell you there wasn't a single good-looking one in the whole town."

"It's your privilege," said Ethan, at this point directing at the boy a glance meant to be punishing, "to criticize the girls in Calgary till the cows come home. But to go around insulting Americans is another thing. Especially when there might be some on this bus. How do you know *I'm* not an American sailor?"

"Because you're a Limey!" someone said.

The boy, who had lit a cigarette, looked up at Ethan through blue smoke a moment, neither chagrined nor unchagrined. But he retreated an inch or two.

"Coming back last trip through the Rockies there was plenty of snow, you know, and we had some Aussies on board," he continued his conversation with the girls. "They're mostly pretty bad too, though some of them are all-right guys I guess, but they'd never seen any snow before, and boy, they had fits. We'd stopped in a little station for a while and I was out running errands, up and down the platform in my shirt sleeves rolled up and just my little white coat on, you know, and these Aussies came out. They'd put on their great overcoats, and hats, and everything but earmuffs. They were wrapped up to the eyes. So they stood there just looking like a bunch of kids. Then they picked up some in their fingers and then handsful of it. 'Look! Snow!' one of them said. 'Oh boy, isn't it wonderful?'"

"The Australians might have seen snow. Perhaps they were homesick, that's all," Ethan said.

"Is that right?"

. . . Homesick, yes; but only latterly, since they'd been living in an apartment, in hotels, in the city again, had it been borne in upon Ethan, and with increasing sorrow, yes, with despair, the extent, the spiritual plenitude of that happiness which had been lost.

Homesick!—And yet what had been lost, on another plane, had only been a fisherman's cabin on the beach, beneath the forest, under a wild cherry tree.

(Ethan Llewelyn looked out of the window at Vancouver Island. He saw nothing at all. Or nothing by which he could have given any form. He supposed that somewhere alongside the roads and in the mountains and on the sea people were doing universal things, but it was too great an intellectual effort to remember what. Suddenly the landscape began to take on a sort of reality but it was not its own reality, but the reality of a landscape seen from a train window, in the sunset, in a film. The film had been called *Looping the Loop,* and he had seen it on a ship going to Gibraltar as a passenger. Now the only reality he could think of was the reality of his cabin. He thought of asking Jacqueline what she saw out of the window but it was too much trouble to speak.

Films had more reality to him than life until he had found his little house, but novels possessed secretly no reality for him at all. Or almost none. A novelist presents less of life the more closely he approaches what he thinks of as his realism. Not that there were no plots in life nor that he could not see a pattern, but that man was constantly in flux, and constantly changing. He woke up a Buddhist, was a Catholic at breakfast, a Hater of Life with the morning paper, and then a Protestant, and then by the time he got to the library was something else, all on account of things he had read or heard influencing him on the way.)

And scarcely more pretentious, he thought, turning to Jacqueline and saying, "Do you remember the night in Toronto I didn't want to live on Gabriola?" And the old waterfront squatter's shack he'd once visualized the drunken Hindu of the Niagara that night living in.

CHAPTER 11 ❧ *Eridanus*

*T*heir house, like the Venetian palaces, was built on piles, on government-owned Foreshore land down an inlet over on the mainland, in the tiny village of Eridanus; they had two rooms, oil lamps, a gold rush cookstove, outside plumbing, a small boat painted yellow, the color of the sun, with a red rim around the gunwale and red oars. In the mornings reflections of the sun on water slid up and down the time-silvered cedar walls; seagulls came onto the porch, demanding their meals, taking crusts from their fingers. Like the fishermen, the Llewelyns paid no taxes, and behind the cabin, which had been sold to them lock, stock and barrel for $100, were forty acres of forest to wander in: sometimes at night curious raccoons came right into the house, and in spring, through their casement windows, they watched the deer swimming across the water, above which hovered, in the hot air of late summer, an endless wayward drift of fireweed-down.

Sometimes too, in the summer evenings, bears stood down on the beach and crunched cockles.

The Llewelyns drew water from their own well: and at the head of a trail through the forest so precipitous it made the trees growing along the dusty main road look three hundred feet high, was a store where they bought their food. Hidden away down below in the little bay of their own within the larger bay, they enjoyed almost complete freedom and privacy, peace and quiet; they swam and sunbathed and if they wanted to sing at the tops of their voices at four o'clock in the morning, or Ethan play the clarinet wildly as the early Ted Lewis himself—it was the flute in Virgil's *Eclogues*—no one would hear them save maybe a heron croaking eerily by on some moonlit fishing trip.

Old Indians on a neighboring reserve said where they lived no two winters seemed the same. The Llewelyns' first had remained mild as spring, or like an extended Indian summer, until spring itself arrived, when snow fell, and the pent-up season spent itself in a week's wrath amid the very buds bursting into bloom. The winter before that, living in the city only fifteen miles away, though they kept physically warm, they had thought dreary beyond measure. But last winter had been tempestuous. Then, the life could be terrifying: at flood tides, in gales and snowstorms, the tumult from sea and forest appalling. The ferocious winter climate of Ontario, whose meanest houses had nightlong-burning Quebec stoves, seemed nothing to that of "Canada's Evergreen Playground on the Shores of the Blue Pacific." Their thin little house was not much more than a summer cabin, without an overnight heater, and almost without insulation. Snow, and of an awe-inspiring new intensity, fell. A new Ice Age descended. The trail became impassable. They wore gunny sacks over their boots, got lost in the dark, and went to search for each other through the forest with lanterns. But rarely when they were together did they ever feel their isolation. Those tempests or mishaps were rare that did not bring them finally some sense of peace, however childlike.

Ships got lost too, in the narrow inlet. In thick fog they heard them—vessels without radar, sometimes no doubt only long tugs or fishing craft, at other times freighters one imagined ancient and benighted, under romantic flags, Liberia or Costa Rica or Peru, and whose crews called out in Greek—trying to find their way through the fjord by the echo of their foghorns from either bank. This also was like getting lost in the forest: it was as if you went ten steps, then stopped; so you advanced in the inlet if you were a lost ship, so many revolutions of the engine, or sometimes for a period of time.

Then you stopped and sounded your whistle and listened for the echo. If the echo came back quicker from one side it meant you were closer to the rocks on that side and you steered away. But if the two echoes synchronized you were in midstream and safe. So, in thick fog, if they heard some craft trying to get her bearings in this way, and she sounded too close inshore, Jacqueline and Ethan stood by on their porch and shouted. Or at night they held lanterns aloft, their gigantic shadows were cast on the fog five fathoms out, high over the sea, weaving and bending. But in a snowstorm there is no echo. Then the ships steered by dead reckoning. And the Llewelyns imagined the horror of steering by dead reckoning, blind, in the storm. For now the snow was bringing on the night and such a storm as shall yield no echo. You couldn't stop. If you stopped you were lost. You couldn't even wait for the tide. Again with lanterns the Llewelyns kept watch, to shout a friendly answer to questioning hail. Perhaps they did not help much but it felt as if they were helping. They seldom locked their front door and they rose at sunrise.

The Llewelyns (and still, in the bus, going to Gabriola, Ethan thought like this, or thought he was thinking like this) had lived by the inlet for more than two years as squatters; they'd gone there in May 1947.

But toward the end of this last summer a loud campaign for the eviction of everyone in the hamlet and the destruction of their cabins started in the Vancouver newspapers, their editors having discovered after a quarter of a century, and in the absence for a few days of suitable headlines concerning sex crimes, or atomic war, that by their continued existence at Eridanus the public were being deprived of the usage themselves of this forest, together with its half-mile of waterfront, to say nothing of the beach, as a public park.

In one sense the reverse was true. The cottages remained, for large sections of the year, mostly uninhabited; and those scattered folk who lived in them the year round were as good as unpaid forest wardens of what was not only a valuable stand of government-owned timber, but, unspoiled as the whole place was, with its paths and old cow trails, and older corduroy roads, here anyone was free to walk beneath the huge cedars and broad-leaf maples and pines, a sort of public park already, the difference being that few troubled to avail themselves of its wild graces, nor had its trees been decimated, or yet begun to commit the slow melancholy mass suicide of those great trees in parks that cannot endure living near an encroaching civilization.

Nor were their poor cabins "eyesores," as was cruelly maintained. Many of them, like the Llewelyns', were beautiful in themselves. But even had they not been so, the hamlet of Eridanus, overtowered by trees, was invisible from anywhere save the water itself whence, with those trees behind, the mountains higher, behind that, and its tall-tackled fishing boats near at hand, swinging at anchor, those despised cabins appeared as nearly the only visible landward creations of man that were *not* eyesores. Seen in this way they preserved, collectively—so blended with their surroundings were they, and setting aside what they might mean to the heart of anyone living there, nearly all such their own builders—a very real and unusual beauty.

And how its existence or nonexistence could be of less interest to the inhabitants of a distant city, whose proudest boast was its own possession of one of the largest and most spectacular public parks in the world they were simultaneously agitating to have replaced by two eighteen-hole golf courses and a parking lot for two thousand motorcars the better to observe the wildlife, it was hard to see.

Nonetheless if one has to be threatened with eviction, to be threatened for the sake of a park is perhaps best. Unfortunately Ethan's legal mind warned him that even this public park, the thought of which with its concomitant hot-dog concessions and peripheral autocourts and motels supplanting their heaven was unbearable enough, might be a charitable chimaera, held up before the eyes of the public by civic chimaeras (in the sense that the former may be considered a foolish fancy, the latter as related to the sharks) whose real object it was to put a railway through, build a subsection, an oil refinery, an industrial site for a pulp mill, a totem pole factory, or a dehydrated onion soup factory.

For, on the opposite bank of the inlet some three miles distant, progress was already making its second greatest onslaught on Vancouver since the Canadian Pacific Railway had been finally joined there in the last century. A Shell oil refinery, with its piers on the inlet, had been remotely visible citywards when they arrived. No doubt it had been there since long before the war. But this had been gradually and stealthily enlarged during the last years, a pyre of oil waste, visible once rarely and only at night, now burned night and day, had become two pyres, and there were rumors of yet further expansion, more refineries, preparations for a pipe line to be run through from Alberta. Not till now had these things whispered a terrible *perhaps* to themselves. For the boom was not quite yet, and from that opposite bank, essentially, more than an age still seemed to separate them.

Just the same, Ethan thought, having once before in his experience been rendered homeless by what men were pleased to call progress, then by nature herself, in a conflagration where a little more progress in the shape of a competent fire brigade might certainly have helped (the schoolchildren were getting off the bus at the farther end of My God Bay, by another store, with a bit of bay this time glittering blue through the trees, and outside which, leaning across the aisle, Ethan caught sight of another headline from the local paper saying MY GOD BAY LITERARY SOCIETY COMMEMORATES EDGAR ALLAN POE'S CENTENARY HERE—he looked again; it was so).

The Greyhound started again with a jerk, rallying to it the soul's cry of *"No cede malis."* Had not this threat of eviction begun to make him suffer as though under some ultimate and irreversible judgment?

Happy, they indeed had been, like spirits in some heaven of the Apocalypse or in some summerland of spiritualists, spirits who had no right to be where they were, which was their only source of doubt, when they doubted it.

But the reverse of their bliss was nothing like infelicity. It resembled terror, a great wind, or a recurrent suspicion of a great wind, the Chinook itself. What he felt dimly they repressed then was anguish on a greater scale than two human hearts were meant to contain, as though their own heart had been secretly drawing to itself some huge accumulating sorrow: alien sorrow, for which there was no longer scarcely the slightest shred of sympathy to be found in the so-called liberal thought of which they imagined themselves the enlightened partakers. Steam, trade, machinery had long banished from it all romance and seclusion.

Once or twice they had thought of calling their cabin the Wicket Gate, after the gate in *The Pilgrim's Progress* Evangelist showed Christian he must pass, in order to reach the Celestial City, or Paradise. The wicket gate that had been made by the blacksmith to prevent his children falling down on the beach. But why call it anything?

Often it seemed a magical thing to them that it had been sold to them by a blacksmith, some species of magician or alchemist himself. Once or twice he came out to visit them, took a cup of tea, chopped some wood vigorously as though he were at home again, then went away swiftly. Once he sat for a long time without moving on a big fir trunk washed up on the shore, with his back toward them, so motionless for a moment they thought he might have died or had a stroke. Perhaps he felt sorry he had sold it to them, or was thinking of the time he had built it?

As a bird wandereth from his nest, so is man who wandereth from his place. Now they understood the meaning of this proverb—with what hunger they always returned to it, saw the pier they had built waiting below the bank, the tide already coming in, their eternal baptistery.

Ah, but it was their own place on earth, and how tenderly they loved it. How passionately—gladly would Ethan have laid down his life for it. But what was it that gave them this life so free and dear, that gave them so much more than peace, what was it that made it more than an ark of timber? Ah, it was their tree, door, nest, dew, snow, wind and thunder, fire and day. Their starry night and sea wind. Their love.

CHAPTER 12 ✇ *Niagara-on-the-Lake*

*F*or to say that the Llewelyns had been unlucky in their houses was an understatement. The first house of theirs in Oakville, Ontario, with its flittering night owls among the Judas trees, in the banging thundery weather, had indeed been swallowed up some eleven years ago, though not before the adjacent segment of lake had become polluted and been pronounced unfit to swim in—and who was to say all this was any more escapable, or less foreseen, than that he should just now, on this day of all days, have had to crane over the aisle to glimpse that ridiculous announcement about the My God Bay Literary Society paying tribute to that other poor devil of Stoke-Newington—and what was the connection—by the expanding borders of, the inevitably expanding borders of yes—and yes, there on the wall was a small advertisement of it as if produced in obedience to his besetting conscience—Mother Gettle's Kettle-Simmered Soup, M'mm, Good!

("All right, Mr. Peter Bloody Cordwainer . . . Go ahead and do it. Grandmother won't let you down, I'm sure . . . She's got a lot of friends in high office. And besides, the Tibetans say you can be comfortable even in hell, just so long as you're clever. And you are, if not so damn clever as you used to be. I've promised you. I'll get in touch with you through old Goddo's wife on Sunday afternoons."

Had he said this? Or Peter: "It's almost worth doing it just to see the expression on all those old stick-in-the-mud faces at Ixion tomorrow." "You forget you won't be here to see them, old man." "That's right, nor will I. That's funny. But I thought you said . . ." "Not for three days, I think, as a rule." "Will I know I'm dead?" "Only if you reflect on the subject." "Well, Schopenhauer does say it's the one thing a man surely has an inviolable right to dispose of as he thinks fit." "All right then, dispose. As a realtor for the next world I recommend this choice lot. I didn't mean that about hell either, Peter. I honestly think things are going to be a damned sight better for you over there. Anyway, you're going to do it sooner or later, so why not now? Have another spot of gin, old chap." "Thanks, old man . . . Ethan, you come too!" "No. You do it. We'll keep in touch. I'll come later. The same way." "Then before you go, I . . . wouldn't you—?" "None of that." "And don't fail me!" So let the bugger die . . . The excuse would not do. No excuse would do.)

Their first house had been the one near Oakville, and they'd lived hardly a year in this pretty home, inexpressibly dear to them largely because it *was* their first home, when the blow had fallen, just before the war: thirteen months later, while they were still searching for somewhere else to live, Ethan's father died, and he inherited the old family home fifty miles away on the other side of the lake. They'd moved into his birthplace in Niagara-on-the-Lake— and how should he forget it? (German troops were entering Romania, the Battle of Britain had been in progress for a month and, a volunteer, he had only the week before been rejected for active service due to defective eyesight, the defectiveness, however, seemingly unconnected with his childhood ailment)—moved nine years ago this very month, October 1940. And then, that second house—

Yet not even the catastrophe of this, an event of the sheerest most eerie mischance, or so it seemed at the time; the house, solid, built to last forever by his great-great-grand-uncle in 1790—two years before that amiable old pioneer (or genial old crook, who as though to establish well in advance such an arrangement need not be *une*

F

fantaésie bien Amiricaine or dependent upon ultra-rapid-or-modern modes of travel, had another more lavish house in what was now Codrington, in the island of Barbados, where, in addition to a mulatto mistress, he kept a pet crocodile) took his seat in the first Canadian Parliament there at Niagara-on-the-Lake—the ancient house of Ethan's birth taking fire in the night when there was no one in it, while they were away for the weekend in Ixion, and burning to the ground for no reason anyone had been able to determine (unless, as there was certainly some cause to believe, it had been struck by lightning, an explanation almost worse than none), not even this had produced in him such a shocking reaction to the outer world of makeshift and homelessness as had now this threat of eviction from Eridanus.

Nor had all the six long years they'd spent in that lovely old place given him such an attachment as had the last couple of years to what was not, properly speaking, a house at all.

And, to save himself, Ethan sought for reasons, trying to tell himself that if he could stand the loss of "the Barkerville Arms," as his birthplace had locally still been called, together with the irreplaceable material loss that involved, surely he could stand, what was besides only a threat, the loss of their little cabin. But from his reasons he derived less than comfort. These were like the devices they'd half unconsciously employed, without being exactly "unfaithful" to their second house, to try "to get rid" of the fire, foreshadowing, alas, those devices they would increasingly use without success to try "to get rid" of Eridanus itself. Now bitterly they discerned truth in the recalcitrating words they'd never thought at bottom were true. For they found they really *hadn't* loved their second house as much as they'd pretended, and to compare that love with their love for their cabin, or their former life with their new life, was an agonizing impossibility. They decided, as though they were the first to make this discovery, that houses like people had destinies, and sometimes fell sick and died. If there were haunted houses, there were also nervous houses, neurotic houses—and the Barkerville had begun, in forced retrocession from the heart, to strike them in this light.

For a house of the New World, anyhow, it had had a long innings. Built and rebuilt, and added to by five generations of Llewelyns, its graceful facade was dignified with a long imaginative sweep of roof over a wing and a second storey put there by old Lloyd Llewelyn's son in 1800, the original house having been just the cavernous cellar and the four back rooms, three steps down from what had become for them the front of the Barkerville. This sort of palimpsest method of building had produced in the end an enormous wooden edifice of narrow corridors with black stovepipes threading and elbowing everywhere through innumerable rooms and connecting with deep fire-boxed gluttonous Quebec stoves, oak beams so massive and inlaid hardwood floors so thick the place appeared constructed to withstand earthquakes and tornados, as it was, and had: trapdoors, beneath which were oubliettes of obscure motive, where British soldiers were romantically supposed to have hidden during the War of 1812; winding concealed stairs; and an attic, attributed to the third Llewelyn, a front and back parlour—ah, that word "parlour" again!—while even their woodshed in its kind of lean-to was not without its historic interest, having once been an outside kitchen. One trouble was, and this not only in retrospect, the house was all too big for them (save maybe for the windows, which were too small, even from outside, as to rebut this implication, the house seeming to say "Look at me," rather than "Live in me"). His father had indeed, in many respects, left a neurotic house, an angry house, impatient of what modern conveniences it had, which, though many, were continually breaking down as though deliberately, or as though the whole place were like some rebellious patched-up old freighter that longed to have done and be broken up. What was still known then as the "servant problem" hadn't improved matters. The Barkerville was too big to run easily without them, but during the war, they could not be had, or would not stay, and Ethan began to find the idea of even one servant in the house so unendurable that Jacqueline (whose original secret ambition might have been to recruit the very snow-shovellers to bring them pure snow to cool their rationed gin) at last counted it simpler to agree with him. The old Negro Pullman porter, James, a man better read at that time than was Ethan himself, stayed on a while as a general factotum, at length died in a bout of canned-heat-drinking, consumed with grief at Ethan's father's death, and refusing to the end to be persuaded, while drinking this hostile beverage, which he strained through an old sock, from that ex-outside kitchen to any more congenial quarters. Ethan himself became devoted to him but when he died was at first almost relieved. For what, he kept asking himself, had there been in his father, which he had missed, to inspire so much affection and respect in another? And, looking back, he seemed half to remember dreams forgotten at that time, dreams of guilt in which his father's loneliness in that house he had done so little to assuage and his own childhood loneliness was merged, dire dreams of infantile uprootings, and night journeys across the sea, even imaginings of his own conception in the house, taking place now as a horrendous violation, now as an act of tenderest love; other dreams where his mother or grandmother seemed pleading with him, gently forgiving, impossibly to undo something already done; which, waking from them always with remorse and sorrow and helplessness on his soul, and always through some fading image of a house, appeared to him as though they must have somehow concerned their first home, and so led back in consciousness in those wool-gatherings of day which were more sinister, sometimes when driving alone to Toronto, or at moments of suspense or boredom in court, or of gaiety on another level, when helping Jacqueline wash dishes after a few drinks, led back in his mind to Peter Cordwainer again, the following out of some insane pattern of beginning retribution, though never to the understanding of it, or the complete desire to understand, or the sincere desire to forgive himself: or to seek help. But Tommy was a healthy, happy child and they thought their own happiness great. Meantime if Jacqueline had rendered the house far more lovely, it did not, in a sense difficult to explain, seem grateful to her for her taste, and its coats of new paint, any more than it was grateful to Ethan for removing its operose porch, stuck on by Ethan's grandfather when he "renovated" it during the Victorian-Gothic era, an era of relative romance and vision one felt the house secretly half-approved, as perhaps did Ethan himself, chronically unable to see that if our era proves capable of being looked back upon at all, it may seem to have been far more so. This much was true: the house could no longer see the wide fields and forest and sweep of lake (where, beneath the ice, according to the local legend revived each winter, lay the two betrayers of the Masonic secrets) and it no longer cared. And if they'd loved it, they now saw, despite the luminous beauty of remembered Christmases, of miraculously wrought Spanish mahogany and family silver within, and falling snow without, that mahogany furniture another redolence of the West Indies, sea-borne hither on sailing ships during sugar-trading days, the house had given little in return and did not love them. Yet how speak of any house as living, apart from its living inhabitants, or their memory, for good or evil, surely an unfructifying object at best, save perhaps to the imagination? Or, without becoming involved with sentimentality, indispensable and most human vice, and that at its rankest, call this object alive, responsive, changeable, sometimes detestable, yet always loving, and with a heart that could break! Or—animism. Men often love their ships (God be thanked) like this: his mother's father, the skipper of a three-master, had gone down with his, rounding Cape Horn. And it was easier to speak of machines in this way: Ethan felt now and then he must have loved his first car something like this, which he had bought himself, after having been denied a car for so long by his father. Yet their feeling for their cabin on the beach at Eridanus was nothing like their feeling for the Barkerville Arms, though sentiment played a part, and pride in ownership (the more strange since they could never really own it) and it was a thing compounded of happy memories of love and summer and the laughter of children, or a child, like any other house, and, like any other, dependent on these for its life to some extent on that plane. But on another, their cabin seemed to possess a life of a kind wholly different from this, of a kind that couldn't have been called forth wholly by its owners, or its past owners. One had come to love it like a sentient thing (and here it was more like a ship) with a life of its own, not that one just imagined as living, or that it flattered and amused one to consider doing so, because one had given it life oneself (unless Jacqueline had bewitched it with magic, in secret, by some spell of her father's). And the trouble was Ethan felt it still did live, even after they had abandoned it, which was something that couldn't be dismissed either, or accepted, at least by him (he hoped, even if it was), as merely some sort of fixation, that term most helpless to convince a hanging jury. Well, this was animism certainly . . . Even Ethan could see their feelings, and more particularly his feelings, involved this, and animism in one of its most extreme and primitive forms—would have been glad to admit it indeed, for by the way weren't all men animists at heart? But what if your animism were occasioned by tactile causes that have almost gone out of the world? by peripheral causes that to you, now, in a different age, had become almost all that made life worth living? by, conceivably, some of the first rationalities of love's survival—or *his* life's survival—as were those very queen-posts and straining pieces to that section of roof being built over there, visible beyond some birches the bus was passing, but which now looked abandoned and left a skeleton? What if your animism were a matter of life or death. And here was the mysterious fact: yes, this much to them about, about their cabin. It was less than a house. But it was also far more than a house. And so now, when they tried to compare the Barkerville with it—not, now, just the two "lives" the competitive "loves" but the two houses themselves, laugh as one might, the poor dear old Barkerville with their little cabin and its great nine-light windows that came, like the Wilderness's, from a dismantled sawmill, and what *it* gave; one thing it gave, at the highest tides you could dive straight out of one of those windows into the clearest, what seemed the deepest and most life-giving water Ethan had ever known. Those high tides rising to the moons of summer, each one higher now rising like the threat of eviction (and the little cabin at this moment, bereft of them, if it was still there, deep in just such a rising tide of October)—their cabin which always seemed gazing outward at the tides; high, slack and rip tide, the first of the flood and the offset to southward; or to the last of the ebb with its weak variable currents;

or the smashing whiteness of the surf at low tide in the night in winter (themselves in bed perhaps, listening to the roar of the surf they couldn't see, far below, for the beach fell off steeply); or gazing at the sunrise or moonrise or star-rise, or these reflected in the tireless waters of the inlet, calm or turbulent, but even when resting always in motion, the stars too in motion on that dark or quicksilver stream, ever-ebbing, ever-returning, the inlet that was neither sea nor river but partook of and gave the best in both; their cabin whose mirrors and mirrored windows reflected alike the flow and counter-flow, flux and reflux of those tides, and the steamers passing upon them (Ethan thought of the engines of huge invisible tankers at night hugging the opposite bank that telephoned through the water to them in bed an aberrant commotion like submarine motor-bikes), and at the back of the house reflected too the green forest itself bending in the wind; why good God, even those garbage removers of theirs, the sea gulls, had the wings of angels! No, comparison was impossible. Moreover *objectively* they must have known themselves half blinded by illusion and Ethan himself more in the devil's clutches than he was; or had become? But this, and irony was the word, he thought again, gritting his teeth in the bus—they had been trying in vain for some time to pass a slow-moving, shabby high sedan tottering before them straight down the middle of the road, with a boiling knocking engine, and a large legend in white letters on a black ground beneath its British Columbia rear-number plate, reading from left to right: *Safeside-Suicide*—was the very thing that made any idea of the loss of their house and their life there so Christ-awful. That he might have been capable amid the circumstances of fostering such an illusion, had it been one, he knew only too well; but then for the same reasons that he had fostered it he must have prevented it reaching near-tragic proportions, for even an illusion was better than, the infantile solution was better than, could indeed be the only alternate—to—

> SAFESIDE-SUICIDE

CHAPTER 13   *The Tides of Eridanus*

*A*lready Ethan and Jacqueline had exchanged glances, much as they had at the headline about Poe, betokening their half-comic acceptance of this phenomenon, the warning sign ahead affixed by the joggling sedan, knowing glances accompanied by the same half-smile now and nodding of their heads that said, as in a musing drawl, "Yes, yes, they're on the job again," glances, in which there was even some perverse jocose pride, that could have meant either "This was put there for me," or "That was put there for us."

But now as the sedan moved over to the right, the bus putting on speed angrily swept past it, Ethan closed his eyes, leaning his head against the back of the seat, but as if suddenly not there, so carried away was he down a whirlwind of his own anguish.

No, he absolutely would not, must not allow himself to think like this. For some while now; though remaining barely conscious of the physical cause, he had been aware of a slow, stealthy, despairing *deepening* of the medium of his thoughts. This too was like a high tide of Eridanus coming in. It was as though he had been watching, on a dark still day, one of those immense black afternoon tides of autumn slowly brimming up beneath the windows: and now were trying not to watch it, on the same day grown gradually a blustery turbulent one of southeast wind and murk and rain, with the branches murderously crashing down in the forest behind the cabin; one of those tides that rose ever higher as they approached, say, the October full moon, that full moon which was tonight, he remembered, the tide already beginning to come in now too in the gulf below them to their right, the invisible tide in the invisible gulf, that same tide they must battle, or whose ebbing treacheries would carry them perhaps, this afternoon, one way or another, on their ferry to Gabriola; yes, and now not so much brimming as lashing and driving up beneath their windows, and with a venomous roaring, devouring, grinding sibilance: it wasn't that the house was endangered by tidewater, for all the cabins were built just to surmount the highest tide, and only once had it happened apparently, when an onshore gale blowing for days and nights and heavy rain had obstructed the normal ebb, that some of the cabins were flooded; but that these tides at their highest might dislodge and set afloat one or other of the huge timbers, left stranded all summer on the beach by the previous spring or winter tides, great writhing snags of roots, usually impossible of demolishment into firewood, which, however, being a menace to navigation, for they could sink a ship, you were legally forbidden to remove yourself by other means, when that could be done, as with a block and tackle, and push or tow out into deep water: for only at the moment that the foundations of his own cabin were threatened with disaster from one of these sudden derelict juggernauts, guilelessly quiescent for the last six months, set floating off by nature at the flood and tearing downstream on the ebb, then maybe, by some converse behavior of the inshore currents, to turn and bear straight back down on his house like an avenging sea-monster, under which, trapped by the crossbraces, in its frantic efforts to escape now, it could become a thunderous battering ram—only then had the fisherman strictly the right to protect himself from it: Ethan and Jacqueline's case was no different, and in wild weather, with the greater velocity of the seas piling up those high tides one was as powerless as Canute to stay, which were already licking hungrily at the flanks of those snags, the danger was far worse: and being so powerless there seemed nothing left to do finally but pray that, if the tide would not, at least that worst of all snags would remain where it was, or if they all must drift, drift in any direction except one's own, pray, and meantime, standing in the back room watching neither timbers nor mounting seas, attempt to suppress too the base but irresistible panic that rose in the soul at that chuckling and hissing and thunder of the fearful water outside one knew lashing up on the surface and beneath welling and creeping inch by inch upon the cabin, perhaps to loose the snags down on it, to attack and destroy its foundations, creeping up inevitably as each hour of each day since the threat of eviction seemed to creep up on the uncertain day ahead of the eviction itself and bring that doom closer.

Ethan felt seized by panic now in the bus. For he'd remembered he never *had* felt that way in Eridanus about the high tides of October. (Scarcely this October when they hadn't been there at all, and he'd been trying not to think about the tides: nor any other October, least of all their first, nor of the yet higher and more dangerous winter tides. Some fear, yes, he might have felt of those in the past as of the winter itself on occasion, those dark, fogbound, snowblinding caliginous spells, of Jacqueline and himself getting lost in the forest, and at the beginning for a long time he had remained afraid of fire) but never that helplessness in the face of fear, never that panic. A current in his mind had gone awry, played him false, a freak thought confused his mind's direction; but without invalidating the power of the emotion it carried that seemed projected, yet not vicarious, as if some part of him at this moment were actually haunting the place. But it was also projected back in time and the time he was thinking of, was, of course and once more simply this last summer again, the tides as they seemed "since the threat," in reality lesser but sometimes menacing flood tides of July and early September when they'd had some bad weather; it was true, and serious threats could arise, and things hadn't been made any easier by a badly sprained ankle. To mention only one added difficulty. But what struck panic into him in the bus was to realize how short a while it was before that he had felt himself a complete stranger to anything like panic, and when summer was a time of sun and joy. Nothing could have brought home more bitterly to him the devastating effect that threat of eviction had had on both of them than their changed attitude, particularly his, toward this other kind of threat from the tides. In their former days on the beach it had been very different. High tides in summer were for picnics on islands, not disaster to the house. Used so long to their lake, either stupidly unmoving or bellowing with shallow catastrophe, even the high tides of autumn and winter usually delighted them, snags or no snags, in fact the higher and stormier and more besnagged the better. As for the snags themselves, inexperienced and poorly equipped though they were to deal with them, and not taking their danger too seriously, since no one else seemed to, least of all the harbor official supposed to patrol the inlet in a motorboat to see there were none there, stranded on its beaches, or mark their position so that they could be officially towed away on a higher tide to some golgotha of snags, they had almost exulted in their challenge.

And they never doubted they would win: for the first time they had both acquired, though they didn't know it then, a complete faith in their environment, without that environment ever seeming too secure. This was a gift of grace, finally a damnation, and a paradox in itself all at once: for it didn't need to seem secure for them to have faith in its security. Or the little house itself didn't need to. The very immediacy of the eternities by which they were surrounded and nursed; antiquity of mountains, forest, and sea, conspired on every hand to reassure and protect them, as with the qualities of their own seeming permanence. The house in Oakville might go: the Barkerville burn down: whole cities, countries, be wiped out; but Eridanus, with its eternal fishermen and net-festooned cabins bordering that inlet of the same name, whose ceaseless wandering yet ordered motions were like eternity, looked from its very air of unobtrusiveness too in winter and rain, lack of the consciously picturesque, as, when a child, poring half asleep by the fire over a picture book with drawings of the Disciples and the Holy Land and modern maps to show where everything is, imagines the Sea of Galilee at the end of the world, somehow transported straight to heaven, its commerce uninterrupted. Eridanus *was*. The most hardboiled side of Ethan, as if untaught by experience, was fooled by this at first: that nature of his as trusting as it could be quick to suspect. What if their little house was knocked down or washed away? he'd asked then. A retreat was not forever. They could always, with a little resource, build another on the same spot and what had they to lose? They'd lost nearly everything already. Not that, he thought, they ever seriously dreamed of losing the cabin but if they did, to begin with, they never dreamed they'd care. That was part of the charm.

For where else in the world was the existence of your home so dependent on the elements (except for fire, never think of fire), why, your very life in it was rendered possible only by gradually achieving harmony with the elemental forces around you, which, one had read, was a human end in itself.

That, among other things, between the cabin and themselves was a complete symbiosis. They didn't live in it, Ethan said, they wore it like a shell.

For in fact they used to welcome and burn most of the driftwood that came their way. Sometimes they'd been dependent on it for months at a time. Logs gathered from the beach, or plucked from the sea, and Ethan's wintry plunges, as Jacqueline's assistant dexterity, had had more often intentions of gay salvage, than of salvation: yet it had been hard necessity too, with the lumber mills on strike, and no wood to be got from the forest save with the sap running, and no other way to heat the house. And salvage of two-by-fours and cedar planks for building and repairs about the house too, or for their porch, to this day left unfinished . . .

While truth to tell, very large logs, even those nearly in the class of "menaces to navigation," could sometimes be secured to the house itself from the beach, left to be sawn up later, so that, unless they broke loose there was scant danger to the foundations.

But at least they had still *been* there. And the beauty remaining never two minutes the same. For one fine morning near high tide they would rise to see a great wheel of carved curling turquoise with flashing sleeked spokes sharp as a fin three miles long sweeping around the bay: crash, boom: the wash of a steamer coming in under the mist—paradisal result and displacement of that far distant and most malodorous cause, a dirty oil tanker which, with all its flags strung diagonally aloft above its bridges and catwalks, looked like a huge floating promenade. Was he wrong and the whole world divine, could the future change the past, would the wash unloose the snags, and those last forgotten, threat of eviction forgotten for the moment, Ethan dived, sprained ankle and all, Jacqueline following him, into the great turquoise wheel, to emerge renewed. Reborn, for five minutes at least.

Now there was only this tide of his mind still rising, and deepening, reaching out toward those other grislier, more menacing timbers that were fears, anxieties, obsessions, horrors, it had not yet set afloat, where they lay still beached, in some cerebral niche, flung hence by some ejecting force, out of reach of the normal tides of consciousness; he knew they were there, would all be coming downstream too. Well, he'd deal with them later. No! he reflected, still with his eyes shut, God damn it, even the beauty of old Barkerville really had been a sort of defunct beauty, it was a bit like a museum, and indeed tourists sometimes asked to be taken through it. This was partly also because by some suspension of descendability between Trisaieul Llewelyn (as Jacqueline liked to call him, thinking great-grandfather sounded better in French) who'd been left it by the last grand-uncle, and Aïeul Llewelyn, the house had actually passed out of the family altogether and had been, in what one wrongly thought of as the last stagecoach days, a notoriously wild pub; whether it was thus it had acquired its name, or from his grandfather himself who, having been obliged to buy it back into the family rechristened it laconically after the spot in British Columbia where he'd made the cash to complete the purchase, or from a coincidence of both, there were no records to show and Ethan though usually fascinated by such things had somehow never bothered to ask his grandmother, when she was alive. Nonetheless

Ethan liked to believe that its period as a pub was the time the house liked best. It endured their tasteful embellishments but contained itself in dreams of riot. Scornful of the age in which it yet lived, it died consciously and furiously, whatever the immediate cause of——

CHAPTER 14   ❧   *A Bottle of Gin*

*B*ut it had not felt like this at the time. The immediate shock of the fire too was a different matter.

Señor, Lord, I wish to be your disciple, Ethan thought on the bus. I say it to you passionately, you are in need of disciples, or at least interpreters, and I, who once lived among fishermen, am in a position to be one, even as the chipping sparrow, who has built his nest near the true disciples, who are fishermen themselves. I am not a Catholic, nor, in my opinion, may one change the religion of one's birth without a feeling of great wrong. I am rid of the idols, except perhaps the sun and moon on the twin spires of Chartres Cathedral, as either hope or a hangover, rise majestically free behind the stubble fields in the weary pilgrimage from San Pres. And on the beach, the edge of the world in a way, what of the sun and moon there, on the twin cylinders of the oil retorts, as the refinery gruffly utters another gust of explodents, how shall I interpret this in a Christian light? Is it well with You? Eternal presence of the Creator, surely we may be inconsistent without being dishonest, as I have heard over the water someone singing on a fisherman's radio.

Now has evil on earth its strong hour, You once said Yourself, through the mouth of some medieval anonymous poet, in the play of your own passion. Of my death ye are not aghast, You said, and then when they killed You, You asked God, how have I grievest Thee that Thou nailest me to a tree. But we are aghast at your death here. Is it well that our hearts are nailed to these trees? The birds have their nests, You said, but the son of man had nowhere to lay his head.

And Ethan thought again of the thunderless gold lightning behind the mountains. It is an esoteric lightning too, like magical powers, and there is the danger that in talking of it we may be guilty of trying to render exoteric the intrinsically esoteric, which, while seeming the most human, is the essential proliferating folly of man, but how shall we be sure of this if we take as anything like fact what is actually happening to an esoteric individual who practices sternly solely what he preaches to his initiates. What do we make indeed of Christ's teaching and the Christian church? Are we to say that the former only begins to repossess its old authority when the latter is persecuted? Or can God change His own mind? However the lightning need no longer scribble exclusively in that void whose secrets are known only to mystics who, as Barbey d'Aurevilly said, "like the lobster knows the secrets of the sea but does not bark." "We have the answer to everything," The McCandless used to annoy me by saying, putting the tips of his fingers together, "except sprites."

But Dr. S. L. Miller, of Columbia University and the Academy of Sciences and the American Association for the Advancement of Science, has just descended to the world of medical research, via the old *Vancouver Messenger* I have in my hand, and hence to myself; I quote: Dr. Miller suggested that *lightning may have had a hand in generating the complex chemicals of which living matter consists* (the path of God's lightning back to God, as The McCandless would say?). He described some experiments in which powerful electric sparks were sent through a mixture of gases such as may have made up the earth's atmosphere in its early stages. Presently it was found that a variety of organic compounds had been formed, including various amino acids—the chemical building-bricks out of which protein, the basic stuff of life, is built up.

Dear Universe without terrors, for no hope can have them, but daily growing more terrific, I am a lawyer, concerned with justice, and have not until today at least considered myself, like Claudel, a poet set aside to proclaim God's revelation as God's spokesman, even though a jingle or so—never indeed until these last days have I progressed further than my eternal poem which begins and ends: Her wing doth the eagle flap, Hungry clouds swag on the deep.

And all this time the tide was inexorably coming in, higher and higher . . .

The fire had happened in May 1946, at about the time that Ethan, who had been, as The McCandless phrased it, "conscripted finally into intelligence," was mustered out of the army, having returned from France less than a week before, after a year's absence. True, he had been obliged to fight most of the war, if not exactly against his will, certainly against his conscience, then to his vast relief so far as Jacqueline and Tommy were concerned, behind a desk in Toronto; later to everyone's quiet merriment behind another desk in Niagara-on-the-Lake itself.

Since on the outskirts of Ethan's home town had appeared an army camp, whose complement of new recruits were detrained, there having been no railway station in Niagara-on-the-Lake within any living memory, right in the center of town; the troop train, the first of any description to be seen there for half a century, approaching stealthily down the middle of the main highway from Ixion—or rather from Niagara Falls—along the disused metals, then drunkenly halting between the Prince of Wales Hotel–Licensed—which during the war opened at 4 P.M., on the one side, and an antique stable housing three cobwebbed stagecoaches preserved as a tourist attraction on the other; not, though, before it had concussively aroused, at least on its first visits, an excitement among the moribund inhabitants of the old capital such as perhaps had not been known since the Johnstown Flood. In this way the train traversed Niagara-on-the-Lake's main street, and, as observed from the door of the public library (which was in the basement of the police station), blocked the end of that street entirely, drawn up across it, hissing mephitically beyond the two-hundred-year-old clock-tower, in complete possession; the approaching troop train no less unlikely

G

a sight to anyone coming out of the Prince of Wales who had completely forgotten the existence of the single railway tracks (which didn't belong to Canada at all but pertained to an old extension over the border of the long bankrupt Lake Erie and Michigan Railroad of America) than had it been, forming infinitely slowly out of a snowstorm in the distance, advancing down the main road, a long sperm whale walking solemnly into town from Niagara Falls smoking a cigar.

Or, Ethan thought in the bus, like something with as little right to be there as an evil spirit tentatively feeling its way into a human brain.

But Ethan had been sent over to France the previous spring, just prior to V.E. Day, in an advisory-liaison-postmortem-legal capacity; he had seen no fighting to speak of, brought up the rear guard of history everywhere. Still, because he'd formerly volunteered for active service as a private (he was astonished to discover in an official capacity how many had done so with an ulterior motive) and been rejected, and now had been in France as an officer, and still seen no action, both his pride and his conscience remained sensitive. And so he stood there with Jacqueline on that fateful Monday of their return from Ixion, unbelieving before this ruination, this dereliction of their hopes, before the bleak rebuke of that charred and ill-odored pile which no longer even smoldered, but at the same time uneasily feeling, apart from anything else he could already feel advancing on him again with paranoic tread, that it must be some holocaustic revenge the war itself had taken on him, a view shared to some extent though from a different standpoint, by his son Tommy, then aged ten, who having spent that weekend with that American school friend whose father was the brigadier general, now on leave from occupied Japan, seemed at first almost delighted by the disaster, seeing in it perhaps some occult hint of his father's military significance after all.

It was Tommy who had greeted them with the news. Ethan had driven Jacqueline to Ixion that Saturday, first having collected the car from the garage where it was being repaired, chiefly with the

idea of taking her to an exhibition of French Impressionist paintings
on loan there from New York, with the intention of returning by
Sunday evening. More amused than hurt by his son's infatuation
with the brigadier's family at such a time, Ethan had chosen to
interpret this as a kind of inherited sensitivity, manly and preco-
cious, in every way worthy of the father, to his desire to be alone
with his wife. But the car had broken down again in Ixion on
Sunday, could not be repaired till the following morning, and they'd
phoned General Heatherington, who agreed to keep Tommy another night and deposit him at school with his son Pat the next day.
That Monday morning they'd returned before noon and driven
straight to the school. Tommy came running out yelling excitedly,
what did they know, Mom, Pop, their house had burned down in
the night! Finding himself a hero, in the manner of the "corpse's
mate" at sea, not only insisted, though let off, on calmly going back
to school that afternoon, but announced his intention of going to a
birthday party at a friend's immediately after it.

Well, Ethan had not seen any fighting, but he had seen great
suffering, and for a while, standing there, in the way the mind
produces the most irrelevant and hypocritical considerations at such
moments, he felt it shameful, remembering his first sight of
shattered St.-Malo, not merely to give way to emotion but even to
cavil. Yet there is no gainsaying the tragedy of any fire or its heartbreak. And, comforting Jacqueline, he knew, despite her apparent
stoicism, it would be long before they transcended it.

What made it all so much the more poignant and hard to bear
was the contrast everywhere about them with the miraculous loveliness of the Niagara spring of that year, evoked for him by Jacqueline in all her last letters to him in France, full of longing for his
return in time to see it with her; how she pictured it for him, that
eastern spring, every bit as extravagant as the tamarind mulberry
and fire-colored autumns, and coming with such a rush and bloom
of life after the breaking up of the ice on the lake; the fountainous
elm trees with their pale green fluttering leaves over-arching the
stately avenues of the deserted town (which a few weeks hence

would be as crowded each weekend with tourists from Toronto and across the border as a Coney Island beach) and the blue lake itself beyond; the white dogwood, the pink dogwood, the celestial clouds of peach blossom, the capricious cardinals so splendidly crested and caparisoned in scarlet (so red, she had written, that when they flash through the trees you don't believe it), the trapezing scarlet tanagers that lived in their orchard, so precariously in a nest of leaves on the end of a branch; the first snowdrops and crocus in her garden; and the fantastic canoe-wood tree; a flurry of snow out of a clear sky (all these details of nature which were to possess far more meaning and reality for him when, in Eridanus, he came to pronounce the names of all birds and flowers and living things with love); but which then, insofar as they were also appurtenances of "Niagara's spring-time beauty" did not yet appear, as they did now, to have been somehow forever outside and slightly withdrawn from them—as if this had been the one curse of truly inhuman meanness his taxless paradise, through its loss, had put on him, "Spiritual Babbit" Jacqueline had once hurled at him—the beauty itself seeming now in retrospect to have a "Trespassers Will Be Prosecuted" notice on it, a "Keep Out" sign; the ferocious taxes that had to be paid for it to have given one the sense at every moment that despite one's owner-ship, even of the orchard, they were beholden for it to some wretched human official rather than to its creator or even them-selves, that the beauty moreover was beginning to capitulate, that nature herself was becoming tame and domesticated and actually looked up smugly as to a superior force at the hideousness of civiliza-tion inexorably surrounding it. And Jacqueline had written of their finding one another again in some renewed springtime of their love, which was what he thought his wife's wild girlish heart meant: and now the words had proved consubstantial with what they described: for here he *had* come back in time to see it all with his little family, and here he was: and now this.

They turned away from the sight, but then morbid curiosity, triumphant even at one's own expense, had to go on looking.

Jacqueline started to cry. "My—my bluebells, my hyacinths . . ."

There was something almost admirable at first in the very completeness of the destruction. If this were the war's revenge, it had almost exceeded its own terms. A bomb might have spared a wall, a room, a floor, left them something to build a hope of rebuilding on. But here there seemed absolutely nothing left but ashes. It looked less like the result of a fire than as if the whole place by some evil magic had been submerged in a great vat of sulfuric acid and simply melted away: house, garden, even part of the orchard was gone, or blasted and scorched, gone, all gone in that sudden infernal cataclysm, that biblioclasm. And they hadn't been here to help, to prevent, to save, if saved it could have been. And still standing there staring, unbelieving, seeing the house still where no house was, and seeing *inside* the house, the as yet undeparted graceful phantasm of staircase and polished bannisters, tallboy and century-old wainscotting and grandfather's clock, they heard the bell ringing from the Catholic school nearby, mingling with the laughter of children (who, in a yard flanked by the cemetery outside the chapel, were playing baseball with the priest), a sound that would always accompany in memory these moments, just as the warning bell tolling along the railway lines on the other side of the inlet would always be associated with their first glimpse of their cabin and Eridanus (and with The McCandless' later comments on it), the bell ringing and ringing wildly, while now before Ethan's eyes rose the terrible shell of St.-Malo Cathedral as he'd seen it not long before his return, and he heard once more its great bell tolling within the hush of the tower, making a mournful incantation of the words he read posted in the vestry:

> Vous qui passez
> Ayez pitié
> d'une Paroisse
> totalement sinistre
> —par le Fer et par le Feu
> —de 6 et 7 août 1944
> —un église en ruines
> —plus d'écoles de filles

—plus de Parsonages
—plus de Presbytère
Aidons nous, merci!

But not even the cathedral had been as "totally destroyed" as their home, its tower and bell survived. Yet, ah God, the fire itself, what on earth *could* have caused it? The fire department did not know, the chief of police had already advanced his theory of lightning, the insurance man was coming to investigate. Was the poor scarlet tanager the culprit, the tanager still whizzing about their heads, brokenhearted, angry as hell, chipping and chirring, still looking for the nest of leaves in the vanished peach tree, was he the miscreant? The scarlet tanager, warbird, redbird, firebird, and firebird of legend: did they make off with lighted cigarettes thrown on the road as people said? had he flashed through some window accidentally left open, dropping the burning cigarette within? *Naturam expellas furca tamen usque recurret,* Ethan thought in the bus, that just an instant, as he opened his eyes again, seemed not in Vancouver Island, but racing through the cavernous avenues of Niagara-on-the-Lake.

"Don't look any more, Jacky. Oh Jesus Christ, my poor darling."

"Don't talk about it. And don't mention phoenixes to me or I'll scream."

"Well if the bloody bird's going to clap its wings at all, I'd say this was a damn good time."

Well, their house was dead. And the world still burned on. Somewhere or other it did, even though it was now supposed to be peacetime. And you cannot look indefinitely at a bad stench. Leaving the car, they walked away, wanting to walk right away, walking hand-in-hand, even from time to time swinging their hands together in interlocked anguish, through the stupid beautiful little town, already blossoming too with more jukeboxes (that all seemed to be playing "I'm Dreaming of a White Christmas") and Coca-Cola advertisements than he ever remembered (and a new advertisement too for Mother Gettle, though fortunately not *the* one) and dragon-red filling stations like Chinese pagodas, all of them feverishly suggesting grotesque fire stations full of imaginary winking fire engines pulling away to the rescue—wanting to walk, as once in their first October there, along the Niagara River through the bronze and amethyst oak forest, "living on the land," as they'd called it, eating raw meadow mushrooms, fallen hickory nuts and two windfallen apples, beside the arrowy, swift, sun-shot Niagara River to Queenstown, wanting to feel this time the remorseless weight of their suffering falling on them there, though all the while their feet were remorselessly taking them to the government liquor store, which was shut. "I guess the only entry is a nolle prosequi," Ethan said, his nose flattened on the window, elbows spread, hands vizoring his eyes, their faces reflected among the bottles in the closed liquor store looking completely cuckoo—which they might well have been. "Probably they've just locked the doors and are boozing our rations away in the back room." And the Prince of Wales beer parlour shut too, for it was only 2 P.M., the Prince of Wales Hotel, where, having successfully eluded so far all kind offers of hospitality with the touchingly gruesome exception of some banana sandwiches and "Grape-up" specially prepared by their neighbor the post-master's wife for their lunch—and hugely appreciated by Tommy, fortunately, who had eaten most of theirs—the Prince of Wales where he intended they should stay—

"And I won't stay at the Prince of Wales! I won't. I won't!" shouted Jacqueline, all at once clapping her hands to her ears. An electric motor-horn in an empty car across the street had been yelling to itself above the jukeboxes, and was still dinning: suddenly the empty car blazed before their eyes: a short circuit somewhere. Now with a promptitude and exactness nothing less than brutal, bearing in mind the late circumstances (which had no doubt encouraged them to take time off that afternoon to practice) the volunteer fire brigade clanged up, while Ethan actively started across the street, accompanied by the chief of police shouting, "Keep away from that car, Captain Llewelyn!" But the grocer opposite had come running out of his shop and put out the fire with a pyrene extinguisher.

Ethan stopped to ask the chief again about their own fire, at which Jacqueline went running like a deer away from the scene. Ethan, his renewed discourse with authority having inoculated him temporarily against a growing feeling now of persecution, guilt, and stark terror, a feeling which was not always to be distinguished from one's grief, followed thoughtfully. He found her in the ruin of the old house, calm and collected, though greeting him from below ground, and holding up, triumphantly, out of the remains of their cellar, a brand from the burning: it was a bottle of gin.

CHAPTER 15 🌀 *Isn't Life Wonderful*

*T*here had to be a bottle of gin, he saw even then, if for a while its significance was largely physical, as they took the God- or devil-sent crock and began to walk half dementedly in the opposite direction from the liquor store—which Ethan, however, had not failed to ascertain from the chief of police would be open at five o'clock for an hour—along the path bordering the shore of Lake Ontario, gazing now and then over the water toward far distant Oakville and within sight of their first home, now long since the fuming province of Mother Gettle. They walked and walked, buying some orange crush and paper cups on the way—living on the land again, they said sardonically—as they did so, almost forgetting the fire, so inconceivable a thing, an innomination did it seem, for whole seconds at a time. Then with blazing hearts they would remember.

The coincidence of the empty burning car did not help. It kept suggesting to Jacqueline, who'd been the last to leave the house, that she might have left a light on by mistake and the fire had been the result of a short circuit. But it was no use speculating. The Quebec stoves had all been out, the oilstove in the basement turned off. Spontaneous combustion was a thousand-to-one chance. There'd been no loose matches lying around to tempt the rodent arsonist.

There was little comfort to either of them in the thought of the insurance, not even should they collect it in full (which, it was to turn out, they did: indeed their hopes now on Gabriola were based on the insurance people having had doubt it was an "Act of God"). They'd lost everything they had, excepting the clothes on their backs—and Jacqueline's loved squirrel coat, the first fur coat she'd possessed in her life (and just the week before had put in cold storage)—the car, and what money they had in the bank. Not one law book of his own and his father's library was left to Ethan. No single one of Jacqueline's cherished volumes had survived. Not one piece of wood from their beautiful irreplaceable furniture. And yet, when one thought again of those who, every day, somewhere in the world, lost, and had lost, were losing, so much more! No honest comfort here either. Much less to Ethan, for whom, now, as for a time he'd felt about the first house, it wasn't the material loss that seemed so unbearable: it wasn't the spiritual loss: it wasn't even the grief: it was this sense of damnation, this time literal, the tangible-intangible feeling of *punishment*. Yes, it was this—no longer like any mere plausible revenge taken by the war—and one's fuller renewed awareness now of that emerging pattern, a destiny in the whole business, which contained a warning, if not a threat, that no matter their material compensations, what had happened, even though not explicably their fault, might happen again, unless they followed a certain course of action, which course it was as if they shadowly knew, yet their orders were sealed.

But with this awareness came a sort of comfort after all, Ethan thought aloud, for wasn't it as though, yes, they were being watched (not in that sense, he said, turning round), they were being tried? Perhaps, he added, with a kind of humor unusual to him, being unintentional, it might even come to give her a faith in "something beyond?" Her answer was immediate, savage, and No! "Have you gone stark raving mad?" Later it developed that Jacqueline saw little more "spiritually" in this horrible day than the beginning of Ethan's real obsession with signs, portents, and coincidences, which from that period forward were so rooted in some ground of primi-

tive logic in his brain that, he sometimes thought, he seldom
questioned that the fire had been occasioned by other than a "supernatural" agency.

But somehow "not to go mad" was certainly an immediate
problem. All very well too for him to counsel Jacqueline to seek
some meaning in the disaster, a belief in some "force beyond" (as if
the words *"Les dieux existent, c'est le diable"* had been written in
vain), when he already saw, from the psychological viewpoint, how
his eventual sanity might come to depend precisely upon a deconversion from his own secret or semisecret beliefs and obsessions, a
deconversion even from any belief in God—either that, or, one day,
its staggering and complete reverse! Yes, how much easier for him
to endure this would be now, could he only believe there were
nothing, if he didn't have to think of it all as a judgment, how
much simpler could he but share Jacqueline's disarmingly fatalistic
belief in blind chance.

In short, despite the assuaging gin, neither of them had yet
arrived at a very realistic attitude. Not half so realistic as that of The
McCandless who, the next day, having been advised of their calam-
ity, telegraphed, together with a hundred dollars (to the complete
obfuscation of the telegraph office—which was in the back room of
the pyrene-brandishing grocer—where Ethan imagined them instantly rendering a copy to the Mounted Police for decoding, as
some important secret document in the current Communist spy
activities), from Medicine Hat:

GREATEST COMMISERATION ON YOUR LOSS BUT CON-
SIDER SOCALLED DISASTER CAN BE BEST POSSIBLE
THING FOR YOU BOTH STOP I TOLD YOU LONG AGO WHAT
PERILS CAN LURK AT THAT GATE OF UNCHANGE UNQUOTE
STOP RELIEVED YOURSELVES TOMMY ALL SAFE BUT SOME-
TIMES SOUL NEEDS ATOMIC EXPLOSIONS WATCH OUT CAN
I HELP FURTHER STOP SUGGEST YOU MOVE WEST AM
LECTURING MEDICINE HAT FOR MONTH YOU CAN STAY MY
HOTEL MOOSE JAW WATCH OUT SUGGEST YOU TRY CON-
SIDER THE WHOLE THING LESS THAN GREY HAIR IN GODS
EYEBROW STOP EITHER REBUILD OR NOT BUT CONTINUE
THE WORK SO MOTE IT BE—LOVE—ANGUS

It wasn't until at least their fifth snort of gin that any comfort of the more obvious kind appeared. For, yes, wasn't there a certain grace about it all? What if they'd been in the house and one of them had lost the other? What if they'd lost Tommy? been hideously disfigured or crippled? Been *all* burned to death? And they ceased to mourn for a time, finding a weird shared comradeship in the disaster, not forgetting to be thankful either for the item spared, and, seated on a bank beneath a peach orchard in bloom where they'd picked sumac long autumns ago, they suddenly discovered a providence in the fact that their car had broken down for the second time, and made wild plans for the future, and, in a morbidly hilarious way, were almost exultant: the phoenix clapping imaginary wings after all as they planned to rebuild on the same site—though they knew it was impossible—rebuild the Barkerville Arms!—and even through "channels" impossible to get enough material to build a two-room shack—but they would rebuild, somehow—plans increasingly vague because they were also so fatigued, and Ethan himself so tight finally that he made a sudden extreme answer to the situation; first having undressed behind a Judas tree on which he hung his clothes, he had a swim.

—Brrrr! Oh God, purify me, forgive this man, forgive me for Peter Cordwainer, let our lives be better after this awful day! The most awful of my life. Of my life but one. (What day was it by the way, apart from Monday? Try not to remember it: bad enough to remember they'd moved to Niagara the first week of October. He didn't want to find out today was Cordwainer's birthday or something either. He vaguely remembered it, or thought he did, as sometime in May. He didn't want to remember the date of his death either . . . Still, he could always shift it a little; it might have been after midnight on the eighth; which would take the curse off the seventh. And off the eighth, if on the seventh. And October was far away, so what was he worrying about?) Swimming in his peculiar histrionic way, in the loved hateful shallow lake cold as the devil; first a smashing, fast, and more than competent crawl: then, slower, like the Waukegan juniper crawling on its belly; *Juniperus pros-*

trata, Juniperus horizontalis; the ginbush, which (according to Mr. Clarence Elliot, the famous botanist) had been cast, for its tempting flavor, like the serpent out of Eden, crawling all the way to America with the Pilgrim Fathers maybe, and finally winding up at the Great Lakes, where it was condemned, as those who oversampled its seductions in gin, never to stand up again, or not for long; the only liquor with a divine curse on it, so why not supernormal powers? so what more natural than that a bottle of gin should have survived their fire? Why seek further explanation? And now faster again: imagining suddenly a hundred people watching him from the shore: not because he was naked but because he always did imagine it, even when as now there was no one but Jacqueline: but taking a desperate joy in the swim because after all it was his homecoming. WAR HERO'S RETURN TO FIRE-RAVAGED HOME. FOUL PLAY SUSPECTED. My house has burned down. Then difficulty with breathing; then ducking like a child, holding his nose (my house has burned down): no mean task since the lake here was only four feet deep: now swimming a powerful important breast stroke taught him by his father in the opposite direction by mistake (do you see me, Jacqueline, even though our house has burned down?). Then turning, falling easily without scissoring his legs into a sort of deceitful South African trudgeon, but hoping the spectators would still think it a crawl, and also how brave he was, saying, "This is guts in a man whose house has just burned down." Oh Lord: and now thinking he was swimming toward shore when he was swimming in the wrong direction again, toward Oakville. Back home to Mother Gettle's Kettle-Simmered Soup, M'mm, Good! My house has burned down. And sudden cat's-paws on the surface too, the lake sulfur-tasting. Or was this imagination? "The lightning is peeling the poles and biting the wires, Captain Llewelyn." The house struck by lightning, in the dead of night, stealthily, nobody seeing it happen, the chief of police perhaps right. Our house has burned down. "The police are not watching now, I hope, and anyhow they will see I am doing something healthy." Ha, ha, the lake getting suddenly rough, and mirages too—or deliriums—in the distance:

Neptune driving a fishing boat with tridents two feet above the horizon in the sun-haze. And now high tearing waves moving fast inshore; like being caught in a heavy sea in the main street of a town, the lake-bottom hard as concrete. You can only progress by walking backward then jumping forward through the waves or letting them meet you head-on. Danger: don't let them see you're afraid. (How many people's lives have I saved? My house has burned down.) Give concentrated exhibition—goddam stupid infantile exhibition, but somehow significant, somehow *necessary*, "the spectators expect it of you"—of wheeling and splashing to demonstrate you know what you are about. (Our house! Our house!) To hell with it; show Jacqueline: swim in! How hateful this sulfurtasting water: coming in in style now, a grand dramatic ending, the smashing crawl again, the crescendo and climax, and final, meaningful, artistically timed free-wheeling. *"And so I say you shall not hang this innocent boy!"* But was Jacqueline watching? She was not. She was sitting, under a tree on the bank, looking sidelong at the ground with a wan smile. She is worried about Tommy. She seems to have other things on her mind besides the fire; the same beneath the surface ever since I got back. She can't go swimming today of course. Anyhow far too early in the year. (Perhaps he should take her on another honeymoon: a bicycle tour, like his father and mother went on big-wheeled boneshakers.) Twenty-eight days on a lunar cycle: thirteen months in a year, like the interminably slow periodicity of the cycles of these lake tides. Ah, the pathetic cross women had to bear! And now the fire on top of everything else. Their wistfulness too, their self-sacrifice, their complicated long-range little plans, and dreams involving a thousand tendernesses: how many of hers must have been concentrated about the house, now all brought to dust and ashes.

And himself: sputtering and snorting and stamping all importantly, the indefatigable, fallible, male engine, which no matter how many times it breaks down, having been thoroughly submerged in water always behaves in this extraordinary fashion: Our *one!*—house *two!*—has *three!*—burned *four!*—down *five!* Just the same he felt a kind of defiant heroism in doing his exercises at such a time, irritating though the sight must be. But Jacqueline had not moved an inch from her former position.

He dried himself on a handkerchief and dressed save for his shirt, which he draped over his shoulder, liking to feel the sun and breeze on his skin (it was *Juniperus horizontalis'* sardonic tribute to life, sober it would have been intolerable today); he came over to Jacqueline and kissed her tenderly on the hair. Still she did not move.

She was wearing a cerise-colored spring suit of which she'd said, joyfully spinning round on her heels the first time she'd put it on, so that the skirt flew out all around her: "Oh Ethan, I feel like a cyclamen in this, with flyaway petals!" Surely it was a color connotative of everything that was exciting, warm, gay, yet innocent and springlike, one associated with fire.

"Jacqueline."

"?"

"I love you very dearly."

"I love you," she said distantly, still looking at the grass.

"Jacky, you never mind, we'll make out, we'll give it all some meaning, things will be far better," he heard his words—not an adolescent youth indeed could have sounded more naïve—words he meant deeply, but as though emerging less from his soul than his suddenly tingling, and half-falsely, renewed physical self, this abrupt sense of well- in the midst of evil-being. "You'll see, darling, we'll turn it into something fine—we'll build a new and better life, we'll—" Stooping he turned her face, puckered with grief, toward him.

But even as she passively submitted to this, she seemed to resist it, the touch of her lips was cold, and, as Ethan gently relinquished her, Jacqueline let her head swing flaccidly back to its former position, like an automaton or a rag doll's. It was as though she didn't want him to see this *grief,* to intrude on it, or to see her face at all, suddenly grey, tragic and haggard as an old woman's. Ethan felt his heart breaking for her. Even though the house had been his birthplace how much more she had lost than he! What pathetic spiritual covenant she must have felt suddenly broken, what inner place of sacrament defiled? And, inexpressibly perhaps to herself, for what it had symbolized to her waywardly of solid hearthstone (and sheet anchor), how much more she must be suffering!

"Yes," she said in the same absent tone, then: "Isn't life wonderful?"

Ethan was silent. He lighted a cigarette.

"Do you remember what you said to me that night, Ethan? After the Griffith movie?"

Jacqueline's voice was now so distant she sounded drugged. Ethan had only heard her voice sound like this once before, just after Tommy was born, but then her face had been radiant. He dropped to one knee on the grass beside her.

"Yes."

"Would you say it again now?"

"Yes."

"What's more to the point, do you remember what *you* said?" Ethan smiled. He was growing chilly and drew on his shirt and sweater. God, where was his cigarette? Had he thrown it away? He had: there it was smoking, down by the shore, by a stone, and he had entirely forgotten the action.

"No . . . No . . . I don't remember," Jacqueline was saying not even bitterly, pulling up grass by the roots, and her beautiful fingers, delicate mementos of the week's passionate caresses, were tensed and nervous.

"That hurts me. You said if we were driven out of our home into a forest with everything gang agley————"

"Into a forest. Go on." Jacqueline gave a faint smile herself. "I bet you don't remember."

"—and our plans turned round in mid-air and thrown away in an old boot, and—would I—oh Jesus. I can't go on, oh my heart's darling!" Ethan knelt and buried his face in her lap silently.

"Stop it, Ethan. Just don't do it. Don't suffer. I can't bear it. Just don't do it, my lamb, my poor lamb," Jacqueline, as if utterly transformed at this moment by some reflex of motherly and selfless compassion, was saying in a consoling and half-authoritative tone, rocking him like a child. "Just don't do it."

"No. And we haven't forgotten our sack of potatoes either, have we?" Ethan stood up. "Ah well; have another snort of gin."

"Yes, please." Jacqueline extended her paper cup. "Why not?"

"And I *am* looking at you like that," said Ethan, "saying 'Isn't Life—?' even though we haven't got a moon, if you understand the anomaly."

"What shall we *do?*"

"Go on. Whatever we decide or you wish. Go elsewhere. But first I'm damned sure you need a rest, a change."

Jacqueline choked on her drink. The portentous ridiculousness, which he immediately recognized, of Ethan's remark sent her into sharp hysterical giggles. "A *change?*" She finished her drink, which seemed to have revived her, and added, her eyes over the top of the paper cup almost genuinely amused, "At the Prince of Wales?"

"We have to get in balance . . . We don't need to spend all our time in the Ladies and Escorts . . . Old Grigorivitch is one of the best cooks in Canada . . . We'd go crazy in someone else's house . . . We haven't even time to get adjusted."

This last, which on the sexual plane at least seemed the opposite of the truth, as well as Ethan's implication that their misfortunes were going to give them a heightened appetite for borscht, provided, once more, for their spirits, the balm of the ridiculous.

"But what you say is *too* true." Jacqueline, leaning right back, drinking from her paper cup, gave a short cry. "We have to get in balance."

"I can't go west or anywhere else without settling a lot of things in Toronto first. To be practical. The insurance—all of that'll have to be settled. Besides we can't very well disrupt Tommy's education from here on a moment's notice."

Jacqueline asked almost shyly, sitting up crossing her arms over her knees, "Do you love Tommy more than me?"

H

CHAPTER 16 🌀 *Lake of Fire*

*E*than was throwing stones into the lake. Burning lake of fire
. . . Suddenly he remembered having once had a grotesque nightmare in which Jacqueline and he had been sitting by this lake, and
he'd started throwing stones. The only important difference was
that in the dream, about half a narrowing cable's length away from
the shore and stretching to the horizon, the whole of Lake Ontario
had been on fire, and in this inferno drowning and blazing forms
gesticulated, though for some reason it didn't occur to either of them
to do anything to help. In the background of the day, in this
dream too, lay some nameless personal disaster which had just taken
place, but despite this, Jacqueline and he were having this perfectly
irrelevant discussion on the lake bank, each word of which seemed
to possess the most singular and priceless importance. This discussion had been rèndered both more pointless yet at the same time
more "important" by the fact that, though in imminent peril
themselves from the advancing flames, it was not in their minds to
retreat an inch or, for in the dream they were apparently too proud,
to ask help themselves, though it also appeared that on the bank
behind, shadowy human hands were held out only too ready to
give aid to them, who were not yet beyond it. Then he'd got up
like this and started throwing stones into the lake, and the cruellest
part of the dream was that he'd felt compelled at first to throw
them at those poor helpless and gesticulating people. Something

or other had dissuaded him from this grisly occupation and Jacqueline had directed the attention of his marksmanship instead to some old tin cans and bottles floating past in the ever narrowing windrow of the lake inshore as yet untouched by the flames. Unprecedentedly the nightmare had had a happy ending, some act of renunciation or self-sacrifice having been made by either Jacqueline or himself or both—he couldn't recollect what—just in time to reverse their doom, but in the dream, absurdly, everything in the end too seemed to depend on his hitting like this, with a stone, an old tin can . . .

"What a hell of a question," he said. "Do you love *him* more than me?" Or had it been, in the dream, a bottle?

Jacqueline had half lain back again, then said abruptly: "Frankly —" And she fell back once more. "No. But do you know, I've come to the conclusion he doesn't love me. Just doesn't love me. Besides I've come to the conclusion I'm a rotten mother to him . . . I've been a rotten mother during the last year. I've been a lot of things the last year I haven't told you about."

"Loud laughter. Is that your tactful way of telling me you've been unfaithful to me?"

"Good Christ no . . . It's hereditary. I just wasn't cut out to be a mother, I guess."

"What are you getting at, Jacqueline? You're a marvelous mother . . . And Tommy loves you dearly."

". . . Not only that but I'm afraid I became a bit of a souse. Nipping away in secret on lonely private drunks."

"Fire cannon and blow up ship! How did you manage that on your rations?"

"Well, they eased up some months ago as you've discovered. And I polished off half your ship-store you left in the cellar."

"Ha! I thought someone had been siphoning off the cargo a little. Well, that's good! We don't have to bother about losing *that*."

"Jesus, you don't know what it is to be here alone in Niagara all winter, I even missed old James saying: 'Now Marse Ethan's just like folks, but ah gets a floodin' at the heart when ah thinks of his father.'—And the goddam snow piling up outside—not like it was on a farm if you understand me, where you felt things growing around you, but just somehow piling up on top of you, nipping away in secret beneath it. Oh yes, the Prince of Wales too. Don't think I didn't go to the Prince of Wales! Three beers at a time and vodka too and shaslik. Grigorivitch was an angel. But then when I'd come out and see the street standing so lonely outside, and those railway lines and the snowdrifts at the end of it and the old stable with the coaches and our Chinese laundryman who got murdered by the way—did I tell you?—still saying 'No tickee no washee' in those days—but those dead sad trees and then the snow blowing up in a terrible kind of flurry and whirlpool in the distance across the crossroads—Oh Jesus, then starting to worry myself to death about you again—"

"But all that time I was as safe as"—it had slipped out and she hadn't noticed—"as houses."

"—and the doctor coming in his sleigh with the sleigh bells going, or on skis. Bringing his bass fiddle and Mr. McClintock too."

"That was nice."

"Was it?"

"That was last Christmas. Oh, Tommy and I had a grim Christmas, I can tell you. He just isn't meant to be an only child."

"Please don't torment yourself like that. What *are* you trying to tell me, Jacqueline. There. Got it. Got that bloody old tin can."

"I guess it's true what my father said. Some people could be born anyway into any family at all, and it wouldn't make any difference. That's not quite what I mean either . . . Their fathers and their mothers wouldn't be their fathers and mothers. Or their brothers and sisters and their mothers and their cousins and their uncles and their aunts, I mean. Maybe some people's destinies are meant to be without children. And you have children just the same, even if you can't. Tell me, did you feel Tommy was glad to see you when you got back?"

"Not very, now you mention it. About the second question he asked me was could he spend the weekend with Pat Heatherington

. . . Look, there's a flicker up on the locust tree."

"Were you hurt?"

"Not much. It's just a phase."

"Not a phase. He gets attached to things, other things, anything not around his home. Oh, and we haven't got a home now, have we? Funny to think of that . . . You know what? He's not old enough to understand about my mother, I mean. But when he does, he'll turn against me."

"Oh Jacqueline, what nonsense! He'll love you more!"

"Attached to his school, horrors on the radio, other little boys, but he didn't give a *damn* about our own house. *You* saw that. The little fiend went trotting back to school pleased as Punch about it. And don't say he isn't old enough to understand that. Do you know what?" Jacqueline sat up again. "Tommy nags me about not having a little sister."

"Can't the fellow wait? To hell with Tommy, for the moment!"

"To hell with him, eh?" Jacqueline was suddenly watching him fiercely, like a captive albatross. "What! Would you like him to grow up feeling as you did about your father?"

"Look here, Jacqueline, I'd do anything for Tommy. He's my son, our son. But it's just like it was in the nursing home that night, when they told me he'd been born."

"What did you say?"

"I said to hell with the child, I want to know how my wife is."

"And—"

Ethan came over and sat down beside her again. "You're more beautiful than ever."

"Darling . . . you remember . . . You once said there were buts in your life—I don't mean that, but that you were too old for me. What if I were to say I'd got too old for you?"

"Oh stuff and nonsense, Jacky. Better calm down—have another drink?"

"Oh well, why not?" Then, once again, she said:

"Isn't life wonderful!"

This time she had spoken bitterly, wearily, cynically, he thought, and now, putting her hands on his shoulders, she gave him one of her old, long, searching looks, but as if meaning through it at this moment to convey the fire were *his* fault, and as though too, which was abruptly frightening, she really *were* much older and wiser than he, and looking at him like this, saw into some deep part of his being, finding there things he had not admitted to himself.

Or no: what was worse, though the fire blazed anew between them, or was ashes in the heart, it wasn't the fire that was at issue; it hadn't been Tommy or anything else; it wasn't the house: it was life, their life, their marriage aborted in its rebirth so miserably by the fire, and now found wanting, or in the balance.

Mysteriously, he felt, she seemed to be telling him she had been deceived by him: that what she'd taken as merely a certain immaturity, childishness, irresponsibility in him—what in part was this—she had been prepared for, had been prepared to love, and had loved; but not to discover that these qualities cloaked a man who had become, of all people, like her father—when she had always wanted to fall in love with someone as unlike her father as possible—a man almost without worldly ambition in the usual sense, who, seeing life's very meaning as an ordeal, perhaps feeling man's purpose on earth at all simply a matter of going through the hoop, had already accepted the fire as some necessary expiation; had married her indeed as a companion to share his loneliness in some labyrinthine path of just such atonements he must tread, whereas she (had she?) had been attracted to him, on the contrary, and with a quite different pilgrimage in mind, not only by what she mistook for those "endearing" weaknesses, but by what also seemed most superficial in him, by the poseur, the actor, who had won her with his likeableness, his good looks, humor, his air of success, his success itself, and everyday sense of adventure: if she'd felt attracted to him by their real spiritual affinities, it was only because she felt that by the fusion of these she must be drawn in the opposite direction from the kind of destiny she was, through her heredity, secretly terrified of, and against which in secret she rebelled so furiously.

But now she saw him as that very kind of man to whom great

accidents happen—if fusion it was also combustion!—as a man who almost relished this, who, if he proposed to take her there at all, proposed to take her to heaven by way of hell, and like it: whereas again, she seemed to be asking, she—what did *she* want? had she wanted? No doubt the impossible!

Yet what, in any event, she hadn't really been prepared for, her look seemed to be saying, as now she held him at arm's length, was for anything as *serious* as this, for this man who perhaps did turn out, after all, as he'd sometimes intimated he felt himself to be— actually damned, who, quite without meaning to, would inflict that kind of damnation on herself; who perhaps actually *was* under a curse, or even mad (oh, Ethan could imagine her thinking, that dreadful old story about Peter Cordwainer he'd told her now long since, so many times she had grown bored with it, that had been to her, or *had to be* to her, just as he feared, all "less than a grey hair in God's eyebrow"—now was he going to persecute them with this again?), no, she hadn't been prepared for anything like this, no matter that gaiety, wittiness, kindness were all attributes of goodness to be sure, and goodness and kindness, she might concede were, together with courage, all that was respected at bottom—a mystical imbalance in itself, as her father might say—by this "cursed" man.

But above all, once more, was marriage to this kind of man any life for a *woman*? could it have been resumed? come to anything anyway? was it not now at an end? Oh, she'd had all too much time to reflect about these things in his absence, and he had no way of knowing how she had changed, and if he suspected she had, he probably hadn't wanted to find out how or why. True it was all pretty complicated, she had to admit. Her life first with her father had been so hard and then, in rebellion from him, so self-sufficient before Ethan met her, that perhaps her womanliness craved dependence on Ethan even while wanting to free herself from its tyranny; but she had little life of her own any more, she'd found that out too particularly while he was away, and in any case now if it was a matter purely of their resumed companionship, she hadn't wanted anything that threatened to be so tragic, so merely a companionship in disaster, especially when, all over again, she thought of those circumstances of her own birth. For not only was there that fear of repeating the cycle of her mother, of going insane herself, there was that whole pathetic business of being a foundling too, a bloody bastard picked up on a doorstep (no matter that bastards romantically seemed somehow nobler than other people), the divided loyalties so much the more passionate in every wild direction, love and hatred of home, longing for and hatred of respectability—all those corollary expressions of her existence that, self-dramatized, were "danger signs," all of which too, once more, made losing the Barkerville far more shattering for her. Yet perhaps just the same she was blaming him, while upon a wholly other plane having a prevision of the future, of which this day could seem the heartless and destructive symbol, for having starved (it grotesquely didn't look much like it at the moment but, in fact, he saw, it was probably so: their societal life had come to consist, largely, as it had begun, in their own society, whether at movies or over drinks at home; and had been as bridgepartyless, horseraceless, danceless, as it was unrelated to any other lighter human activity, long before one could blame this on the war), starved the purely frivolous side of her nature, that part of her which could not help wanting to see life, as she'd put it once, as a kind of pleasure cruise (if not exactly like one on the old S.S. *Noronic,* moronically blowing its siren now, to attract its complement of all of seven passengers, alongside at Niagara-on-the-Lake's dock, preparing to make its first translacustrine trip of the season), whereas she might, disenchanted, have gained the impression that he tended to see life, Schopenhauer-wise, more like a stretch in a penitentiary: a penitentiary mostly officered by brutes, criminals and stool pigeons it was one's primary object to outwit with as much grace as possible, and in which it was one's highest privilege sometimes to be able to laugh: "This week is beginning well," as the condemned prisoner observed, on Monday morning, upon being led to the scaffold. Yes, that he really had turned out a creature of hate, rather than of love, that the Heathcliff faction in his soul was real and abiding and implanted in his character—was not the most dishonest and plausible thing he had ever done to pretend to lay all the blame for this at the door of his own child-hood?—a character that hadn't been essentially mollified, for all the "goodness and kindness," by their marriage . . .

Ethan couldn't believe that at bottom she had wanted anything "obvious" from "life" for the lack of which she was blaming him—why should she?—again the war had scarcely given them a chance at the "obvious," if a better chance than most—or that, as if over-night, she now found she "conformed." Certainly he'd never seen that the birth of a child had changed her much in this respect, and all the less could he see it happening if Tommy really was proving a distress to her, which he didn't for one moment seriously believe. He'd known her complain of the lack of that "social life," but put to the test it nearly always turned out she despised it almost as viru-lently as her mother had: doubtless she'd lacked friends here, but that was her fault as much as his. (There had been no lack of friendliness.) They'd made very few friends to begin with, and the reason for this had seemed as complicated to others as they were—unless they started reflecting on the matter—simple to themselves. Given every opportunity, she was not a "joiner" or a stitcher of socks or shrouds, a social busybody contributing to that noble cause shadowed forth in the image which always reminded him of the whole overstuffed stupid world doing eternally what it was told by its gruesome parents and groaning and straining forevermore on a pot: the war effort. But what in heaven's name did they need with friends or a social life if the only true common ground they met on was the magnificent dangerous though scarcely gregarious one of romantic love? And if it were the only ground, what then?

—And yet, to have returned to her like this, only for them both to be greeted so immediately with this conflagration, as of *them-selves,* did not this seem in some sort too to cancel all *knowledge* of one another? to raise the question, had they ever known one another at all? time to become "adjusted" or no, was it not rather as if they'd become—or was this just the shock of the fire again and alcohol's mutual alienation?—all of a sudden like the hero and heroine of separate films, playing in separate but adjoining cinemas? It could seem like that to her, or that his action of returning had somehow begotten this doom.

But Ethan saw he was mistaken. Jacqueline was grasping his hands very tightly and she was biting her lips. Yet there was a curious light in her expression, an infinite pleading. She had not spoken cynically at all but sadly. And knowing he had half-suspected all along what she was going to say, his heart filled with pity and grief for her.

"Ethan . . . Ethan, listen. I'm not sure," Jacqueline gripped his hands more tightly. Rain began falling softly in the lake, describing its peaceful intersected circles. It was a *lluvita,* a handful of rain, and the tiny spring shower stopped as softly as it had begun. "I hadn't wanted to tell you, you know, since you'd just come home, and all . . . I have to see the doctor again, but I don't think—listen, I have to get this over with. I don't think I can have any more children."

CHAPTER 17   *A House Where a Man Has Hanged Himself*

—And how the wind blew and the birds sang, and the sun shone, that day on the way home—on the way home?—the goddam golden robins all waking up again in the wind and sunshine and starting singing after their siesta, as if they too knew that the liquor store toward which Jacky and he were hastening, to get there before it shut, opened at five o'clock, the empty gin bottle now bobbing in the lake with an absurd motion, and an absurder message in it scrawled by Jacqueline, "Good luck to whoever finds me" (Ethan found it himself a fortnight later); the golden robin that was the Baltimore oriole and knot expert, and master builder, at its complex work of nesting, whistling in its rich contralto; they had seen the two orioles making their nest together earlier in the afternoon, the Llewelyns themselves the watchers on the threshold, watching them weaving happily their wonderful nest of fibres and plant down and hairs and string (rebuild, *we* shall rebuild), the female thrusting a fibre into the nest and then, this was the wonderful part, reaching over to the inside and pulling the string through with her little beak, tugging with all her might to make everything all "a'taunto," solid and tight, he hadn't fully appreciated this either till they'd got to Eridanus, but that was what the birds had been doing (their bus went rushing over a bridge crossing a swift river with the sign: *This is the River Amor-de-Cosmos. Drink Grape-up!*—and "I shall build a house myself, or with Jacqueline's aid, even if I need a book for that too," Ethan thought, while the same Mounted Police car they'd seen before choired past in the opposite direction:—no), she would make no mistake, that little bird, and so to make certain she would thrust in another fibre, or the male would, and that was what they were doing now, having resumed the work after the siesta, repeating exactly the same process, though now they had nearly finished, so that looking at their work, this small while later, Jacqueline and Ethan could see how their little home was all so knotted and felted and quilted together that though it was tossing wildly in the lake breeze (that bore to them with a scent of grasses, over the deserted golf links down the thirteenth fairway, the charred creosote smell of their own burned house), it looked as if it would last for years, and they imagined it tossing there for years, braving all the tempests of the storm country, seeing beyond too, through the trees on the right by the twelfth green, the boarded-up house of the matricide, one of Ethan's former clients, dead by his own hand before he was arrested or brought to trial; the daffodils and dandelions growing together in the overgrown garden—where someone was standing, after all, some faint Maria Chapdelaine motionless there—a man who claimed to have seen a polar bear kill a walrus in one blow by banging it on the head with a block of ice, an action that seemed unfortunately to have impressed him too much; his house forlorn as Cézanne's painting "Maison de Pendu" seen the day before yesterday in the art gallery at Ixion (which was on the fifth floor of the Department of Mines and Resources): a house where a man has housed himself: a house where a man has hanged himself; and now the windy whistling empty golf links themselves with their blowing spiny spring grasses and sand dunes and stricken stunted thorn bushes like Wuthering Heights: "I lingered round them, under that benign sky, watched the moths fluttering among the harebells"—the course! but ah, what further hazards lurked before them there, what roughs and bunkers and traps and dog-legged approaches, and dongas and treacherous blind (and nineteenth) holes, and final, it was to be hoped too, bright fairways; and the ecstasies of bobolinks twittering and bobolinking in the blue, bobbing on the links, or bringing rushes of rollicking song downwind, like imagined tintinnabulating harebells, like tinkling bluebells, darting over the "moat" of the old fort—the bastion now the out-of-bounds at the short fourth: *"Ein Festerburg ist unser Gott,"* Ethan said (observing at this moment that the old *Noronic*—"Bask in the warm breezes of sunny Lake Ontario on the boat deck of Canada's favorite pleasure boat"—was halfway to Toronto) and where, among what appeared cunning contracallations, they found an antique long-lost golf ball of forgotten make named the "Zodiak Zone"; the blithe bobolink, friend of hay and clover: the merry bobolink that was also called (ex post facto knowledge too) skunk blackbird, *le goglu,* Dolichonyx oryzivorus; the bobolink that said clink.

CHAPTER 18   🌀   *The Element Follows You Around, Sir!*

CALLED TO THE BAR

Once too often

Barrister Beats Bastille

Captain Ethan Llewelyn, famed criminal lawyer, was called to the bar once again last Saturday night. But evidently he stayed there too long. The ceremony enacted in the courthouse Monday resulted in suspension of his license to drive for one month and a fine of $50. Alcohol impairment charges against him were dropped. The lawyer fell afoul of the law himself on the Toronto-Ixion Thruway where he was questioned in his stalled auto by a passing prowl-car officer.

True to Form

Long noted as the "helper of the little man," Captain Llewelyn, who admitted having had two drinks "at a farewell party for myself," explained that, true to form, he had stopped five minutes before to give a push to a carful of youths who had also stalled on the road, then in restarting had "conked out" himself. Asked to explain why on the wrong side of the road he replied that his car, of English make, had "apparently run dry too"

[114]

and had no doubt stopped on the left side "out of habit" or "as a protest" or "simply because it preferred it."

Not Sozzled Samaritan

This explanation apparently being received dimly he was hauled to the Toronto bastille but later released under his own recognizance without bail. Later he explained to newsmen, "I must have been suffering from belated shock, and thought I was still in Europe. Anyway don't call me the sozzled Samaritan." Captain Llewelyn has only recently returned from France. The noted lawyer's house, the Barkerville Arms, in Niagara-on-the-Lake, and long an attraction for tourists, was completely gutted by fire weekend before last, threatening surrounding potential industrial property valued at over $500,000.

✿✿✿

Elephants may be fed whiskey and warm water in limited quantities on ocean voyages.

✿✿✿

The pile dwellings of the Nocobar Islanders in the Bay of Bengal are among the world's most ancient type of homes.

—No, he had not forgotten that little item in the *Toronto Tribune,* nor was likely ever to forget, now, that last filler. Nor their towing the MG away—it was still the same one (and one of the few of its kind, that special 1932 four-seater convertible MG Magna "University" model), like the sporting hearse—and taking him to gaol in that very unsporting hearse the Black Maria: nor the gaol itself, so familiar to him from the outside looking in, nor the friendly cop, who knew him, who said, "Don't worry, Mr. Llewelyn, we've had some of the best people in Toronto down here, as *you* should know, sir." Nor the unfriendly one, who didn't, and who, when he kept on talking about the fire, had shoved him in the urine-smelling "tank" for a while. "And what's *your* name?" he asked another fellow sufferer there . . . "Oh, I'm just an old murderer."

"Somehow not to go mad . . ." Yes, but now it was as if the subjective world within, in order to combat that threat, had somehow turned itself inside out: as if the objective world without had itself caught a sort of hysteria. Caught it, maybe, from poor darling Jacqueline, who, though she'd been magnificently sporting about his arrest, indignant on his behalf, tender, even managing to be humorous, now became subject to occasional hysterical fits herself, into which she could be startled more and more easily. And there appeared to be no febrifuge against this double sickness, this interpenetrating fever of madness, where effect jostled cause in a wrong dimension and reality itself seemed euchred. As (or was it by reversal?) in those plays where the players mingling with the audience make their exits and entrances over the orchestra pit (as once in those days perhaps, he remembered, when Niagara-on-the-Lake's old cinema had been an experimental theatre) and watching them you abruptly discover your companion not to be the girl you brought to the show but the Hairy Ape himself—or Claude Rains, in *From Morn till Midnight*—insanity and nightmare seemed to flow into life and back again without hindrance, to the frenzied infection of both.

During the previous fortnight at the Prince of Wales, between their fire and Ethan's arrest, there had been a succession of violent thunderstorms, and it seemed to them they heard the fire engine wailing almost every night. Yet curiously, because there'd been no fires at all in Niagara-on-the-Lake for many years, three more fires, following their own, *had* broken out in those two weeks, two probably caused by lightning, one quite inexplicable, all three occurring at night, though all, unlike their own, minor. These fires all struck on the side of the old Barkerville ruins remote from the Prince of Wales. But now, on his return from his weekend in Toronto which had ended so ignominiously (a trip, however, which already had as its object the eventual severing of his connections with the Toronto branch of his firm, the farewell party for himself had been no joke), now four more fires struck close to the Prince of Wales itself. Fatigued and tight, Ethan and Jacqueline, who was also, under doctor's orders, fairly heavily sedated, actually slept through the first of these fires, started by lightning striking a woodshed behind the old stables with the cobwebbed coaches, though it wasn't fifty yards away. On the second occasion Ethan woke to find the red conflagration raging right outside their bedroom window and Jacqueline already in a frenzy. Shrieking—imagining, she said later, the Barkerville itself in flames—she half dragged and carried Tommy from his room out into the street. Fortunately it wasn't the hotel, only another woodshed that was burning. Having, with the aid of the understanding Madame Grigorivitch (who, an exiled Ukrainian, was no stranger to such sufferings), succeeded in calming Jacqueline, Ethan helped the firemen put out the blaze, tripped over the hose, gave himself a black eye.

Jacqueline greeted him back in the hotel room with a mocking smile and half a bottle of gin, where earlier there had been none.

"So we have to keep ourselves in balance?" she said gaily.

"___"

"My poor lamb."

"How's Tommy?"

"Sleeping like an angel. Now. He kicked and screamed of course and wanted to go to the fire."

Ethan observed after a time, eyeing her as well as he could over his glass, she was holding a compress over the other eye: "If Francesca was a girl anything like you, I don't see that Paolo can have had such a grim time after all."

"Did you save anything?"

"Apart from the surrounding potential industrial property valued at more than five hundred thousand dollars, since you ask, yes. We—we shot a bear—saved L'Hirondelle's woodshed. Part of it . . . But it was pretty damned funny."

"What was funny?"

"No one knows how it started. No lightning tonight. No explanation at all, the firemen said."

She woke him up later: "Did anyone have anything more to say about *our* fire?"

"Nothing new. No one apparently saw it till it was too late," he said deliriously. "God damn it!"

After five hours of towering nightmare Ethan woke in sunlight,

I

determined to go on the wagon forever and pull them both together. This determination lasted until midday, when the liquor store caught fire. Nothing was lost save a few old packing cases and a bottle of whiskey *blanc vieux* Canadian, which exploded. Once more the pyrene-wielding grocer, who'd been talking to the manager of the cinema next door (outside which it said *Coming! The Wandering Jew*), was the hero.

There wasn't any explanation for this fire either, though the fourth one, occurring the next night, in a cottage on the lakeward side of the Prince of Wales, was caused by an overturned kerosene lamp. A terrific thunderstorm shook Niagara-on-the-Lake after this, though lightning did no damage locally that was reported. It would have been uncomfortable, under normal circumstances, despite the minimal damage from these outbreaks, to realize that in this way, living in the Prince of Wales, they had been surrounded by an actual ring of fire. As it was, the effect of the knowledge was devastating. Jacqueline, exhausted and sedated, and often tight, seemed to him to be only partly aware of what was happening. And what *was* happening? (How much of it actually *had* happened, he wondered later. Yes, but all of it had happened, he thought, from some bloodshot sphere behind his closed eyes in the bus. And happened to *them*.) After all, it hadn't been called the Storm Country for nothing, had it? Storms were to be expected. Yet the besetting sense of the unnatural, of *cauchemar,* penetrated even Jacqueline's wall of defenses. For such storms were not to be expected in May. They were almost unheard of. They were the properties and effects, the *Klangmalerei,* of the lakeside dramas of July and August. And the conclusion, in Ethan's state of mind, grossly exaggerated by alcohol, seemed inescapable: not satisfied with having taken their home, it was exactly as if something, some "intelligence," was searching for them *personally,* or *him* personally, all over the town, and preparing to strike again.

But now its strategy became confused, dispersed. Though storms continued to break overhead, some force seemed to have abduced the lightning, as well as the plague of fires themselves, in the opposite direction, in fact every other direction. Phenomena went galloping and gambolling over the whole countryside, though now and then, as if to show it had not forgotten after all, the "intelligence" would strike a chord again in Niagara-on-the-Lake itself. Now they really did hear the fire engine clanging rebelliously after fires nearly every night; but distantly, those of Queenstown, and perhaps Ixion, and Hamilton as well. Now more than ever, on country roads, the lightning was "peeling the poles and biting the wires," the lake must more than ever have tasted of sulfur, though Ethan had not the heart to sample it again.

This was sad, perhaps he thought, because between storms the weather was very hot.

Sometimes the "intelligence" expressed itself almost benignly. The barber and his wife limped home one Saturday evening from an outlying pub, took refuge under an elm, were struck by lightning, and came home at the double, forever cured of all rheumatisms from that day forward. They had need of their new-won agility because that night their own house, on Niagara-on-the-Lake's outskirts, took fire. A fireball went bouncing solemnly across their lawn and in through their kitchen window from which Mrs. McTavish sprang screaming, though landing unhurt. The fireball set a few curtains ablaze, then the flames died out of their own accord.

More of the chief's famous "ground lightning" felled more trees, or half-felled them, or was reported to have felled them, across the road bordering the golf course. The intelligence was coming back. One night Niagara-on-the-Lake rocked with the celestial tumult overhead as in the grip of an earthquake. Bangs and crashes sounded across the fields shuddering with lightning where Jacqueline and Ethan had gathered sumac and teazle to decorate the Barkerville. An abandoned farmhouse five miles away went up in flames. And a little tree house, without the tree being even scorched. On top of this, apparitions, or "mysterious lights," were reported to have been seen moving in the many overgrown and neglected graveyards of Niagara-on-the-Lake. Thunder returned to Niagara with redoubled violence as of huge aerial battles above the lake, sounds of celestial snooker. And now the whole town itself (or all but the most level-headed members, among whom should have been included, relatively, Jacqueline herself, and even Ethan himself) became involved in this tumult, this tempest, this kind of celestial disorder of the kinaesthesia. Rumors of every kind started, grew, swelled, and like fireballs themselves, having bounced in through a few kitchen windows, were dissipated. A phantom sailing ship with all its topmasts blazing with corposants was observed sailing in an easterly direction. A sea-monster, with horns like a goat, 119 feet long, was reported cavorting down the Niagara River. Psychic investigators investigated. People left their doors open for Jesus to walk in. The priest sprinkled holy water on the threshold of Jix Gleason's "Osteopathy and Manipulative Treatment." And, it was said, "in many homes." And lastly, M. Grigorivitch's setter gave birth to a blue dog.

Meantime Ethan, in order not to remember the exact date of their fire, for in that way he saw himself acquiring another obsession, or perhaps not to have to think of "May" at all, found himself each night in bed trying to think back instead over all the October sevenths he could recall for the last seventeen years, and it seemed to him since Peter Cordwainer's death there had always been a misfortune, or the beginning of a misfortune, at or near that date. And this, that at least it wasn't the first fortnight in October, was, apart from gin, one of the few consolations he had at this time.

In the meanwhile too, he had finally, or almost finally, severed connections with the Toronto branch of his firm, though it wasn't as yet clear whether he would be able, as he hoped, to join another branch of it in Vancouver. As he hoped? The truth was Ethan did not hope for anything at this period. To go west seemed simply a blind solution, about as good as death. He did not work, had none to do, but hung around the town, himself like some earthbound phantom, haunting the place of his nativity and earthly disaster. Occasionally it would occur to him he was not meeting his ordeal as he should. Yet he really did nothing about it, despite repeated half-hearted attempts.

Jacqueline, for her part, was alternately sporting and mean. That she might be waiting for him to take a sterner and more decisive attitude himself toward both their lives scarcely ever occurred to him. One night, having upbraided him for not "going on the wagon," as he had several times promised, when he announced once more he *would* do just this, she upbraided him instead for his blatant hypocrisy in daring to pretend anything of the kind, so that, in no time at all, he found it convenient to imagine that he was being "driven to drink" by her. While Jacqueline equally, having made similar resolutions, would see herself as "driven to drink" by Ethan. At other times Ethan would suddenly find himself alcoholically unable to comprehend why Jacqueline, having lamented for so long her lack of exposure to anything convincingly supernatural, should now, with the evidence, as he saw it, right under her nose, reject all interest in it. That she might actually be scared half to death by terrors she couldn't, or wouldn't, give name to he couldn't see either. Nor could he see—or see seriously—that his own entertainment of such thoughts at such a crisis might be a presage of almost as complete a breakdown in himself as, complementarily, these very phenomena might seem to indicate in the world of causes about him. Yes, he said to himself again, it's as though nature herself is having a kind of nervous breakdown. Why not? Human beings have them. Perhaps Jacqueline is having one.

He went to talk to the pyrene-wielding grocer about it: this indeed—to talk to any human being—was a relief. First, he'd confined himself to talking only about their own fire; then there was the second fire, the third fire, the four new fires; now Christ knows how many fires there were to talk about.

The grocer thought a long time, then he said: "H'mm. It's like the element follows you around, sir."

"How do you mean it follows you around? . . . You're damn right, of course."

"Like when you get worms," said the grocer, wrapping Ethan's purchase of two tins of orange juice. (It was extremely important that the grocer should think of him drinking that orange juice, as if he had no eyes in his head to watch him marching off afterwards straight across the street to the liquor store.) "Missis gets worms—fortunately she's a very smart woman—preserves the worm. Damn big worm. Doctor congratulates her. Then he says: 'Funny thing. I haven't had a case of worms in five years and then—bingo!—five cases, all this afternoon, all different families. You're the fifth,' he says."

"Worms!" said Ethan. "God damn it, man, having your house burn down's not like worms!"

"No, I meant all these crazy fires, coming after yours—same damn thing, Mr. Llewelyn ... We were burned out once, in Whiskey Creek, Saskatchewan. Moved to Swift Current, Saskatchewan. Place where there'd been no fires for donkey's years. Soon as we get there—bang!—five fires, all in the same month————"

"What's that? *Three* bottles of gin? I can't give you three," said the man in the fire-scarred liquor store. "I will give you three though, since it's you ... Yes, fire," he sighed. "Well, we were lucky. Compared with you, I'll say ... Don't know how ours happened either ... Hell, it's like they say ... It's like the element follows you around, sir."

"Thank you.—Would you mind saying that again?"

"Worst damn thing that can happen to a man."

Coming! The Wandering Jew.

It had not been so unwise after all, insofar as anything he did could be said to be wise those days, and whatever his ulterior motives, to have insisted they stay at the Prince of Wales. Not only did the racket downstairs in the evenings help to drown the increasing noise of their own dissensions, or poor Jacqueline's conniptions, when there were no thunderstorms to drown it, but the kind-hearted Madame Grigorivitch proved a tower of refuge and a sadly needed mother to Jacqueline, and Tommy too (who, since his father's arrest, had not ceased to be the corpse's mate, but now in a more literal sense; and was even in a kind of half disgrace, persecuted by his former friends, while supported by newer wilder factions, good or bad for him as it happened to be), who otherwise must have got completely out of hand. She was a mother on occasion to Ethan also, feeding him bottled beer in the kitchen on those nights he found it impossible to sleep, no matter how tight he was. Their conversation always ran as follows:

"Are you by any chance related to a Russian movie director called Dovjenko, Madame Grigorivitch?"

"I tink I muzz have know him as a little boy. Tink he is my cousin, perhaps."

"I saw this film he made and it was wonderful, when you forgot the propaganda. There's this scene where someone had to kill his brother in a forest—"

"Dovjenko Ukrainian peoples . . . Here, drink you beer."

"Now Dostoevski . . ."

Then, comforted in a sort, he would return to Jacqueline, uneasily sleeping under her sedative, and lie quietly beside her in the dark . . .

CHAPTER 19   🍂   *Fire Fire Fire*

As one device to send himself to sleep he tried reciting the Lord's Prayer. Rarely did he get so far as "And deliver us from evil," though when he did, he repeated this phrase many times. Starting again, the prayer became dislocated. For "Our Father which art in Heaven," he would find himself saying something like "our fire which art in fear." And out of the word "fear" instantly would *grow* fears; fears of the next day, fear of seeing advertisements, which he now seemed to in almost every newspaper, for Mother Gettle, at almost every street corner—in fact there were two hoardings on the main street, including the new one, and he could scarcely avoid seeing *them*—and there were always the tins of soup, in the grocery, to be reckoned with; fears of the next day's ordeal, with people looking at him queerly on the street as if he'd been responsible for all the fires (or still loathsomely sniggering over his arrest), fear of yet another evening darkening to its end with a sense of guilt. And out of the fears grew wild hatreds, great unreasoning esemplastic hatreds: hatred of people who looked at him so strangely in the street; long-forgotten hatreds of schoolmates who'd persecuted him about his eyes at school; hatred of the day that ever gave him birth to be the suffering creature he was, hatred of a world where your house burned down with no reason, hatred of himself, and out of all this hatred did not grow sleep. In order to combat the mental sufferings of the day, and perhaps also to distract attention from his black eye, Ethan had now let his beard grow. So in daytime his anguish was swallowed up by another sort of self-consciousness, that excruciating consciousness of the beard. Indeed he *was* the beard. Even now in bed he was the beard. Our beard which art in beard walking down the beard. Give us this day our daily beard. And deliver us from beard.

"You don't think you'll fool the Mounted Police with that foliage do you, Captain Llewelyn?" the chief of police greeted him heartily on the library steps, where they led down to the basement of the police station. "Ha, ha, ha!"

"I wasn't fixing to fool the Mounted Police, I was fixing to fool *you,* ha, ha, ha," answered Ethan, always delighted at so much attention from the "Law," at least when it was as avuncular as this. "How goes the ground lightning? Have you caught the roving arsonist?" He wasn't so sure, now, on second thoughts, he would have liked what the chief of police had just said, had he not addressed him as "Captain."

"God damn. There is no arsonist, far as I can see. Oh, in cases like this, nearly always some crazy firebug springs up, takes advantage of the situation. Oh, we'll catch someone setting fire to a house one of these fine days, all right . . . Yeah, but I've seen nearly as bad as this too one time . . . Antigonish."

"——?"

"It's the name of my home town," said the chief indignantly. "Now you take these here polterghosts . . . Oh, I've been called out on them things too in my day."

Ethan lit a cigarette. It was imperative that the chief should not smell his breath, or think he had a hangover. He had acquired a cigarette holder now, perhaps for analogous reasons to the beard, but he didn't fit the cigarette into it, just left it in his pocket. He hadn't lit the cigarette either, for that matter, but now he did.

"Poltergeists! Are you meaning to suggest my damn house was haunted?"

"I don't say that, Captain Llewelyn. No. But now take these here polterghosts. In Antigonish, say. I've had experience of these damn

OCTOBER FERRY TO GABRIOLA

things. Bolts of fire, pianos jumping around, weights sprung out of the grandfather clock like pouncing serpints at my detective sergeant one time, and I don't know what all. The priest sometimes seems to fix it up. Only you can't pin this stuff down. Can't arrest anybody, you know."

Ethan glanced round him nervously and seemed to hear himself saying: "Well, it couldn't have been us, could it? Doesn't there always have to be a little girl in the family when there's a poltergeist?" Now what had he done with his cigarette? What if he should set fire to the police station? But there it was, smoking away on the steps. And the chief set his boot on it, as if absently. "Anyhow, what can lightning have to do with poltergeists?" he said. "Lightning's responsible for half these fires, isn't it?"

"What do you make of it yourself?" the chief of police inquired, "as a Captain of Intelligence?" with, Ethan thought, a suddenly searching look. "You're right. There's no sense to it . . . There *is* usually a little girl, well, *some*times a little boy, connected with these things too, to begin with, now I think about it. That's what that book I read said too. Some little girl suffering from this here shitzo-frenzia; what you call it. And then the whole town catches this here shitzo-frenzia, goes haywire—and God knows, Captain Llewelyn, *this* whole town's got it too, if you ask me . . . Talking mongoose too, I read about . . . What they used to call witches is just polter-ghosts too," he added more formally.

Ethan asked severely, feeling, however, a sense of horripilation, his hair prickling along his scalp: "It wasn't a poltergeist or a witch short-circuited the battery of that car over there three weeks ago, was it?"

"Ah, hells bells!" The chief, as though reciprocally, removed his cap and scratched his head. "It's just one of them things. But I'll be frank. I've got these polterghosts on the brain a bit, having had experience of them before like, in Antigonish. It's them fires that don't burn things up proper that get me down," he went on, with unintentional cruelty. "Well, you might call it a kind of cower-dice." The chief pronounced it to rhyme with price. "Now you're a reading man, Captain Llewelyn, and I shouldn't say this, because I'm a Catholic, but there's a book in the library down there tells you all about it. One of these sickic investigators put me on to it. Oh yeah, I go down there to the library sometimes, when there's nothing doing, chew the fat with Miss Braithwaite. You wouldn't believe me, that damn place used to be a regular meeting place for drug operators. Smuggling the stuff across the border. Made me feel uneasy too, this goddam book . . . I ran in a husband and wife once for conspiring to commit arson for their insurance," he went on, as Ethan shuddered, "and now sometimes I feel I did wrong. Put their little girl in too . . . It sure as hell upset me, this book . . . Me and the Missis were all set to win at the police whist drive that night, and after I read it I couldn't keep my mind on the game."

"Who wrote it?"

The chief assumed a literary air. "Just go down there and ask Miss Braithwaite for *Ten Talents*. That's the name. She'll fix you up. And tell her I sent you." He hesitated. But seeing that Ethan was still waiting for an answer he added, in a slightly aggrieved voice, "Booth Tarkington."

"Booth *Tark*ington?"

"I was real surprised myself. Used to read his Penrod stories when I was a lad. You ever read Penrod?"

Ethan, shaking his head, reflected that all he knew of Booth Tarkington was the wonderful, if mutilated, movie of *The Magnificent Ambersons,* made by Orson Welles. "But I read somewhere a while ago the poor fellow was going blind," he said.

"Is that so? Well, that's too bad . . . I was real surprised that he should have written such a book. Of course I couldn't read it all, just glanced at it, like. Very different style from Penrod. Real deep stuff. But it sure gives you the lowdown on all them polterghosts. Well—"

"See you in Antigonish!"

Ethan, in fact, had been in the act of going down to the library too, not to read anything, or to get a book out, but simply to give the good impression locally that he had, so to speak, "gone down to the library." Now the thought of the chief's book deterred him: it seemed a bit too near the knuckle . . .

Coming! The Wandering Jew.

At the Prince of Wales he traversed the lonely Men's side of the beer parlour and dropped into the kitchen to have a look at M. Grigorivitch's dog. It was blue all right.

That night the bandstand went up in smoke.

"Christ! You begin to think you must walk in your sleep and do it yourself," Ethan told the grocer.

"Well, you just don't want to let yourself get that way, Captain Llewelyn," counselled the other in a kind tone, placing Ethan's cans of orange juice in a brown-paper bag. "Two tins of Mother Gettle's soup, you said?"

God knows why he bought them! He wasn't going to insult Madame Grigorivitch by asking her to warm the tins up, and Jacqueline and he had no gas ring, fortunately. Presumably it had been his idea of, for once, "facing reality." He dropped them into a garbage can.

"There's the devil in it," he told the man in the liquor store, cautiously looking round for the Mounted Police. *Fear may only be defeated by defiance or faith.* The comfortingly crafty thought was also in his mind that if these fires really *could* be conceived of as being produced for "them personally," then, perversely, they might be construed as the work of some really well-meaning intelligence, who had chosen this relatively harmless method of making him "rationalize" what had happened to the Barkerville. But his friend did not contradict him. In more senses than one: gin, since the day before, was unrationed.

So, after a period of comparative restraint, were the recurring phenomena. A dirt-laden fog settled over the whole area of Niagara-on-the-Lake and Queenstown, causing hydroelectric poles to catch fire through short circuits and, as the papers said, "knocking out some electricity," while even hydroelectric officials termed this fog a "strange phenomena." And seventy-nine-year-old Mrs. Annie Mc-

Morran, the mother of the golf professional, who lived opposite the club house, watched with fear as a lightning bolt appeared to flash down her chimney and send a red-hot ball of fire rolling across her living room. Then Tommy dropped his own thunderstone down the chimney.

"I know who did it, Daddy," he announced delightedly one day, out of breath, having run all the way back from school to make this disclosure.

"Who did what, son?"

"Burned our house down, of course!"

"What!?" stammered Ethan, aghast.

"Oh," said Tommy airily. "Small boys. They think you're a Communist *spy*."

Ethan carefully and controlledly stubbed out the cigarette he'd been smoking in an ashtray beside him. "You know what W. C. Fields said when he was asked how he liked small boys, don't you?" he asked.

"No, what?"

Now, confound it, Ethan had to search in all the other ashtrays in the bedroom for a smoking cigarette and on finding the cigarette he'd put out even feel the end of that to find if it was hot before he was sure it was the one he *had* put out.

"No, what, Daddy?" Tommy repeated.

"Boiled!"

Though Ethan was instantly remorseful about this harsh jest, Tommy thought it the funniest thing he'd ever heard in his life, and after that their relations improved considerably. "We get on just like a house on—" Ethan said to Jacqueline.

"Yes. Just like a house on."

That night lightning knocked out electrical power all the way from Niagara-on-the-Lake to Ixion. Electric company emergency crews worked all night restoring it. The fog, however, had moved away. Nonetheless the postmaster's wife, she of the banana sandwiches and the Grape-up, reported that the lightning had knocked a telephone from her hand at eight fifteen the same evening. She spent the night with friends and when she returned found another bolt of lightning had smashed a wall plug to pieces. Jacqueline went to Ixion to see an aunt; the lightning burned out the motor on the 8 P.M. tram she was taking, delaying service for one hour while the crippled vehicle was towed off the line. Flashes of lightning blasted the local radio station off the air and damaged a service station. New violent unexpected storms began now at all hours of the day and night with rain, hail, and loud claps of thunder. Then the brigadier general "got his," as he termed it, in much the same way as the postmaster's wife. Only he received such a paralyzing shock from the telephone he was hospitalized for three days. Towering thunderheads appeared in the sky, lightningless, went away again. Then, just as everything seemed normal once more, something stranger still happened, considering the comparative flatness of the land: a giant mud slide oozed down and buried one end of a power station between Niagara-on-the-Lake and Queenstown, which, according to the papers, would keep industrial plants normally served by the station on staggered working hours "for a considerable time."

It was true these last peripheral events did not so directly affect the Llewelyns. They were more affected by a decision Ethan took at this point. Though his driver's license was now once more valid, having consulted Jacqueline when she was off guard, he sold the car. He wasn't going to drive again, or let her drive either. Unfortunately, this sad commendable decision, for they loved the car, whose motive had really involved the final severing of their connections with Niagara-on-the-Lake itself, regarding which he'd felt his will to act becoming more and more sapped, had the opposite of its intended effect. Instead of helping to free them, it was as if now he'd neatly imprisoned them. Indeed he couldn't have erected a more formidable obstacle to the final winding up of their affairs here. There was no bus to Toronto. Telephone service was often impaired. In order to go by train, it was necessary first to take a bus to Ixion; two hours drive, then another three to Toronto itself. But there never seemed a bus to Ixion. A seaplane could have made the trip in five minutes, but there was no plane service. While the

Noronic was tied up at the dock, "pending greater safety provisions." There wasn't even the old troop train any longer. Jacqueline now saw herself deliberately trapped in the Prince of Wales Hotel. She was; so was he. He saw it himself. He couldn't take a hint. Obviously something more than the loss of their own house by fire, fireballs, the all-dreaded thunderstone, the very disorder of the heavens themselves, and whole divisions of polterghosts was going to be necessary to drive them out of Niagara-on-the-Lake.

CHAPTER 20   🍃   *The Wandering Jew*

*O*ne evening, after a bitter quarrel with Jacqueline on the subject, and walking with averted head through the beer parlour downstairs, he went off by himself to the local cinema to see *The Wandering Jew*. Or his beard went off by *it*self. It was the first show, the feature already half over. Nonetheless he had become so obsessed with the notion that, with his beard, he might have been taken for some figure advertising the movie itself it was at least ten minutes before he began to concentrate on the film. (Worse still, what if someone in the cinema should imagine he really were the Wandering Jew? Or, in some yet more complicated manner, imagine that Ethan thought himself the Wandering Jew, and what if he were the Wandering Jew—and what if the Wandering Jew were a Communist spy too! to see a film about himself?) "Subjectively"—it was a variation of the old idea which rode him—Ethan wondered if this wasn't an almost universal experience, when life was going desperately, and you dropped into some lousy movie to get away for an hour from yourself, only to discover that, lo and behold, this movie might as well have been a sort of symbolic projection, a phantasmagoria, of that life of yours, into which you'd come halfway through. This old film, with its menacing, almost inaudible characters and clanking machinery of which you half knew the plot, and bad, sad music, its hero (oh, that beard on the screen didn't fool the Mounted Police in Ethan, he knew who *he* was) going to his predetermined ruin, when to evade ruin was now your only hope, or you hoped it was: in fact you'd thought you were fractionally evading it by coming to the movie in the first place. And against such a predetermined doom, as against one's fate in the nightmare, finally you rebel! How? when the film will always end in the same way anyhow?

Yet perhaps it was at such moments, with hangovers in movies— as in pubs, hamburger stalls, lavatories, on ferryboats, in addled but profound prayer, in drunken dreams themselves—that the real decisions that determined one's life were often made, that lay behind its decisive actions, at moments when the will, confronted with its own headlong disease, and powerless to save, yet believes in grace.

. . . Much good that was doing poor old Buttadeaus, or Caragphilus, or Ahasuerus, the striker of Jesus, at the moment, either to believe in it, or appeal to it! *"A fugitive and a wanderer shalt thou be in the earth, ran the curse of the Lord,"* someone was saying in a crackling voice on the screen. *"And as with Cain, the Lord appointed a sign for him, lest any finding should smite him."* It was a flaming cross on his brow, that he covered with a velvet ribbon. Altogether worse than Ethan's black eye. And it was not, at the moment, saving him from being smitten. So the Wandering Jew was in a sense Cain too, ghastly notion; especially since (apart from that little matter of Abel) Cain appeared to Ethan one of the few humane people in the Old Testament. But what else was it the Wandering Jew—not the legend, simply the words, the phrase— reminded him of? Inner Circle. Inner Temple. (The Inner Temple had provided Ethan's own admission to the bar.) *From Morn Till Midnight.* London. Somehow London.

No. It was Niagara-on-the-Lake's cinema itself, which had something in common with his own first approach to the arts, that had reminded him of *From Morn Till Midnight.* The cinema in which he sat (he remembered again) had been built as an experimental theatre a quarter of a century ago, in those days of the early O'Neill

K

in Provincetown, of *The Long Voyage Home,* in fact. Where the Wandering Jew now bemoaned his fate, the Hairy Ape had once beaten his breast, though without, unfortunately, attracting any attention from across the border, as had been the idea. It had closed for some years and reopened as a cinema, still privately owned, and following a policy somewhat similar to the one in Toronto where Jacqueline and he had first met, and all this he knew because his father, who had never seen a decent play or film in his life, but who liked a finger in every pie, had long been one of its directors. This project failing, as well as other more conventional policies, it had now become a movie house apparently showing anything so long as the piece was at least ten years old, and in this way, with still a fair sprinkling of English and foreign films, it occasionally put on something interesting. *The Wandering Jew*—too theatrical, too slow, poorly directed, lighted, portentously acted—still showed no signs of being among their number. And he recognized none of the actors, though the Jew himself, an excellent part, was effectively played.

Ah, now he knew what he was reminded of. It was of a play he had never seen, of the advertisement for a play that had been running in London, years and years and years ago, when he was a boy. *Matheson Lang in The Wandering Jew.* He remembered the advertisements for it now, along the upper sides of the red two-decker buses, but mostly it was a huge poster in the London tube stations that had fascinated him. The poster, shaped to the concave tunnel, and half the length of the underground station, showing the wretched Jew, his eternal sea-gown scarfed about him, struggling against the wind, in thunder and lightning, among riven trees; yes, he saw the hoarding again now plainly, as if once more before his eyes. Because it had been just after his eyes got better. What wild romance it had denoted for him! That was what life was: to see— even to *be*—*Matheson Lang in The Wandering Jew! . . . New Theatre. Nightly 8:30. Matinees Wednesdays and Saturdays. A Play in Three Acts by*—by whom? Inner Circle. Inner Temple. The tube was known as the Inner Circle and there was an underground station, the "Temple." By F. Temple—No, J. Temple Thurston!

That was it. *The Wandering Jew*, a play in three acts by J. Temple Thurston. Most likely this was a movie made from that play, and if he hadn't been so upset by his quarrel with Jacqueline, and self-conscious about his beard, he probably would have noticed that Mr. Thurston—whether the playwright would have been grateful for this or not—had been given credit in small letters on some placard outside the cinema.

Just the same, the dreadful story of the poor Jew cursed by Christ never to die through the centuries—as if Christ could have been, *be* Christ, and put a curse on any man, least of all one who struck Him (had he, Ethan, struck Him? he, Ethan had struck Him—) the legend must have stemmed from one anti-Semitic source—could not lose all its force, or its power to move even to tears. Isn't Death Wonderful? it should have been called. For it was death that was all the Wanderer's longing; death precisely what no one was going to give him, death, the thought of which filled him with the same euphoria, meant the same thing as life for the lovers in that other, never to be forgotten, Griffith film, like that illness which is said to possess deep-sea divers, who cannot resist going lower and lower, until they drown, "the rapture of the depths"—not that the Jew, alas, ever seemed allowed to approach that close to drowning . . .

"*I plunge into the ocean; the waves throw me back with abhorrence upon the shore,*" here he was saying, and in a flashback, suiting the action to the word. And now reporting no better luck with other, recently more familiar methods. "I rush into fire; the flames recoil at my approach; I oppose myself to the banditti; their swords become blunted against my breast." Bloody woe, it was as bad as bad as the tank in Toronto. Yet that was nothing to the unkind treatment he was receiving from the volcano he'd just hurled himself into, from which he was now being spurned on an angry stream of lava. And all he got out of this was to be suspected of witchcraft.

"*He is looked upon as an alien, but no one knows whence he hails, he has not a single friend in the town: he speaks but rarely, and never smiles; has neither servants nor goods, but his purse is*

*well furnished, and is said to do much good among the towns-
people. Some regard him as an Arabian astrologer, others declare
him to be Doctor Faustus himself . . . He is of majestic appearance, with powerful features and large, black, flashing eyes."—"His
hair hangs in disarray over his forehead . . ."* H'mm. Not unlike
Sergeant Major Edgar Poe, in fact, late of the American army, and
points south. Or what about a large flashing black *eye?* So now, my
God—and couldn't one escape fire even at the movies?—they had
got him, were going to burn the poor devil at the stake as a sorcerer.
They were burning him. The flames shot up. But it was as one
might have expected. Ahasuerus had proved, once more, incom-
bustible. Not even his beard was singed. Some of his lower garments
appeared scorched, otherwise he was unharmed. Yet instead of
taking this sportingly as evidence of his innocence (as, say, the
English might in Joan of Arc's case), innocence, by this time heaven
knows, of everything, his captors had to turn him loose with further
maledictions on his head, to begin his wanderings afresh, coming
through thunder, the film ending now, to sombre crepitant chords,
with a windswept lightning-crackling landscape, the tableau exactly
like that of the old hoarding of Matheson Lang in the whistling
London underground. (And what more than lonely Wandering Jew
was not he, Ethan, at last, to whom figures on hoardings had begun
to have more validity than human beings!) But he was just lonely
without Jacqueline. Together they could have enjoyed the film, bad
as it was. She would have closed her eyes at the moment they set the
torches to the stake, as she always too dramatically did when any
character was being maltreated on the screen, opened them to see—
perhaps—Donald Duck . . . It was not until Ethan had sat halfway
through the cartoon following the feature that he began to perceive,
with fear, a certain horrible relevance in that fire which had burned,
yet not consumed . . . Or did he mean irrelevance, when he
thought how completely their own house had been burned? Bah!
Really, he must get hold of himself, go and look at the Kokoschka
in the art gallery for a while (where first the image of the troop
train as an evil spirit feeling its way into a human brain must have

occurred to him). But with these reflections Donald Duck itself became horrible, and he watched the antics of the ill-tempered bird with gloom, as though seeing upon the screen his own passions hideously caricatured . . . There is no worse place than a cinema, either, in which to be conscious of the too many drinks you've had too many hours before, especially when in combination with the drinks you are proposing not to have afterwards.

The feature began again: THE WANDERING JEW—yes—*From the play by J. Temple Thurston* . . .

Ethan stayed to verify that much, then, like someone plunging headlong into a bar, sought refuge in the little public library, which stayed open till 9:30 P.M.

"Good evening, Miss Braithwaite. Do you have a book here called *Ten Talents?*"

"Who is the author, Mr. Llewelyn?"

"Booth Tarkington."

Miss Braithwaite, with puzzled politeness, and a half smile, called her assistant. "Do you know anything about these *Ten Talents*, Kitty? By Booth Tarkington, Captain Llewelyn says."

". . . We have *Seventeen. Alice Adams* . . ."

After some discussion it was decided by Miss Braithwaite, politely (and correctly) that Booth Tarkington had written no such book, and by Kitty, that it was out.

Ethan, as reluctant to provide a further clue by mentioning the chief of police had recommended it as he was publicly to pursue further interest at this time in a work about poltergeists, asked could he "browse" awhile.

It was an interesting little library, in the old tollbooth, beneath the police station; the volumes mostly of the Victorian era, with complete sets of Howells, Meredith, Mark Twain, Mark Rutherford, and a startling array of translations from the nineteenth-century French classics: the Goncourt brothers, Zola, Flaubert; *Crime and Punishment* was there, in Constance Garnett's translation; so was Lawrence's *Studies in Classic American Literature;* but twentieth-century fiction seemed scarcely represented save by the seven-day books, current best sellers, lying on a shelf above Miss Braithwaite's head.

There existed a separate section for "religious and occult" volumes, and aware of a certain ratification, even admiration, for his beard in this place, he browsed awhile without undue anguish. The section was well stocked with a surprising number of recently printed works of this nature, for which, one surmised, the war had been the invisible salesman. Ethan almost immediately—so immediately it was as though the volume had been waiting for him—found what he was looking for, took the book over to a table and sat down.

Booth Tarkington had not indeed written *Ten Talents*. And *Ten Talents* was clearly not the name of the book the chief had in mind. Booth Tarkington had merely written an appreciation for a book named *Lo!* by a writer named Charles Fort, and a piece of its cover, with a quotation, was pasted inside an omnibus volume of works by the same author, among them *Lo!* itself, and a book called *Wild Talents*. It was this more inclusive volume Ethan was glancing through; "A writer whose pen is dipped in earthquake and eclipse"—Booth Tarkington. The chief's mistake was complicated, but it wasn't difficult to see how he'd made it, especially if he'd had one eye on Miss Braithwaite. While the name Charles Fort probably meant as little to him as to Ethan.

But *Wild Talents* hadn't much concerning actual poltergeist phenomena, though there seemed other large sections throughout the omnibus dealing with that subject. Fort, an American who had died in 1932, obviously a genius if ever there was one, the possessor, together with the appalling insight, of all the scotomas and quirks of such dedicated powers, had obviously also been a pioneer in his approach to this type of research: one felt much intelligent opinion had come closer in recent years to accepting some of his views on such phenomena—insofar as Fort had any, for dogma in any form seemed his principal foe—accepting them even as a possible cause of otherwise inexplicable fires, and it must have been these parts the psychic investigator had referred the chief to, under the impression their content was strictly "psychical." The joke, to some extent, was on the investigator. But then the whole book, wherever you opened it, was so compulsively entertaining on the surface, even with all its enormous weight of documentation, it was easy to be deceived, so hard was it to concentrate on a given spot. The immediate thesis of *Wild Talents,* insofar as one could take it in so rapidly, was as logically compelling as it must have been acutely discomforting to Ethan, had not the author's personality everywhere provided such robust assurance one soon forgot oneself. In no time at all one had been pleasantly convinced that certain unexplained fires (apart from those that seemed the undoubted work of poltergeists, whatever *they,* finally, were) had actually been *feared* into existence: that on occasion, feelings of sheer hatred or revenge toward other human beings had been sufficient to cause, without admixture of purposive "magic," disaster, otherwise inexplicable, to others: (So why not to oneself, Ethan thought, as psychiatry implied, by hatred of oneself?) Moreover, that motives, not acted upon, could produce the same result as those same motives had they been translated into action . . . It was one thing to have felt this instinctively, quite another to see it in cold print. For what criminal lawyer could not recall some instance in his own experience, where a confessed crime of murder or theft had offered the only conceivable motive and explanation for some secondary collateral, apparently covering crime the criminal could not, in either the physical or legal sense, possibly have committed?

None of this formed the main thesis of the whole work—Ethan was skipping back and forth in the omnibus from book to book by this time—into another book called *The Book of the Damned,* into yet another called *New Worlds*—all of so obviously extraordinary a kind one felt astonishment that its author's name had not long since become a household word. Surely few writers were ever capable so swiftly and convincingly of disaffecting a reader from the regular bounds of his cosmos. Although in one sense Fort didn't widen them, he narrowed them. In ten minutes more Ethan had become convinced that the source of Niagara-on-the-Lake's black fog—for here, by Jupiter, were *their* black fog, and the mud, and the fireballs, and not only these but rains of periwinkles and frogs too—were perhaps unknown lands situated at relatively no great distance in the dark nebulae, that celestial visitors of all kinds were no uncommon occurrence, that the object shaped like a man seen passing over Vicksburg, Pennsylvania, the report of which had once so perplexed him, was possibly no less than he seemed to be. And now, on every page he turned to, he seemed to see examples of the kinds of phenomena which had plagued them so frequently of late, cited as having been reported innumerable times before throughout history, or at least the last hundred years; everywhere in the work they were given veredicity—yes, everywhere Ethan was looking, as if once more those pages had wanted, were demanding to be looked at tonight—here they all were again, the black fog, the mud, the unexplained fires, the fires that burned, the fires that did not burn, or went out, or did not wholly consume, the wandering mysterious lights in churchyards in rural places, and now again the fireballs, the flying saucers, the auxiliary prodigies, in fact everything save M. Grigorivitch's blue dog, though no sooner had he thought that, than here was an example cited of a dog who had said good morning and vanished in a "greenish vapour." Mr. Fort had drawn the line at the dog who said good morning.

The cumulative effect was terrifying: yet, for all that, Ethan thought to himself again, oddly reassuring. It was all something like going into a house reputed to be—that one had always thought was—haunted, in the company of some amiable Don Quixote, and perhaps a barrel of amontillado. Or a hogshead of gin. But haunted by spirits? Not a bit of it. Such notions were really the work of romantics. The only haunted house was the human mind. And the human mind was that of a magician—how The McCandless would have liked this bit!—who had forgotten the use of his powers, but from time to time could not help using them. All of which by no means discounted the possibility of other "intelligences" inhabiting those regions so much nearer than were supposed, those near those—now he thought of it—far too near regions. Only nothing was *super*natural. Everything would be explained when the time came. Even those "imperfect" conflagrations could be explained, were not really supernatural—and it was perhaps almost a disappointment after all, could be—

Jesus.

The man of one of our stories, J. Temple Thurston—alone in his room—and that a pictorial representation of his death by fire was enacting in a distant mind—

Suddenly Ethan's eye fell on a passage that almost made him drop dead with fright. What?—J. Temple Thurston? death by fire . . .

The man of one of our stories—J. Temple Thurston (he read, again)—alone in his room—and that a pictorial representation of his death by fire was enacting in a distant mind—and that into the phase of existence that is called "real" stole the imaginary—scorching his body, but not his clothes, because so was pictured the burning of him—and that, hours later, there came into the mind of the sorcerer a fear that this imposition of what is called the imaginary upon what is called the physical bore quasi-attributes of its origin, or was not realistic, or would be, in physical terms, unaccountable, and would attract attention—and that the fire in the house was visualized, and was "realized," but by a visualization that in turn left some particulars unaccounted for.

Ethan glanced yet again at the passage, saw that was what it said—almost incomprehensible when so isolated, but God knows it said enough—noted the page and the end of the preceding paragraph: "It was during a thunderstorm and the woman had been killed by lightning," which seemed irrelevant (though another storm was at this moment beginning), took out the book and ran up the steps leading from the basement of the police station.

The knowledge, in any case, could scarcely be borne alone. He'd narrowly escaped having to bear it too, being locked up in the darkening public library, that, as he hurried out, had been on the point of closing, himself forgotten, to be bailed out perhaps, at the frantic sounds of his knocking, only by old Chief Tollbooth Tarkington himself, in cautious search of subayuntamiento polterghosts.

Held Over. The Wandering Jew. Cameo Cinedrome. Ethan's feeling of panic was now succeeded by a mysterious sense of elation, even self-congratulation, flooding through his being as he hurried through the hot lightning-flickering dusk under the few remaining elms thrashing overhead in concussive gusts (he wondered later if Mr. Fort was right, and this sensation perhaps an atavistic one, common to all men, who suddenly seem to feel, if only for an instant, and on a sublunary plane, their own lost magical powers restored), hurried past the clock-tower, over which a frantic homing seaplane was flying soundlessly, like a bird with long shoes, into a patch of hyacinthine sky in the west—hurried home to the Prince of Wales Hotel . . . *King Storm Whose Sheen Is Fearful*.

He found Jacqueline, who had previously announced with fury she was going to bed, after having seen to Tommy for the night, wildly drinking beer and talking to M. Grigorivitch in the almost deserted Ladies and Escorts. She greeted him with a radiant and friendly smile while M. Grigorivitch went off to get them one on the house.

"What's the book?" she said cheerfully.

But Ethan's calm had left him, and having tried to tell her his story about the cinema, the Wandering Jew, and the library, his hands trembling, he couldn't find anywhere the passage in *Wild Talents* about Temple Thurston.

"Give the book to me . . .

" 'Upon the night of April 6, 1919,' " Jacqueline found immediately these words which she read aloud, " 'see the Dartford (Kent) *Chronicle*, April—Mr. J. Temple Thurston was alone in his home, Hawley Manor, near Dartford. His wife was abroad.' "

"But *Jac*queline———!"

" 'Particulars of the absence of his wife, or of anything leading to the absence of his wife, are missing. Something had broken up this home. The servants had been dismissed. Thurston was alone.' "

"But that wasn't the passage—"

" 'At two forty o'clock, morning of April 7, the firemen were called to Hawley Manor. Outside Thurston's room, the house was blazing, but in his room there was no fire. Thurston was dead. His body was scorched, but upon his clothes there was no trace of fire.' "

"But *Jacqueline!*"

" 'From the story of J. Temple Thurston I pick up that this man, with his clothes on, was so scorched as to bring on death by heart failure, by a fire that did not affect his clothes. This body was fully clothed, when found, about 3 A.M. Thurston hadn't been sitting up drinking. There was no suggestion that he had been reading. It was commented upon, at the inquest, as queer, that he should have been up and fully clothed at about 3 A.M. The scorches were large red patches on the thighs and lower parts of the legs. It was much as if, bound to a stake, the man had stood in a fire that had not mounted high.' "

"Great *God!*" Ethan felt a tightening of his throat at the roots of his tongue. "But Jacqueline. The *end* of the Wandering Jew, in the movie———"

"All right, Ethan. I get it." She looked up at him with frightened eyes. "But wait—let me finish . . .

" 'In this burning house nothing was afire in Thurston's room. Nothing was found, such as charred fragments of nightclothes, to suggest that, about three o'clock, Thurston, awakened by a fire elsewhere in the house, had gone from his room, and had been burned, and had returned to his room, where he had dressed, but had then been overcome. It may be that he had died hours before the house was fired.' "

"But that's absolutely inconceivable! That isn't the passage I read at all!" Ethan burst out.

" 'It has seemed to me,' " Jacqueline pursued, calmly reading on, " 'most fitting to regard all accounts in this book as "stories." There has been a permeation of the fantastic, or whatever we mean by "untrueness." Our stories have not been realistic. And there is something about the story of J. Temple Thurston that, to me, gives it the look of a revised story. It is as if, in an imagined scene, an author had killed off a character by burning, and then, thinking it over, as some writers do, had noted inconsistencies, such as a burned body, and no mention of a fire anywhere else in the house—So then, as an afterthought, the fire in the house—but, still, such an amateurish negligence in the authorship of this story, that the fire was not explained. To the firemen, this fire in the house was as unaccountable as, to the coroner, was the burned body in the unscorched clothes. When the firemen broke into Hawley Manor, they found the fire raging in Thurston's room. It was near no fireplace, near no electric wires that might have crossed. No odor of paraffin, nothing suggestive of arson: or of *ordinary* arson. No robbery.

" 'The fire, of unknown origin, seemed directed upon Thurston's room, as if to destroy, clothes and all, this burned body in unscorched clothes. Outside, the door of this room was blazing when the firemen arrived.' "

In the same way he had felt himself flooded by that strange sense of elation after leaving the library, Ethan now felt the fright this had cancelled coming back, but in a far more powerful form, as though now he were being overwhelmed by a sea, a huge breaker of primeval terror, and as if the obsessive thought of fire itself had produced the compensatory image, the opposite symbol of water—or it was like an incoming wave from the burning lake of fire in his nightmare—and now, as the feeling receded, he were left sprawling in a titanic undertow.

At the same time he saw clearly the blazing door, the unscorched clothes, the imperfectly burned body of the poor playwright alone in his room, saw the closing scenes of the movie again, the Wandering Jew bound to the stake. "It was much as if bound to a stake, the man had stood in a fire that had not mounted high"; the imperfectly burned undying Ahasuerus, his imperfectly burned dead "creator" "in a fire that had not mounted high, as if bound to the stake"; and fearing to see these things too clearly, found himself remembering too some words of the passage he had been unable to find again in *Wild Talents:* "that the fire was visualized by a

visualization that in turn left some particulars unaccounted for";
"that a pictorial representation of his death by fire was enacting in a
distant room"; "that into the phase of existence that was real, stole
the imaginary"; then————!

But he now became conscious of something more frightening yet
taking place in his mind. It was a feeling that permeated the high ill-
lit yellow walls of the hotel beer parlour, the long dim corridor
between the two beer parlours, on which the door now seemed to be
opened by an invisible hand (revealing, lying flat on her back, a
good woman weighing 350 pounds, from Gravesend, London, who
had so far resisted all efforts to be lifted—it was fruitless, as Ethan
well knew, who had tried before: she went through this performance almost every night about this time, and then, at ten forty-five,
just before closing time, would get up of her own accord and go
home, as though nothing had happened), a feeling which seemed a
very part of the ugly, sad, red-and-brown tables and chairs, something that was in the very beer-smelling air, as if—the feeling perhaps someway arising, translated to this surrounding scene, from the
words themselves—there were some hidden correspondence between
these words and this scene, or between some ultimate unreality and
meaninglessness he seemed to perceive adumbrated by them (by
these words, under their eyes, in the book on the table—and yet for
an instant what meaning, what terrifying message flashed from all
this meaninglessness), and his inner perception of this place: no, it
was as if this place were suddenly the exact outward representation
of his inner state of mind: so that shutting his eyes for a long
moment of stillness (in which he imagined he could hear—God—
distantly, pounding, the tumultuous cataract of Niagara Falls
twenty miles away) he seemed to feel himself merging into it, while
equally there was a fading of it into himself: it was as though,
having visualized all this with his eyes shut now he *were* it—these
walls, these tables, that corridor, with the huge woman from
Gravesend, flat on her back motionless in it, obdurate as the truth,
this beer parlour, this place of garboons hard by the Laurentian
Shield! But in this new reality not even the goodness of its landlords

served to redeem it. Nor any other benevolence of fellowship, gaiety, the relatively innocent drink it purveyed. For his visualization appeared to include everything that ought to have been ordinarily invisible *too,* Sergeant Major Poe's "unparticled matter" rendered palpable to the gaze, so that it was like *seeing* all the senseless trickeries and treacheries alcohol had here imposed on the mind; all the misery, mischief, wretchedness, illusions: yes, the sum of all the hangovers that had been acquired here, and quite overlooking those that had been healed. Ethan now held this collective mental image for an instant completely, unwaveringly, on the screen of his mind. Image or state of being that finally appeared to imply, represent, an unreality, a desolation, disorder, falsity that was beyond evil. Satan was in a sense perhaps a realized figure in the human psyche. But even such a Satan could not, and for that reason, dwell in this region: or if this were in his domain, he held no sway; or, by some more than legal fiction, so far beneath the abysmal was it, his law sounded here faint, unheard, confused—like the recurrent sounds of the motor in the refrigerator. Yet this seemed the home also of more conscious mental abortions and aberrations; of disastrous yet unfinished thoughts, half hopes and half intentions, and where precepts, long abandoned, stumbled on. Or the home of a half-burned man, himself an imperfect visualization, at the stake; this place where neither death nor suicide could ever be a solution, since nothing here had been sufficiently realized ever to possess life. Ethan opened his eyes. What was he saying to himself? Had he really *had* some sort of vision—the feeling had not altogether departed—some kind of "mystical" experience "reversed?" Some form less of an illumination, than a *disillumination,* a kind of minor St. Paul's vision upside down; certainly it had arisen, if in an unorthodox manner, from an almost complete and mysterious identification of subject with object: and had been accompanied, paradoxically, by such an astonishing sense of ecstasy, one felt one could never begin to describe it, even to Jacqueline, even to her father, who, if anyone, should be equipped to understand it, without somehow leading to the propagation of a lie, an ecstasy which still persisted, though diminished, an icy perverted ecstasy now before "reality" asserts itself—and waking indeed you discover your clothes to be neatly folded up in the icebox where, alas, no drink has been providently left. Ethan came to his senses abruptly. Grace had at least penetrated to this more immediate mundane region in the shape of another beer, and he drank it greedily. It wasn't that there was anything particularly original about such thoughts, any more than there had been, he now saw, in the form of his "disillumination" (on the contrary, as to aesthetic content it had perhaps hardly more merit than a parody based on a misreading of T. S. Eliot, or for that matter, Swinburne), yet the intensity, the conviction, was still there, this impression as of something overwhelmingly important that had just occurred. And he saw something important *had* occurred, and quite apart from the experience, its "mystical" validity or otherwise to another, and something of striking obviousness. What was important was that he was now convinced there must be some complete triumphant counterpart, hitherto based on hearsay or taken on trust, of that experience he had had, or almost had: as there must be of that abyssal region, some spiritual region maybe of unborn divine thoughts beyond our knowledge . . .

So why, then, should he have rushed to the conclusion that the extraordinary thing that had happened tonight with the Wandering Jew and Temple Thurston and Charles Fort, that this collision of contingencies, was in its final essence diabolical, or fearful, or meaningless? Why, to the conclusion that he had somehow magically produced it himself, then that any message in it for *them* was necessarily terrifying? Mightn't he equally well consider that he'd been vouchsafed, was so being vouchsafed, a glimpse into the very workings of creation itself?—indeed with this cognition Ethan seemed to see before his eyes whole universes eternally condensing and recondensing themselves out of the "immaterial" into the "material," and as the continued visualization of their Creator, being radiated back again. While meantime here on earth the "material" was only cognizable through the mind of man! What was real, what imaginary? Yes, but couldn't the meaning, the message, for *them,* be simply that there *had* been a message at all? Yes, could he not just as well tell himself, as Cyprian of Antioch, that here God had beaten the devil at his own game, that magic was checkmated by miracle! Ethan drank half another beer. Gone was his fright. In its stead was awe. In the beginning was the word. But what unpronounceable Name had visualized the Word?

"Nothing mysterious at all," Jacqueline was saying calmly. "I simply looked up your Temple Thurston in the index, since it didn't seem to occur to you."

"I didn't know there *was* an index," Ethan almost shouted, as thunder, a single colossal explosion, struck overhead.

Other more distant thunderclaps crashed and banged around the peninsula, then all the lights in the Prince of Wales Hotel went out.

Outside of war, there is no noise on land or sea as shattering and extreme as that of a thunderstorm in the Storm Country, in the Great Lakes basin, and it seemed useless, with this going on, which possessed its own peculiar uneasy exhilaration, in the intermittent dark and blaze, to attempt to explain to Jacqueline, as if she needed any further explanation, the significance of poor Temple Thurston's unscorched clothes, his scorched body, the Jew at the stake.

M. Grigorivitch drifted in, carrying candles, their gold flames wavering in the draft. "The lightning is peeling the poles and biting the wires, Captain Llewelyn," he moved on with his candles to the other tables.

Then there was dead silence and the lightning started again soundlessly on its own accord and the impression was of a child playing with an electric torch, switching it on and off in the hotel garden. "I must say Fort didn't show much pity for poor old Temple Thurston," he heard Jacqueline saying, though it was the kind of thing he might have said himself, and perhaps indeed he had said it: "It's an inconceivably horrible world, why does anyone bother to live in it?"

"Have you ever heard of Charles Fort before?" Ethan, almost certainly, had asked.

"No."

"Your father never spoke of him?"

"No . . . Not that I know of . . . I think he's writing of the Qliphoth, though; the world of shells and demons. It was one part of the cabbala of which Father would never speak."

"Do you suppose Tommy's sleeping through *this?*"

"Like an angel."

Suddenly, just the same, cobalt lightning filled the room, and he saw Jacqueline's face across the table, her dark eyes, enormous, staring widely at him.

"But you *must* have read this passage," all at once she cried through the thunder. Then, as the lights came on again: "Here. Look for yourself. Thurston, J. Temple. 912f. It's the only page reference it gives in the index."

"But I told you—I didn't *look* in the index. Why the devil *should* I?"

"Well, try to remember the number of your page then."

"It added up to 7 . . . 1051. Let's try that."

There, sure enough, was the passage, and Ethan read it to her: "The man of one of our stories—J. Temple Thurston—alone in his room—and that a pictorial representation of his death by fire was enacting in a distant mind———"

"Very well then! It was an oversight of the person who made the index," Jacqueline said stubbornly.

Thunder sounded like a single plane, high, in windy cloudy weather, that, going fast downwind invisibly overhead (the wind blowing in the opposite direction below) sounds like forty planes, as they sat looking at each other with scared eyes across the table.

And though they searched till closing time, in candlelight, and under electric light, and with candles again, all through that omnibus of Charles Fort's works, nowhere did they find any further reference to Temple Thurston; there was no hint that Fort had ever heard of him as an author at all, and certainly not the author of the play, *The Wandering Jew,* at the end of which "bound to a stake, the man had stood in a fire that had not mounted high . . ."

L

And perhaps it had been another Temple Thurston.

That night a house, on the lakeside of the Prince of Wales, took fire, and Ethan felt himself being borne solemnly homeward on a litter to the Prince of Wales Hotel, with its triple signature of fleurs de lis over the door: a cage of lovebirds, lofting slowly out of a window, and floating down toward him, had struck him on the head . . .

He had gone to the rescue with the volunteer fire brigade at 2 A.M., clad in his pyjamas and an army greatcoat. Not that this was a serious fire either, even for the lovebirds, or himself, but it did the trick. They went west.

While one of his last memories of Niagara-on-the-Lake was of the lurid vitrified lake itself, reflecting the fire: and of the grocer, who had nobly arrived with his fire extinguisher (M. Grigorivitch, the electric light having failed once more, leading the way, beyond the desolate Men's beer parlour, to the shadowy stairs, with white face and upheld flambeaux)—of the grocer saying, "H'm. It's just like I said. The element follows you around, sir!"

CHAPTER 21 ✸ *Go West,*
Young Man!

And Saskatchewan and Saskatchewan and Saskatchewan: said the train: and Saskatchewan and Saskatchewan and Saskatchewan. And Manitoba and Manitoba and Manitoba. Five thousand miles at thirty miles an hour. Five hundred miles of prairie were. ablaze. Beyond the Great Divide, they looked down on the wild beauty of lakes and ravines and pastures of British Columbia with all the boundless and immeasurable longing in their gaze of two children of Israel shading their eyes before a vision of the Promised Land. And when from the Rockies they had descended through the Fraser Valley, the first thing they saw of Vancouver was, from the train window at Port Moody, across the water on their right, a swift-flowing inlet, a fisherman's shack, built on piles, blazing . . .

CHAPTER 22   ✇   *"A Little Lonely Hermitage It Was . . ."*

Oh, hell! . . . Ethan opened his eyes and smiled. He nudged Jacqueline. A man was getting off the bus, carrying a brown suitcase, on which, in gold letters, were inscribed the initials R.I.P.

Once more the Llewelyns exchanged their knowing smiling nods; once more their faces reflected in the window took on that look of hope and excitement, as of two strangers.

Even though here came old Safeside-Suicide again, boiling and sputtering past: to be overtaken this time without difficulty; while the man with the suitcase, falling behind in the dust, grinned and waved his hand . . .

For it was a glorious day after all, if here in Vancouver Island too, this weather could change with explosive suddenness. And the blue gulf had opened below to their gaze again with its green islands, and Mount Baker in the distance on the American mainland, and for a time they watched this lovely view almost gratefully.

A man knocked his pipe out on a garden wall. To their left another man went through his gate into his house. A woman, hanging washing between two trees, clothespins in mouth, stared after the bus. A child lay, elbows in grass, gazing dreamily out to sea while his father pointed. Youth of Raleigh.

Rest in Peace . . . R.I.P. and *rip* was also a body of water made rough by the meeting of opposing tides and currents. It was to become torn apart or split asunder. It was to divide or separate the parts of something by cutting or tearing. It was a rent made by a seam giving way. It was a tear. And to go ahead or proceed head-long. And to break forth into vehement, often profane utterance. Yes, and a mean, vicious or worthless thing or person. Riparians, that's what they were too, for had they not lived on tidewater, on—or half upon—the inlet bank? Were they not riparians more-over—ex-riparians—of the very regions at which they were so hungrily gazing, across the Gulf, beyond, even, Gabriola Island—or at which he was so gazing, as to gain one moment's peace from torment, never mind an eternity of it?

They were. And how could one not remember it? For they had been travelling as it were along the upended base of a triangle of which Eridanus itself on the mainland could roughly be considered the apex, an apex that was a great deal nearer Nanaimo than Victoria (despite everything, their decision to visit the island capital first had been a decision to postpone as long as possible making any decision at all about the house in Gabriola), so that, by drawing close to Nanaimo in their journey northward they had also drawn so much closer to their old home that those very peaks and ravines of the mainland across the sea, distant as they still were, now pos-sessed the terrible familiarity of ancient landmarks to the heart.

Yet it hadn't always been easy to explain how their existence on the beach over there, under those mountains (the illusion too, of whose nearness was growing more uncanny by the moment, for the mainland mountains, above which swam a few peaceful sunlit clouds, Michelangelesque, were now extraordinarily clear, whereas the intermediate Gulf Islands were blurred with haze or smoke) could possibly be accounted an improvement, let alone so ideal. The factors it contained of the "primitive life" had often seemed to Ethan himself, until that life came under attack, however mild, a subject for satire more than anything else. Tommy, in his vacations (for he was at an "English boarding school," St. Jude's, in Van-couver, which occupied his emotions to the extent that he sometimes flatly refused to leave the place on weekends), simply saw it as so much rather rugged "camping." And although there was no questioning its hardship, at least in winter—how beautiful it could be then, with the snow-covered cabins, the isolation, the driftwood like burnished silver—the wonderful excruciating absurd shouting ecstasy of swimming in freezing weather—there had often seemed to him at first something false about it, especially from his point of view, since a disproportionate share of the real burden fell on Jacqueline, who, humiliatingly, proved in many respects more practical and adaptable than he, moreover, to play the game seriously, perhaps they should have had no money at all.

"Back to nature, yet not all the way. Rousseau with a battery radio, Thoreau with a baby Austin," a friend had said.

"No, we haven't got a car."

They had never bought another one, and this was indeed the key to a certain apparent hypocrisy arising from the situation, for while Ethan proudly argued, Jacqueline loyally agreeing, that this preserved their "independence from the machine," he knew, to the contrary, this tended to make them too often yet more dependent on it in the shape of buses. What he really wanted was to be free of the whole false view of life, false comforts constrained by advertisements and monstrous deceptions, what more valuable gesture could they have made in this age? But Ethan could not expect Jacqueline to share the courage of his convictions, when he was not in full possession of those convictions always himself.

Nevertheless, he maintained they'd found that due to their new life "even a car could be dispensed with." The real reason was more complicated: and in no obvious way, involved with fear, for they'd both virtually stopped drinking before they'd lived a month on the beach: to Ethan perhaps a car represented a residual responsibility of an alien world best left behind, a world where, with oneself at the wheel, inexplicable disasters might be expected to happen.

"As every nature-lover and hitchhiker knows, Ethan," his merciless friend had pursued, "who's ever begun a walking tour in Detroit . . . Besides, even at best, if you ask me—you're right—it *is* damned unfair on Jacqueline."

"You don't know her father, old boy."

As a matter of fact The McCandless had paid them a surprise visit late their second May, arriving in the top of his form, a gigantic volume of anogogical research into Gothic literature by a Finn, half hidden by his Gothic cape, under his shiny coat sleeve, and as he reached the end of the forest path, and their house with the inlet came in view below the steps, greeting them with (indeed they heard this Spenserian incantation going on in the bush some while before they saw him):

> "A little lowly hermitage it was
> Down a dale, hard by the forest's side
> Far from resort of people that did pass—
> In travail to and froe . . . A little wyde
> There was a holy chapel edifyde—"

The McCandless was pointing straight at the Chic Sale and it was at this point they caught sight of him.

"Daddy, you wretch!"

"Ha ha ha, my children! . . .

> "Wherein the hermit dewly went to say
> His holy thinges each morne and eventyde
> Thereby a crystal stream did gently plan

(it was true a stream ran by their path but by this time of year it was a mere trickle)

> From which a sacred fountaine welled forth alway . . ."

All in all they might have thought he was being yet more sardonic than the friend who'd gibed at them about Thoreau. But it seemed The McCandless could quote nothing later than the early nineteenth century. Not that they didn't appreciate the joke. Nor that, for his part, during his stay, he probably meant to impugn their precious beach life. His point seemed to be, as if that new life involved a task he'd magically conjured up for them himself, their own attitude was one in question. For him Eridanus apparently wasn't a place to be enjoyed, so much as another test of their love, to be endured heroically, come through. Ah, they were coming through all right too, and how cynically proud of them he sounded. It didn't seem to occur to him, no matter how often they insisted on this, to what degree they might genuinely exult in their life, or if it did, he was at pains to conceal his feeling. Perhaps he had some real prescience of what was going to happen in the end and discouraged them for that reason. Unfortunately, right from the start, there seemed all too much tactile basis for his kind of congratulatory discouragement. Their inlet they were so proud of had, disloyally and hurtfully, chosen that afternoon of his arrival, due to someone having opened the wrong valve of an oil barge moored at the refineries distantly visible citywards on that opposite bank, to become sleeked for miles with a vast scum of crude oil. Simultaneously, the weather turned chilly, and it rained intermittently every day during his whole visit, though it stopped each evening just before sunset. That first afternoon too the coal stove fell apart and the roof leaked. Even the forest, with their beloved pines and cedars and swaying alders, did not escape The McCandless' cheerfully commiserating sarcasm as, the first night, they sat on the platform after dinner beneath the gloomily dripping great trees towering over them to watch a ghostly feeble Ryder moonrise and he said in sepulchral Scottish tones:

" 'The tops of the lofty forest trees waved mournfully in the evening wind, and the moonbeam, penetrating at intervals, as they moved, through the matted branches, threw dubious shadows upon the dark underwood beneath.' "

The works of people like Mrs. Radcliffe seemed to hold a peculiar fascination for The McCandless, though truth to tell, the fantastic Gothic literature book he'd brought with him (which, the work of an erudite Finn, Aino Railo, and called *The Haunted Castle,* he had ceremoniously presented to them as a belated Christmas gift) abounded in analecta of this grandiose nature, usually having some mystical significance, many he appeared to have learned by heart for the occasion, perhaps to impress his daughter with the knowledge that English literature, at least of the romantic period, which was Mr. Railo's point too, was not wholly devoid of the profounder implications of "holy gibberish."

That they were succeeding in living rent-free, however, commanded his unequivocal Scottish admiration (in a place which, for all its lack of conveniences, must have, if in America, set them back in summer at least $500 a month).

He stayed with them a week, maintaining throughout this hilarious, half-hurtful and mock-esoteric mood, drinking quantities of Canadian Scotch, seeing omens and cabbalistic paths everywhere, posting letters to them from a neighbouring village and delivering them himself, stamped and postmarked from the store an hour later, pretending this was magic, setting, in the rare bursts of sunlight, glasses of whiskey on the porch tables to "radiate the creature," picnicking with them on an island they'd rowed out to between showers, thinking to escape that relentlessly ebbing and flooding oil, only to find themselves at high tide completely encircled by its viscous peacock feathers, an island where nevertheless he sportingly affirmed that he was Prospero, and themselves Ferdinand and Miranda; it having become now his favorite thesis, no doubt also thanks to reading Mr. Railo, that *The Tempest* had been consciously based by Shakespeare upon certain ordeals in the Eleusinian mysteries—cutting himself a hazel wand at midnight. He insisted on sleeping each night, drunk as a cock on blackberry brandy, and with no more covering than a terrycloth dressing gown and a couple of horse blankets, upon the bare boards of the platform.

Next evening, as they sat on the platform, the inlet was still covered with that gruesome carpet of dirty oil spreading everywhere over its surface. The tide was at high slack, the breeze only a fluctuant cat's-paw. Voices were audible for miles across the water. Part of the trouble was the colossal stench arising from that oil slick at this stage of the tide. It was something that contrasted weirdly with the blasts of heavenly fragrance wafted, at the least shifting of the wind, from the forest—a contrast resembling and not less improbably than that between floating ambergris and its distillation in perfume. The perfume permeated partly by the scents of Jacqueline's spring flowers, but drawn out by spring showers and the blossoming trees in the depths of the forest, from wild cherry and wild crab apple and wood violet and wild rose there, as though the whole woods had undergone a saturation of perfume stronger than heliotrope or night-scented stock, at the same time nothing cleaner or fresher could be imagined, unless it was the salt sea smell of the inlet itself when it was running clear and pure.

Every bit as peculiar, and twice as terrifying, as this olfactory contrast was that between the sense of relatively ineffable peace otherwise on their side of the inlet, a quiet broken only by the dripping of water from the trees, or the beginning notes of the western nightingale, and the unholy, plangent yet strident and ever-increasing tumult now arising from the other side.

The short stretch between, two miles distant, and half as long, was thus all they saw of that other bank and the refinery had become to them, as it were, its ideograph, as well as that of all this "new activity" upon it, which, so far, having consisted in the refinery itself being expanded into a little town with, of late, a name on the map, Shellco, had all seemed marvelously innocent. Not merely had Shellco seemed quiet and unobtrusive enough but once accepted as part of the landscape, as an entity aesthetically pleasing, even a cause for outbursts of lyricism by Jacqueline; with its cylindrical aluminum retorts and slim chimneys like organ pipes against the green grass a "fairy city of dawn," of "rosy metal of an unearthly hue": while at night, though it showed a little constellation of a few tasteful and colored lights, it slept still and soundless beneath these as an innocent toy model city beneath a Christmas tree—as, specifically, that toy model of Moscow Ethan's father had not finally given him, albeit it more resembled a toy New York. But now, as if it had happened overnight, or behind their backs, and just for The McCandless' benefit, its aspect, and with it that of the whole opposite bank where unfamiliar demonic magenta lights were abruptly winking on and off, seemed frighteningly to have changed. Gone all of a sudden was the innocent little constellation, the quiet lights gleaming ashore at Shellco. A few nights before, an oil-waste burner that had suddenly started fountaining like flambeaux over there on the refinery town's slope had prompted them to think an unbidden fire had started and, when it died down, had been put out. But tonight, suddenly as if just now, this same sword-shaped pyre had reappeared, only looking ten times fiercer and taller, so that a fiendish lurid light coruscated from the whole refinery, each of whose cylindrical aluminum tanks reflecting the flambeaux in descending degrees of infernal brilliance, in turn sent those reflections wavering deep within the dark stream, wherein too, when a cat's-paw ruffled the surface, all the reflections in the water dithered together with the image striking down directly from the fiery torch itself, the reflections and the reflected reflections all wriggling and dithering and corkscrewing frenziedly together diminuendo like red-hot slice-bars in a stoker's nightmare. Those luminous digladiations gave at first the impression of taking place in sinister silence but in fact there was a hellish if magnificent din: from the oil-waste pyre came a whishing, whistling, consistent rushing roar, mingling with a noise like rattling giant chains which appeared to come from behind the oil tanks, sounds of machinery, half-submerged in the high lament of huge invisible saws in far sawmills northwestward. While they watched and listened, a coarse cerise light switched on, illuminating in large capitals erected against the grass slope below— someone having omitted to supply the initial S—the word HELL: on top of this, to The McCandless' grave delight, the moon came out . . .

And the twin beams of searchlights from the forgotten legions of the city began to sweep, attenuating themselves to a vast height, crossing and recrossing the low cloudbanks like broom-bewildered ghosts on stilts, or mounted on falling fire-ladders down the sky. While beneath, good God, here was their city of "rosy metal of an unearthly hue" with a vengeance! In place of their well-behaved Meccano structure some lurid flickering City of Dis indeed, suffusing all the lowering sky westward with a bloodshot volcanic glare and firing the windows and mirrors of the little cabin, and, as now with the moon's arrival the wind began to blow strongly and steadily out of the refinery's quarter, from the southwest, overwhelming them from across the water with a new and deadlier assault of unique oil-smells, bringing on their gusts an added wild clamor, this time probably from the city too (though again seeming to suspire to the refinery alone), a tumult, steadily increasing in volume, like the plucked strings of a thousand Jews' harps, and the flexitone whinings of flailing metal, and a moaning rising to a pitch and then falling and dying to reascend again, surcharged now, in a lull of the wind, by those immediate coastwise concussions, zinzulations of shingle-mills, Byzantine warnings, chimes and chuffing of engines along the railway lines, wails of locomotive steam-whistles, and harmonium chords from diesels.

All this being punctuated at intervals, as the wind shifted slightly once more, by the clear pure fluting—first the introductory note, then the clear flutelike rising carolling song—of the hermit thrush sitting in the wet dogwood tree behind their woodshed.

"It was the nuns at a convent chanting the requiem for a soul," The McCandless observed.

The requiem continued a little longer. "I don't think there's a convent but there's a monastery over there somewhere," Ethan said.

But the next morning it was as though the doleful noise had never been.

"And," The McCandless was saying, "Satan—or one of the others —to be the personification of that which tries simply to intercept you in the course of performing your higher will?"

"Mmm," said Ethan, whose handsaw, at the moment quivering, became trapped by the imperceptibly loosening sections of the dividing log. He found a wedge—one of the kind they knocked into cleats to secure the hatches on shipboard—and hammered it into the now splitting wood until the saw was freed. But now the wedge itself was driven in too far without the job being done, so he found a carpenter's hammer and brought it down with a crash with such a mighty blow that the sawhorse itself collapsed. And still the log had not split.

"You need a claymore for that job," said The McCandless.

Their little yellow boat, whose sternline that morning was made fast to the sawhorse, rolled on its beam ends, scended to a pitch where its bow hit the forward mooring post, a horizontal two-by-four, projecting from the unfinished front porch and hanging over the water. And each bump hurt his heart, he felt it contract and he looked toward Jacqueline with concern, but the tides weren't brimming high enough to threaten the garden, yet he waited for the noise, and all the tender anxieties for their little household it aroused, each one separate and stabbing his heart with love, to subside a bit before speaking.

"I remember that Lamb says somewhere, helpfully, 'reason shall only visit him through intoxication,' and he's very good too I think where he speaks about the difficulty of doing *any*thing, of the 'springs of action being broken.'"

The berserk flare had died to a small quiet jet, a cool religious flame against the green bank, making the scene at Shellco appear almost pastoral, while the only sound to be heard was that warning bell of a train beating along the coast, but turned soft, nostalgic, homelike, as The McCandless said, it being Monday:

> "'Tis sweet to hear a brook, tis sweet
> To hear the Sabbath bell . . .'"

The joke here was, Ethan thought, in the bus, that, unlike Niagara, no Sabbath bells were permitted to chime at all in Vancouver or its vicinity, certain delegations of workers, those "bloated capitalists" of the New World and arbiters of its taste, perhaps, who knows, the oil workers, having complained to the authorities that their sound kept them awake on Sunday mornings. It was true that, not far away from the Llewelyns, about a mile behind the oil refinery, in a region where the bones of a race of giants had been lately discovered, existed a monastery possessing some of the most fluent bells in the Western Hemisphere, cast from the same mold, it was said, as those of Westminster Cathedral, by certain dignitaries of which the bells themselves had been presented. But the monastery neither possessed a campanile nor had sufficient money to build one strong enough to accommodate the bells. And had they erected the campanile they would not have been allowed to ring the bells. So the bells, tended by a sad monk, languished on the ground in a kind of outhouse built for their tongueless purpose. They could be seen, on payment of an admission fee . . . A little way behind that monastery too, on that opposite bank, was the city's most formidable prison, its chimney visible on a clear day, that very prison where, in an elevator shaft painted bright yellow, on December thirteenth, the boy Chester—

And this prison possessed a bell too that never rang, though Ethan had never seen it.

And it was a little later on that Monday that The McCandless burst on them once more, like a spectre, from the forest path, where they stood below the steps, between the well and the woodshed, chopping shakes from a block of cedar with an adze.

It was The McCandless' birthday. Jacqueline had never told Ethan how the whole business of birthdays and anniversaries within her family had been managed in her childhood, but so far as her own was concerned he suspected that it was only after she'd had a child of her own that birthdays had taken on a kind of ambivalence, since they never ceased to cause her some measure of pain, though she referred to it with amusement as "The McCandless' little astrological problem." She was meticulous about remembering Tommy's birthday, and his own, the same went for The McCandless, though the only anniversaries of any moment to the old magician were the equinoxes. Yet they set great store on The McCandless' birthday, on those rare occasions when he'd been geographically available. This could almost have looked like a form of revenge on her part but that it could conveniently be celebrated, and to some extent subsumed, by an occasion when one could also be celebrating something else: Empire Day, though the Empire could not be said any longer to exist.

This had certainly been a week of strange weather, too early in the year to have attracted normally more than the odd boatload of sightseers—Rotarians, nuns, Americans, Communists—were not to-day the Monday toward which the weekend tended: Empire Day, the last Monday in May, and moreover that day on which, traditionally, British Columbians took their first swim of the year, as on

Labor Day their last. Tommy should have been out to visit them today, but had begged off to attend, so he said, a meeting of Junior Forest Wardens. It was a day of flags. And not to be found flagging in outward patriotism the outcasts of Eridanus, evincing that extra share of patriotism noticed in convicts during wartime, also displayed, from their cabins, the Red Ensign, the Union Jack, and even at one place, the Jolly Roger. From the Llewelyns' house as a token of international goodwill, the twin flames of the Union Jack and the Stars and the Stripes fluttered and flapped in the trade wind side by side at the two small mainmasts raised on either side of their pier.

It was one of those rare occasions when Ethan had been actually prepared quite to forget the special pride and pathos of their isolation. He had been looking forward to exhibiting to The McCandless the unrivalled interest and color of their rich poverty in the purely bourgeois pleasure that Eridanus was really capable of, feeling in itself with, and floating and flowing past in their own back yard and their windows, of showing him that the true aristocrats of the inlet were the fishermen in their huge halibut boats, often, at high tide, seeming on a higher level than the eyes, as they splendidly sailed downstream, often four or five abreast, magnificently and recently painted in emerald and cobalt and white, deep-waisted and constellated, fore and aft, almost medieval-looking, yet lavishly modernly equipped. But the gorgeous sea procession hadn't arrived, this Empire Day, and though at any other time he would have been relieved, because they caused a huge and ruinous commotion as their united wash swung inward against the beach and the house, today he felt a faint disappointment.

But it was the signal of departure, The McCandless, the oil and the bad weather vanishing almost simultaneously, leaving their heaven quite without a stoop in its soul (after a day or two) for not being apparently recognized as such.

CHAPTER 23 🌀 *Adam, Where Art Thou?*

Yet Ethan was a man who always had his ideas of the good life (he could and indeed had lived quite happily once in New York, to be sure before he knew what "happiness," to him, could mean): and it could not be said that these ideas at first had been essentially changed by their life at Eridanus. Rather they had become, in common with most of his other ideas—he'd felt this as a gradual process while living there—harmonized, *accordés*.

He'd begun his retreat by finding himself, before a week was out, deeply shocked all over again by how little he knew, despite all Jacqueline's efforts, and his own, to widen his horizon during the past years. How close the stars as they rose over the mountains, and were reflected in the inlet, among the reflections of the pines. Yet of their names, their behavior, it came to him, he still knew nothing. He hadn't even known till Jacqueline told him that Eridanus was also the name of a constellation, far less that it was the river, in Virgil's *Aeneid*, which watered the Elysian Fields of the Earthly Paradise, something that was probably not in the mind either of the English skipper of the freighter S.S. *Eridanus*, of the Constellation Line, just at the moment he ran his freighter aground here, a piece of history filling a more forgivable gap in one's knowledge that had been supplied by their friendly neighbors the Wildernesses—those then paradoxically unbaptized waters. And this renewed sense of his ignorance had not been borne upon him with shame, but by a sort of love, a speechlessness, in which his feeling for Jacqueline had a part. It was as if a new aspiration had come into existence, a longing to be better, a more worthy man, more worthy of love, and of giving love. And he was in love; he fell in love again with Jacqueline. There was no other way of saying this. And everything seemed to help. Even the knowledge she could have no more children, which in any case meant reevaluating their lives on a wholly different basis, but which had threatened to separate them, only served to draw them closer together. The same aspiration took the shock when now suddenly he realized how little still he'd read in general (yes, again, after all these years, and despite Jacqueline's encouragement, though this time the aspiration was more genuine, he wasn't as before half trading on his ignorance), read not merely of astronomy, but in philosophy, history, or literature. He'd ended by suspecting that he might be in no very different position in regard to the law, that despite his practical experience for all that he was aware of it as a living changing thing he was like the man in *L'Education Sentimentale* (he'd borrowed Flaubert's novel, together with an adze, from a cheerful if distant neighbor Roderick Fairhaven, a Scottish schoolmaster) who had attended his law lectures for a fortnight but given up the Civil Code before the lecturer had reached Article 3 and abandoned the Institutes of Justinian at the Summo Diviso Personarum. And indeed, in Canada, too often it was *not* a living, changing thing. Quebec still used the Code Napoléon. Some of the laws in British Columbia seemed to him of an unbelievable barbarity. And instead of being adapted to changing circumstances and continually reformulated, as he now began to feel they should be, by those not only acquainted with the principles of the law itself, but with the highest of all arts, the intricacies of psychology and medicine, when a new law was made it often turned out more barbarous and intolerant than the old. Obviously, in a few years, Canada would be bound to revise her entire legal code. Temporary retirement did not disqualify him from making certain proposals to

M

the right quarters, indeed who was better qualified in some ways than he to make them? That didn't mean he could not become better qualified in his own eyes.

So Ethan, taking advantage of a sensible arrangement by which books could be sent out from the City Public Library to rural places, had begun to read intensively though not, because of the erratic contents of the library itself, with much method. He pored over what he could get of Aristotle, Dante, Kant, Bishop Berkeley, Spinoza, Michelet. And what reading he'd already done he tried as best he could to revise. Fragments from William James, Jung, Dostoevski, whose volumes were nightly piled by his bed, jostled in his dreams with bits of the *Book of Changes,* Keyserling, *Moby Dick, Wilhelm Meister.* At night too, Jacqueline loved him to read Shakespeare to her, and they both laughed their heads off over Stendhal's wonderful "The Telegraph," with its almost exact description of the local political situation in Vancouver. His reading led him back to his former reflections on the "good life" and hence into strange paths indeed. Having received one month by mistake a package of books on modern architecture he discovered himself, all of a sudden, to be an admirer of Le Corbusier, Frank Lloyd Wright, in general agreement with the socio-architectural tenets of Lewis Mumford. From the objective standpoint, of course.

But even before The McCandless' visit he could not say that his "appreciation" of the Shellco refinery, for instance, had been "sentimental" in the sense that he'd had to adapt the place to some category of shared *gemütlichkeit* (which was the opposite of their attitude toward the wilderness, and the mountains anyway) before being able to stomach it at all. He didn't regard it as obviously "ugly." No, if there had to be oil refineries, that at Shellco, he'd seen detachedly, was probably a pretty good one, oil-waste pyre and all. Even after it had showed itself in its true colors on that discouraging occasion, or what had appeared to be its true colors, he saw, with the same detachment, that it possessed "drama and beauty." Certainly he had thought if those pyres went on reduplicating themselves without anyone doing anything about it, none of the workers who lived hardby would be able to get a wink of sleep at night, but that was another story. He was able emotionally then, for some reason, to dissociate himself from what the place meant . . . Whatever it meant. Probably the oil workers were happy enough where they were in those adjacent repetitive houses of sensible design back on the hill. After all, not everyone could have the privilege of living right on the water like themselves. What was it the great Ludwig Mies van der Rohe had said, "Less is more." From which it was but a step to "everything for nothing." But since man was by and large incapable of appreciating everything for nothing, even when he had it in his grasp and right under his nose, what was the use of blaming the machinations of real estate operators for depriving him of it? "Modern architecture should be structural architecture." That was their little house too, all right. But if he was not sentimental about it, it was because he didn't need to be . . . After that painful week with The McCandless bad oil slicks were few and far between: when on occasion there was one, those tides of Eridanus, at their work of pure ablution round the shores, soon cleansed the filth away, in the space of a tide, a few hours, so that the inlet was running cleaner and swifter than ever, though it was true that a particular accident with the oil valve had caused such a commotion among the rate-payers who lived near, though not *upon,* other distant sections of the inlet, or had pleasure boats anchored in it, that the steamship company had been obliged to pay for some pure ablution on their own account, to the tune of $10,000, setting to work hosing down the beaches with detergents, which a local cartoonist pictured as being siphoned off from the barrels of the local beer parlours. And when a second oil-waste pyre was added at Shellco, the brilliance of both seemed somehow tempered: and whether people had complained about the noise or not too at some point, the pandemonium never, since that evening with The McCandless, seemed so awe-inspiring again . . . Or perhaps it was that the Llewelyns had simply *absorbed* Shellco, taken it in their stride, and so come almost to forget it. The mountains and the stars were still there: so was their forest, even if it had to be an oasis of unspoiled wilderness in the midst of an abomination of desolation, that only added to the beauty of their side of the picture, to *their* drama. And the swimming was better than ever. So what were they worrying about? They were not worrying. Not even the memory of Mother Gettle moving in on their home in Oakville made him worry now, did it? While the nightmares of Niagara began to partake of the diffident quality of some half-forgotten waking dream endured under morphine.

The only thing that worried him was when he went to town; then he felt guilty because he would not put in an appearance at his law office. He read the Code of Hammurabi and came to the conclusion that Babylonian law, severe as it might have been, was probably less inhumane than Canadian law. "Penalties attached to perjury and false accusation assured that malicious actions were seldom brought," he learned, and "the utmost pains were taken to protect the rights of the individual." So said his authority, Carleton. One exception, however, seemed to be the survival of the dreadful *lex talionis,* whereby if under certain circumstances a man accidentally brought about the death of a child, not he, but *his child* must be killed. Therefore—though this had been much later, it was early this year, only a few months ago—when a sixteen-year-old boy named Richard Chester was sentenced to hang for the rape and murder of a girl a little younger, a boy who also had lived in a shack on government property incidentally (though in the city down a creek on a mudflat where his father, a fisherman, kept his boat), as a consequence of which all such cabins everywhere were promptly termed by the authorities and the newspapers "rats' nests of vice and spawners of crime," when Ethan began to compose a public defense of this boy (and was he really thinking like this, was he, Ethan Llewelyn, in the bus really thinking like this?), he did not of course invoke this particular point of Babylonian law in the hope of obtaining an acquittal . . . in fact he did not base his defense on any point of law at all. In fact . . . in fact but upon a passage in Herman Hesse's novel *Demian.*

Ethan read, with enthusiasm, Thomas Mann. He even read a book about the cabbala sent him by The McCandless after his visit which, though its high-flown "occult" diction struck him as peculiarly loathsome—bearing out one of its own theses that the higher a certain kind of mystic rose in such a hierarchy the more he was in danger of leaving his intelligence behind and his good taste as well—he found not only extraordinarily interesting but, as a method of thought, profoundly helpful. In fact he could sum up no better their life on the beach than to say it had been, in a manner, *his* cabbala, in the sense that, if he was not mistaken, that system might be regarded on one plane as a means less of accumulating than of divesting oneself—by arrangement, balancing them against their opposites—of unbalanced ideas: the mind, finally transcending both aspects, regains its lost equilibrium, or for the first time truly discovered it: not unlike, Ethan sometimes supposed, the modern process of psychoanalysis. "Rebirth"—every morning waking up to make the coffee, splitting kindling, doing the smallest, or the most onerous chores. Yes, Ethan felt exactly as if he'd been reborn, mentally and physically. Never before had he taken such an exultant delight in sheer physical labor. But then (and here came all these thoughts again, like damnation now, redundant and weary as the thuddings of Ravel's *Bolero* on a favorite sad old cracked record) never before had he taken such a delight in swimming itself, in sailing a boat, in sunlight and sea wind and the flight of gulls, in making love to his wife. While this sense of *mens sana in corpore sano* was enhanced by an extraordinary strengthening of his vision —his eyes always his weak point which had been bothering him again, seeming enormously to benefit from salt water and the use of coal oil lamps.

Sometimes his feeling of well-being was almost too much for him and he'd take his old clarinet—still Virgil's flute in the *Eclogues* —into a secluded place in the forest he was on good terms with, and play such wildly ecstatic hot music all by himself that when he stopped it seemed that all the birds for miles around were singing like mad. Or sometimes when Jacqueline felt like talking to Primrose they'd take his instrument down to the Wildernesses', who lived in a similar cabin in a similar bay about three quarters of a mile down the beach, and with Sigbjørn, who was an unsuccessful

Canadian composer, but an excellent jazz pianist, at his cottage piano, they'd all have a jam session: singing the Blues à la Beider-becke, the Mahogany Hall Stomp and heaven knows what. Or they'd play Mozart, after a fashion. But mostly the Llewelyns were alone and happy in one another. Seabirds and wildflowers were friends they both knew by name. Those complexities and conflu-ences of those tides so entranced Ethan at first that he had passages of the Harbour Board's tide book by heart and he concocted a special tide calendar for Jacqueline which she hung on the wall. He found endless amusement doing sculpturings in driftwood, but above all he was, or had become by force majeure, a more than enterprising woodsman and carpenter, in short something of a pioneer. And though Jacqueline might be handier than himself when she put her mind to it, as the majority of bona fide native Canadians were handy by upbringing and instinct, to Ethan, throughout his former life so troubled by clumsiness, the intransigeance of objects, this was triumph indeed. And then just when life to him for the first time had meaning, ritual, direction, its holy of holies, when for the first time in his whole existence he had found this ecstatic joy simply in *living,* the summum bonum and the reality of heaven as physical pleasure, as Berkeley (not yet then Bishop) said, had come this bloody awful threat of eviction.

Because it was no more than a threat, if one more than likely to be implemented, to begin with Ethan imagined that from the very life which was now in jeopardy could be drawn the moral strength to meet it.

"Colleagues, Criminals and Escorts, Spectres and Emanations, Fellow Poltergeists—my God" (putting his binoculars to his eyes and walking out to the end of the pier), Ethan said, "there's old Mount Baker out this morning, or is it Mount Hood? Out very clear and beautiful, halfway up the air over the middle of the Shell Oil Refinery, very clear and beautiful and just like an American ice cream cone, or an advertisement for one, being served on high at a perpetual soda fountain, perpetual reminder of the high standard of living pertaining below in the State of Washington, with the highest suicide rate in the Union. How often do we think, in this post-antediluvian world, of the significance of this drunkenness of Noah, *Noah inebrians*. Known better to all we Oaxaqueñian drunkards confined in intellectual reserves as Cox-Cox the Pop-eyed Pilot Man. How pleasant to delimitate this magnificent thickness of things here in America and Canada in this way. How often do we think of the significance of British Columbia? We are not styled B.C. for nothing. For if Christ should ever come down to earth again He can be assured of a welcome in every way as rewarding as His old one. Not because we are to America as Palestine to Rome, unless economically, but because of the multiplicity of Messiahs between Los Angeles and Vancouver who would challenge His priority. What time the British pound, alas, goes spiralling down to emerge as a pistareen. You don't know what a pistareen is, Jacqueline? You know what it sounds like, but not what it is. It is a debased coin, and as such the best symbol of the age in which we live, all of us together in the soup, under the soupistareen."

Yet rarely had he felt less at the mercy of circumstances: besides, it would not be the first time he had met disaster with courage, or with what he could tell himself was courage (and here came all *these* thoughts again). Moreover they'd never looked upon their little beach cabin, however beloved, as a permanent thing. That impermanence, indeed, the ramshackle tenuity of the life, were part of its beauty. The scene, too, that confronted them through their casement windows was ever-changing; the mountains, the sea never looked the same two minutes on end: why then be afraid of change? A few months before they'd have laughed at the idea—it wasn't as if they'd meant (till then!) to stay there their whole lives. For one thing, though Ethan had travelled fairly widely, he meant to take Jacqueline abroad and one summer soon they'd planned to take Tommy to Europe, go back to England, visit Greece—

But it seemed that the threat was worse than any reality could be and perhaps they hadn't, despite all, thought of Eridanus as a home until they were threatened with losing it. Sometimes he felt they were a bit like William James' people who might have been so happy living on their frozen lake, merrily skating in the sparkling sun, had they only not known—it was his tragic image for man living without faith—that the ice was slowly melting beneath them. Or, in a waking dream, he'd think of the ancient people of the north, driven out by the Ice Age, and searching for a new Eden, and then it would dawn on him there had been no Ice Age (unless that one in their imagination their first winter), they had not been driven out, they'd left of their own accord. And to speak of Eden, would Adam and Eve who had defied death by eating the fruit of that tree (which The McCandless liked to claim was symbolically no less a transcendent thing than the Tree of Life embodied in the cabbala itself) have fled at the mere *threat* of being sent forth, of the cherubim and the flaming sword? that glittering sword in the night like a scintillant oil-waste pyre? And yet, it was indeed as if Ethan had heard the dread voice in the Garden: Adam, where art thou? . . . And they had gone.

CHAPTER 24 🌀 *"The Wretched Stalking Blockheads—"*

*T*hey hadn't gone very far. They hadn't gone any farther to begin with than, once more, an apartment in Vancouver's West End they'd sublet while looking for another house, and after a week of that it had been seriously in Ethan's mind to go back again, eviction or no eviction. But the cabin had been "lent" to a man named Wolverhampton, a schoolmaster at Tommy's school.

Perhaps it wouldn't have been so bad if they'd managed to get their old apartment in the West End, where they'd lived on first coming to Vancouver. Maybe some essence of those old makeshift days of companionship would have been rediscovered there, some essence of that old hope and desperate attempt at renewal, before they'd ever tasted happiness on their beach. For had they only known before, in those dark days, what joys lay so close, awaiting them! That hope had not been illusory, even so, and perhaps some ghost of it still haunted there, to work another miracle . . . Or so he'd felt until they'd found their old digs could no longer be rented, or exactly called—unless by some outrageous euphemism—an apartment in an apartment building at all.

So immeasurably happier by comparison, however, did those days spent there begin to appear that Ethan quite forgot how near breakdown had seemed to them both. Dishonor and anxiety had prowled through the ruins of his being like marauding cougars. Jacqueline's forthcoming operation shadowed their whole lives, while the horrors of the case Ethan was working on had exacerbated everything.

But Vancouver in May 1945 had been new to them too and then these rooms they'd taken seemed comfortable enough, at any rate a relief after Niagara-on-the-Lake and the Prince of Wales, and even, at times, fun: it had been on the top floor of what must have been one of Vancouver's first such apartment buildings, a truly majestic old pile (as it still was) whose service elevator shook their bed, of antique patent, which slid out of the wall from a dark recess, from whose depths, in early spring just before they left for the beach, they were continually having to rescue pigeons fallen from their nest down the air vent. The janitor was a friendly soul who let Jacqueline, despite a bylaw to the contrary, put crumbs on the windowsill to feed the birds. Moreover through their windows then they had had a pleasant view of blue shutters and colored roofs, lined with chestnut and maple trees, down which plodded the milkman's horse with its white wagon, and the rag-and-bones-man's horse with its green wagon, beyond which, looking westward, they saw church spires sunk in a valley, the white fangs of mountains beyond nearer mountains crowned with evergreen forests, and, from time to time, though they hadn't known it at first, or attached any significance to it, down a vista of paralyzing grandeur, the nearer narrows of Eridanus' inlet itself.

From their windows looking the other way too they saw Nanaimo and the Victoria boat come in and occasionally, when it was clear, Vancouver Island, and perhaps other Gulf Islands, though they hadn't given it a thought then. Maybe they'd even seen Gabriola without thinking anything of it or knowing its name. Jacqueline had fallen out of touch with Angela. They went for walks through Stanley Park, taking Tommy and their misery past Lost Lagoon, with seabirds swimming on the lake, and the tennis courts where you could play for nothing, and later watched freighters tottering into harbor like drunkards, their arms upraised at sunset.

Only a block away in one direction was the windy promenade skirting English Bay, with beneath the promenade in a grotto an aquarium housing a tough old octopus, a miserable wolf eel, and the wheel and engine room telegraph of the first paddle-steamer to come to British Columbia (which it had done by way of Cape Horn): above, between the promenade and the bay was a row of delightful ivy-clad old houses with large airy light rooms and shingle roofs, sometimes with cupolas added later, and even stuffed owls gazing gloomily from their upper window-sills, and with gardens full of roses blooming even in November going right down to the sands, on which among the silvered driftwood cows were to be seen wandering, one such house being evidently a sort of farm.

On the other side of the promenade, in the center of a carefully mown island of green turf sloping up from it, an eternally empty circular bandstand stood alone and locked, from which you could see the indoor swimming pool, whence it was only a two-minute bus ride to the city's main street with its neon lights, shops and cinemas and at the end of this, conveniently, were his law office and the law courts.

What had given this west end of the city its peculiar charm was that there was scarcely one transverse tree-lined avenue or alley that did not open upon some vista of the mountains. This—because this was hardly to be avoided altogether even in those sections of town where people had done their best to avoid it—and something more human, that seemed to inhere in the lines of those first old pioneer-built houses, some perhaps started as shacks, but houses one conceived of as having for so long shared these lovely views and vistas: and in the later but often wonderful cupolaed fantasies and widow's-walks of the despised "nightmare" Victorian period: it was also the curious surviving air of innovation, of the ramshackle, in the former, upon which age had nonetheless conferred a beauty of weathered dignity and even solid permanence, combined with the once devil-may-care gaiety and enthusiasm evinced by the homes of that Victorian era (upon whose lasting gimcrackery of impromptu aerial ladders and crow's nests obsolescence had conferred a corresponding pathos) that breathed a certain soul of brooding romance, a Hansel-and-Gretel magic, of watching continuity into the place. Such were the amenities of Vancouver's West End in their "old days": a romantic enough place for wandering lovers to be happy in for ten days (or forever) if they knew how, or no better, in any case a place bad or good according to what you wanted to make of it, or your mood, a live-and-let-live sort of section too, like a separate town in itself, where the occasional policeman was polite as a London Bobby and who, when asked what you could do on Sunday, would smile and say, "Well, you can always go to the aquarium."

To be just, some of these amenities, including the aquarium, not to mention the octopus and the wolf eel, still survived, or had the appearance of surviving, and were features equally available from or adjacent to their new apartment in the West End, which due to a great influx of population into the city during their years on the beach, was the only place to rent they could find. But to Ethan the changes in the West End seemed so many and disastrous that no doubt he only began to see its old virtues now they were so fast and patently disappearing. For this part of the city was itself evidently in the grip of that same "clean-up" campaign whose tentacles had reached to their hamlet eight miles away as the killer whale swam. CLEAN-UP OF VANCOUVER DEMANDED BY ANGRY CITIZENS, yelled the headlines. TREES, EYESORES, MUST GO. And with that down were coming all the horse chestnut and the maple trees lining the beautiful leafy avenues and alleys. Bulldozers grunted up and down the beach of English Bay, long since bereaved of the cows (mourning which pastoral delight Ethan quite forgot how many whole villages had been pulled down in sixteenth-century England and their people evicted to make way for the sheep), rooting away and cleaning up the silvered driftwood that alone to him had lent it character, though to their relief many of the houses with rose gardens going down to the sands still stood, and the Llewelyns feeblemindedly hung on to this fact like a talisman of their own survival. But everywhere else, it seemed, the shingled houses were falling like ninepins, each day cupolas tumbled off the poor old steamboat Gothic buildings being torn down, like the trees, to make way for more soulless Behemoths in the shape of hideous new apartment buildings, yet more deathscapes of the future. No longer was the milk delivered by a wagon and a good-luck white horse but in a vehicle resembling a mechanized death slab. And if there was some economic sense in this change, to regret which was senti-mental, the same could scarcely be said of other changes. The fake modern buildings going up everywhere were proving far more deserving of literal cold-blooded condemnation than even were those they replaced. Their roofs leaked, their staircases collapsed, their toilets would not work. And besides a soul-destroying ugliness these new buildings all had in common, both within and without, was a curious-seeming out-of-dateness. Not in the sense that the steamboat Gothic houses could be said to be out of date. It was that those had the aspect of potential ruins, of a sort of rubble, even before they had been completed. So that when, very occasionally, a new building went up of fine modern design, and which might almost have done credit to a Ludwig Mies van der Rohe, and with some obvious intent and claim to permanence and solidity it was lent a kind of horror by its crumbling neighbours, as if it were not moored there in a "growing community" but something in a partially dismantled exposition shortly to be moved away, yet which meantime blocks the view.

Why Ethan should have expended so much emotional energy about these matters was a mystery even to himself. For there was no true correspondence between their past life and that which seemed doomed here; little in common between their little house and any of these doomed houses (unless it was the doom), life in which must have been to him, after their beach, little better than the living death of an apartment. Yet he couldn't stumble on the demolition of such a house at this time—the bulldozer in some cases pulling out the whole lower story then reducing the remainder to a heap of rubble in a few minutes—without feeling as though something within

himself were being demolished, a sickness and sadness and helplessness in his soul that would last all day. To think that that poor
house where so many lives had come into being, that had been
occupied before most residents of this city had even arrived, should
be used in that heartless, and as if deliberately callous fashion. Yes,
murdered. And in vain he told himself there might be good reasons,
repeating to himself that it was all simply an inevitable progress,
that, in the words of the paper's real estate subdivision promoters
were merely carrying out demolitions in connection with replanning
in locations where coordinated planning had not been done originally. Bah, who gave a damn about their "coordinated replanning,"
especially when in so many instances this did not involve new
houses at all.

One of the blackest desponds caused by their new apartment
could not, however, be laid to "progress;" from their windows they
had no view of the mountains at all, this being totally blocked by
their old apartment house, which was in process of transformation,
despite wrathful public protest, into an overflow correction house or
subsidiary bridewell for juvenile delinquents, for those, that is, the
authorities had decided were in no fit state to be hung, and behind
which was going up a new YMCA. They did, though, still have
trouble with pigeons, and of two different kinds. First the janitor
threatened to call the police when Jacqueline, having innocently
disobeyed the city's edict against feeding birds, pointed to the state
of a neighbouring convent roof as for ratification by a higher law;
then the janitor and the landlady—they were both Irish Catholics, in
which they differed from the more carefree nuns of the convent who
were French Canadian of a Franciscan order—turned out themselves to be police informers. Ethan was not surprised. They had
made from the start a fetish of the propriety of the place, of how
they'd cleaned it up from some former condition of disrepute, and
how they only took the most reputable of tenants, inquiries into
whose past lives were exhaustive. Never having heard of Ethan
Llewelyn the lawyer—and maybe not believing in his existence—
they had gone out of their way to make dark references to a certain

"disbarred lawyer," a former evicted tenant who had once lived there with a practical nurse.

Ethan had been suspicious of their odious landlords from the first, but he'd also been sorry for them until he caught them eavesdropping for the second time. "But even if we can't feed them, we can't stop the pigeons from their eavesdroppings," Ethan said pointedly, at the desk that evening. Informers! It was the vocation of the times, the Communist scare. Set Judas to betray Jesus, you only ended by betraying Christ all over again. And indeed to Ethan at this time, there seemed informers and secret police and spies everywhere, outside each drugstore, lurking at each street corner. The ethos of Vancouver had certainly changed. Meanwhile their landlady whom they been sorry for because she had only one eye, and was known as Old Eagle Eye, would even inform on a passing drunk. The malevolent bitch would sit glued to her telephone all afternoon just waiting for one to pass so that she could call the police . . . And gone was the smiling happy-go-lucky policeman who directed you to the nearest bootlegger after hours and so English you felt that beneath his uniform he kept the bottom button of his waistcoat undone. Nothing but police cars arriving with a noise of fire engines or storm troopers. Or silent ghost cars and prowler cars with officers in plain clothes. Finally Ethan couldn't see a priest without thinking he must be a police spy. Vancouver was being cleaned up indeed.

The mephitic blasts of steam heat, the feline omnipresence of the janitor always halfway upstairs or outside your door, scenery withdrawn behind the YMCA, the gesticulating shadows of the juvenile delinquents, the miserable and tyrannic rules, that interdict against feeding sea gulls, always remembered at the last moment, and the beak beating against the window, the carefully silent drunks downstairs—the telephone!—the disastrous thud on the door of the evening newspaper, always picked up with the sickening fear it would bring news of the irrevocable and final eviction, the injured venetian blinds in the kitchen always half-shut against a glimpse below of a single monkey tree in a garden bordered by monstrous chicken croquettes of shrubbery, the wretched policeman, who being in uniform was perhaps not a policeman, strutting and skulking past the Safeway Store, where the clean-shaven old man had said to Ethan, as he drifted round with Jacqueline, steering the perambulator, the reference being to the beard he'd let grow again for the first time since Niagara-on-the-Lake: "Are you trying to set us a new fashion or what, young man?"

"I don't know . . . I grew it for a joke. Then I got kind of attached to it and I didn't like to shave it off. But I'm going to just the same."

"That's right," said the old man, who obviously had once had a beard himself. "We all have to get attached to something, else," he added, "*we* go down, down—!"

CHAPTER 25 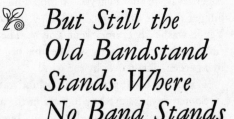 *But Still the Old Bandstand Stands Where No Band Stands*

*A*nd down down it was anyhow, what with *Time* and *Life* on the table with their bouncing advertisements of a bouncing life with Big Cousin that never was on land or sea, or if it was, in his opinion shouldn't be, haunting you each weekend, and criminal slanting of the news, which Jacqueline absorbed with guileless interest, as without knowing it, so increasingly did he, so that their conversation began unconsciously to reflect these opinions, or disgustingly react from them beyond all fairness and judgment, whereas in the country the magazines simply seemed a welcome weekly joke, to be treated in large with the same amused contempt that intelligent Russians presumably reserved for *Pravda*. And the horrible expense. Christ Jesus how he hated it all. Where had *their* life, *their* time gone, where was the sea (it was just outside round the corner, but still where was it?), the forest? the smell of salt, pines, and evening smoke? Where were his beloved chores, objects, tools? The stars, the seabirds, their boat, their companionship, the well, the sunrise? And from the top of the steps between the wheelbarrow

N

and Jacqueline's watering can, a sudden view of cavorting whales . . . Two advantages alone was Ethan able to see in their return to civilization, you could take a hot bath in more comfort, and there was a good gas stove, and both of these seemed equally—the latter irresistibly so and daily to someone somewhere in the city, if the paper was to be believed—temptations to suicide . . . Let the bugger die. He often felt like killing himself out of sheer boredom. Yet it wasn't that time went slowly. The days passed with a terrible meaningless swiftness, like the pages of a book abandoned in a garden, blown over by the wind . . .

Like a real book, perhaps, left behind in their garden . . .

Sometimes he stayed by himself in the apartment, letting Jacqueline house-hunt alone, afraid to go out, but also afraid to stay in, not daring to show himself at the window. He had the idea increasingly that he was being watched, and maybe he was quite right, he was:

"Anyhow you're quite right about your landlord," the public prosecutor told him over the phone.

The occasion of Ethan's calling him was an unpleasant incident of the night before wherein an old and valued friend of the Llewelyns' having dropped in at their apartment, had, on leaving, mistaken the janitor's car outside for the taxi he'd hired for the night—which had pulled around to the opposite curb, whereupon the friend had found himself being arrested for trying to steal the car even before he had time to see his mistake, so swiftly had the police arrived in screaming force at the behest of the janitor and Old Eagle Eye following his movements, which, since these were not altogether steady, it had needed some fast talking to explain away. "Not two days go past without your landlord making a complaint to us about some tenant in your place," the prosecutor went on.

"Even anyone who calls there with one over the eight, Ethan, we get his car number right away, though we don't pay much attention to it any more."

"You don't eh? Then how come you got your strong-armed stinkweasels there so quick?"

"I guess the bastard's so proud of having cleaned up the joint from what it was," the other continued, disregarding Ethan's question. "Or rather afraid we'll forget he has and raid it again."

"What was it"—Ethan heard the prosecutor purring a while.

"An abortionist's clinic," he said finally. "For the ladies of the West End. Hell of a scandal about it a year before you came to the coast . . . But probably he thinks you're a Communist, living out there on the beach like all the rub-dubs and canned heaters."

"I'd like to know what the hell——"

"You're not, are you, by the way."

"Yes. And an anarchist too."

"Look after yourself, my boy."

A house of abortions! What could be more appropriate, it characterized their new apartment perfectly and for all time. And their old one become meanwhile a house of correction for juvenile delinquents. Perfect!

Now they had had twenty-four days of drought; nothing could grow, not even weeds in the vacant lots. There was a shrill cold dry north wind and it was half cloudy, half cold sunlight; there was a sharp metallic smell and the mountains looked like steel.

Then came the other wind, cloudy and different; a soft sky, a soft day, with a big wild boisterous damp wind, but soft, it was almost like spring and one thought one could feel things growing; bits of Scotch mist hovered in the air when the sun came out, a moist south wind with a different smell, silky and fragrant.

The first thing that happens in a city is that the weather dies in the soul, though people may talk of nothing else, using it was the only medium for conversation, much as people still will talk idly, gossip in the terms of long-forgotten heresies, mysterious codes of honor, not knowing the significance of their own metaphors. "Depositaries of marvels," The McCandless said, "which they do not understand."

Their first spring on the beach Ethan had understood, even if vicariously at first, the infinite pathos of weather, of a day, and in this the difference between himself and Jacqueline. In her there was always the tender balance between inner and outer weather. But as for him, he had had to go to a movie to become aware of it. Spring for him had been the Shaftsbury Pavilion, where a film would use the music of migrating birds to the sight of blowing grasses. For the first time in his life that spring he had seen Blake's angels in the cherry trees in bloom.

Few writers seem to be aware of this. True, it was the lyricist's stock in trade. But usually so far and no further. Nothing was more unreal than a novel, even a realistic novel. Think of the vast French tomes dealing with all the intricacies of love but which never would mention the anguish of waiting for VD to develop: the bad weather of love which, even if counteracted, would be found to exist in some other spiritual form.

But a house of abortions! In this very room life that was to come into being had been stilled forever by one prick of the knife: in every room in the place it was as if sordid murders had been committed . . . Women had writhed, screamed, become hysterical—they still did for that matter. Even as such he could not help thinking it must have sometimes been a jollier place than it was now "cleaned up," and greeted from time to time, by someone at least, with a sigh of relief.

With these gruesome reflections Ethan, half hidden by a curtain, was watching the antics, down on the sidewalk of the street, of exactly that kind of drunk known unkindly by the police and the newspapers as a rub-dub or deadbeat, who had evidently strayed from the skid road (where he perhaps lived in a shack under edict of eviction) into this part of town and lost his way, poor devil, in a mental blizzard of canned heat, watching the circumspection of his movements, his piteous attempts to control himself, to maintain his equilibrium, asking the way of a child now.

He thinks he is not seen: not a bit of it, from a hundred windows malignant eyes are watching, and already Old Eagle Eye herself is at the phone, ringing up the police, a real orgasm of ringing, and even though he had done nothing but ask a child the way to the nearest beer parlour, probably he was dying to take a piss, tomorrow he will find himself in a line-up with some poor devil facing a ten-year sentence and a whipping as a sex maniac.

(And this kind of train of thought was quite genuine with Ethan at this period. It had not taken long for what had become so precariously balanced within himself to be overpoised again.)

Ethan thought to warn the man, to shout. But it was too late. Here the police car came braying already. No, they hadn't seen him. But they would soon. Poor fellow. Yes, that was it. Confident no one could see him, now he was peeing blithely against the convent wall. And that would never do. Sea gulls might do worse on the roof, and men pee in calm legal collective security against the side of Antwerp Cathedral, but to piss against a convent or any other wall was downright stupidity for a human being in Vancouver, even when your bladder was bursting, and there was not a urinal visible for five miles, for though they'd build anything else, it was a well-known fact the inhabitants of West End were so pure that they preferred to think they had no natural functions at all.

Well, maybe that was funny (Ethan had prayed and the bum, piloted by a kindly Chinese, and buttoning his buttons where no buttons were, had got away down a side alley), as well as half true. But, as Jacqueline told him, the imbalance had set in. Ethan not only began to hate the apartment house of abortions but Vancouver itself with an almost pathological savagery.

Its soul seemed to him like one of those sportsmen who count their civic reputation of the highest value, are noticeably quiet, sober pillars of the church, object publicly to risqué movies and symphony orchestras on Sundays, neither drink nor smoke, and call the police themselves on the slightest provocation. And certainly, Ethan could point out to Jacqueline, who often was only too glad to have a good bout of loathing for Vancouver too, this wasn't just imagination. That the city could be seen as, was, just such a strangler and murderer was no more than truth. So miserable a place had it apparently become to live in that at this period literally not a day passed without a suicide, usually by gas, or a murder of the most horrible type.

The trouble with Ethan's sweeping indictment was not that it didn't contain some objective truth, but that it was based not so much upon his experience as on his personal reactions to the current articles in that dreaded *Vancouver Evening Messenger,* with its eternal rapping and probings and so devoted to tolerance and freedom of thought that, having lost interest in the evictions on the North Shore for the moment, it was running a series of leading articles urging all public-spirited citizens to turn into the authorities the names not merely of those of their neighbours who evinced "dangerous un-Canadian leftward tendencies," but "personal eccentricity in any form."

Poor old Vancouver! That there were columnists on that same newspaper who took anything but that point of view and who sincerely were interested within their limits, in "tolerance and freedom of thought," was beside the point to Ethan; that the newspaper's pages might be open to the expression of almost any opinion whatsoever, however fantastic, a personal and complicated frustration; and since he had not noticed these fair-minded writers had ever carried their tolerance to the pitch of being tolerant of the squatters who lived on government beaches, Ethan found himself reacting mostly to that which aroused his own venom, which, being aimed nowhere, or at an abstraction, ended only in poisoning himself.

The city authorities, however, had not lost interest in evictions.

For one day they saw the sinister men against the skyline on the ridgepole. They were pulling down the most beautiful of the old houses between the promenade and the bay. It was the first of thirteen such houses whose demolishment would permit the widening of the approach to Stanley Park. A five-car lane instead of the narrower avenue than at present, where the promenade proper merged with it, was divided from the bay by these houses and their rose gardens sloping down to the sands. Nor had the Llewelyns been spared on that first day, for they could not resist going closer to look, the sight of the few remaining effects in the house being moved out, and the naked scaffolding so *white:* the poor cedar two-by-fours, though more than half a century old, still looking so new, so fresh. This was no bulldozer's job where the house-wreckers smashed the house to smithereens in one grunting blow: they were taking, torturing, the house to pieces, it seemed bit by bit. It was almost as if they meant to eat it; piling neatly its strips of white flesh to one side in the trampled garden, as though the house were a carcass they meant to carry away piecemeal and devour at their leisure. Then, next day, the roof-tree demolished: the calamitous wrenching sound of clawbars ripping nails from boards, a scalariform scaffold to windward and a few last bookcases carried out, and the workmen with saturnine heartless smiles whistling back up the front steps— left intact for that purpose—through the empty door frame, into the empty shell. And the next day without its ridgepole, without its front door, where once had hung a Christmas wreath, the house so demolished it had almost lost its tragedy, so bowed down with tragedy was it; and the next, a heap of boards by the waterfront; and the workers' clawbars smacking their lips for the final demolition. Ah, dead Tie-Beam, dead King-Post, dead Wall Plate, dead Pole Plate, dead Purlin, Christ, how he hated the heartlessness of man who could do this without ever having known what happiness was, Christ, how he hated his country, how he hated all men, and so felt the warning, that he himself was going to die, *lex talionis,* and a good thing too. Better that he should than Tommy. He felt this warning and saw, in his mind's eye, all the other houses being pulled down, one after another—but perhaps they would get a re-prieve—a boy was whistling to his dog from the last doomed house . . . And what made it worse, it had turned out that Jacqueline had been led to believe she could rent from its owners what was now this heap of boards. Hoping to please Ethan, she'd kept this unselfishly secret from him, divulged only a few days before they saw the men on the ridgepole, when she'd found out her hopes had been too high (like the rent) of having a pied-à-terre for their house-hunting that was not an apartment but a beach home from home where Ethan could swim. Worst of all, the owners, who were shortly to depart for California, and had now gone, demanded a huge deposit of $500 before being willing even to consider leasing the house, so that at one stroke, since they must have known what was likely to happen, all sympathy for them was now lost. Amid the wreckage a woman could be discerned darting about, wringing her hands, and crying heartbrokenly, and speaking in loud angry tones to the workmen in a language like Russian, possibly. But maybe the owners, descendants of the original builders, could be forgiven; unlike their forefathers, money being the only language they knew, they had made one final assertion of their home's worth in terms that could not be met.

Well, gone was another piece of life. And what were they going to put up in its place, in the name of God, a five-car lane: but who wanted a five-car lane to a park that would end by being logged and a five-car lane itself. More deathscape, more *potlust*—bah! cleaning up the place! Because the poor houses could be surprised in a state of dishevelment, because they would give a bad impression of backwardness to our cousins south of the border (which, on the contrary, American tourists would welcome), because they were *not new*. It would soon be the same everywhere. Canada's beauty was in its wildness, and if you like, untidiness. It was the only originality it had. If one loved it, it was because it was—Ethan had been going to say—a sort of bastard. There might be beauty in the effort of trying to tame it, but the result was something else. Final success would be its death—or the work would have to be undone, the striving start again—

While Ethan in his confused emotion advanced such loose arguments as these, which were, he saw, perfectly useless, not to say irrelevant, and probably meaningless too, and had the effect only of irritating Jacqueline, they were walking along the promenade in the gale that met them after they were out of the "shelter" of the doomed houses, walking in the direction of the park, toward the still empty old bandstand on their right (it would have been empty this time of year anyhow but no band had obviously played in it now for more than a decade)—trying to get some feeling of the beach back, of an old beach walk, from the sea gulls shivering with blowing feathers farther ahead on the steep grass seabank or hopping backwards there at the onslaught of sea and spray against the seawall, under-propped by those waterlogged snags beach-dwellers know as "dead men," walking past the sweaty chill aquarium, smelling of bath houses, where the octopus, now grown much older, still lived out its sour existence of disused bagpipes, and the terrible wolf eel, now much more miserable, with its expression of sadness and the attenuated face of a prostitute by Edvard Munch, uncurled its slow damnation, or hid its grief beneath a stone.

As they came abreast of this bandstand itself Ethan suddenly announced with triumph he had been composing this jaunty ditty in his head for the last five minutes, with the object of cheering Jacqueline up.

> They are taking down the beautiful houses once built with loving hands,
> But still the old bandstand stands where no band stands
>
> With clawbars they have gone to work on the poor lovely houses above the sands
> At their callous work of eviction that no human law countermands
>
> Callously at their work of heartbreak that no civic heart understands
> In this pompous and joyless city of police and moral perfection and one man stands
>
> Where you are brutally thrown out of beer parlours for standing where no man stands
> Where the pigeons roam free and the police listen to each pigeon's demands
>
> And they are taking down the beautiful houses once cared for with loving hands
> But still the old bandstand stands where no band stands.

CHAPTER 26 🍃 *"... Stalked*
Fatefully ..."

—And to cheer her up because they happened also to be on their way to visit Tommy in hospital. Tommy's school term had already begun when they left the beach for town but he'd spend a Sunday afternoon with them in Stanley Park. He cracked two ribs when the supporting chains of a swing they'd left him to play on alone for a few minutes had given way. His injury by reflex action had caused a colonic complication, not apparently serious, but giving anxiety enough, and the boy considerable pain.

But Ethan's poem was not having the right effect.

And though, to their relief, Tommy seemed much better, surrounded by grisly comic books he was sitting up in bed between the legend *Fasting* and a portrait of the infant Jesus, in whose hand were two shingle nails, being shown by St. Joseph how to build a cross. On their way back from the hospital to the apartment Jacqueline became more irritable and depressed than ever.

Lex talionis, Ethan thought again, whereby if under certain circumstances a man accidentally brought about the death of a child, not he, but his child must be killed. But Tommy had not been killed. What if he had been killed? What if his injury should cause complications that lasted for life or, if he should take a turn for the worse, die now ... Perhaps poor Jacqueline was just depressed

because it was the same damn hospital where she'd had her hyster-
ectomy. Moreover she'd had another dreary day, this time in his
company, of fruitless house-searching. The sight of that house in its
final death throes had put the lid on things.

"It's all the fault of the damn beach," she broke out suddenly.

"You can't blame Tommy's accident on the beach."

"Yes, I can. If we hadn't been quarreling about it in the park that
Sunday we wouldn't have left him alone on the swing. And I can't
see why he doesn't want to stop with us at the apartment if it's not
because he's got the idea that home's a bad place anyhow."

"They only accepted him at St. Jude's on condition he'd board
there . . . And we only got the apartment on condition we'd have
no children with us."

"But he doesn't even like to visit us here."

"Who would?"

"Maybe if we can get a decent house we can *live* in for a change
it'll be different."

"Live in! . . . We'll never find a better place in a million years
than our little cabin."

And the quarrel really blazed out into the open when they got
back to the apartment, which Ethan had entered however this time
with a sigh of relief like a man going to bed, or one who has at last
eluded his enemies for a while; even if his enemy was only a beard,
he'd felt its unusually hot pursuit of him this afternoon.

"What you don't see is that I'm only too glad to get away from
your goddam shack!" she burst out at him, her eyes looking black
and wild: she was in what they called her "wild Assinaboine
mood"; but the horrible thing about such quarrels was that they had
a dramatic falsity and banality that seemed implicit in the very life
they were quarreling about, viewed from the corroding standpoint
of the city with no respect for the *religio loci!*

It was as if they had exchanged sunlight on water for photographs of sunlight on water, cool commotion of blowing grasses and
pennyroyal, or reeds and the rippling waters, the soaring love with
which they followed migrating birds, for the tragic incidental music

that always accompanies documentaries involving blowing grasses, rippling waters and migrating birds, and soon they would not be able to have told the difference, perhaps prefer the incidental music for which they had to be as thankful for as the films. Soon they might not even have that.

"And anyhow what right have you to identify life in this apartment with life in a new house?"

"God forbid I should do that. And please don't call it a goddam shack."

"Why don't you give me a *chance?* Look here, Ethan Llewelyn, what you've selfishly overlooked is the fact that that beastly cookstove was a tyranny for a woman, that the lack of conveniences was much harder on me——"

"Though not so damned hard as you make out a case for their being."

Ethan was remorseful. What he had really overlooked—he thought he only saw it now—was that the threat of eviction had poisoned their life in Eridanus for Jacqueline more completely and fatefully perhaps than for him, to such an extent (and here came all these thoughts again, here in the bus) that she had not been able to live without transferring herself in advance to the thought of another home: and while he had felt there was something traitorous in the facility with which she was able to do this, the truth seemed—for under her hands the "goddam shack" had become beautiful, or more beautiful, that in order to bear the loss of Eridanus and their life there—and it was the Barkerville all over again (and in the bus it's the recalcitrating words about the Barkerville all over again, bound to these thoughts like Ixion to his wheel) she had to pretend. Or were they simply engaged in some elaborate form of *ignoratio elenchi?* not talking about the cabin at all, Tommy being the point at issue, their anxiety for him become their anxiety about the beach. Or was there some other underground process of substitution at work, some buried jealousy on her part, or the cabin become the child they could not have? Moreover not even the threat of eviction had really poisoned that life, he saw. He was capable of thinking of it now, quite as if it still existed, with a boundless impatience, an immeasurable longing—

"And I *did* hate it! *Do* hate it—Hate it! Hate it! Hate it!"

Ethan was watching her as she said this, her furious dark eyes, her sweet sleek cap of dark hair that curled slightly around her face; she was wearing a beige, some sort of beige, turtleneck sweater, and a full black skirt with a wide red belt and high-heeled red shoes—in the country she wore slacks oftener than shorts and he'd forgotten, for a moment, what pretty feet and beautiful legs she had—and as she spun around in her anger, her skirt flying out like a dancer's, her hair flew out a little bit from her head, and she almost stamped like a child. Though Ethan wanted to lose his temper still further, he was extraordinarily excited, as well as angry, and picking her up, Jacqueline still half fighting with him, and how light and little she felt—he tottered with her to bed in that stifling apartment in which one felt sealed as in a tomb.

"Tommy hated it anyway," said Jacqueline later, still not quite repentant.

"Do you remember last Hallowe'en?"

Jacqueline sighed.

"He can't have hated the prospect of the beach so much," Ethan went on, "since he wangled the whole weekend off from St. Jude's for his Hallowe'en celebration."

"Do you remember how worried the poor child was all day it was going to rain?"

"Do you remember how worried *we* were?"

"Do you remember——"

"Do you—"

The cloudy October night with the inlet dark and Styx-like. And the mountains and mountain shadows immense in the gloom. And themselves alone on the beach, not one light in the fishermen's cottages, but with such a sense of from the dark night withdrawn, and of love within the cabin and of being a little family so happy in one another. While outside the salmon had stopped jumping, and the only sound was a barking dog; or the distant sounds of foreign firecrackers like faint machine-gun fire from the opposite bank. And the refinery lights too bright, still portending rain.

And Tommy's excitement at the rockets all lined up on the windowsill to go to the moon: and the wonderful names of the fireworks: the Brocks Crystal Palace, Jack-in-the-Box, the volcano-shaped Volcano, wrapped in black and orange paper, with a pattern of irrelevant lightning flashes, the Illuminated Light cylinder dressed in red and green, the Flower Pot, and the Electric Fountain: and the Golden Rain, the Aurora and the Glittering Cascade; the Guy Fawkes Mine, and most exciting of all, the Three-Bead Hooter, from Hong Kong, manufactured by Kwong Lee Duck and Co.

Jacqueline first lighted a Titania's Magic Wand, two Titania's Magic Wands, it being as if, she said, God were trying out a few experimental worlds and stars and suns and calculating how long they would last, and whether the aesthetic principle involved could somehow outlast the worlds He created, save did that matter? asked Ethan, since the form of the snowflake was within, mattered even less, by the way, since both were nearly duds, except to Tommy, who began to assume an air of ruin, which was hurtful, for his parents felt themselves to be on trial, were perhaps even trying to woo him to the beach.

But still it hadn't rained anyhow. So for safety they began to set the fireworks off, shooting them out to sea, from a child's bucket filled with sand, one of their fire extinguishers, which they placed at the end of the pier where Jacqueline, from the glow of her lighted punk, charged an object named the Midnight Sun that, in the bucket, looked like a sharply cone-shaped dunce's hat in a Mexican lake bed. Not very successful. Then Ethan produced a livid beer parlour of malodorous light, from which issued a hurricane of flying onions and Christmas bells, a horrendously beautiful spectacle, with the luminous balls slanting then bouncing upon the pier, as they were not meant to do, and dying so impressively that Tommy observed, "What I'd like to do is bang, boom!"

So Jacqueline made a magic of cerise fire, which exploded into a fountain of multitudinous silver and gold fire and sparks that elicited from their son the response, "That's better than the sparkler." And Jacqueline, trying to conceal her disappointment, saying, but with such an air of being importantly a mother that Ethan had to laugh:

"Now I want you to notice the smell of the punk, Tommy. Something like a peculiar incense. It has a smell so completely its own. You light your punk and it just glows on the end."

And then, Mount Vesuvius erupting backwards, the Glittering Cascade a mere trickle, the Roman Candles short-circuiting, the Guy Fawkes Mine a complete dud, and Tommy's disappointment that they hadn't a Catherine Wheel.

"I had one and then I put it back," Jacqueline explained, "because I decided it was too dangerous."

"Yes, old man," said Ethan, "you have to nail it to a post and when it spins, if it comes off, it can shoot off in any direction, and might even set fire to the house."

Then Tommy, soon mollified with some more sparklers, saying, "Mother, you look just like the Statue of Liberty." And not being allowed to set off the larger fireworks, setting off two sparklers spluttering at once himself and dancing madly round the platform with them, yelling, "Yippee, I'm an Indian!" And then getting more and more excited. "I want the one that's made in Hong Kong. I like particularly the Three-Bead Boomer."

"Isn't any Boomer, old chap. What you mean's the Three Bead-Hooter. Here we are. Made in Hong Kong."

"That's just what I meant, that old Three-Bead Hooter——"

And Jacqueline, at the end of the pier, bending backwards away from the sputtering fuse, having touched her glowing punk to it, in a manner that, in the opposite direction exactly balanced the seaward declension of the rocket, that neither boomed nor hooted, but was not less impressive for that, so Tommy said.

"Now it's your turn to pick a firework, Daddy, Daddy—"

And Jacqueline, like a child herself saying, "Dozens! Such wonderful names!"

And the Electric Fountain, seeming for at least five minutes to be a dud too, only dull red fiery worm, then suddenly Zip: burgeoning forth magnificently into a shower of golden fountainous stars, expiring in a steaming livid Paracutin, and ending in a fizzle.

"It looked like Versailles and lasted no longer than the treaty."

But the rain still holding off and the evening becoming triumphant, with Tommy, getting more and more excited, like a drunkard who can't stand the space between drinks, crying, "Choose a firework! Choose a firework!" wanting them to go off continuously.

And Jacqueline saying, "I just want them to go on."

And himself, like Tommy, who wanted them to go on. And the ecstatic moments of light like those burgeoning fountains and exploding fireworks that never unhappily did go on.

"Let me be your angel . . . Didn't I find you the little house on the beach in the first place?"

"Ah yes . . ."

Jacqueline had been lying facing him with her head on her arm; now she raised herself on one elbow, and though he couldn't see her face very well in the twilight, for the days were drawing in (he had pulled the curtain and they hadn't, as they still thought of it, "lit the lamps"; maybe out of habit, for lighting the pretty blue and silver and copper lamps at dusk had been a ritualistic action demanding some concentration and care). Jacqueline's eyes looked enormous and pleading.

"That's what we're both trying to do, my heart's darling."

"You don't give me much cooperation."

"And what a hope there seems to be!"

Post coitum omne animal triste est . . . That again was not always true in the cabin. It could be succeeded just as well by exhilaration, bursts of humor, and purification of a swim, racing along back to the house looming up above you, your eyes in a sea squall, dizzied with mountains and sea gulls and pines. But who wanted to be exhilarated in a bewhiskered slippery bathtub with a view of the toilet seat?

But there was another objective reason for Ethan's gloom that began to fasten on him as if it were that octopus which lived in the aquarium. When he said they'd never find such a house as their cabin in a million years he really meant it. Ethan simply did not believe that the sort of conjunction of favoring yet opposing circumstances which had maintained Eridanus' existence in balance for so long could arise again, or be discovered elsewhere to have arisen. *Another* Eridanus was not to be found. Where else could you find the freedom, the privacy, the absolute privacy, and yet when you needed it, the friendliness, not too far, not too near, where else find all man's simple needs so simply satisfied? It was unique: in one's praise, as in another's denunciation, as when the papers cruelly said, "No other city in the Pacific Northwest has stood for such a disgrace to their waterfront! Look at Seattle! Put these hovels that look like so many marine growths to the torch and keep going!"

And now, in October again, when the summer people had gone and Eridanus was nearly deserted, the tugboat's whistles sounding through the fog over the water; in the forest the sunlight striking down through patches of fog, making oases of celestial light, the silence, the steepness of the forest path, the moss growing on the bark of the trees reaching out of sight, the ferns growing in the moss: and the silence of the pretty little cottages where such simplicity and happiness lived for a moment, but don't you believe it! There is nothing that the brute blind muzzle of the world loves to do more than destroy this kind of happiness, once it has rooted it out, in the name of the future it cannot see.

"Ethan, look here," Jacqueline was shaking his arm, as they lay on the bed, smoking. "Ethan—It's absolutely ridiculous to say we can't find another place where we could be just as happy. It may be different, it may not be another Eridanus, but even Jean Taschereau said——"

"I know what you're going to say. That British Columbia is a large place. About twice as large as France, in fact. And that because Jean Taschereau found somewhere up in the dry belt where you can still stake a claim and buy land for two dollars an acre on some lakeshore or other, there's no reason why we shouldn't. But I hate

o

lakes, and so do you, after living by the sea—salt water I mean—and anyhow the whole thing would be far too isolated, I don't want to bury you in the wilderness."

For the paradox was that it was humanity, sparsely represented as it might be, that had given Eridanus its beauty, not nature alone.

"What!" Jacqueline cried, sitting straight up in bed. "Do you mean to lie there and tell me that Eridanus was *not* isolated, that you were *not* burying me out there in that Christ-awful godforsaken hole!" She lay down again abruptly, groaning, while Ethan, wounded, wrestled with this further ambiguity. "To you that was *not* your idea of burying me in the wilderness?"

"Not altogether. We were near enough to here, to Vancouver——"

"Oh God! Vancouver! Oh Hangover—If that's not wilderness I don't know what is. You have only to step off the highway into that forest beyond McHeath Road to be lost—hikers are always getting lost—we got lost——"

"—Where we could go to concerts." (Ethan reflected that they'd been to only two this year at that, and now the season was over.) "And haven't you just reminded me that you *found* the godforsaken hole?"

"Oh!"

"You couldn't see so many intelligent and brilliantly produced plays in a London season as we've seen here in the last year," said Ethan, who now would even defend the city in order to defend Eridanus. "I found it exciting to be in at the birth of a new theatre in this country."

"Bah!" Jacqueline now automatically took the other side. "Just give it a few more months and those enthusiastic amateurs will be back to Noel Coward again."

"Of course I never dreamed when we saw Sartre's *No Exit* a few months ago that we were going to find ourselves in exactly that same hellish apartment of his."

"If it's hellish it's largely because you make it so."

"They've had some first-rate exhibitions at the art gallery. Nobody, Jacqueline, whose mind was not absolutely provincial could take a snobbish attitude toward that, even though most Canadians seem to . . . No, I *didn't* 'bury you in the wilderness.'"

"I don't see how anyone could have a more provincial attitude than yours is."

"Oh, come off it, Jacqueline. What with your misology and my misoneism——"

"What kind of social life do I have, anyhow? There's nobody to talk to most of the time except a few old fishermen."

"At least the fishermen don't gossip."

"Like hell they don't! Ha ha!"

"Stop shouting. The janitor'll hear us, or somebody'll complain . . . Well, at least we don't hear them gossip."

"I'm not shouting any louder than you are. And you know perfectly well they gossip as much as anybody. Don't be sentimental."

"They're away half the year. And the summer people kept mostly to themselves, except for the Fairhavens, who're swell, and what about Sigbjørn and Primrose Wilderness? And I thank heaven we did get to know so few people! and it's you yourself who are turning this into an obscene quarrel and making me say all sorts of things I don't mean. That's what your wonderful civilization does to a fellow! And get this. I'm *not* an enemy of human consciousness, simply of——"

"I simply cannot understand you," said Jacqueline dreamily, lying down on her back and looking at the ceiling. "What the hell has that got to do with the argument?"

"It's no use asking me why I love it," Ethan said after a moment. "I can't tell you. I'm not sure I know. In fact, I don't know that I don't hate it as much as you do."

"It seems to me your attachment to the place is really insane!" cried Jacqueline, sitting up again.

"—and if there's something pathological about his attachment," Ethan said, laughing, in his father-in-law's accent, "not to be attached, considering how much they got for nothing, would be more pathological still." He took Jacqueline in his arms again, but this only made her more angry and she shook herself free.

"All *right,*" she said in the staccato tones of someone who has made a final decision. "If you want it so much, why don't you *fight* the eviction? You're a lawyer, aren't you? Then find some law."

"Oh, Lord . . ."

Yet here Ethan was involved in another paradox. It wasn't a field of law in which he was well versed, though he could easily enough look it up, but certainly it seemed to him there was little legal basis on which to fight such an order should it come, and certainly not before it came, squatter's rights, if not fishermen's privileges, having long since been abolished; and even had he "found some law," by which to delay the eviction, it might only have imperiled those few fishermen whose houses, having been mounted on rollers against just such an eventuality, could be towed away to another government-owned beach where they would possess delimited foreshore rights, but which, alas, by no means posited another Eridanus, more likely beneath the railway tracks. No, to fight might even bring down in addition to an eviction order on those left, a writ of *fieri facias*, or something or other even more ghoulish, for some huge and unpayable amount in back taxes. In fact, Ethan sometimes thought, it was as if almost their life had argued the presence in the background of some beneficent tolerant spirit, behind the intolerant civic facade; it seemed ungrateful even at the end to confront this with any insistence on legal rights, even had it not been true there were none, unless love itself could stake a claim.

"Our garden! Our little boat . . ." Jacqueline was sobbing.

"Don't grieve, honey lamb. We'll find somewhere, you'll lead us to it, as you did before. You'll see."

"But it isn't a question of just *some*where."

"Well if we can find *any*where to live at all, not in absolute limbo, where you can have a garden, with conditions as they are we'll be lucky."

"Perhaps we should live on Vancouver Island . . . Ethan," Jacqueline suddenly stopped crying and sat up, blinking excitedly, like a child, "I'd almost forgotten about Angela. Maybe she'll know of something."

"Doesn't she live on Saturna Island, or some place with a Saturnine name like that?"

"Gabriola . . . it's a lovely name."

Jacqueline jumped out of bed and ran, naked, without stopping for a robe, into the living room where he could hear her pulling out drawers in the desk; she came dancing back in a moment, making triumphant leaps, waving the maps, and excited as a little cookstove when the kindling catches in the morning and you have to turn down the damper. She snapped on the light and got back into bed where they rested their elbows with the maps between them.

"Then in Gabriola perhaps," Ethan said at last almost hopefully. "We wouldn't be too far. You wouldn't be buried. We can get all the books we want posted out to us from the Victoria Provincial Library under that new arrangement. And Nanaimo has a good chamber orchestra, I've heard. And we could easily come to Vancouver for a weekend. And who knows," he added, invoking with mock grimness an old private joke—for objectively this conversation sounded truly dreadful—"we might even sometimes treat ourselves to a flight to Bellingham, in the good old U. S. A."

"Nanaimo. *That's* where we have to go to get the boat for Gabriola, see . . . Darling . . . darling . . ."

Ethan, wrapped in a blanket, was standing tiptoe on a chair to see if he could catch a glimpse of the ship whose siren had just sounded from the bay, maybe the Nanaimo ship itself. But all he could make out were those ventilators on flat roofs that looked against the evening sky like the head and shoulders of Easter Island idols and beyond that the sky was very clear to the west with a few long gold and vermilion streamers, dove-grey and wild magenta clouds in three layers were blowing overhead with a few whisking off at an angle: in the east it was very dark with rain falling in perpendicular sheets at right angles to the billowing blue-grey clouds. King Storm whose sheen is fearful. But in fact there was just this one isolated shower in a clear sky.

And then, against the door, the thud of that disastrous evening newspaper.

"They want to turn this whole place into a vast bloody great Black Country, a Lancashire, or Staffordshire of the Pacific Northwest," Ethan said, giving her the second half of the paper. "Or another Ruhr or something. The curse on British Columbia used to be that it had too many miners and not enough farmers, well, the same curse is turning up now in another form."

"But just now you were blaming everything on shortages and a coming depression. And only two percent or something of the country's arable anyhow, isn't it—Oh, dear, don't let's take the paper if it's going to spoil everything every evening. Why don't we just tie ourselves to the bed and never do anything at all?"

"But it's the boom we've really got to fear," Ethan said grimly. "You'll see, Jacky. That's coming in a few years, together with the inevitable revived war economy for the *next* war. Your poor little bit of property won't be safe from desecration no matter where you are. And then, when they've totally ruined most of the beauty of the country with industry, and thoroughly loused up the watersheds and the rainfall, and the last old sourdough has traded in his gold sifting pan for a Geiger counter and staked out the last uranium claim—as it says here—some jeezly fool will drop an atom bomb on the whole business, and serve them damn well right too! It's a pity this paper hasn't got that character of Flaubert's—what's his name, Pellerin?—on their staff of artists. The only thing lacking is a picture of Progress in the form of Jesus Christ driving a locomotive across a virgin forest."

Ethan's hatred was perhaps expressive of despairing love. Quite against his better judgment he believed that some final wisdom would arise out of Canada, that would save not only Canada herself but perhaps the world. The trouble is, the world never looks as though it's going to be saved in one's own lifetime.

—In Gabriola perhaps. Ethan looked thoughtfully out of the bus window at the Gulf again; after the quietude of the inlet, with its silent flux and flow, after Eridanus, what would Jacqueline make of an island shore exposed to the full smashing fury and monotony and idiot clangor of the more open sea? What if, once there, she couldn't bear to live by the sea at all, and wanted to live inland?

"Kelp—" a voice was saying in the bus and Ethan listened a moment. "When they put their heads up and shake their hair that means the tide is slackening . . . tangle like a head . . . grew the opposite way about . . . I was watching for slack water . . . hadn't the tide with me . . . If you went two feet that side you'd have the rocks . . . I stood there looking for the rocks . . . The banks were filled with bracken and hay . . . where they came up and shook their heads I knew I was safe . . . twenty-five or thirty feet long, alongside a wicked rock but where they grow there's deeper water . . . Too strong for a little boat like that . . ."

Yet—in Gabriola perhaps. In Gabriola he hoped. Sometimes he felt—this was no doubt why he kept thinking about the "lot"—that the only way he could console himself would be to build a new house, himself, with his own hands, that resembled the old. Sometimes when he remembered the small lost objects, those lares and penates left behind, as not worth removing, the old wheelbarrow, the watering cans, the bookcase he'd made of orange boxes, their usage once dear to them as a continually renewed benison, it seemed still a betrayal on his side of the lonely cabin itself to think about the skipper's house, as if, should Jacqueline's loyalty have to fade, he must, for both their sakes, keep his alive. And deploring this childishness at the moment, on the bus, it was only to find himself thinking about the lot again. Lot. The human lot. And Lot's wife too . . . Yet why not the house? It would save much intermediate trouble and anxiety. And poor Jacqueline would be thinking again even now, at this instant, yes, as if he were the same man, and he was the same man was he not? that at the skipper's house there would, after all, be plenty of work for him of the kind he enjoyed most. And in a way she was right; he could build on a room, two rooms, put up shelves and cupboards where they were needed, reshingle the roof: the skipper probably had a vegetable garden, but they might plant fruit trees, and if they could move in right away, he thought with a sudden access of tenderness, it wouldn't be too late for Jacqueline to set out bulbs, so that by next spring, besides the skipper's flowers there'd be daffodils, snow drops, Stars of Bethlehem———

"In Sonora Island I came upon dwarf rhododendrons—they were

on the logs drifting down—a common purply color like I saw them in the nunnery . . . There's a lagoon I could show you there. But the British navy doesn't know it's there . . . Charlian Harbor . . . You could see evidence of cougar excreta . . . the deer hair, they don't digest it . . . don't spit on your hands, Jimmy, that will put blisters, he said so anyway . . . And all along I was gathering flowers. I had a girl at this time . . . At Port Grenaugh I've gathered wild daffodils . . . And all round that shore French currents growing and the water, the edge of the water, was alive with salamanders——"

"What makes a bad sea in the Irish sea is the seas fighting one another."

Ninebark, birdfoot clover, would they find those on Gabriola? Ah, the happy day they'd spent yesterday at the Botanical Museum in Victoria. Happy? And Christ the pathos of this, the brave pretense on Jacqueline's part that it was all just like their old life again when nothing could perhaps better symbolize their fall from grace than those hours, enjoyable or not, for had not that life—as Schopenhauer—Schopenhauer?—might have said, become like a running away from nature to look at a museum of dried plants or a landscape in copperplate and pretend you were enjoying it more: yes, and enjoying what more, might one ask too if Swedenborg—Swedenborg?—were right and nature herself were dead, no more than a reflection, less than a museum of dried plants herself to that which she reflected? . . . Ah, Wake Robin, Sea Rocket and Ocean Spray—Blazing Star and Love Lies Bleeding. Why should he always think of wildflowers?

—Death Camus and the Destroying Angel.

CHAPTER 27   ❧   *Useful Knots*
and How to
Tie Them

The bus drew up at a grade crossing to let a log train pass. A full minute later it was still passing and, Jacqueline noticing some seats now vacant on the driver's right, the Llewelyns edged forward to watch the timber piled on the open cars slipping away from them. It was a very long train, clicking along slowly.

"It's nothing but knots."

"—I'd hate to have a house built of that stuff. It'd just fall down."

"Why do they bother to cut it?"

So ran the encouraging conversation between two men across the aisle. The cars did indeed seem full of impossible snags; the train was booming, a soft continuous thunder of trampled boards above which you could hear the crossing's little comment as the wheels rolled over the metals: *clunkety-clunkety-click-clunkety-clunkety-click*. Ethan now became aware of another agitation, closer at hand, less loud, but more insistent. A mountain mist had suddenly swooped down on the Greyhound, their bus having turned inland, a slight drizzle, and the driver had set his windscreen wipers in motion on the two front windows immediately ahead of the Llewelyns. Though the two wipers, which working in opposite directions, together possessed a consistent rhythm, they did not perform in exact unison, the right pendulum having swung to the leftward limit of its arc always an instant before the left pendulum had swung to its rightward limit. Sometimes it looked as though the left pendulum were trying to catch the right one, to trap it, at some always elusive moment of conjunction. The commotion this made was, to Ethan, first interesting, then stupefying, at last, in concert with that of the train—that now appeared at least a mile long—with its diminishing cargo of sad snags in the open cars under the mournful drizzle, and the wholly alien rhythm arising as each car trundled across the road itself—absolutely maddening.

"De-clock de-*clack* de-clock de-*clack* de clack de-clonk de-clonkety-clack!"

"—*clunkety-clunkety-click clunkety-clunkety-click*—"

"De-clonk de-*clack* de-clock de-*clank* de-clack de-*clonk* de-clonkety-*clack!*"

"—*clunkety-clunkety-click clunkety-clunkety-click*—"

Ethan now became aware of something else. He had a hangover. The snags in the cars under the drizzle were more than sad. They said horrible things to him. Not that it was a bad hangover. Six or seven small beers in a pub last night, less than a pint of gin, well diluted with orange juice, shared with Jacqueline before turning in, and he hadn't been aware of it when he woke up—

"De-clonk de-*clack* De clonkety *clock* de-clack de-*clock* de-clockety-*clack*."

"—*clunkety-clunkety-click clunkety-clunkety-click*—"

Of a hard-drinking profession, Ethan had been used to drinking fairly regularly, but moderately, most of his life. About once a month he had liked to get pretty tight: so, for that matter, did Jacqueline. But at Eridanus, little by little, without deliberate discipline on this point, he found that he had dropped the habit, "walked away from it" as they say, altogether. Simply, he found his happiness where he was and in what he was doing, even though he still kept liquor in the house, Jacqueline still liked to drink, and himself to see others drink—indeed most teetotalers he suspected of secret crimes. "One may be happy watching others though one drinks no longer," his father-in-law would say, on one of his occasional visits, paraphrasing Voltaire and pouring himself and his daughter a huge Scotch and splash. "It is an obscure feeling resembling the fantastic passions retained by the dead in the Elysian Fields!" "Yes, with the difference that it's perhaps the first time I've been really alive," Ethan laughed. But ever since they'd left and gone to that apartment Ethan had been drinking every night again, not much, less than he used to, but still too much, and sometimes in the morning too.

The worst part of it was that the desire for a drink had suddenly overlaid any decision, or thought of any other goal, save a pub. A glass of beer—to be frank at least six glasses of beer—now seemed more important than a house. Even than Gabriola. And that such might be a sympathetic enough human feeling didn't make him tolerate it the more in himself. He wished his own quitclaim to the whole tyranny—though since he was not an alcoholic and never had been (had he been it would have been quite a different matter, of course), why the word "tyranny" should have occurred to him was not quite clear.

But perhaps it all came back to Eridanus again. The moment he became conscious of a hangover these days, however slight, his persistent suffering at the loss of their old life interacted within the misery to create something like a physical force, like a cold wind rushing through him. This suffering, which he hadn't been able to conquer save by alcohol, was somehow more a tyranny than the alcohol itself, which, while it made it worse finally, he *could* conquer.

Anyhow, apart from this cold wind, his condition was nothing to speak of, was it? First the noises of the windscreen wiper, and the freight cars continually crossing the road, that were now lulling him, had exacerbated him. Then, a moment ago, so far as he could recall a moment ago, there had been nothing but that faint sensation of overexcitement, of needing a drink too much. Just now there had been a feeling as if a tiny wheel that had been coming loose in the machinery of his brain had dropped off, nothing painful, but inducing a sense of unreality, as if he were strapped into his seat, and upon a plane, not a bus.

No, it was more as if a needle had quietly, unheededly, fallen out of a soundbox in his head—an apt image, for now he scarcely heard the windscreen wiper, the endless passing train, the pattering drizzle. And now—was it once more?—there was this vacancy in the brain, this blankness behind the eyes, that immediately it became aware of itself, as at this instant, seemed peopled with mental threats and anxieties and terrors, projecting themselves through into the outer vision—imposing themselves on reality there—with glowering fading shapes of ruin and catastrophe and sadness. Medicine might contradict it, but it seemed possible to look the picture of health and even be in excellent shape while this kind of thing was going on, Ethan reflected. Besides, he hears no voices. His hands are steady as the Ripple Rock. With them, unaided, he proposes the heroic plan of building a house . . . And, equally, he knew it was not the desire for a drink at all, but a longing, a longing that every day grew a little less, for a swift swim in the cold inlet; and how he had loved Eridanus at this time in October, when the tides were high in the early morning and early evening, so that he could dive into deep cold water before breakfast and dinner, dive even right out of the window, into the inlet where the clouds were reflected six miles deep in the water, and it was like flying among these clouds, half fish, half bird, deep among the minnows and reflections of pines and kittiwakes—and ah, the white light on the sea these early October mornings, the clouds rolling away, the freshness, the newness, the sparkle and cleanliness—A longing for the pure intoxication of sobriety possessed him—

STOP! LOOK! LISTEN!

Mother Gettle's Kettle-Simmered Soup. M'mm, Good!

It must have been there all the time of course, the advertisement staring him in the face; perhaps the mist had obscured it, or the high-piled timber on the open cars trundling by, while now there were some curiously meaningless empty cars that he could see right over; but it had been in his mind anyhow, all the time, he had been expecting it sometime or another all morning, but not *this* one, not the one with Cordwainer himself on it, not this comparatively rare one, showing a twenty times life-size cartoon of Peter, a lively, handsome, grinning youth of fifteen, gulping a great bowl of steaming soup and saying, "M'mm, Good!"

"Don't, Ethan! Oh, *don't* look like that." Jacqueline took his hand. "Remember what we said this morning? Please, darling, dear Ethan."

"But my God, you haven't——"

"Of course I saw it. I hoped you wouldn't."

"It's the one of Peter as a boy. That's the absolutely final . . . That's the bloody last straw. We might just as well cut our throats now."

"Ethan . . ."

"But don't you see, Jacky? I'll never get away from it. They'll probably put one up across the road from any house I try to live in."

Jacqueline withdrew her hand. "Oh, undoubtedly. They must have heard you were coming and put that one there on purpose for today."

"Please don't be harsh. I can't stand it."

"I'm sorry."

And at this moment, as abruptly as the machinery of a phonograph with self-changing records clashes into action, it was as though within him a totally different consciousness had taken over. Since the first full awareness of a hangover (or of its total extent, its regressive downward economy and meaning, of the steps too, also no doubt downward, that are going to be taken to "recover" from it, since this awareness is in effect often the beginnings of a new drunkenness), this other consciousness, familiar and feared, had been swiftly rising to the surface of his mind and had now taken command. It was as if the mind of another person, coexisting with the first but utterly independent of it, had begun to work over much of the same material, but with what a different viewpoint!

For up to now, Ethan's method of thinking—that is the way he had been thinking, or thought he had been thinking this morning up to this point—involved a process akin to composition: not as though he had been composing a brief, exactly, but had been loosely composing a mental dossier, preparatory to making a brief on behalf of an accused he proposed to defend. But the actual and frightening and certain knowledge at this moment that he had been *consciously* deceiving himself all morning, actually suppressing and misrepresenting the very events of his life for the sake of making them fit into a bearable pattern, came with the force of a revelation. If the first consciousness was the counsel for the defense, this second was the counsel for the prosecution.

Nor that this second consciousness or self was any more rational than the Jesuitical and selective one that had just abandoned him, it was less so, and equally selective. But so implacable was it, in its voracious accusation, that Ethan, when in its grip, almost excused that other half-lying and plausible consciousness for existing, in an effort to keep him sane. For no one could endure the battering of this second consciousness very long without giving way, if the nature of its activity, its repeated and dreaded assaults, were not a symptom that he had long since done so.

"De-clock de-*clack* de-clock de-*clack* de-clonk de-clonk de-clonkety-*clack!*"

"—clunkety-clunkety-click! clunkety-clunkety-click!—"

Mother——Gettle's——Kettle -——Simmered——Soup.

The isolated words leaped at him between the snag-heaped cars, now passing again.

Symptom: But what if, speak harsher truth though it might, there were latent or arrested or even actually present in the remorseless and vindictive motion of this mind—washed up like driftwood tortured into obscene shapes by these waves of suffering glutting some cavern within—the symptoms of mental sickness?

This might actually be his soul with which he was not thinking, a soul that had become sick almost to death, that perhaps had been sold to the devil, a soul that could only plot the most merciless revenge on him for what he had done to it, and that sick though it was, and speaking though it did partly with the accents of insanity, also spoke true.

Mother———Gettle's———Kettle -———Simmered———Soup— ——M'mm———Good!

But it hadn't been till after their house in Niagara burned down that Ethan had begun to see—or imagine he saw—a certain hideous pattern in his life, a sort of curse, and even then he had connected it less with the house burning down at first than with the bottle of gin that was left. He thought it was perhaps during that ghastly night at the police station that his obsession (could he only believe it an obsession) had really begun to take hold of him. No, he did not believe that it was until then that he had really seen any "significance" in the manner of their losing their house in Oakville. At the time the simple sorrowfulness and unhappiness of that event cancelled all else. No doubt he had remembered that Peter Cordwainer had been the only son of the advertising manager of Mother Gettle's Soups—from the horrible to the ridiculous is but a step, and vice versa—but that was as far as it went, or rather, that was another reason for forgetting it, least of all attaching any significance to it, for whatever the facts, Peter (whenever he'd thought of him, which was, mercifully, rarely) remained a painful and ravaging memory. Now, in this mood, it seemed inconceivable that he could ever have thought of anything else, from the day Peter died. And this, October seventh, was the anniversary of the day Peter *had* died, exactly twenty years ago. As he had known of course even before he opened his eyes this morning, waking in the hotel room in Victoria. He had lain there as if made of stone, partly trying to get control of himself, partly not wishing to wake Jacqueline, for it was barely dawn. But presently he had known she was awake and was gazing at him, though he still kept his eyes closed; then, suddenly, she took him in her arms, tightly, trying to give him her will and strength and comfort. He lay quietly for a moment, then he tore away, turned his back and half sitting up began to pound the table beside the bed with his fist.

"What's the use! What's the God damn use! Why, of all days, have you dragged us out *today* to look for a house? Can't you see there'll be a curse on anything we find?"

The devils, the sickness, in full possession, he had raved, cursing her and their life with every obscene and violent term he could conjure for their destruction . . . Jacqueline had given him a phenobarbital, and he had fallen into a heavy, nightmare-ridden sleep. When she woke him gently, a few hours later, sitting on the bed beside him, he was still under the calming influence of the drug, and they had talked quietly, even hopefully; they had agreed, or some part of him had half agreed, that if they did find a house today it would mean they had "turned everything around," that the curse would be vanquished. Over a hearty breakfast, her high spirits (real or pretended) and half a benzedrine tablet had brought him, cautiously, to a state of mind where he almost *could* forget the day, until some casual mention of Edgar Allan Poe had reminded him: it was the day Poe had died too, one hundred years ago.

"*—clunkety-clunkety-clink clunkety-clunkety-clink—*" and the train was past, appearing to go much faster as they saw it from behind, receding, and folding up, like a concertina, running into the future. What future?

OCEAN SPRAY INN, NANAIMO 6 M. LICENSED: he now read with satisfaction on a hoarding on the other side of the grade crossing.

What was so fascinating about grade crossings, even frightening—far more so at night in inter-urban districts with their gasping stammering stop signs swinging aloft like the be-davy-lamped vizored heads of decapitated coal miners in a nightmare, the warning bell shrilling in endless hysteria—or, as they occasionally still called them here, level crossings, where two distinct forms of destiny, under separate control, each fractionally assumed the other's field? That did not account for their eerie, and for motorists too often, it would appear, fatal hypnotic fascination. In this respect they seemed stamped with a similar damnation to crossroads—why did they once bury suicides at the crossroads?

Stop! Look! Listen! Or it was as if one had been waiting for something to pass out of a wholly different life, a Behemoth flashing for one brief breadth over that luminousness which is our own life, to disappear into another immensity.

But disappeared, at least audibly, the train had not. For all its melancholy cargo it was a train and meant to let them know it. And now as their bus trampled the highway again, through the forest across an intervening field, with a sudden noise of speeding wheels on iron, came an impassioned hullabaloo—that familiar barking drum-roll, swift harmonium-peddling sound as of violent accident in the organ aloft, accompanied too by subterranean pertussal whoops, diatonic supplications, echoing of expiring concertinas—which was transforming itself, was transformed already, into that powerful protracted chord of the emotions known as nostalgia. The train was yelling insistently as a baby. To the other alarums was now added the frantic beating of a bell. At last the train seemed as if winding the whole pandemonium up and hurling it into space like a discus thrower. The wailing went bounding from mountain to mountain, slithering into silence. Eurydice! Eurydice!

But the frantic beating of the railroad knell had become the bells of the University of South Wales, twenty years ago on the night of October the seventh.

"It was a freezing night," Ethan said suddenly. "With a red moon, like November." He heard Jacqueline beside him take a quick, faint, indrawn breath as she turned toward him from the window, but he wouldn't look at her, wouldn't meet her eyes. "We were at school together too, you know, Boy Scouts together too, Peter was an expert on knots, even then . . . He was the patrol leader of the Tigers. That was about the time they made that drawing for the billboard."

"I know."

"It was right at the beginning of our second term at the University. I thought he looked rather strange and wild-eyed when he opened the door, but I was a little tight already, and when he first told me I didn't pay much attention, I was playing the phonograph, I had a new record of 'In the Dark.'"

P

"Ethan, please stop." Jacqueline spoke urgently, her voice rising a little.

"Once I'd got it in my head, or half in my head, that he was serious I tried to argue with him. At one point I was quite dramatic, warming to my subject, as I pictured for him his poor mother and father . . . Of course it was going to be a bloody mess anyhow, he *had* driven his car away without stopping, and the man he hit had bloody died. And he'd have been sent down, right enough."

"Ethan. You were only nineteen, a boy. You can't go on the rest of your life like this."

"I could have stayed with him, all night if necessary, I could have stayed, I could have stopped him."

"He'd have done it the next night. He was going to do it whatever you did or said."

"You think so, do you? You don't know anything about it. I tell you, in the end, I talked him into it. I told him to go ahead. It gave me a sense of power. Of course, that was after I went out for the second bottle of gin. It was terribly cold for October, that night, there was a heavy frost on the grass and ice crunching underfoot like broken bones. They were all tight in the pub—'Let the bugger die!' they said—and the barman said, when he sold me the bottle, 'I'm doing you a favor.' I've often thought of that. When I got back Peter had the rope out and was tying knots in it. That's when I got fed up and began to sell him real estate in the next world. A la Swedenborg: 'My grandmother,' I said, 'will be a great help to you. I'm sure she has friends in high places.' "

"For God's sake, Ethan, stop it! You're indulging yourself, you're simply wallowing in a pathological sense of guilt."

"—But he declined the gambit, he lost his nerve when I offered to help him."

"You know perfectly well you're distorting this. For all you know when you left he'd promised not to. You don't remember."

"Quite. I don't remember. For all I know he may have promised that he would do it. I don't remember."

"Well then—"

"The next thing I remember I was running back to my digs and the clock was striking twelve. I was staggering and running and gasping and I recall passing the hospital, where they held the inquest the next day. I had to be in my digs by twelve, you know, and I just made it. I was still blind tight and raving hungry. I stuffed myself with cold ham and passed out with my clothes on."

"And once during the night," Jacqueline said, in a cold voice, "you woke up with your heart pounding, and decided the whole thing was a nightmare and went back to sleep."

"And toward dawn I woke again. A heart seemed beating in my ear, a heartbeat that was growing fainter and fainter."

"And you thought: Well, if I went and roused my landlord, and got the police now, Peter'd be indicted, maybe imprisoned—"

"And would certainly be sent down. And as a consequence would certainly commit suicide anyhow. So I went back to sleep. Next morning I found his farewell letter in my coat pocket. I had a shocking hangover but I noticed he wasn't at our first lecture so I went round to his rooms and found he was dead. They had already cut him down . . . Of course I didn't tell the truth at the inquest, partly for Father's sake, partly to defend myself."

"And partly for Peter's parents' sake. Oh, Ethan!" Jacqueline put her hands over her face for a moment.

"But to almost everyone else except Peter's parents I was perfectly frank. I accused myself, somewhat unnecessarily, they all said. Because the point was I didn't *know*. Or did I? . . ."

There was just that blank, and what it did was murmur to him, what profundities reiterate as refrain for him, beneath its poetic and disastrous undertones of the soul, what, indeed, but these words:

Mother . . . Gettle's . . . Kettle- . . . Simmered . . . Soup.

And this, October seventh, was the anniversary of the day Peter had died. Ethan would like to have forgotten it too but was bound to remember it for a wholly irrelevant reason: it was the day Edgar Allan Poe had also died.

Ethan had often been told he looked rather like Edgar Allan Poe . . . And his reflection in the rearview mirror, now opposite him, leaned forward, out of the past, as if to corroborate this. Yes, yes: there was the dark, the Byronic resemblance: but he didn't like those red veins, those broken blood vessels in his nose. Did Edgar Allan Poe have a red nose? In any case his was a healthier face. A compassionate, burned, dissolute strong face, his face nodded in approval. But his face could not see those veins; he had some kind of disease perhaps . . . Perhaps. Suddenly he saw his whole life had been like one long malignant disease since Peter's death, ever since he'd forgotten it, forgotten it deliberately like a man who assures himself, after it begins to disappear, that the first lesion of syphilis is simply impetigo—like Thomas Mann's Dr. Faustus, in fact—forgotten it, or pretended to have forgotten it, and carried on as if nothing had happened. The face in the mirror, a half face, a mask, looked at him approvingly, smiling, but with a kind of half terror. Its lips silently formed the one word:

Murderer!

CHAPTER 28 ❧ *Wheel of Fire*

*E*than took a deep breath and, as Jacqueline turned from the window, he smiled and took her hand. Well, anyhow, even if Captain Duquesne's house was no good, or Jacqueline didn't like it, *their* house wouldn't have to fall down, that was sure. Failing the skipper's place a new house would be built of good timber, cut on their own land, if they bought the lot, each tree selected by himself and felled where it would not leave a slash to desecrate the forest.

He produced a pipe. The mist had rolled away, the sun was shining brightly once more, and a slash was precisely what they were passing. Though on the other side was a pretty park. Or it was worse than a slash which, strictly, is the fire hazard created by loggers who leave huge logged-off areas uncleared and full of inflammable brush. Here fire had already created a disastrous ravagement. As far as the eye could reach there seemed whole mountainsides of burned and dead trees, whole forests that looked as though they would never grow again. The abomination of desolation sitting in a holy place. It was too easy to judge the loggers. Man makes the mistake of thinking that because life is so prodigal in expenditure of itself that its resources are everywhere inexhaustible and that there is no such thing as death without rebirth. Velleities and portentous thoughts. Who was to blame? The monopolists claimed that the original foresters were all socialistic and paternalistic. The loggers thought their business was to log and move on, and the government theirs to clear away and it *would,* but never did, or never chose to, never having the money. Only big business enterprise would, it was claimed, have the money and the forethought to do that. Ethan didn't know the truth or where the blame lay. Interacting causes: but then, whoever thought emotionally of interacting causes?

But whoever was to blame you couldn't imagine anything much more dead than this dead death. The only live thing Ethan could make out in the whole scene was a crow, fluttering above a blackened stump, and it was hard to see what that was doing there, unless it had been sent on purpose to depress him as a bad omen. One crow sorrow, two crows joy, three crows a wedding . . . But Ethan, wherever he looked, could not find a second crow.

You cannot prevent the birds of sorrow from flying over your head, but you can prevent them from building nests in your hair.

Damn this pipe, too. It did not draw well and had evidently been manufactured by someone with little love of pipes. The cost of removing its intricate yet absolutely pointless nicotine trap, which had involved breaking its stem once already, had probably been more than the pipe itself for which, partly because he had taken so much trouble with it, or more probably because Jacqueline had given it to him, in all simplicity, he had a sort of singular patience of protective tender love. Well, it was an old one, Jacky had bought it just at the end of the war, but that there'd been trouble in obtaining imported briar seemed no reason why pipes, if there had to be pipes at all, should be manufactured so narrow in the bore you couldn't get a pipe cleaner through them. He struck another match, tried to light it again. There was something wrong with the match too.

Oh hell! First the cedar, which would stand the dampness, for the pilings and foundations to be sunk. And for the floors. Then the fir for the walls and rafters. He could take it himself to the sawmill to be cut into the two-by-fours for the plates and uprights and rafters, the two-by-twelves . . . and the V-joint. Yes, if he felled the timber this month, and had it all cut, he could build next spring. Of course, it ought to season longer . . . There probably wasn't any shingle mill on Gabriola, but he could split some shakes for the roof himself, the outside walls too. While the inside walls would be knotty cedar, the wood itself, smoothed and oiled by hand until it shone like knotted gold.

Mother Gettle's Kettle-Simmered Soup . . . Oh God! there was something alive beside the crow, and godammit if it wasn't Mother Gettle. Ubiquitous in her way though she was, somehow he hadn't expected to find her here so soon again.

Beaming, ten times larger than life, from the roadside hoarding, aproned, spectacled, and looking more unctuous than ever, she stirred away at her simmering cauldron, ladling and sniffing, for it was another animated advertisement, this time the gigantic ladle went round and round and then was lifted, neon-lighted, to her nose, as though to say that every drop of the soup was, despite all difficulties and shortages, still being prepared with her own motherly hands just for you alone—as for them had it not!—and moreover even at grave risk to her life, so that by the mere act of buying that relatively insipid concoction one participated in the pioneer danger, for now certain armed and wild figures on horseback could be seen advancing in the background outside the kitchen —Indians—as one approached closer still one saw they were murmuring with one accord: "M'mm, good!"

The damnation on the left had now given way to scattered suburbs beyond which the mountains seemed to grow higher, their tops lost in clouds. They had entered a long straight road, with sidestreets, running slightly downhill between hoardings on either side. It was a road of infrequent autocamps, steambaths and Quonset huts containing neighborhood dentists and naturopaths. On the right the view of the sea was blocked by warehouses and factories, some in process of construction, though the mountains on the mainland were still visible, with the white American volcano rising above, and nearer, once or twice, between chimneys, or moored freighters, tantalizingly, could still be made out part of the island in the Gulf.

She Stirs for the War Effort. Buy War Bonds.

But their bus, caught in a sudden jam of expensive-looking American cars, cars like sulfur-bottomed whales, quite beautiful in their futuristic way, with huge-peaked cap windows at both ends that seemed coming toward you when actually they were going away from you, and which had been emerging steadily from the side roads, perhaps there was a factory making such cars in Nanaimo, and these contained executives going home for lunch, or maybe they were coal miners, their bus was moving so slowly for the moment they could hardly resist peering closer at the hoarding.

Clearly a wartime relic some sign inspector had overlooked, this represented, while still an aproned and spectacled, a far more martial Mother Gettle, wearing the uniform of some unspecified Waac or Wave with even a row of ribbons showing above the apron, while she stirred away with a look of quiet determination; meantime a little procession of walking wounded soldiers could be seen advancing in the background outside the kitchen, where the Indians had been, among whom, from his air of greater alacrity and higher upheld nose, though on crutches, could be discovered Mother Gettle's own soldier son hobbling along—upon further inspection it could be seen that they too were murmuring, "M'mm, good!"

Now in fighting fettle. Mother Gettle stirs for you. Support the War Effort. Buy War Bonds.

Perhaps it was not an oversight on the part of some sign inspector. Perhaps with canny prescience they thought the advertisement would do as a hand-me-down for the next war too, so the Llewelyns decided . . . The jam had broken up and their bus was putting on speed.

Nanaimo 3M. Hotel Ocean Spray, Licensed. Where they would live in the meantime, subtle fellow, should he build the house? Commuting to Gabriola?

The American cars, somehow really beautiful, began to disappear ahead or up and down more sidestreets, while now, as they approached the town the hoardings came thick and fast, on either side of the road.

Mother Gettle's . . .

Ocean Spray Inn 3M. Licensed

Sore Muscles?
Minard's KING OF PAIN
Liniment

Licensed Ocean Spray Inn
Nanaimo 2¾ miles

GABRIOLA ISLAND FOR GAIETY
OUTINGS, FERRIES DAILY

*Is it nothing to you
Oh ye who pass by . . .*

GOD IS LOVE
WHAT SHALL IT PROFIT

a man if he gain the whole
world and lose his soul?

Ethan pointed the billboard out to Jacqueline, the gaily colored yachts, the regatta, going round a headland, it was a pretty and tasteful poster and he was sorry she hadn't seen it, but it was too late.

Baby's Hot Little Head

Drink Coca-Cola Ice Cold

Mother Gettle's Kettle-Simmered Soup, M'mm, Good!

PREVENT FIRES! DO YOU WANT THIS TO HAPPEN TO YOU
Use EDDY's MATCHES for safety. No afterglow.

WHAT SHALL IT PROFIT
a man

BUILD YOUR OWN HOUSE NOW!
McBean Realty Corp

Have you repented? Believe in the Lord Jesus Christ
and you will be saved.

OCEAN SPRAY INN 2M. Licensed

Falling Hair?

Is it nothing to you
all ye who pass by

KING OF PAIN
LINIMENT

It crossed Ethan's mind again that the advertisements for the Ocean Spray Inn, Licensed, might be illegal, but somebody had got away with it; at the same time he had been thinking what it must be like to walk down this endless road between these billboards, past midnight, when it was absolutely empty, in the opposite direction, under a full moon rising over the mountains, penniless, shoeless, homeless—not to say drinkless, Godless, soupless—with a groaning hangover having been that morning given twenty-four hours to get out of town by an unsympathetic judge, and then later to wake shivering and delirious among these acres of dead burned trees, under that full moon, even if it were a cut above the subterranean dungeon in which one had spent the previous night; but, he said, smiling, and putting an arm across Jacqueline's shoulders, that it was common to assume that this kind of scenery was modern and represented some awfulness peculiar to American civilization. The dear little pigs bouncing with glee over their reduction to sausages, the irrelevant cigarette posters with their cynical appeal to man's hidden fetishism, or even secret ambition to be a Guardsman wearing a busby outside Buckingham Palace, or desire to go to bed with a drum majorette—

| *Jesus came into the world to save sinners* | Is your soul saved? |

"Well, isn't it?"

"—And then for whatever ails you afterwards there's always the King of Pain . . . No, of course not . . . One tends to think of Coca-Cola as a symbol of all this and that the whole thing not only started in America but is typical of American civilization, which seems to me certainly pretty unfair to the States."

Ethan went on to say that he thought the industrialization of Europe had really started when the flow of gold and silver from Peru and Mexico ceased, of which latter country Vancouver Island —and supposedly Gabriola for that matter—had once been a part. When the galleons no longer sailed from Acapulco and Callao loaded with ingots, in that hour was the stage set for the eventual hegemony of Coca-Cola *bien frío*. Only it had all begun in Italy, in Europe. There was this Hofmannsthal—or Broch—who said nature had been tamed and the terror had gone into the cities, etc. For with the industrialization on a large scale, so with advertising, the declension of the Lancashire countryside to a grassless slag-heap, and the addition of Carter's Little Liver Pills to English rural delights.

"Preston, Lancashire, in 1939—I remember this from some old pictures and newspapers my old man showed me—that is, a hundred and eight years ago, if not by billboards, was certainly dominated by advertisements. *If you want a good boot go to France*. And remedies for *That Most Excruciating and Painful Sickness of Man: Tic Douloureux*. Come to that I remember another newspaper he showed me with the first news of Nelson's death in the Battle of Trafalgar. The whole front page of the paper was all advertisements."

"But some English newspapers still do that."

"Yes. 'Noblemen and Persons of Fashion—Immediate supply of money supplied at low interest. Discreetness of primary importance,' was followed by 'Cures for bilious disorders and rheumatism and overindulgence in free living—' for which you were advised to take somebody-or-other's pill."

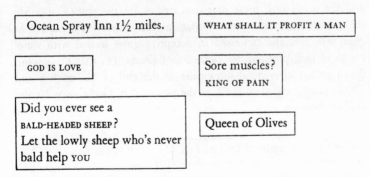

Ocean Spray Inn 1½ miles.

WHAT SHALL IT PROFIT A MAN

GOD IS LOVE

Sore muscles?
KING OF PAIN

Did you ever see a
BALD-HEADED SHEEP?
Let the lowly sheep who's never
bald help YOU

Queen of Olives

"And when was the fire of London?" Ethan said, "1666, something like that, wasn't it? Well, you can go right back to then. What about Defoe's description of the plague the year before: 'Anti-Pestilential Pills Incomparable drink against the plague, never found out before. Royal antidote against all kinds of Infection.' They had placards all over London, Defoe says . . . Actually I'm talking nonsense, to some extent, about advertising-cum-industry. During the plague London maintained a terrific coal trade with Newcastle-on-Tyne . . ."

Ethan had been talking to cheer Jacqueline up, and without regard to the accuracy of all of his remarks. Moreover he'd been talking in what she called his "court voice," and somehow it had sounded unreal to him, as though someone else had been speaking. This sense of unreality was now suddenly succeeded by an astonishing, almost preternatural sense of reality. All at once, without knowing why, he felt as if he were seated at the center of the infinite itself, then, that this was indeed true, that the center of the infinite was everywhere, just as its circumference must be nowhere. Everything seemed part of a miraculous plan, in which nothing stood still, everything good was capable of infinite development, everything evil must inevitably deteriorate. Even the billboards and advertisements took on a new significance, seemed even to be existing on another plane, as if man's spiritual pilgrimage on earth too were eternally between these hoardings, these advertisements for spiritual soup, and the soul's rest, these drastic remedies for the spirit's anguish, these fierce warnings and exhortations that concealed a motive of gain, where truths expressed in deceptive guise jostled with statements of fact, profundities clothed in ugliness, lies that must wind down to the ultimate shadowy lies at the end of the endless and always beginning road, until, as the poet had it, God's great Venite change the song.

| Ocean Spray Inn Licensed 1 m. | DINE AT GRILLO'S CHICKEN 'N THE STRAW |

(It was hard not to hate Chicken 'n the Straw)

Did you ever see a
BALD-HEADED SHEEP
Try Nil-O-Nal 30 days

HAVA JAVA
SHU RENU

Arthur Lee Simpkins
Singing everything from Grand Opera to Boogie!
Eli! Eli! The Lord's Prayer! Pagliacci! Musical Comedy!
Ave Maria! NO ADVANCE IN PRICES.

Totumland rotunda—*Mr. Blanding's Dream House* and *The Long Voyage Home*.

Ethan looked again: so it was. Jacqueline had seen it too, and they both began to rock with silent merriment.

Ocean Spray Inn. Licensed ½ mile.

Nor did one escape the Borden Cow with the crumpled horn, milked by the maiden all forlorn, who married the man, who owned the dog, who worried the bald-headed sheep, who killed the rat who ate the meat in—

McBean Realty Corp.
BUILD YOUR HOUSE NOW

GOD IS LOVE

WHAT SHALL IT PROFIT A MAN
if he gain the whole world and lose—

Ocean Spray Inn ¼ mile Licensed.

And now at last a kind of triumphal archway, over which was written:

WELCOME TO NANAIMO UNLIMITED
CITY OF THE FUTURE

From the Nanaimo Junior Chamber of Commerce.
Suddenly they were in Nanaimo itself, which did not look much

like a city of the future. The notion prevalent in these last frontiers of the Western world that a town had only begun to come of age when industry moved in and the trees began to be knocked down, and its natural beauty began to disappear, was analogous, Ethan thought, to the popular superstition that one had not reached manhood before acquiring a dose of clap; the only difference was the clap could be cured . . . Nor did Nanaimo look at all like a mining town. One searched in vain for the slag-heaps, the windlass wheel spinning at the pitheads.

It was a pleasant surprise. Very clear and neat and pretty, it stretched from the foothills down to the curving harbor sparkling in the sunshine, with streets running uphill from the center of town like the spokes of a wheel.

Their bus prowled slowly through the steep streets of the outskirts, or rather what had once been the outskirts, of Nanaimo, its air brakes, as if commenting protestingly or enthusiastically on the approaching end of the journey, making sounds of tearing canvas, deflating toy balloons. The impression made by the town was peculiar, something like in a dream that seems of vast symbolic importance while it is going on but which you already suspect will turn out on waking to have none at all, or a significance wholly other. In dreams too there is sometimes an air of forgetfulness about architecture. Doors appear in the wrong place, rooms have no entrance, windows open on nothing. Such was almost one's feeling here. But because new houses were springing up on every side, one's first impression was of a certain new prosperity that seemed to contradict, too, the acute housing shortage one knew to exist. Some of these houses looked as though they never would be finished, while others, more nearly completed, even prematurely inhabited, had exteriors of tar paper striped with lathes, and bare grassless yards. For all their newness they had already an air of impermanence, of the irreparable damage caused by delay. It was as if these houses did not want to be. He turned to say something of this sort to Jacqueline and was stopped by the expression of eagerness and hope on her face as she still gazed out of the window.

God knows how deep was her need for the sense of permanence and stability they all too prophetically never possessed in their cabin at Eridanus, however much they loved it. Yet it was different with her! Ethan was not at all sure, he thought again, he had ever wanted anything more permanent and stable than their cabin had seemed to him at first.

As a matter of fact poor Jacqueline was staring straight at an apartment house, or what was now an apartment house. Ye Sandringham Taverne. No Vacancies . . . Alas, this was the fate of most of these old houses of stone, of half stone, and solid worth. A decency, a sort of faded wisdom and vision sat there, like an all too palpable ghost. There it sat anyway, the old house, a relic of what was called the late Victorian era, large, solid, secure, serene, evoking still a stealthy half-insane essence of family solidarity, security, safety, personal chivalry, of the days of white flannels and imperial quart bottles, benign summer evenings with white girls and magnificent tennis in tricky twilight, with its domed tower, from a window in which a haunted face seemed eternally to peer, with its porticoes and arbours too, and latticed railings, set in a formal garden of clipped English holly trees; it was the same vintage as some of the beautiful-horrible, romantic, and altogether fine old houses in the West End of Vancouver. It even still had a hitching post in front, while a black cat walked daintily around the precarious edge of the dome. Good luck?

What it came down to, Ethan thought, at the end of this fourth year of the atomic age people had come to disbelieve in the future so thoroughly that the creation of the permanent, or the excellent, no longer seemed worth while. They were like Ethan himself at this moment, who could see no farther than the end of his own nose, over a beer in the Ocean Spray.

Permanence and stability! But a house built to last, one that had lasted a hundred and fifty years, and was sound and strong and more beautiful than ever, could still go up in smoke. And fire! The Barkerville was burning and Ethan closed his eyes a moment.

Vous qui passez
Ayez pitié
d'une Paroisse
totalement sinistre
—par le Fer et par le Feu
—de 6 et 7 août 1944 . . .
. . . Aidons-nous, merci!

And the bell of St.-Malo's cathedral still pealing through that blackened hush, that shell, beyond which the workmen trundled their wheelbarrows through the acres of rubbish. In 1946 he'd made a flying trip to France for his law firm.

Ocean Spray Inn. Licensed. 440 yards. To the left, just beyond the bastion.

As the crow flies, no doubt; as two crows fly. As one crow plus one black cat flies, maybe. For, with anguished gears, they were going up another hill, almost in the reverse direction, with no sign of the pub.

"Some of these old places, been up eighty years; look at that damned old thing—" someone was saying on the Llewelyns' right, and Ethan followed the man's gaze toward the house so cruelly referred to. It was an old shingled house, of beautiful proportions, with a neglected garden full of dusty fading lesser willow herb, fireweed, and asters, that was being pulled down evidently right over the heads of its inhabitants, still living in it. Sagging, hauled out of alignment with its foundations, the steps to its front porch had already been removed, the top windows, that once must have commanded so fine a view, had no panes in them, and as Ethan watched, a child swarmed up onto the porch to join the family apparently living entirely in the one bottom room. Eviction.

> *Condemned. This house unfit for human habitation.*

And now, over a hump at the top of the hill, a sudden extrusion of mass-produced houses, houses built without hands with a vengeance, built without the slightest thought of what man really wanted and needed—and oh, God, what was it he wanted and needed! undoubtedly he must in a measure have wanted and needed this or he wouldn't have got it? ugly, standardized houses in a long row, boxes crowded together in an exact row as though dropped there by a conveyor belt.

Yet where one saw how here an effort had been made to plant flowers, there a defiant verandah had been added, it transcended everything for a moment to feel this was somebody's home, his place for his poor ways on earth.

Pasa Thalassa Thalassa! The beer-dark sea.

In fact, there was no doubt a good proportion of self-built houses going up among these others, a proportion that in years to come was likely to increase with the steady rise in carpenters' wages. And actually it was not always easy to distinguish the creations of these heroic amateurs from the rest. These were probably the lived-in homes, with exteriors of tar paper striped with lathes. Shortages and delays . . . Nolle prosequi—a stay of proceedings. It was a case where one didn't have to ask for an entry of nolle prosequi, one got it just the same.

And with sudden fear he realized that Jacqueline and he were no different, they had never finished their cabin in Eridanus, bought with the porch only half built. Well, the house was on government land, there was an element of common sense in their attitude. But the threat of eviction having actually come, then was the time, if any, defiantly *to* finish it. They could have left their house as beautiful as it could be. But they hadn't, and now this troubled him terribly.

Yes, but hang it all, it was as if the whole world were beginning to fear eviction, to reason like this, he thought all over again, striking another match and trying to light his maddening pipe. And had there ever been a time in the world when disaster of some sort did *not* threaten? It was better to finish your agony square and true, and hurl your challenge whole in its teeth!

Q

They were passing a Catholic church, simple and beautiful as the Protestants criticized them for never being: white, dainty, and unpretentious as a humble birthday cake. Church of the Guardian Angels. Outside there were several taxis starting off: a funeral. Ethan thought of his first important case he had defended, one of manslaughter, and purred. Delay . . . For some time, without his knowing it, they had been following the funeral itself, that had left the church to precede them through the tilted narrow streets. Now he saw the great elongated hearse ahead, the five black shrouded cars, the mourners inside.

Circum ipsam autem libamina omnibus mortuis.

Their bus, still frustrated in its efforts to pass, wailed like the wind in the rigging of a ship. They had been going by some sensible, really charming and homelike modern houses, and a few fine and prosperous old houses with lawns and rhododendrons blowing in the sea wind that had sprung up. A pleasant residential section. A new wing was being added to one old place: the house, half-timbered, as in Cheshire, England. Edwardian, false, but handsome. Ah, why so large a cost, having so short a lease, dost thou upon thy fading mansion spend? Still, a grave. There was something permanent for you at least, you would think. Not a bit of it. Not even in the grave would you escape the machinations of real estate. You'd think you couldn't be evicted from a grave, but you could. In Niagara-on-the-Lake it happened all the time.

Ethan watched the long, jet-black, sinister, purring hearse ahead, on the roof of which two sea gulls, perhaps mistaking it for a coal barge, had, ludicrously, almost just alighted; on either side of the intervening cars in mourning, in the manner of the ever-receding phantom candles hovering among the pines in the funeral scene in the French film of "The Fall of the House of Usher," Jacqueline and he had seen last winter at the Vancouver Film Society, numerous foaming and ghostly glasses of beer, ever withdrawing from reach, seemed importantly to be bobbing. Nearer my bier to thee. Roderick Usher rose at six, and found himself in a hell of a fix . . .

On their left a pretty girl wearing a short scarlet coat, her hair blowing back in the wind and a big dog galloping beside her, came tripping down the sidewalk. She crossed behind them (the scarlet tanager) going down toward the sea that spread far below to their right again.

"That's a pretty color. I always like color. I liked to work with color. Aye, that's vermilion, that is."

The speaker was an old man, with impish features and an alert blue eye, wearing a mackinaw and a velour hat whose brim barely grazed the top of his seat's back before Ethan, so small was he.

"Vermilion, we used it for trimming the coach wheels." He was speaking to a much larger and more powerful old man seated in front of Jacqueline, with the cropped bullet head of a Dane or German, who was listening intently, and after a moment Ethan became possessed by a strange feeling that every word the old man was saying—whose remarks had probably been elicited not merely by the color of the girl's coat, but also by the contrast between that purring mechanized contraption of death ahead, and those majestic, if no less sinister, hearses of old drawn by stately horses tossing their funereal plumes he must have remembered (room for one more inside, mister!) these and the screaming tires of the bus itself,—that all the old chap was saying was addressed mysteriously to Ethan himself; and moreover that almost every phrase had another meaning, perhaps many meanings, intended for his ears alone.

"That was in the days when I was an apprentice," the old man went on. "And they still had coaches in the Isle of Man. And how—well, you've seen the old wheels with an iron tire—well, they shrink them on. Now the wheelwright has delivered the wheel to the blacksmith, and the blacksmith builds a ring of fire—sometimes for a big coach wheel it has to be twenty feet when you think of the circumference—now they have the iron welded together and they put it in the fire: they don't let it get quite red-hot, it's still black, they have to get it just right. Then, when it's ready the blacksmith with his two helpers, they take it out of the fire with tongs, and they force it over the edge of the wooden wheel, and then it smokes *something awful,* it damn nearly sets fire to the wheel. So then they run like mad pouring water on it. Now you understand it has swelled in the fire, and now it shrinks quickly, and now it has clasped the wheel forever—"

CHAPTER 29 ❧ *Just Behind
the Bastion*

Gabriola?" the man repeated, the checking-room clerk in the bus station, "Hey, Ed, where's the Gabriola boat?"

Ethan was inquiring, while checking their bags and waiting for Jacqueline, about the Gabriola ferry from the attendant who, standing on a platform slightly above him, seemed unnaturally tall, so that Ethan, himself a tall man, had to look up at him. (Like the bar man, the drawer, now in the Ocean Spray, required by law to stand on a dais, the better to observe that none of his patrons were adding a bit of the creature.)

. . . Suppose one were to throw a professional, a truly profound McCandless expression into one's face, as though one weren't so much concerned with merely looking at the forecasts (it need not be so shameful, it could even be unselfish to steal a glance at Jacqueline's "horoscope") but were pondering at the same time, like a gnostic geometrician of the Middle Ages, the duplication of the cube, or the trisection of the right angle, not to say the Symbol of the Divine Trinity in Unity. No, it would be almost as embarrassing as being caught weighing oneself. In fact, the two occupations seemed mysteriously to be related. For here a weighing machine offered: *Your weight and your destiny* . . .

Slut machines . . .

And the *Colonist:* probably the Vancouver papers hadn't arrived yet. He was always half afraid to buy one, too. CHILDREN SINK IN $10 MILLION TYPHOON. MOUNT ARARAT IN ERUPTION. Your weight and your destiny. *Time* and *Life* . . . Why in heaven's name Canadians should read these magazines was beyond him but they did, he did, Jacqueline did. Well, why was he reading the damned thing if he didn't like it? He had a choice of other magazines more disinterestedly devoted to one's fate, an enormous number of them indeed, more than he ever remembered seeing on one newsstand before. In addition to *Astrology* magazine, there were *Astrolabe, Ephemeris, Nostradamus Today, The American Astrologer, Astrology and the Atom, Astrology After Hiroshima, Canadian Astrology, The Canadian Astrologer, Canada's Destiny, Canada's Coming of Age, Omarr's Almanack of Warnings, Nanaimo's Horoscope, British Columbia's Rising Sign, Your Destiny, Astrologically Speaking* and *Birney's Predictions.* And once more Ethan found himself thinking of old Defoe's description of the days at the beginning of the plague—not of the preventive medicines this time, but the prognosticatory literature. There wasn't much difference even in the titles. In those days it had been *Lilley's Almanack, Gadbury's Alogical Predictions, Poor Robin's Almanack, Fair Warning,* and *Britain's Remembrancer,* and, Come Out of Her my People, lest you be partakers of her Plagues.

The sea wind blew in their faces as Ethan and Jacqueline walked down the main street. Nanaimo all at once was as strange as Port-au-Prince. But that Nanaimo had a beautiful setting had little to do with this. The feeling was, or was at the moment, that of themselves as lovers setting forth in any new town, however drab. There was also a certain dismay, as though the sinking sensation when the bus stopped—no matter that you were physically longing to get out of it, for it to stop—and you were obliged to get out, had been protracted, mingling with this sense of strangeness and adventure. Yet when all this was shared with the person you loved, these moments, even if filled with some immediate irritation, even a sort of fear, were looked back upon with an inexplicable desire: these were the happy times.

They came to the post office with its flag galloping slowly from a tall clock-tower: ten to twelve: and there, at the foot of a wide, steeply sloping ramp, the approach to a long cavernous grey building resembling an English railway station, mounted on a pier, built on piles marching far out into the harbor, was the "dock." C.P.R. was inscribed across the building's forehead, set in the middle of which another clock said twenty to twelve. Men with masks over their faces were working on the roof, spraying it with grey paint.

A mighty ocean liner, with three slanting maroon and black funnels, and six harmoniously raking masts, lay, half a cable's length away, dramatically moored alongside.

The prisoner in the dock . . .

No Smoking on Pier. Auto Ferry This Way. No Dogs on Newcastle Island Resort. But there was no sign about Gabriola.

And the prisoner in the dock was a liar. It was not a mighty ocean liner. It was the little passenger steamer for the mainland, built in an exact replica of an ocean liner. And for some reason, today, Ethan felt disenchanted by this familiar legerdemain, which seemed like a trick played on him personally. For this was the sister ship to the vessel on which they'd crossed from Vancouver to Victoria, should they take it they could be in Vancouver in a few hours, thence "back home" in Eridanus before nightfall.

Outwardly, taking Jacqueline's arm, Ethan felt himself responding to her mood of excitement, being amusing, considerate (though she recognized the island boat she saw no significance in it, and he did not invest it with any for her) and interested in everything: on the other hand, as the harbor steadily withdrew itself from sight the nearer one approached it, and the mainland boat disappeared, and, as reaching the foot of the ramp they entered through a sort of bar door, an enormous baggage room filled with crates, boxes and trunks, leading to another vast windowless room with three ticket offices all closed, he began to feel out of touch with himself again.

His soul might have been walking far away somewhere, in a snow-storm, through a street of dolls' houses. It was haunting Eridanus perhaps . . . *And now it has clasped the wheel forever* . . .

But equally he was aware—what seemed to be an open ticket office, now appeared far ahead at the end of another long room with glass windows—that he was being haunted by himself again, though this time in a different way. He was being haunted by a tune. It was one of those odd times when the guardian mnemonics of ancient records, ever waiting their opportunity, in the brain's packed lumber room, and finding, as they suppose, their master absent, prepare to have a field day. Their first number was "Aunt Hagar's Blues," played by the Virginians, on His Master's Voice. Probably he hadn't heard the record for over a quarter of a century, back in English days. One of the greatest of American blues, its sombre recording by the Virginians made, as it were, a funereal yet majestic accompaniment in his head to their steps echoing through this depressing endless building, in which they hadn't yet encountered a single soul. But Aunt Hagar's final effect was exhilarating, it made you happy.

The record reminded him strongly and poignantly of his youngest brother, who had been lost at sea on that trip in 1931, off the Norwegian sland of Aalesund, with a Norwegian timber freighter on which he was working as a coal trimmer, a vessel in ballast out of Preston, Lancashire, bound for Archangel, though she'd originally been destined for Newfoundland, which was why Gwyn signed on, he wanted to come back to Canada. How young Gwyn had loved this record! And how happy it had made the boy when Ethan had brought it home from school for him, that time eight years before that, shortly before Ethan himself had left for Canada again. "But you haven't forgotten 'Aunt Hagar's Blues,' Ethan?" "No, you little idiot, it's in my trunk." The record had been broken, to his brother's bitter disappointment, but Ethan had managed to patch it with the gummed back of an envelope so successfully "Aunt Hagar's Blues" played well, though always punctuated by this regular click he still could almost hear now, as the needle passed over the crack. Clickety-clack, te-clock, te-cluck. And ah, how well Ethan remembered the last time he'd seen poor Gwyn; it had been on a short visit to England some three years before he was married, the two of them drinking beer after beer in Exchange Station, Liverpool, till time for Gwyn's train to leave for that fatal port, Preston. *Skibets Reisefra Prester til Arkhangelsk:* in his mind's eye Ethan could still see the *hyrkontrakt* his brother had displayed so proudly. If only he had dissuaded him from going! When, after all, he was not going where he wanted to go, to say the least. And what was it young Gwyn was trying to say to him now?

"Gabriola? Sorry, we don't run the ferry."

A kindly-looking official resembling a stationmaster, who none-theless spoke sharply—behind whom, on a littered desk, was a small alarm clock that had stopped at half past eleven—and who was wearing on his coat a ribbon denoting, Ethan recognized, a high Canadian reward for valor—was looking up at them questioningly through the glass window with the little semicircular hole at the bottom.

"Where is the office, please?"

"Don't think they have one."

"We were told it was on this pier."

"Couldn't tell you, lady. Don't think they run it in winter time anyhow. There's nothing there."

"But we have friends living there," Ethan said.

"Oh? Well, I guess you know more than I do then."

"We could phone the hotel there?"

"No hotel on Gabriola, mister. Oh, might be one in summer, sort of camp, but there's nothing there this time of year." The man was drumming with his fingers on the ledge. "Why don't you phone your friend?"

Ethan listened to "Aunt Hagar's Blues" for a little while. On the other side was "The Hooking Cow Blues." "The Hooking Cow Blues" was not quite so good as "Aunt Hagar's Blues."

"They don't have a telephone."

"But there *must* be a ferry!" Jacqueline cried.

The man gazed at her with interest. "Don't hold us responsible for it. The C.P.R. doesn't run the ferry."

"Then who *does* run the ferry," Ethan said patiently. "Perhaps we can find out from them."

Well, perhaps you can," the official turned away, "but they don't even like to give us their schedule."

"But *who* are they?"

"Oh yes, just a minute . . . Smout Ferry Company."

"Smout Ferry Company. Well! Where are Smout Ferry Company?"

"Back up the ramp. You'll find them—just behind the bastion."

"The bastion?"

"Yes. You can't miss it. They're just behind the bastion."

"But what's the bastion?"

"You can't miss it. Just go along the waterfront."

"But—" Ethan began, then stepped aside. A small line of people was beginning to form behind them, evidently to buy tickets for their minuscule Leviathan for the mainland, that at this moment, after three attempts, managed to put a stop to their conversation by emitting an almost life-sized roar.

"You'll see them! Behind the bastion!"

Ocean Spray Inn. Ladies and Escorts. Gentlemen.

At the top of the ramp Ethan stood a moment, undecided, gazing up at the great windows (in one of which, like a ghost, a lone waiter hovered, motionless) of the massive beer parlour leaning above them on the cliff. Temptation resisted. He took Jacqueline's arm and they began to walk along the waterfront, but seeing nothing that might be taken for a bastion climbed a staircase between houses leading to a street on a higher level. This maneuver shortly brought them back to the Ocean Spray, so they retraced their steps along this street, from which the sea was visible only in snatches between houses.

The Llewelyns, this time avoiding the staircase, gazed about them with interest. At first it seemed, hopefully to Ethan, like a whole street of old English pubs, many with their signs creaking outside in the wind. Then one saw that while these possessed the mien, the half-timbered zebra look of certain old English pubs, they were all tea shops, coffee shops or cafés, called Ye Olde Lygone Arms, Ye Coach and Horses, Ye Olde Cocke, and the like. But the street had little need to fabricate for itself an extraneous romance of the antique, any more than might have had, say, the alchemist's quarter in Prague, during the Middle Ages. For it was a street of calculators of nativities and dreamers of dreams.

Ethan now thought with pleasure of Daniel Defoe again. In the *Journal of the Great Plague,* he seemed to recall, Defoe had expressed wonderment as to where, after the pestilence itself, all those prognosticators, not to speak of their literary works, had gone, if they had not indeed vanished from the face of the earth altogether. Defoe's curiosity had he been alive today and in British Columbia, Ethan said to Jacqueline, would have been satisfied. For obviously they had not vanished: they had, after sojourning, with metaphysical aid, for several centuries underground, all turned up in British Columbia. And those who were not functioning in Vancouver or Victoria were very evidently practicing in one way or another, in this very street in Nanaimo.

Certainly a large number of the houses, as well as cafés, seemed occupied—*Madame Q. Messages From Flowers. Please Knock at Window*—by spiritualists, clairvoyants or seers. But it was in Ye Olde Cocke and Ye Coach and Horses, to judge from the cards in the windows, that they plied an important part of their trade, as though, while their homes might be their consulting rooms, these were their clinics, practical and diagnostic experience. Ethan remarked it was a pity the cards were not more consonant with the signs, that neither Friar Bacon's brazen head, nor the sign of Mother Shipton, nor yet that of Merlin himself were in evidence, something that would have combined the signboard idea with a more accurate evocation than that provided by Ye Coach and Horses of what

was to be found within, and would have been, besides, more histori-
cally consistent . . . *Madame Zog, Famed Albanian Seer, in this tea
shop, 1–3, 4–7 daily. Teacup readings or crystal.*

YOU'RE A HARD MAN MCBEAN!

it stated in the window of Ye Olde Cocke Tea Shoppe, and the
Llewelyns paused.

—MCBEAN, and so are many of life's simple problems, Methodology is interdependent with astrology because the success or
failure in all human effort is influenced if not actually controlled by
planetarium, thus methodology cannot succeed if in direct conflict
with planetary movements. From childhood Draco the Druid had
been fascinated with celestial complexes, studying the travels of
many "wandering" stars and their influence on all humans born at a
time when the "wanders" return to certain established proximities to
nonmoving planets. With this knowledge Draco the Druid is frequently able to dissolve difficult perplexing problems which are
always creeping into human affairs. This year may contain "good
luck" for you. Why not consult Draco the Druid personally or send
for your horoscope at a cost of only $1.00. Give day, month, year and
place of birth. Address Draco the Druid Diviner. At Ye Olde Cocke
each day 4–6:30 P.M. 43 Main St., Nanaimo. Personal appointment
by phone. Marine 777.

"That's good stuff, isn't it?" Ethan said. "What would The
McCandless think of it, Jacky?"

"It's marvelous," Jacqueline murmured, giggling. "But I rather
think Father wouldn't approve, you know."

"Scientific too. Oh yes. I'm absolutely scientific, that's why I've
got such a big practice. And I'm on the level too. I don't just tell
people *anything,* or just from the *month* they were born in, like
some of these crooks. You gotta get the day and year and place . . ."
The Llewelyns crossed the street, laughing, probably a bit hysteri-
cally though the fresh sea air had revived them, and began to walk
back on the opposite sidewalk, always keeping an eye out for the
bastion. "Of course when I do a real horoscope like that—I mean
what with all those 'wanders' creeping into human affairs and all—

it takes time, you understand, and I gotta charge for it . . . Cigarette, ma'am? Trouble is, I half believe in it, don't you? Though naturally, as in other professions, it rather depends on the talent of the practitioner."

"Thank you, Mr. Draco. You seem to have quite a going concern here . . . No thank you, Ethan dear, not in the street . . . But tell me, won't you lose some of your—ah—clients by hibernating out here rather than operating in a bigger city?"

"Bound to, either way. We always count on losing nearly all of them or they wouldn't consult us in the first place."

"Pardon me," Jacqueline was saying, "but we're trying to find the office of the ferry for Gabriola Island."

"Eh?"

The elderly man who had turned to them might well, at first sight, have been Draco the Druid Diviner, or even The McCandless himself had not one instantly recognized him as a species of military British pensioner, and in fact this did not entirely let out the possibilities. He was dressed in a large loose cloak, a kind of tweed domino, a deerskin Sherlock Holmes-like cap giving the effect of a hood, knickerbockers, black stockings, and heavy hobnailed boots: the cloak imparted a lairdish McCandless quality to him too, now one thought of it, and in features and carriage he reminded Ethan not a little of Jacqueline's father: the physical effect was impressive, even fierce, though the voice was jovial, reassuring, as if its old colonial imperiousness had been mellowed down through long practice addressing squirrels and ducks in the park. Holding himself ramrod straight he narrowed his eyes at them, cupping his hand round his ear as Ethan repeated Jacqueline's question.

"Ah yes, yes. Well, old boy, it's just behind the bastion, what?"

"Thank you," Ethan smiled. "But where is the bastion?"

"Why, there, old cock." The sympathetic fellow directed a punishing yet somehow chivalrous look across the street, toward the gap opposite at the head of the staircase they'd climbed from the waterfront. "There," he repeated, pointing with a sort of shooting stick. "The bastion, of course. Right behind the bastion."

"What is the bastion? Bastion of what? *Where* is it?" Jacqueline cried.

"I'm sorry to appear stupid, sir, but we're strangers."

"Why the bastion, of course, old boy."

"We're sorry to appear stupid, but we're strangers here," Jacqueline repeated.

"Why the bastion don't you know . . . We English built the bastion, old boy, Hudsons Bay Company . . . defense of civilization, all that sort of thing. Historic landmark."

Ethan reflected it was not unusual for those North Americans who've never read Dickens to think this type of exaggerated, and still much mimicked, and, to him, almost touchingly nonconformist British lingua franca, or pidgin-Blimp, had originated fairly recently, even as recently as the British vogue for imitating the speech of P. G. Wodehouse's characters, but all at once he found himself thinking of Mr. Brooke, in *Middlemarch*.

"A museum, that's what it is now. Museum, you know, all that sort of rot."

Twitching his shooting stick under his arm, the brave old bird pointed once more with a skinny yet swollen forefinger straight across the street where, sure enough, not thirty feet away, to the right of the staircase, set back a little from the sidewalk, but half-hidden under the lee of some overshadowing scaffolding erected against the building behind it—where a board said NANAIMO TOWING COMPANY—sat, as it must have been sitting in fact for the last hundred and fifty years come to that, all the time, an ancient white structure like a tiny sailless windmill, hexagonal, with two tiny cannon not over two feet long, crouching on little wheels on a grass plot, guarding its ancient doorway, above which hung an anchor.

"Right there, old boy."

The Llewelyns gazed at each other, suddenly seized as by a stupor, a sort of momentary, mutually helpless catatonia.

"You say the Gabriola Ferry Company is *behind* the bastion?"

"Yes, there it is, old boy."

"But I don't see—you mean—" Jacqueline wailed, "that building with all the scaffolding up in front is it? But that says Nanaimo Towing Company."

"That's right, madam. The Smout Ferry. Behind the bastion . . . God bless you."

"God bless *you!*"

Ein Festerburg ist unser Gott.

Finding the door ajar they walked in. They stood a moment behind one of two desks in half-guilty silence, guilty because there seemed nobody in the office, which made in sudden retrospect the manner of their arrival, clambering absurdly over and under the scaffolding, almost felonious. Just like a prisoner in the box, Ethan thought, preparing to voice his se defendendo. He now suspected someone might be in the back room that was hidden by a filing cabinet, and rapped on the desk sharply. Order in the court . . . No one. Everybody was evidently out to lunch and the door, on which it said SMOUT FERRY, GABRIOLA TICKET RESERVATIONS, and REAL ESTATE, had been left open by mistake.

Oh Mr. Smout, please show your snout.

But it was certainly the right place. Doubly, or too much the right place, because, like those barber-cum-watch-repairing establishments (Ethan saw no clock here at all) in Oakville, Ontario, it combined two offices at once. They might even find out definitely about their prospects for a house in Gabriola itself here, as well as the ferry, but this idea for some reason frightening him he tried not to grasp its significance.

The immediate impression, however, was that while the real estate side of the office was in operation (there were stubs in the ashtrays on the other desk) the "ferry" side, where they were standing, and where there were no ashtrays on the desk, only a calendar with the September leaf still not torn off, had suspended operations during that month. Well, that needn't mean the ferry wasn't running either. He looked at Jacqueline, who was rouging her lips in a mirror on the wall. How pretty and fresh she looked!

But no, the glow of excitement had faded from her face and her eyes, she looked suddenly tired and despondent, almost heartbroken, like a child; she was trying to conceal it, and suddenly he took her in his arms as she began to cry softly.

> BOY-OH-BOY
> *Cheap Living*
> *Only $8250 full price with terms.*
> *Substantial Red. for Cash.*

This five-year-old bung. has two rooms only but these rooms are nicely decorated, large, bright and cheerful. This is a grand opportunity for retired couple or young married couple trying to get a start.

> IT'S SIZZLING HOT!
> THIS $10,000 SNAP
> Only 14 years old

This much loved bung. nestled under lofty poplars, so tastefully dec. such cute light fix. . . .

> BARGAIN!!!!
> WE'RE ON YOUR SIDE!!!
> PLEASE READ CAREFULLY!!!
> *Owner is asking only $9950 full price*
> $5000 cash and $75 monthly

Very cute and clean older type bung. . . .

> HARK! THE SOUND OF THE SEA!
> GARDEN OF EDEN!
> THIS WON'T LAST LONG!

This attractive 4-rm. bung. situated on very lovely double land-scaped lot with fish pond. Only $18,000 . . .

But in fact the office was enough to make one gloomy, darkened by the scaffolding—the scaffold!—outside, and now it grew still darker. All at once there came a distant, and as if waterborne, but protracted sound of shunting—gods playing snooker—thunder: Well, that needn't mean a thing either. Thunder in October rarely did. Already it was brighter. It was rather as if the day—like the extraordinary Aztec Tiger Flower whose petals began to fold every time a cloud came over the sun, and died at sunset, though next morning, from another stem, there was another flower—had started to close, then opened again, its petals. Garden of Eden. This won't last long. He kissed her and then to cheer her up set the little jingle running through his head, despite "Aunt Hagar's Blues," to a murmuring tune of "Mr. Gallagher and Mr. Shean":

> Oh Mr. Smout, please show your snout!
> Oh how is it that you're in, and yet you're out?

This made her laugh and cry at once as they gazed round them at the walls: at the pictures of sailing ships, steamboats, the S.S. *Beaver,* the first steamboat to come to British Columbia, in 1850, round Cape Horn, perhaps also of the Gabriola Ferry itself, certainly the *Princess Guinevere,* the prisoner in the dock, and the *Mauretania:* photographs of houses for sale, bastard-mansard, big bow-wow windows, some quite pretty, with swimming pools, apparently in the Yukon: though they saw none situated in Gabriola: a newspaper clipping pinned to the wall: *Rules in House Buying. Be Practical about Your Dream House:* and in a frame, behind the "ferry" desk, a nautical verse, of jaunty motion, decorated with suitably marine embellishments. Suddenly it seemed of first importance that the ferry *should* be running, and his longing to get to Gabriola became, in the instant, greater than that even for a beer. The verse ran as follows:

> *What of the night, watchman, what of the night?*
> *Cloudy, all quiet, no land, yet all's right!*
> *Be watchful, be vigilant, danger may be*
> *At an hour when all seemest securest to thee.*

R

How gains the leak so fast, clean out the hold
Hoist up the merchandise and heave out thy gold—
Now the ship's right—
Hooray the harbor's near! Lo, the red light!
Crowd all thy canvas on! Cut through the foam,
Christian, cast anchor now, Heaven is thy home!

CHAPTER 30   ❦   *The Ocean Spray*

*I*nside the Ocean Spray Inn, on the almost empty Ladies and Escorts side, the view from those same big windows looking straight out over the harbor and the Gulf of Georgia toward the mountainous mainland must have been about the best in the world, Ethan thought. Nothing could have been fresher, swifter, more wholesome, more brilliant. There was a tremendous sense of sunlight, and even sitting here, inside, you could feel the fresh sea wind and smell its sea salt.

Not a cloud in sight, so the thunder must have come from the mountains of Vancouver Island itself, behind them.

The sea was blue and rough, striated with lighter polar blue, the horizon line jagged with deep indigo and white peaks of the mainland mountains.

And there, far beyond a lighthouse in the immediate foreground, whose tower rose waggishly from its substructure of red roofs and white walls, lay Gabriola Island itself, the bartender was saying, or its tip, maybe seven miles away, shimmering like a mirage under the noonday sun.

The Llewelyns sat looking at this happy view without speaking. Anything like it these days was almost unique in Canadian "beer parlours," which tended to combine the more lugubrious elements of the funereal and the genteel.

"Yes, that's Gabriola, sir," agreed the waiter. "Just beyond Hangman's Point there, sir."

"Just beyond——"

"And there's a ferry that runs to Gabriola Island, of course?" Jacqueline put in hastily.

"Ferry? Oh, absolutely.—Four?"

They gave themselves over to the enjoyment of the view again, sea gulls and lighthouses, blue sea and mountains—how grand it was! It touched your heart, too, filling it suddenly with a wild pride in your own country, a giant, yet so youthful, a clod of springtime mould after all. You felt proud even to be looking at such dramatic beauty, as if you participated in all that dignity and cleanliness and sense of space and freedom; were, in some manner, clothed in this wholesomeness yourself, *were* what you were looking at. Do you see those mountains? That is ourselves, part of us.

It was a sudden feeling of love for one's land that had little to do with patriotism, but seemed part of a true pride. Ethan felt a pang: they were both looking past Gabriola, from which their toy passenger steamer was keeping an offing, straight over in the direction of Eridanus. And at the same time he became aware that this was perhaps the main source of his pride. Perhaps the view, even though not their old view, really *was* part of them, its beauty they somehow deserved, had earned (so it seemed in this mood, until one remembered again): those wild forested mountains and the sea were the meaning of their whole life in the little house in Eridanus. In a way he couldn't have explained, they weren't looking at the view, but at something in themselves. Or that had once been in themselves. It was what they meant when they turned to one another, crossing the Second Narrows Bridge some stormy winter afternoon to stare through the streaming windows of their bus down the inlet through the wild weather, with the clouds sweeping low over the evergreens and only the lower slopes of the mountains visible, so that no place on earth seemed more grim and desperate and tempestuous and impossible, and looking forward to the lamps of evening still half an hour distant in the house to say, half-humorously, with such longing: "We *live* there!" And now?

"Hangman's Point," Ethan said aloud.

"I never saw so many lighthouses in my life."

"Nor I."

They counted seven from where they sat, planted on rocks near and far, the white towers of vigil all rising from port-wine-colored roofs and white walls of their keeper's houses, all with much the same pretty architecture. A lighthouse was surely the last thing you associated with a home: yet these scattered beacons on the rocks, these *farolitos* testifying to the extreme danger of the coast (and the extreme danger of living in such isolation: in his experience Ethan could remember more than one tragic crime committed in a lighthouse) not only were homes, but quite obviously and obstinately loved as such—around the nearer ones they could even see where efforts at gardens had been made, and among the rocks of the nearest lighthouse, roses still blooming, in defiance of the spray. And on a near island they saw a lovely little white house, built on piles: they looked at it, shining there against the bronze, russet and burnt gold of its maples (Jacqueline loved to name the colors) faded sage-green of alders and dark bottle-green of pines.

Flying shadows of herring gulls, glaucous-winged gulls, violet-green cormorants swept across the big C.P.R. building at the foot of the ramp. Their passenger boat for the mainland was now no more than a smudge of smoke, but a sister ship was coming in, her three yellow funnels, white bridge, foxglove-flower-shaped ventilators moving straight against the blue sky.

To the right, a half-mashie shot below the window, in a small sequestered harbor at the foot of the staircase, threescore freshly painted fishing boats with spiky masts swayed meekly at anchor, or were lying against a wharf. An old freighter was anchored out in the roadstead, just before them, an empty ship with water being pumped out of her side, riding so high she looked gigantic, ΑΡΙΣ-ΤΟΤΕΛΗΣ. Two men were working aloft, on the cross trees of the mainmast, doing something to the topping lift of a derrick. Derrick, it was a derrick because of the first hangman. It certainly was a curious place to meet Aristotle. Far to the left, remotely, a sea-weary-looking steamer with a great list, not much more than her stern visible, was taking on cargo.

"Loading coal for Australia," said their waiter, arriving at this moment, a tray of beer balanced on his palm, "and the funny thing about that there coal is, it don't come from Nanaimo at all, but from somewhere in Alberta, I heard."

"Oh?"

"If you ask me, Nanaimo's getting too big for its boots these days," the waiter said, "ashamed to be among common working people like anyone else."

"And you're quite sure about that ferry to Gabriola?" Jacqueline asked again, shyly, as the waiter was going.

"Sure, there must be one, ma'am," the bartender, a stout, fatherly man called over from the bar. He had been rinsing glasses, and was now drying them. "Only question is, is it running?"

"That's right," said the waiter, "they might have stopped the summer service by now."

The bartender, glancing from time to time out of the window at the scene outside, began to pile the glasses one within another in a stack on the counter, a dull-seeming occupation, about which, Ethan now understood from the bartender's glances of satisfaction at the stack, the position of which he altered now and then, evidently to suit some aesthetic whim, there was, on the contrary, something almost godlike: it was a creative process, an act of magic: for within each glass lay trapped the reflection of the window, within each window the reflected scene outside, extended vertically by the glasses themselves, the reflected windows flowing upward in a single attenuated but unbroken line in which could be seen a multiplicity of lighthouses, seabirds, suns, fishing crafts, passenger boats, Australia-bound colliers, the minuscule coal rushing audibly down the minute chute, minute S.S. *Aristotle* with minute Greeks working on the derricks. Ethan touched glasses with Jacqueline and drank.

It was now the end of the luncheon hour. People strode in the wind up and down the ramp. A bearded man in a bright red and black plaid shirt riding a chestnut mare stopped at the top, right under the window, to readjust the horse's blanket and cinch. A dark sedan with some faded gilt lettering on the front door—DEPARTMENT OF MINES AND RESOURCES—also drew up, revealing within, next the man driving, a stout dowager in a seal coat lighting a cigarette. Ethan touched glasses again with Jacqueline and took another draught of beer watching, with one's eyes, where, diagonally across the street, sat the bastion.

". . . Last ship to pass through the Panama . . . down to New Orleans . . . country where you can have some standard of living, like the U.S.A. . . .

Sailors. The voices came from next door, from the Men's side; Ethan, peeping, thought he could see the speakers through a crack in the partition dividing the two rooms.

"Cargo of lead ore from Patagonia, in Argentina, for Trail, B.C. . . . Vancouver . . . lumber and general cargo . . ."

These partitions were usually movable, for at crowded hours the Men's side was much fuller than the Ladies and Escorts: the partition would thus often be found slowly moving in on the territory of the latter, producing, sometimes, if you were obliged to leave your lady for several minutes, on your return a certain eerie feeling of perichoresis. An isolation that was, at the same time, begotten by an interpenetration. But this arrangement seemed an exception, though Ethan could make no sense of it. Alterations were evidently in process on the other side, as the bars appeared not really contiguous, but divided by a corridor, on the farther side of which was yet another partition, or maybe a wall, Ethan couldn't make out. The sailors, either by choice—there seemed a full sea wind blowing through this corridor that may have made it seem a home from home—or because the Men's bar was full, were sitting thus at a table in a kind of no-man's-land between the two.

"I'm English and I hail from Manchester—and don't forget it!— but I'm married to an American girl in Mobile, so when I'm outward bound I'm homeward bound too."

"Outward bound . . ." the voice came from their first meeting,

in the little movie theatre, in thunder and snow . . . *"But are we going to heaven or hell? But they are the same place, you see . . ."*

Voyage, the homeward-outward-bound voyage; everybody was on such a voyage, the Ocean Spray, Gabriola, themselves, the barman, the sun, the reflections, the stacked glasses, even the light, the sea outside, now due to an accident of sun and dislimning cloud looking like a luminosity between two darknesses, a space between two immensities, was on such a voyage, to the junction of the two infinities, where it would set out on its way again, had already set out, toward the infinitely small, itself already expanding before you had thought of it, to replenish the limitless light of Chaos—

Blue, blue, deep blue: a white fishing boat slid across the foreground, which telegraph wires just outside the window intersected; and holding up the glass to the light and drinking the beer, one might have felt, forgetting everything, as though drinking down the day itself, and having drunk that the day was still there (there was another beer, this time Jacqueline's) in its inexhaustible coolness, its prospect of happiness to be engulfed once more.

But Jacqueline had scarcely finished her first glass of beer and now—Ethan had just drawn her attention to the scarcely perceptible *kaoiling kaoiling* of another very distant freight train—an expression of supplication came over her face.

"I'm sure we'll find a place on Gabriola, sweetheart," Ethan said.

But even as he said it, hoping it was true, he was aware of a certain sinking sense of fear that had been with him all morning, as though part of him did not want to find it, to commit himself finally, something of the feeling one has at the moment of commencing a long voyage (however much one has dreamed of and longed for it) or the feeling he had had when he finally resigned from the law firm in Toronto and started west with Jacqueline, and he knew she felt this too, though if Gabriola proved impossible he felt already their exhausted and bitter disappointment at the same time. And yet, finally to leave Eridanus, even though they knew they must, they had been warned of the new park that would encompass that stretch of forest and waterfront, warned that they were to be evicted, and even though they had never intended to live there permanently, still, to leave—

"Ethan," Jacqueline said, taking his hand.

"Yes."

"Do you remember, 'when you see the light in the sky, you'll see——' "

Two years ago last spring, in May, the Llewelyns, having followed the path through the forest ("follow this trail through the bush until you see the light in the sky, then you'll see the cabin you folks are looking for, at the bottom of the steps," the old fisherman had instructed them), and there below them, beneath a wild cherry tree in full bloom, its chimney capped by a bucket, shingled roof needing repair, its strong cedar foundations standing right in the sea, for it was high tide, they saw, for the first time, their third house, their beloved cabin. It was shimmering, awash in light; the reflections of the sun on the water sent forever millwheel reflections sliding up and down its weathered silver cedar sides. They stood there, looking at one another, in the lightness, greenness, the heavenliness of the forest, and always this first glimpse of their house was to be associated too, perhaps from memories of the carillon-sounding Sunday mornings of Niagara-on-the-Lake, with the unearthly chiming of a church bell through the mist. Actually the sound in Eridanus came from a freight train walking along the embankment on the other side of the inlet, its warning bell . . .

Entering the house with the key they had received from the owner, they gazed round the two rooms, slightly dusty, damp-smelling from disuse, but essentially clean, and bare of all but necessary articles: the wood-burning cookstove, table by the window and two plain wooden benches, the cupboard for the dishes; the second room with a bed like a ship's bunk set into the walls, and chest of drawers in one corner. Could they possibly—could Jacqueline—live in such a place, without electricity, without plumbing, without even running water?—There were two pails to be filled at the well. Jacqueline gazed round her, pulling off her white gloves she looked totally out of place. Ethan walked out on the porch, leaving her still gazing, with mute abstracted nods and astonished eyes round the rooms. But a moment later she joined him on the porch, and looking across the water toward the mountains: yes, she had said yes!

And then—"I know how you feel," Sigbjørn Wilderness said to them, last summer.

"God knows we've thought about it enough, but if you bought it would you like it?"

"Why not?"

"Well, we couldn't keep our houses on the beach then, we'd have to build houses back from the water twenty feet, I think it is——"

"Oh God, I'd forgotten about the Harbour Board."

"And then we'd have to cut it up into lots and chop down all the trees over twenty feet high and put in water mains—in short, you might as well just go round the point and buy a lot in the subsection. But hold on, we've been here ten years . . ."

But Ethan couldn't hold on, not like that. For between knowing that you are going to die, and knowing that you are going to die sometime within the next year there i a difference.

And once more, that day, the warning bell had sounded through the mist, more frantically, and it had been high tide, and afterward they had stood in the house in anguish—and oh, my God, how was the house *now?* Perhaps at high tide the logs were banging underneath with a chewing breaking ruinous sound (and they not there to protect it) so that the house shook, hearing this, the *house* hearing this, for it was as if the house knew, with no sentimentality about it, knew its every timber and crossbrace precious to them, as if the house had heard that bell too, coming over the water, till the sound had driven in its last weary nail, the sound which was also like the cathedral bell—

> Vous qui passez
> Ayez pitié

CHAPTER 31   ✷   *Twilight of*
the Raven

*W*ell," Jacqueline sighed, releasing Ethan's hand, "I guess we'd better go and see if the skipper's back from lunch."

"Let's wait a little longer, sweetheart."

The post office clock struck the half hour: one long deep solemn note. Ah, but to go, suddenly seemed now like a final treachery.

Yet what held them still? Why were they sitting here in the Ocean Spray Inn? What were they dreaming about? Was it the dawns, the delight of swimming at sunrise, the strangeness and marvel of looking out of a window almost level with the sea into the sunrise, the smells of coffee and bacon around them: the dawns like burning cathedrals too, like bonfires, and always the three trees held in the frame of the sun . . . Jupiter and a half-moon at rising . . .

Sunrise! Twilight of the Dove. He remembered a sunrise in early spring: the sun first a bubble of light, then an arrow, then a white forest fire. Then, kite-shaped, silver, the upper segment enormous, gleaming, the lower appearing as stars in fog, shining through the morning mist as points of diamond light, like the particles of sugar before them spilled on the table over their coffee. The group of trees on top of the mountain were silhouetted gigantically against this upper part, and for a time there was nothing to be seen in the whole world save those giant firs high in the sky, against this segment of white light. Then the fog began to drift shoreward and the complete sun appeared, higher and naked of the trees, like a faceless moon for a moment, then, suddenly brilliant . . .

Or was she thinking of last November, the frost melting in stripes on the porch, yet her chrysanthemums and even a few roses still miraculously in bloom; or the rain, and how, sitting at the table by the window, she loved to watch the rain falling into the sea.

And the great storm-driven mounting dark tides of January when they thought they would be washed away to sea—it was the day the killer whales came crashing and cavorting down the inlet and they had been working all afternoon getting in a load of wood and repairing the stove—to wake before dawn of that next morning, to save the house from the battering of logs, waking, as he told her after, from one of those queer dreams when you seem to be reading, a dream of wheelbarrows and watering cans, whales, woodashes, tinsnips, asbestos and salt water. And what again of the house without them, of timbers battering at the foundations—broken into perhaps, windows shattered, abandoned by the Sea-Centaur, leaves drifting in over the sill, incursion of damp, rats . . .

Or was she thinking of the windy evenings of this month, October at the little house, evenings of clouds and sea gulls blowing four ways at once, the black sky above the trembling alders, jingling their delicate green jewelry, and the gulls, white, white, soaring against the darkness, wild ducks doing sixty downwind, and golden-headed kinglets feeding in swift chiming multitudinous flight through the leafless bushes in autumn. Or in summer, how once in their forest they had come upon a city of foxgloves in long grass, in a wild clearing, the slender spires and the sun-greened leaves . . .

"No, I'll go," Jacqueline said all at once, getting up. "You stay here, darling, and drink your beer."

"Damn it, no, that does seem a dirty trick." Ethan rose, though it was a fact their waiter was coming with more beer.

"I'm away," Jacqueline said, brightly patting him on the shoulder, and she was gone.

Ethan stood at the window and Jacqueline, pretty, dainty, below in the street, turned by the bastion and waved her green-gloved hand, then turned again and, smoothing her fur coat and skirt down over her knees against the strong wind, turned yet again, kissing her hand, and went into the alley, steep, falling away into steps leading seaward, their staircase between houses of the hour before, but which from above looked quite different—she had disappeared amid the scaffolding—the scaffold—as if it might once have been the glacis of the fort itself, down from the forgotten counterscarp of a dream. Bastion. The final bastion of human consciousness . . .

Ethan stared after her with a sudden dreadful pain: what if she should never come back again? Simultaneously he became aware of two unusual things happening below in the street, where a man on crutches, supported by an extraordinarily pretty girl, were approaching, a touching sight. Ethan now saw that these two people were drunk as geese, the man had dropped one of his crutches and was hopping, trailing his bandaged foot to a wall to balance himself: both were roaring with laughter. And Ethan was surprised to find that he was regarding these people and this attitude with the most intense curiosity and approval, at the same moment, reserving his astonishment for something yet more unusual. For the bastion, so it would appear, was speaking.

"A vast expansion by land, sea, and air," it was announcing proudly, "is hastening Nanaimo's destiny. The huge multi-million Harmac Kraft Pulp Mill is making marked progress. A multi-million dollar expansion program—in three years."

Ethan had just made out that the source of the voice was a loudspeaker mounted on its cockloft, when another waiter appeared officiously at his elbow.

"Sorry, sir, you'll have to move into the Men's if your wife is gone."

"Gone? She'll be back in a few minutes. She's just gone to inquire about the ferry to Gabriola."

"Sorry, it's not that—it's just that we saw the goddam inspector, sir," the waiter said.

Ethan took his two remaining beers through the no-man's-land.

"—potential outlay of twenty-two millions," the bastion roared, "a three-hundred-eighty-foot wharf and a fifty-inch pipe with a storage dam—" past further evidence of alterations in progress, and stepped into a fluorescent floodlit scene of such astounding hideousness he nearly lost his senses.

Though its boundaries seemed yet to be determined, if the purpose were not to leave them flexible as now, this newly renovated Men's section proper of the beer parlour appeared to be finished to the satisfaction of whatever inverted genius had created it. Finished. It was the end.

Ethan swam toward a seat, against a noise like a boiler room. It smelled like a recently but not very well-disinfected public lavatory, and accustomed as he was to the huge viewless ugliness of beer parlours—at worst, at night, on the crowded Men's side, little better than anterooms to the "tank" at the police station—this one appalled him. But it was the color scheme that was really remarkable. Jacqueline was good at describing such horrors and unconsciously he began to think of it as if through her eyes. But it struck him that these colors were new to him, and must have been new to her, brewed, perhaps, in some infernal, more than Mother Gettle's Soup cauldron, containing a hitherto unimagined amalgam of pigments and abominations, to create an ugliness the world had not thought of before. Considered as a painting, as a work of imagination, on the other hand, Ethan surmised, a modern master could scarcely have improved on it, for the room seemed to be the perfect outward expression of its own inner soul, of what it meant, of what it did, even of what awful things could happen in it. What made it all wrong was that the creatures that inhabited it were alive, though at first one was not sure even of this, alive, were moving, or almost moving, seemed to be, however cancelled by it, human beings.

But the colors. "Vomit yellow and ashes of raspberry," he could hear Jacqueline saying, laughing, with fastidious hatred (she had once described a similar scene); and how he missed her already, with a sharp sense of pathos and self-reproach at having let her go out alone; "criminal grey, decayed salmon, and exhausted orange, with a dash of little shit brown." And the same effect repeated in columns of mirrors, carefully designed to look broken, under a ceiling of dried blood.

The light turned the denizens of the place into corpses, their flesh a yellowish grey, with purple lips and cheeks. Near the lavatory, under a neon cerise floodlight, something sat in the corner; a sack, it looked like, under those macabre lights; not a sack, it was square, more like a wardrobe, and draped with a spotted filthy wrinkled grey canvas under these cerise ceiling lights that glared down like three pairs of mechanical eyes. And the carpet, for there was a carpet, seemed to be composed of some sort of evil fungus, in which growths struggled with each other, ash-colored and slime black. The windows were either boarded up, like those of prisoners, he thought, in the citadel of Parma, against the view, or the glass was a thick corrugated verdigris green.

"Well, some folks objected to the windows," another waiter came up with Ethan, saying. "You know, walking by outside and seeing folks in here drinking."

From without, the flesh must not be tempted, nor, from within, the soul invited, even if limited vice were legalized. But Ethan recalled that some years back the Reverend McCorkindale, Prohibitionist, was of a different opinion: he complained that he could *not* see into beer parlours from the street, this, he asserted, being his right under the Act, which stated that the interiors of beer parlours must be visible from outside, a defection that moved the reverend gentleman to threaten that churches might hire detectives and lawyers to enforce the law.

"Yeah, they're going to fix up the Ladies and Escorts too. Put in improvements, like this here, soon's they get around to it."

"I'd like two more beers, please . . ."

"Well, they didn't make these improvements for the peace of mind of you rub-dubs in here, and that's a fact," the waiter added cheerfully, giving Ethan his change and looking round him. "Glorious, isn't it?" Ethan followed his gaze toward a pane of corrugated horror the color of certain wilted cabbage roses, but still bright and hard, within a door, to a sinister divertissement arising in one corner like a black box with two ship's ventilators facing away from each other like cocked eyes, and now a serpent of livid light swimming so savagely around a clock you could almost hear it hiss.

"Glorious," the waiter repeated. "Suitable to the age, I sometimes think."

Ethan, chuckling, now observed a mural on one of the boarded windows which, Pompeii-wise, was evidently intended to express the lost scene outside, and that a row of electrically lit imitation medieval English lanterns, perhaps as some kind of concession of "atmosphere," contributed not a little, apart from the floodlights, to the ghastliness of the pervading light. The gentle sun, idling among the swift waters of the Gulf, could never have thought, every time he unwontedly entered here, through gangrenous glass or door, or by refraction, what an awful thing he had done.

NOTICE

Forbids profane or obscene language, singing or the playing of any musical instrument. This regulation must be strictly enforced.

Ethan took his pipe out but didn't try to light it and found that, stooping forward, he was sitting in a deliberately uncomfortable attitude he could not, for some reason, change. But glancing round him he saw that his half-prayerful and uncomfortable attitude seemed native to the other haunters of the place. Sitting on their chairs of imitation leather, covered with new, already cracked paint in bright brick red, as if they would slump off and collapse at any moment in a heap, their neglected beers standing on the swimming steel tablecloths enamelled in fire-engine red and gunmetal blue, they appeared intent on the fungiform carpet, bowed over it, in noisome prayer, or talking to themselves.

—Well, he *shouldn't* have let Jacqueline go alone, that *was* sure, it *was* a weakness, perhaps equivalent to a disastrous failure. Perhaps, even thinking of the ferry and no more, he didn't want to be certain of anything any longer. On the other hand, it was the kind of thing she liked to do; even if, as seemed to him highly probable, they'd have been able to find out all they needed in this pub within the next half hour without going back to the ferry company at all; before that time her longing impatient spirit (which, unlike his, had already bravely accepted and freed itself of the past?) would have flown a thousand times to Gabriola.

Ethan was not impressed by these excuses, and felt unhappier by the moment.

Christ, what a miserable place was this. And pretty soon their beautiful Ladies and Escorts too would be "improved," as the waiter had said. And in a few years . . . By that time British Columbia's strange partial prohibition would probably be repealed, but would that make things any better? There would be, in addition to the fifty-inch pipe with the storage dam in the harbor, jukeboxes in the Ocean Spray, though the notice forbidding profane or obscene language, singing or the playing of any musical instruments would remain the same. Still, things would get "better"—as they said—after first getting worse, no doubt, and with saner liquor laws, the Ocean Spray might even get its view back. But Gabriola? What the hell would it really matter, finally, if he bought the vacant lot or the skipper's house? There too, all too soon, there might be a "view" no longer, though by that view he meant something quite different and something overwhelmingly more irrevocable. The Ocean Spray might have its innings again. It was their own souls, as never before, as finally, that were threatened by this ugliness, these mechanical eyes, this evil fungus, that ash color, that glass of thick corrugated verdigris green.

Christ, how lonely it was in here without Jacqueline. And though it seemed a little absurd, an unbearable pathos now attached itself to her doing what she was doing, alone.

Ethan felt a sudden need to strike up a conversation with somebody, even to join in that conversation coming from a group in the

S

corner that looked sinister as a hanging jury, and where they seemed to be saying over and over again:

"It's no good, this kind of life."

"No, that's what I said to him, it's no good."

"No good."

"No good."

"No, it's no good."

"How do you feel there, Shorty?"

"No good."

"Ha ha ha!"

"Oh, shut up."

In addition to the isolated ones muttering to themselves at lone tables, there were other groups of drinkers, drinking together; three hunchbacks, several longshoremen, probably out of work, since it was after the lunch hour, and a scattering of lumberjacks wearing lumberjackets, in addition to the sailors, who in the corridor on the Men's side, commanded all the view that was left of life, and they had now risen to go. But the acoustics were peculiar; often you could not hear what was being said in a conversation close by, but sourceless voices, volleys of obscenity, would detach themselves in this manner, from the farther end of the room.

"It's no good this kind of life."

"No, that's what I said to him, it's no good."

"Oh, shut up."

Ethan now saw that, seated near him (at the next table to a giant of over seven feet in a red-and-black striped mackinaw, with black curled hair flowing down his back, probably he was an all-in wrestler) was a Negro, whose face had been so hideously disfigured—perhaps in a fire—properly speaking he had no face at all; every smile he tried to create turned into a distortion, and Ethan rose, wanting to say something both friendly and wise to him, perhaps about the weather.

But the eerie system of lights reflected in the columns of broken mirrors produced a vertiginous effect similar to that in the Vancouver aquarium where the arc lamps are so placed their reflections shine up from beneath the water of the tank, seeming to shift positions as you approach, and the whole place becomes fluid and swaying; and having risen and started off, as he thought, to the Negro, Ethan found himself going in the wrong direction, and when he regained his bearings he thought the Negro had not smiled, and had probably not wanted to speak to him after all: Ethan returned to his seat.

A fatuous presumption anyhow, on his part, interference with another's privacy. And yet—why did he not have the courage to speak to him? Ah, how could one do it . . . The Dweller on the Threshold . . . And, as so often happens when an impulse of love meets some self-created obstacle, Ethan felt the love itself changing into the very force that inhibited it.

See who it is that watches by the threshold . . . And all at once he was seized by an appalling, unreasoning fear, not the less intense because, having been at the mercy of a semblance of it from time to time recently, he recognized a further reason for it.

For life—the mundane or dramatic round, the wanderings into court, the brushes with the bench, the cross-examination of Crown witnesses, the courtroom tragedies and comedies, the arguments on points of law over a drink, even the suspense of waiting an important decision, the sheer routine, all these things were paradoxically, in one "caliginous" aspect, and as if it had all come about by an opposite process to that which had taken place in this bar—life was *like* this bar, from which you could not see out; take all that away, he thought, remove the barrier, and the verdigris pane, and enter the realm of yourself; never mind the beautiful view, the seas are in—

Twilight of the Raven. A lonely man is dining on breast of turkey, cauliflower, French fried potatoes, cucumber, tomatoes, celery stuffed with cheese, fruit salad, vanilla ice cream, bread and butter and tea. Only a little piece of cauliflower is left on the tray when it is returned to the kitchen. He drinks too, a two-ounce portion of Hennessy's Three Star Cognac . . . But he has no breakfast.

Twilight of the Dove. Sunrise! The sun, first a bubble of light, then an arrow, then a white forest fire. Then, kite-shaped, the upper segment enormous, gleaming, the lower appearing as stars in fog, shining through the morning mist as points of diamond light, like the particles of sugar before one, spilled on the table over morning coffee.

Sunrise, twilight of the Dove, and a thick morning mist is creeping out of the hollows into the prison cabbage patch. The diner of the night before has no breakfast. Instead, he rises in answer to a summons. He is wearing prison clothes; a faded grey work shirt, blue denim trousers that are too tight for him, grey felt slippers. Outside the cell door he bends to kiss the silver cross the priest raises to his lips. He is not nervous. He walks without a stumble the seventy-five feet to the execution chamber, wrists strapped behind him. A bare light bulb suspended over the trap lights the yellow walls. He fixes his eyes on the wall and does not blink an eyelid. The hangman, Emile Banville of Montreal, dressed in a dark business suit, secures a brown leather strap around his ankles. He places the new yellow noose around his neck. At six five the eight uniformed guards stationed in front and on both sides of the trap turn to face outward. The chant of Latin from the priest is the only sound, and the man, Michael Robert Richardson (or Ethan Glendower Llewelyn), drops noiselessly into the former elevator shaft, painted bright yellow. Death is pronounced, the body is anointed, the rope is taken away; a fine new one, unlike the flag used to drape a corpse's body at sea.

After the inquest the body will be given to a person the hanged man has described as his only friend. At six forty it lies on the stretcher on which it has been carried from the elevator shaft, surrounded by warden, prison doctor, sheriff, and guards . . .

—And this ritual murder is, gentlemen, as all of you know from reading your newspapers, no unique or isolated performance. It is all too familiar. One might almost say, from the frequency of the occurrence, that it has become one of our main cultural activities in British Columbia, others being somewhat hampered by censorship and the guardians of our morals. Just as the reports thereof, from which I have drawn freely, the reports which are protests against it in general (but more rarely in the item) are our quid pro quo for creative literature. This ritual, this is our true beginning of a drama, our Tragedy of Blood, our *Titus Andronicus*. Possibly with the rise of an indigenous literature, or of a drama, a theatre in our province, our country, possibly with our gradual assent into maturity, with the abolishment of our brand of prohibition, the cleaning up of our beer parlours, our slums, our other rats' nests of vice, possibly with this push forward into maturity, if I may so express it—else we shall sink back into childhood and degeneracy, there is always a moment when the choice is made—it is possible that our evil and horrible deeds may be sublimated to all our civic satisfactions. Possibly, I say possibly, gentlemen, with the rise of a great tragic drama, this vicarious apology for it as expressed periodically upon the scaffold may cease, and the psychologic need for these recurrent tableaux vivants . . . So it was not to spare your feelings that I have not yet described, far less criticized, the skill or otherwise with which, in real life, the final part of this degrading ballet, this Grand Guignol, is performed. For from the newspapers, to the everlasting credit of the reporters and columnists concerned, this must be fairly familiar to all British Columbians too.

But I shall remind you—though who could forget it?—of Henry Wade's appalling description of Danny Schultz breaking away on the walk to the scaffold, and being chased all over the jail by frantic officials, who, after half knocking him out with a thrown chair, then slowly strangled him to death. The lunatic hangman, Charles Arundel, oily, sombreroed, pale eyes glaring, shaking hands with himself and taking a sweeping bow when he hears that staccato crack which denotes the neck is broken. Something, as Wade pointed out, that all too rarely happens! As for instance, the case of Dudley, who hung unconscious four minutes before he began to writhe and twist; then the hangman, who'd gone to have a drink, was summoned back, and wrenched his hands free when he started to climb up the rope, uttering hoarse and frightful cries of terror and despair. Then Arundel mounted the stepladder and tearing

Dudley's hands from his throat, pinioned those frantic hands to the dying man's sides with his own arms, and stepping from the ladder, swung on the body until the wretched creature was dead.

I, too, have witnessed events nearly as barbarous. Often the victim takes twenty minutes to die. Sometimes he is decapitated . . . And there are other horrors, though it might not at this point seem so, too obscene and gruesome to mention . . .

But I am not taking your time to present a case either for or against capital punishment in general. I am not going to take your time by prolepsis, gentlemen, either in its literal or chronological sense, or to attempt to seek in my words the all too obvious frontier provenance of this horror, for reforms will undoubtedly be made. One reform, for example, I know, for I have it on the highest authority, to be almost certain: a murderer will no longer have to wait through that last night till the sunrise, but instead will have the privilege of dying at midnight, since for one thing, at that time it is easier to assemble jurymen, less disturbance is caused among the inmates of the prison, and, most important of all, it obviates the necessity of cooking meals for the guards, who have otherwise to come in early for dawn hangings.

No! What concerns us here, is the next December 13, at dawn, in the year 1949 in British Columbia, a child, a boy of fifteen, is condemned to die in this unspeakable manner, in that former elevator shaft, painted bright yellow, and without, so far, this barbarism having elicited a flicker of tactile public protest.

Guilty—or technically guilty of a lesser offense, gentlemen—this child perhaps is. But guiltier by far are the adults who condemn him. And guilty are those citizens from whom I have not yet read one comment that shows a desire for a judgment based on unbiased truth. And anything like such comment we are not likely to get from many sources, for the callous and simple reason—why?—why, it is too damaging to our self-esteem. And there is another more potent reason—fear.

For to expose ourselves too publicly upon such a matter as this, fellow citizens, involves a grave risk. For to speak out in this instance not only might involve an individual danger to the speaker, but to the whole community in which he lives, thus not only laying himself open to the opprobrium that society will fasten upon an outcast, a pariah, but by that outspokenness making outcasts even of his friends, or people who now claim to be his friends, but would then—they would say to themselves, naturally—deny being so.

That this boy should be condemned to die, by a jury who seem to have arrived at their fateful verdict informed by the crassest sentimentality, and an absence of psychological or even medical knowledge, would be bad enough. But he has been so sentenced for a crime which there is no evidence to show that he committed deliberately, or had any intention of so committing.

You are of course all aware of the rough circumstances of this tragic case, the seriousness of which there is no need to gloss over; that the boy, Richard Chapman, aged fifteen, caused the death of a girl, also fifteen, a school companion, after allegedly having attempted to rape her.

But was it murder? Was it rape?

Were one speaking mainly in legal and juridical terms of defense in regard to assault per se, the fact remains that there were no marks of violence upon the body, and that actual assault had not taken place.

The girl died by suffocation, but no account seems to have been taken of the probability that death itself was accidental, or that it could have been, say, the result of a reflex muscular action, caused by sheer terror, a terror operating on both sides; that when the girl became hysterical, the boy accidentally suffocated her in an effort to silence her screams.

There is not the slightest evidence to show that the boy was in any way degenerate or vicious, on the contrary, we are told that he was quiet, a "good boy." He could easily have fallen victim to a psychological aberration, or simply lack of wise advice on these very points, a victim of his own natural ignorance, in short, a victim of his parents, as, unless a miracle occurs, he must perish a victim to *our* ignorance, as a martyr to *our* hypocrisy. For one thing is clear: a terrible thing like this could have happened to any one of us, to the gentlemen of the jury themselves, yes, even they themselves, when Chapman's age, might have perpetrated in all innocence what has been characterized and so sensationalized as an atrocity.

Are the people of British Columbia unique in that they have never passed through the fears and bewilderments of puberty?

Let a more competent voice than my own speak of this period common to everyone, the voice of one of the most distinguished figures in the world, who will, in all likelihood, be the recipient of the Nobel Prize this year or next. I refer to Hermann Hesse, who, in his *Demian,* says:

> As to every man the slowly awakening sense of sex came to me as an enemy and a destroyer, as something forbidden, as seduction and sin; what my curiosity sought to know, what caused me dreams, desire, and fear, the great secret of puberty, that was not at all in keeping with the guarded happiness of my peaceful childhood. I did as everyone else. I led the double life of a child, who is yet a child no longer. My conscious self lived under the conditions sanctioned at home, it denied the existence of a new world whose dawn glimmered before me. But I lived as well in dreams, impelled by desires of a secret nature upon which my conscious self anxiously attempted to build a new fabric, as the world of my childhood fell in ruins about me. Like almost all parents, my own did nothing to help the awakening life instincts, about which not a syllable was uttered. They only aided, with untiring care, my hopeless attempts to deny the reality, and to continue my existence in a childlike world which was ever becoming more unreal and more mendacious.
>
> In the average person this is the only time in their lives that they experience the sequence of death and rebirth that is our fate, when they become conscious of the slow process of the decay and breaking up of the world of their childhood, when everything beloved of us leaves us, and we suddenly feel the loneliness and deathly cold of the universe about us. And for very many this pitfall is fatal. They cling their whole life long painfully to the irrevocable past, to the dream of a lost paradise, the worst and most deadly of all dreams . . .

"And so I say to you——"

"Hooray!"

"Bravo, Mr. Llewelyn!"

"It's no good, this kind of life."

"That's what I said to him, it's no good."

"Ha ha ha."

"Oh, shut up."

"Yes, we like that, Mr. Llewelyn. Especially that bit about the irrevocable past, and the dream of a lost paradise. Is it not because *you* are still clinging to such a dream, to such an irrevocable past, that you, who of all people might have done some good, who would in fact quite possibly have been retained to defend the boy, did not raise a finger to help?"

"I?"

"Yes. You. Did you not say, 'For to speak out in this instance not only might involve an individual risk to the speaker, but to the whole community in which he lives?' And what kind of community could Mr. Ethan Llewelyn be speaking of, pray, but some unique and suspect community, one against which society is prejudiced, and what community could that be, other than that of your own—you squatters on those float houses in Eridanus? For it is certain that no other *community* would be risked in such a dramatic manner by intelligent action. Only that which (according to you) comprises your own lost Paradise, your own irrevocable past, in short, that of Eridanus itself. That you were loath to draw attention to Eridanus in such a manner while you yourself were living there, may or may not be an unselfish action. But in any case it is a strange sort of unselfishness that would give precedence to this and allow a child to die."

"That's what I said to him, it's no good."

"No good."

"No good."

"And you have omitted to state that there have, in fact, been many protests."

"Yes. For example, *I* said: as a mother of two boys and a girl I feel you should do all you can to prevent the gross injustice that has been wrought on the condemnation of Richard Chapman hanging. Let him have a chance to learn as all must learn."

"Hang him!"

"And for that matter, you have forgotten the counter-protests. As I wrote: Under Canadian law we all know that persons accused of murder are given every opportunity to defend themselves, irrespective of the cost to the public. If there are any extenuating circumstances the sentence is commuted. If none whatever, the death penalty should be imposed, regardless of age——"

"Hang him!"

"And I said: There is something seriously wrong not only with Canadian justice but with ourselves, if children such as Richard Chapman can be sent to face the horrors of an execution without more than a whisper of protest from the general public——"

"Spare him!"

"But I countered: In reply to 'End Barbarous Punishment,' personally I think she should have her head examined: she writes about how the cruel delay must touch the hearts of every father and mother. Doesn't she think that rape and murder also touch the heart of every Canadian father and mother? I think I would gladly take the hangman's job myself. Like it says in the Bible, an eye for an eye—it's true, is it not?"

"Hang him!"

"What with all the filthy magazines that are allowed to overflow our newsstands—I have been hoping that a more able pen than mine——"

"With so many potential murderers around by the way of drug peddlers and drunk drivers, it is a crime to wreak vengeance on an immature youth——"

"Hang him!"

"Spare him!"

"—If there is a difference between a mind warped by sex and a mind warped by drink, I fail to see it, as the results are the same."

"Hang him!"

"It's no good, this kind of life."

"No, that's what I said to him."

"How do you feel there, Shorty?"

"Oh, shut up!"

"Every passing day brings nearer the doom of the fifteen-year-old youth, and I should like to plead with all my heart————"

"And I said: It would be a Christian and honorable gesture on the part of our government, in honor of the prospective visit of our Princess Elizabeth to Canada, to grant a reprieve to those who have sinned against us and now wait for the hangman's noose. Life imprisonment must, of course, be given those poor creatures in order to protect society, but in honor of our future Queen, let us temper justice with mercy."

"Save him!"

"Oh, shut up!"

"It's no good, this kind of life."

"But you, Ethan Llewelyn, what did you say? What did your able pen do, your pen more able than mine, or your still small voice, the one voice, the one pen still able to save him?"

"Hang him!"

"Hang him!"

"The appeal for clemency of Richard Chapman, the fifteen-year-old rapist has been refused by the Cabinet today. Richard must keep his date with the hangman next December thirteenth."

"Hang him!"

"Hang Ethan Llewelyn!"

CHAPTER 32   *Twilight of the Dove*

. . . Yes, hang him, Ethan thought. He eyed his own uneasy shifty figure in the mirror, still buttoned up to the neck in the long grey overcoat, seated sidewise to the table in the same uncomfortable frozen attitude, squinting at the several uneasy reflections in the mirrors; the other men, sitting in similar attitudes, some pretending to read newspapers, each with that sidelong corner smile; smiles of hope that one would be recognized as unique by some fellow being; smiles of depravity; smiles of despair. People did not come into this room either, as sailors come up on deck, but "made entrances," their bodies muscle-bound and out of step with self-consciousness, all of them with this unctuous smile flickering at the corner of their mouths. And yet, should one speak to any of the denizens of this loneliest of homes, with what friendliness would one be greeted, more likely than not, so great was man's need for love. Hang Ethan Llewelyn, but what good was that going to do the boy Chapman, perhaps wearing such a smile himself, half thinking he was doing, or even had done, something heroic, half smiling at the shadowy impossible knowledge that, most heroic of all, he must hang.

But hadn't he already left it too late? That figure in the mirror seemed to be saying to him, aren't you beginning to lose the courage to make any decisions at all? Was it not much as if the new life of

his which was set toward a rebirth had become an abortion? Fear—
to be sure it wasn't always on the surface, but neither was it a
sudden or occasional thing—fear had essentially dominated his days,
as if it were a moon: a moon of fear ringed by doubt. Ethan
doubted, and not for the first time that day, whether he'd been
seriously looking for a house . . . All you think about is the next
drink and perhaps all you're looking for, all you long for, is your
own death. Perhaps essentially he was afraid of finding his real self,
afraid of discovering himself to be a criminal, a murderer even, or
one whose destiny was suicide, in which case there'll be no need to
hang Ethan Llewelyn, he'll do it for them . . .

How could one set at naught such thoughts? In Eridanus he
might have defied them. But now he felt he couldn't find any
strength for defiance, any source from which to draw that strength.
You've lost your faith in yourself, old boy. But then, for the matter
of that, he had no faith in anything else, in anything at all, to speak
of, except Jacqueline of course, though he wouldn't say he hadn't
searched for one—both of them had—and with far greater persis-
tency than they'd ever searched for a house.

Ah yes, the search: in the Gospel Center, the Backslider in Heart,
in the Faith Thriller at the Reel Pulpit, and at the metropolitan
Tabernackle, Does it matter, Virgin or Young Woman, and at the
First Baptist, "No Prowl Car comes for the social snob but if we
avoid our fellows in need we shall one day hear the condemnation
of the Judge of Life": the search in the Unitarian Church, "Beautiful are the gasworks in the evening light, beautiful is the humility of
a strong man," and, "Sportsmen, also those who doubt miracles, are
invited to hear Rev. A. Dinsbury in Grace United, who Sunday
evening will speak on A Big Game on Poor Ice," and in the terrors
and comforts of the Spiritualists' trumpet: in the Theosophical
Society: the search within oneself; in love . . .

But it was as though this search for faith too had become like a
longing for death, if not death itself, a certain knowledge that soon
he was going to die: and it was as though, suddenly, in this hell
Ethan felt the warning of this now—perhaps it was not by accident

that they had found themselves following a funeral—felt this warning, and it was a good thing, too, that he was going to die, he felt it at the very center of his visceral consciousness. And a moment it was almost as if he were dead already, surrounded by warden, prison doctor, sheriff and guards . . .

Ethan was aware of another waiter, hovering near, who, catching his eye, now came directly over.

Ethan stood up, took a step forward, feeling a sense of complete unbelief, as must that Calgary farmer on the prairie, who suddenly had come upon his brother, struck by a bolt of lightning, while controlling the harrow's four horses from behind, his brother in the saddle, the horses lying in pairs to left and right, his clothes spread over the surrounding prairie, his cap cut in two as with a pair of scissors.

"Mr. Llewelyn, isn't it? Don't you remember me, Henry Knight?"

"Well. What do you know. Well, son of a gun. Henry Knight," Ethan said at last, holding out his hand, which the other grasped firmly.

"The same, sir. Well and happy too . . . thanks to you, sir," he added in a low tone.

"Well, what the hell, Henry, you old bastard. I don't know what to say. Will you have a beer?"

"Not on your life. You have one with me."

"Son of a gun."

"Son of a gun."

From the horrible to the absurd was but a step, as Henry himself might have said. As Henry went to get the beers, Ethan chuckled to himself. A murder charge would hardly seem the subject for humor, but the case of Henry Knight had been, from beginning to end, a source of mirth. It had also, back in 1936, been his first murder case, strange though that was to reflect on now. Henry came from New Toronto, and his specialty was making barrels for people shooting the rapids in the vicinity between Queenstown below Niagara Falls, and on occasion for shooting the Falls themselves (he had helped to construct the barrel in which Bobby Leach, later to be killed by slipping on a banana peel, had successfully negotiated Niagara) and he had been arrested in a church. People living near the Church of the Nazarene in Oakville had complained of weird noises coming from the building at midnight, and Henry, who not unnaturally resented being interrupted in the midst of a recital, and who moreover considered that the Church of the Nazarene should provide him with the privilege of sanctuary, had not only resisted arrest in the church itself, but had escaped on the way to the police station. In the scuffle one of the policemen, struck, it was averred, by Henry, had collapsed and later died. Henry Knight was charged with murder, it was later proved that the constable had died of heart failure. Ethan finally had successfully defended him from the second charge of manslaughter, and he received a suspended sentence. The case had not been made easier by the defendant himself who had prejudiced the jury against him by loudly expressing the opinion that churches had no right to be closed, that a country that was so full of interfering miserable busybodies and stool pigeons, as he put it (he was an Englishman) that they would inform on a man playing the organ in church, better think twice before calling itself free—an opinion that was interspersed with gratuitous quotations, and misquotations, from Thomas Hardy and Dickens, many of whose passages he had by heart, and repeated vociferously at the most inappropriate times.

"But the church was shut. You could be charged with breaking and entering anyhow."

"The church should have been open, Mr. Llewelyn my lord. All churches should be open, in my humble opinion, or they're not churches."

"To every drunk who comes along?"

"Well, I was a bit organized, you might say, and I don't remember it overwell. But I can tell you this—what got me mad was that anyone should be so mean a rag of a thing as to inform the police of something like that. What kind of a country is this, I ask you, where a man can't play the bloody organ in peace?"

"If you were sober enough to remember whether you struck the policeman or not——"

"I was sober. And I didn't strike the policeman. If he fell down it was his own fault."

The conversation of two human beings, meeting by accident, under happier yet obviously delimited circumstances, after such crucial times, often tends to resemble the irresponsible running patter of comedians.

"Well, *I've* been in the can since I last saw you," Ethan said, as they raised their glasses.

"Saw a nice little bit in the paper about that . . . Were you guilty, sir?"

"Guilty as hell. Well, technically, in a way."

"Nothing to that . . ." Henry was silent, then: "Well, I was a bit organized that night, as you might say . . . I saw where you lost your home. Worst thing that can happen to a man."

"You ever burnt out?—ah yes, I remember."

"Twice, don't you remember? Well, I got my brother here with me now. He's been on the ships. Came over from England after the war."

So it was Henry's brother in the Ladies and Escorts. "I thought his face seemed familiar."

The sailors were trying to attract Henry's attention and he started to go, but another waiter came to the rescue.

"Well, you're not making any barrels in these parts, are you, Henry?"

"Well, I was *over* a barrel, you might say, if it hadn't been for you—and you 'ave my undying gratitude, sir."

"Think nothing of it. Are you playing the organ these days, Henry?"

"Well, you know, I don't *tell* people I play the organ."

"You couldn't play it in here, anyhow," said Ethan, standing up, as Henry prepared to take his leave.

"Ah, there're worse places than this," Henry drained his glass, "where there's no untried refuge left for a moment's shelter from the terrible truth, as Charles Dickens says."

"Sounds more like Hardy. But maybe sometimes we'll have a duet if we settle down in these parts. I've taken to the clarinet . . ."

"If it's no worse than that, sir, you won't come to no harm!"

Henry Knight rode off on Rosinante a little way, but since he always, Ethan remembered, like to make a good exit, cantered back again almost immediately, as if to pick up, on the fly, an empty glass.

"Nothing will speak to your 'eart with the sweetness of the man of strings, as Thomas 'Ardy said," he began.

"Hardy? I'm surprised at you. Isn't that Kipling? Or maybe even really Dickens this time."

"No. Serpents is serpents, sir, as Thomas 'Ardy said. And harmonious and barrel organs be miserable sinners. But clarinets were not made for the service of Providence, you can see it by looking at them."

LAW REGARDING MINORS

No person under the age of twenty-one years may be served alcoholic beverages in this establishment. Infringement of this law renders the offender liable to a fine not exceeding $50 or imprisonment for a period not exceeding six months. This law must be strictly enforced.

—Well by God, he would do it, he would do *something*, not do nothing, cost what it might. Chapman's appeal had been refused, but there still should be time to organize powerful and intelligent public protest. And to do so he must get himself really fit as soon as possible. He would certainly do it, and in that case he'd have to sacrifice building a house. He would buy the old skipper's house, letting Eridanus go altogether, putting the whole thing behind him, and this, if he were to be completely honest, and all of a sudden he

T

meant to be completely honest, not merely for Chapman's sake, or Jacqueline's sake . . . For he knew only too well the nature of the work that lay ahead should he build the house himself, with just one carpenter to help, if he could get one. Digging into the hardpan of these shores would be like digging into cement. Yet even that was preferable to pouring cement for the foundations, he thought with a sigh. This last was such an unsympathetic job to him, perhaps because unfamiliar, familiar only through having seen others do it, that Ethan could almost take pleasure in thinking beyond it to the strains and mishaps incident in hoisting, by himself, the heavy stringers and foundation posts. No, there would be no beer. One thing led to another: cut it out altogether. Well, perhaps there would be one little beer. Or at least there would be now . . . The winter ahead would not make it any easier. And stupid to have thought of it cooling: it would scarcely be beer weather. For if he really proposed to build in the spring, he'd have to put the foundations in during the very worst of the weather, with the hardpan frozen (one little bottle of whiskey was more like it, tilted, concealed in a dark crab-swarming hole between granite rocks where also stood propped his cold clawbar) sodden with icy rain and sleet, or God knows, if it was a bad winter, lying, until March, under three feet of ice and snow. And on top of this (and in spite of all this talk of coming prosperity, of fabulous riches and development) would be the inevitable delays at the sawmill, the difficulties for the "small man" of getting materials, as Henry Knight was just saying, wiping the table:

"So you're going to try and build, sir. But hell, Mr. Llewelyn, you can't even buy enough nails to build a chicken coop . . . Everything goes to the big fellow these days."

"No, I'm not going to build, on second thoughts . . . But we were thinking of buying a place on Gabriola. By the way, Henry, do you know if the ferry's still running?"

"Gabriola ferry goes at five, weather permitting. Just go down the ramp and turn left where it says Newcastle Island."

—No, he wouldn't build. For there were doubtless a host of

other, hitherto unforeseen objections and difficulties, such as those at this moment suggested by the complete momentary abandonment by all the waiters of the Men's side of the beer parlour, leaving him and the other infernal drinkers alone. Even Henry Knight had vanished before he had time to ask him another question. Yes, these were the days, perhaps these were always the days should you come to think of it, when everyone took his own time and people let you down without explanation. Ethan saw again the unfinished houses on Nanaimo's outskirts.

But at the same time, suddenly, perversely, he saw the thin slanting shafts of November sunlight striking through their forest as Jacqueline, from a moss-covered log, watched him admiringly at his work of undercutting. There was the steady ringing smack of the axe, a tree shuddered (he hated more than he loved to cut trees, all trees, all trees but this one, but it would not be spring, the sap would not be running, they would deprive no birds of their home), cracked and fell thunderously. Their home grew before his eyes. And at the thought of these things, of judgment proved balanced, vigilance rewarded, of Jacqueline's joy when their dream actually began to take shape—the first windows—he was filled with an extraordinary happiness. To hell with the skipper's old shack. He would build the goddam thing himself, alone, if need be . . .

"Mr. Ethan Llewelyn wanted at the bar, please!"

"Ethan! There is a ferry." Ethan came up beside her as, already seated she put her hand on his arm, shaking it. "Listen, darling, listen, I've found out all about it."

Ethan took her hand, sighing, as he slowly sank down into his seat beside her, at the view through their windows which seemed impossible after the Men's bar, like an emergence from hell, the sea, the lighthouse and the sea gulls, the sapphire Gulf, the steamers— there were now two more freighters anchored out in Departure Bay, for that was its name, the drawer, pleased at their return, had just told them—the ships with their air of *Quand partons-nous pour le bonheur?*

"Not until five o'clock, eh? . . . Well I suspect you're hungry.

Themistocles also ate before the Battle of Salamis. Or will you have a beer?"

"Why not? Oh Ethan, how exciting!" Jacqueline leaned on the table, chin on her hand, obviously quite unconscious of the beer parlour itself, which had filled up slightly on this side, though they had not lost their old places, and gazing at him with that clear bright candid look, her dark eyes at once earnest and half laughing, so often conjured to his mind whenever they had been separated, even if for a short time. This time it had only been half an hour, though it seemed longer.

"In which time, however," Ethan said, "it is possible to drink quite a number of beers. But as the glasses only hold five and a half ounces, have a dummy bottom, and are only filled three-quarters full, the stimulus can scarcely be said to be commensurate with the apparent quantity."

"It'll do you good, my poor lamb, you've been under such a strain."

"That should be preserved," Ethan was saying, "in the thesaurus of unlikely remarks by modern women," as Jacqueline gave the order to Henry Knight's brother.

"Four, please."

"Only I have an excuse. Sort of an excuse."

And leaning over Ethan told her in lawyer's whispers, cupping his hand over his mouth and speaking directly into her ear, of his encounter with Henry Knight. Jacqueline had never met old Henry Knight, but long ago his name had often kept them awake. It took them back to Oakville and the year Tommy was born. Strangely, for all their recent jocularity, the convention of legal reserve, as an old banker client of Ethan's liked to term it, would still have forbade introductions: in fact, the presence of the brother, whose privity he could not assume, almost forbade recognition, without some further sign from Henry himself. It was a startling, yet eminently reassuring anomaly, in a world of bad manners, that after all their low comedy on the subject he had to behave as if it were one of Henry's most closely guarded secrets, and himself a total stranger.

"Well, as you were saying, Jacky, Captain Smout—"

But at his name they had to laugh for awhile.

The captain had still been out for lunch when she arrived, but Jacqueline had talked to a pleasant girl in the office till he came back: the captain was a very obliging person, and he'd given Jacqueline the cerise schedule she now handed to Ethan—"All sailings subject to weather and tidal conditions and change without notice."

"You didn't ask—" Ethan took the package of cigarettes she was trying to open from her.

"No, they don't know anything about the skipper's house, it isn't advertised for sale." Peering into the tiny mirror in her purse Jacqueline took off her hat and smoothed her dark hair with her long nervous fingers.

"What about the other lot?"

"H'm-um," Jacqueline shook her head, putting on lipstick, "we have to go to Gabriola to find out."

"Hemlock," a voice suddenly broke out. "Hemlock has been despised for some time, hadn't got that pitchiness—Oh, t'was good for making seats—"

"It splits too easy, when it's 'drive a nail into it'! . . . Lasts for ever and aye in a flume, though."

Jacqueline smiled, meeting Ethan's eyes. The men were carpenters, or boat builders, seated beyond the partition in the place lately vacated by the sailors, talking about wood; and since they couldn't help hearing, the Llewelyns listened a moment, while Ethan thought: how much longer in the world would one hear such conversation as this?

"Arbutus—tried making an axle for a wheelbarrow at one time . . . Wore away with the sand and wet . . . Wore away quite then where it was turning in boxes . . ."

". . . Fir in the rowboat's thwart—"

". . . little spits would come out like freckles, in fir."

The Llewelyns sat drinking their beer, smoking, and looking through their beautiful windows. A plane, high up, flashed like a day star. Another passenger boat from the mainland was steaming into harbor. A girl wearing a short scarlet coat tripped down the ramp happily, her hair blowing back in the wind, and a big dog galloping beside her—it was the same girl they'd seen from the bus, and now Ethan recognized the dominant voice beyond the partition as that of the man who'd been seated in front of them in the bus, and who'd been prompted by the color of this same girl's coat to talk about coach wheels in the old Isle of Man.

"Aye, cedar is very soft and kindly that way . . ."

And now it has clasped the wheel forever.

"Do you think Tommy'll like Gabriola?" Jacqueline said all at once.

"I think he'll tolerate it as long as it serves his dramatic purposes. From the way he pores over dramatic criticisms these days I rather think his ambition is to be a second George Jean Nathan—and God knows Canada could use someone like Nathan. Who incidentally said the last word on the subject of nature from Tommy's point of view. 'I suppose the country is great stuff for people who've been born in it and don't know the difference, but for anyone who can't tell a redwood from Hendrik Willem Van Loon I'm not so sure!' Well," Ethan added laughing, looking through the window toward Gabriola, over a sea that seemed, in the last few minutes, to have become much rougher, spray was drifting right over the road and there were whitecaps beyond, only a cognation of impassive ducks, scoters, rising and falling on the billows inshore, apparently fast asleep, prevented it from seeming actually menacing.

"What I think should concern us is not the five o'clock ferry going over to Gabriola, but whether there'll be one coming back. What if we can't find Angela in a pinch? Do we sleep on the dock?"

"But there's this hotel, too. I told you—didn't I tell you? But we have to phone for reservations."

"Well . . . Are you happy now?"

They clasped hands across the wet rickety table.

"Oh yes!"

"You bet your life I'm happy too," Ethan said.

Through the window they watched an eagle shooting downwind until it was out of sight.

"Oh? Thank you, operator. Well I'll try again in a minute," Jacqueline was saying, and Ethan heard the operator's faint voice rattling as his wife held the receiver a moment longer.

"You know how it is," the voice was saying, "these places, he's probably gone off somewhere."

The phone booth, chairless, stale-cigar-smelling, was in a narrow dark hall wedged in between the Ladies Rest Room of the Ocean Spray and the clattering kitchen of a restaurant, in which could be made out, every time either one of them stepped into the corridor, through which the wind sucked in a freezing draught, four Chinese cooks darting up and down the narrow space between stoves and counter, slapping food on the plates.

Why on earth *was* it so difficult to find out about Gabriola? They had taken turns at the telephone trying to make contact and there was something eerie in this attempt to communicate with an island across the water that only a moment since you had actually been able to *see,* something disturbing too, in the disparity between the cramped smelly booth and the sense of the rough sunlit sea, with the lighthouses and the white peaks beyond, the windswept blue gulf across which, or under which, their voices must travel in order to be heard. Should they be heard.

"Wait a minute, they're answering," said Ethan, who had taken the receiver. Or it was like one of those strange telephone calls between the villages of Wooler and Yetholme, famous in a point of criminal law, calls which, though the villages themselves were only fifteen miles apart across the Scottish border, nevertheless had to go three hundred miles through Newcastle, Edinburgh, Galasheils—"Yes?" he said.

The voice on the other end sounded more as if from Siam, across a howling hurricane; a wraithlike voice, like one's idea of a spirit voice in a séance, or one of those forms in Dante, grown voiceless from long lack of speech, a ghost that cannot speak at all unless addressed first. "Yes," Ethan repeated, "but you're a hotel, aren't you?"

". . . nobody here . . ."

"What?"

". . . gone . . . I'm just the caretaker."

"What! You mean we can't get a room at all?"

"Nobody here . . . Andersons all gone . . . Sorry."

"Oh dear! Wait a minute, *please* wait," cried Jacqueline, snatching the receiver from Ethan. "Can you hear me? I can't hear you at all."

"Yep. I can hear you fine."

"Please speak a little louder. Can't you possibly put us up for the night? We've come a long way—"

". . . All gone away. I'm just the caretaker . . . Did you want to eat? You want your meals? I don't know . . ."

"Oh, just anything! It would be so kind of you. We'd be so awfully disappointed."

"I don't know . . . But I hate to see anybody disappointed. Might fix you up somehow."

"Thank you. Oh, thank you!"

"And I bet you never seen a ship that was *really* taking coals to Newcastle before, missus," said Henry Knight's brother to them, when they came back for another beer after lunch, less with a desire for a beer than for the view. "Well, there she is." And he pointed through the window to where, on the left, the rusty vessel was still loading coal into her hold.

"But I thought you said she was going to Australia," Ethan said.

"That's right, sir. So she is! Newcastle, New South Wales, Australia."

Libra's year ahead. Difficulties of the Fourth House . . . *Time* and *Life*. Have you ever seen a bald-headed sheep?

CHAPTER 33 🐚 *The Dock*

*O*n the post office the flag was galloping more swiftly in the fading light and the clock said a quarter to five, as once more the Llewelyns went down the ramp; they had had just enough beer and were in a highly good mood.

Walking with his arms held straight down at his sides, Ethan carried their suitcase in one hand, in the other a jug of wine (Grape Wine, it stated bluntly on the bottle) in a shopping bag.

"This way," Ethan turned left.

"But it says Newcastle Island."

"Never mind, it's the Gabriola ferry, darling."

No dogs on Newcastle Island Resort. No dogs allowed on Newcastle . . . Product of China . . . They were hurrying down another lesser ramp, a gangway, whose foot rested precariously upon a floating landing stage beneath, to which this last statement, inscribed upon a large empty packing case pitching with the stage, lent a note of exoticism, of mystery, overshadowing for a moment, perhaps because the float seemed almost to have risen above it, the presence of a small steamboat, wallowing and pitching alongside.

The pitching boat, its gunwale now above, now below, now rolling away from the clanking rising and falling landing stage, was scarcely more than a launch, had no discernible name, and had been newly painted yellow. Mingled with the smell of fresh paint a terrific cleanly harsh smell of salt and fish rose to their nostrils from the harbor. Taking things all in all Ethan reflected that they ought at this point to feel sick but the smell was so violent, as if everything putrefying had been purged out of it by the sea and wind, that instead they were exhilarated.

Trespassers using this dock—the prisoner in the dock!—do so at their own risk. Smout Gabriola Ferry Ltd.

"They do. It is." Ethan helped Jacqueline on board from the crazily scending and skreeking pier. Skreegh, skreigh, shreek, skrak.

The ferry had a tiny funnel, a broad flat afterdeck, and a kind of open anteroom under the bridge, with narrow benches running down the sides, to which they now made their way, bracing themselves against the thrust and swing. A few bags and one or two wooden crates were stowed casually in here, among which Ethan now set down the shopping bag with the wine and their suitcase.

But there seemed nobody aboard. Nobody at all. Well, well; and not even the lifeboats had names on them. No mystery about that; perhaps it was because of the ferry having been recently painted. Yet could this really be the ferry for Gabriola? Apparently. Apparently. It was. For here, on the bulkhead, in the anteroom again hung the cerise Gabriola Island Ferry Service Schedule, a duplicate of the very one Jacqueline had been given by the skipper behind the bastion, while beneath that appeared a notice of a school meeting on Gabriola Island, with, below that, some quoted extracts from the Public Schools Act. In addition there was a blackboard covered with indecipherable chalked figures—Forge—they made out—possibly they were tank soundings: while between an axe and a pyrene extinguisher was pinned an advertisement: Gabriola Convalescent Home, Mrs. R. Tullyweather, R.N.

Skreegh, skreegh, skreek skrak went the landing stage.

"What's the female Royal Navy doing here?" Ethan asked.

"It means Registered Nurse."

"I know. But it never occurred to me they'd have a convalescent home on Gabriola, somehow."

"Do you object?"

"To the contrary." Ethan lit a cigarette. "One's glad to know people go there to recover from something."

They were walking around their ferry boat which besides being nameless appeared to them unfinished. At the stern was nothing but a gap, across which stretched a chain connecting the bulwarks. Above rose a sort of pseudo-poop, just the skeleton, like a roof in progress of building with planks set at random for the workers to move around on. Nameless lifebelts, like strange white millstones against the prevailing yellow, hung here and there. While the two yellow-painted nameless lifeboats were suspended from their davits on either quarter. So might Charon's boat have appeared, Ethan thought, when hell was nearly brand-new.

For Charon himself there seemed merely a little glassed-in wheelhouse forward of the funnel on the bridge above the anteroom itself. The door was locked. There was an alleyway on the port side of the anteroom but a sign, No Admission Except on Business, and an instinctive caution forbade one investigating further, even though there was not the slightest evidence even here of anyone actually on board. The fact seemed to be that they were for the moment in the unique position of being absolutely alone on a vessel that negotiated responsible waters. With a little skill they could have commandeered the ferry and sailed her anywhere they pleased, even to Australia.

Ethan laughed at this fancy. Well, actually they couldn't have got beyond Cape Flattery before the Mounted Police would have nabbed them. But a sense of adventure, yet of cold fear had possessed him for a moment. It was difficult to say where this fear came from, but could it be that in life we sometimes have intimations of an after, or another life? I am here. But by the way, am I here? Were *they* here? No, nothing certainly could have been (despite the strangeness) more mundane. The poop, the lifeboats, the chain, the bridge, and now the anteroom, the locked door, even the accident of being alone on the ferry—if they were alone—didn't seem unusual when you thought about it, the anteroom again with its crates and notices, the harbor behind, the town of Nanaimo. And perhaps nothing could be more common than this fear: perhaps man feels it every day but merely says: "Well, but I have a train to catch and old Jones to see. I'm too busy to think about the immortality, or otherwise, of my soul." But this seemed only part of it and now Ethan thought he knew where the fear came from, and this too was a common experience. It was that everything had become, all of a sudden, so extraordinarily familiar. From the main wharf building the painters spraying paint had disappeared. The passenger boat had long since gone. The big ramp was empty. The little ramp was empty. The words on the schedule, "All sailing subject to weather and tidal conditions and change without notice," were here for them to read over again. This scene, with the empty ferry pitching ominously with its clanking of subterranean chains, the landing stage rising and falling beside them, wallowing and groaning and creaking, and Jacqueline now beginning to walk nervously by herself about the open deck. Had he experienced it before? stood right here many times before, wondering: would the Gabriola ferry perhaps not sail at all? Or had he dreamed it? And if a dream, had it an unhappy or a triumphant solution. Was it a nightmare from which he woke in a cold sweat, and which was never finished? And why did he have such a sense of adventure about this, a sense of destiny, as though the gears of decision were really being engaged—

> Trespassers using this dock do so at their own risk.

Jacqueline was shivering and Ethan helped her wrap her scarf more closely about her throat. The sun had dropped behind the mountains, leaving the town and the wharf in shadow, though it sent a glow into the sky, and light was still dancing on the sea a little way out from shore. But if they didn't start soon, it might be dark before they arrived, once the sun set the dark came quickly in October . . .

"Don't they *want* it, do you suppose?" Jacqueline asked, delighted. They were standing in the anteroom before another notice, a petition, from the British Columbia Power Company, on behalf of the inhabitants of Gabriola Island, for the installation of electric light and power; but no signatures were affixed to the petition and the Llewelyns smiled with private understanding, and pleasure mixed with a sudden sharp pain: their cabin in Eridanus had given them a romantic attachment to oil lamps. On the other hand too, more practically, it reminded them that they had no flashlight.

"Ah—!" cried Ethan, and he lit his pipe triumphantly as now two people, a shabbily dressed man wearing a drooping hat, and a taller woman with a heavy wool scarf wrapped round her head and drawn up over her chin, came down the ramp to the plunging and whining pier. The woman, likewise shabbily dressed, and all in black, seemed pale and sick; she was helped on board by the man, evidently her husband.

Suddenly a small crowd of people appeared. First came an elderly lady with a bandage over one eye, then another elderly lady leading a child with braces on her teeth. A tall, thin, blond young man, treading carefully, was followed by an attractive dark woman in tweeds, and a man in a smart navy blue overcoat, sunk in thought, carrying a small brown bag. Next a party of youngsters pushed noisily on board. Two men in shirt sleeves, careless of the frosty sunset, carried a washing machine down the ramp. A bewhiskered old man in a mackinaw muttered along by himself. Lastly a young couple about the Llewelyns' age ran for the boat, laughing and talking. Refugees, with the unanswerable emblem of the enemy God born triumphantly in their midst.

Everyone seemed to know each other and the anteroom was soon the scene of familiar greetings and inquiries.

The ferry was moving rapidly away from the landing stage.

The Llewelyns, seated in the anteroom, looked at each other with the tender, insulated private amusement of man and wife: someone must have cast off while they were stowing their bags more securely. And this despite the fact that Jacqueline had still not seen anyone yet resembling her obliging skipper of the Smout Ferry Company—indeed neither of them had seen anyone on the bridge, let alone at the wheel. Well, perhaps their skipper had been on board all the time and their quartermaster was one of the washing-machine bearers. The engines thrummed steadily . . .

And powerfully too, with the deep rolling monotonous song already of a deep-sea ship:

> Frère *Jac*ques
> Frère *Jac*ques
> Dormez *vous?*
> Dormez *vous?*
> Sonnez les ma*tines!*
> Sonnez les ma*tines!*
> Ding dang *dong!*
> Ding dang *dong!*

The old man in the mackinaw stared at them openly. The young couple had disappeared through the door, not shut again, but presumably unlocked, and somewhat embarrassed by the old-timer's gaze Ethan wondered if that way led to some concealed lounge after all, on the upper deck, where Jacqueline would be more comfortable. But so swiftly, in such circumstances, does the sense of being a neophyte take root in the soil of the uneasy conviction ever ready to receive it, that man owns nothing in this world, is allowed nowhere, that Ethan, whose old profession of all professions might have taught him disregard of such feelings, made no move. There was always the fear too of embarrassing someone with prior rights to one's own: what if one should open the door and something secret should be revealed? Yet, ah, they *had* actually started for Gabriola, and Ethan could feel, just as he could feel Jacqueline's own mood, the strangeness and thrill of this communicating itself to him. Or perhaps he shared in the excitement and happiness communicated to *them,* rather than him, a happiness in which there was still that shudder of fear, like the anxiety the ferry would roll over too far at this moment and their jug of wine be broken. But which was like—

he thought as they happily linked arms again—the mood of the bus once more, a mood of verticity, of active resignation and relief, upheld by the delicious sensation of being truly underway for their goal.

Frère *Jac*ques
Frère Jac . . .

. . . They had sailed exactly thirty yards over to the main C.P.R. wharf, where, the starboard bulwarks of the ferry having been paneled back amidships to permit its onset, they were maneuvering beneath a gigantic upslung iron gangway, an appurtenance of that wharf, and the property of the same company where they had inquired earlier for the Gabriola ferry (they could even see the ticket office at a little distance, and even their stationmaster asleep within, dreaming, perhaps, of forgotten campaigns) and now the ferry, sidling and rolling broadside on almost into the position earlier occupied by the toy passenger steamer, now drifting farther away, now nearer, as the gangway jerked and bounced down to fill the space between boat and wharf, and then, high above them, menacing, remained suspended.

"Let her go!"

"Down she comes!"

There was a rattling and a clattering of ropes and chains and pulleys as the gangway amidships, like a medieval drawbridge spanning a moat, settled into place. Bang. But no: it was rough, a tricky operation, and now the ferry—for there was a furiously seaward-flowing current—had rebounded so far away the gangway's foot was barely resting on the brink of the starboard scuppers . . . At last it was done. A car was rolling aboard, and they all had to stand back well into the anteroom to keep out of the way. The car was driven by a woman, leaning nervously over the steering wheel; she was scared, and finally the smaller of the washing-machine men still in his shirt sleeves (they were both members of the crew?) had to finish the job of parking it, turning the car carefully, backing and turning, and shouting, above the howls of a large uneasy dog in the rear seat, up at the still invisible skipper to edge his command yet once again closer to the wharf.

The car was followed by another automobile and a small truck.

Evidently not wishing that she felt let down by this delay too—and perhaps how much more!—Jacqueline was gazing, not at the cars being loaded, but at their fellow passengers within the anteroom. Jacqueline was peculiar about people, or rather, had become so of late. Both peculiar and inconsistent. "That Anderson Lodge creature." She never would have said that a year ago of someone they'd never met and who in fact had put himself out to be kind. He saw again, watching her, and with an increased perception, that this was due to an obscure and contradictory loyalty to their life on the beach. She had reacted, momentarily, from her huge relief that they could be put up at the Lodge in Gabriola; and the Anderson Lodge, far more than had been the case with the Smout Ferry Company, was already associated in her mind with the irrevocable. Now, watching her still, and with a new understanding, Ethan saw too why, since the threat of eviction, she had sometimes referred to their old neighbours on the beach with sudden spite: certainly it was not because like the newspapers she looked down on them as squatters and fishermen or worse, really thought them beneath her (Jacqueline was singularly free of snobbery for a woman and her mind was anything but provincial) but rather because they, the Llewelyns, had almost ceased since that blow to be neighbourly enough. They had almost ceased returning kindnesses as they should, and as of old. And they lacked the fatalism of the older fishermen who, long used to evil, grieved, shrugged their shoulders and went on living there till disaster drove them out, because they knew that was what it was to exist. It was a kind of unconscious rebellion against the isolation that suffering, and an inability to live under the inevitable hammer, had driven them into. It was that, as he'd felt once before in their apartment in Vancouver, in the last months, more, alas: it was perhaps *her* way of casting herself loose from Eridanus itself. But now—and he tried not to let himself be hurt by it if truly there were no hint in it of backward yearning—there seemed no mistaking her look of almost wistful affection. Ah, he could feel she was thinking, the woman in black with the scarf over her face, the woman with the bandaged eye (who, with the other, surprisingly, was reading, in French, *La Chartreuse de Parme*), the impish old chap in the mackinaw with the velour hat, the man in the navy blue overcoat, the attractive woman in tweeds, would these one day be their neighbours and friends? Perhaps one day they would all be familiar—each separate, each known for his or her special qualities, tragedies or comedies, problems to be sympathized with—instead of merely an indiscriminate group of hats and coats. Even the two nuns, now reading their prayer books, but perhaps still thinking of their ice cream and the country store after their little day's outing, might be familiar, and the priest with the gentle eyes, and wearing such big shabby boots, and who had just wakened up with a start and was looking round him bewilderedly, as to say, was this Gabriola already? Dear me, I didn't think we were making as good time as all that.

And perhaps one day the ferry itself with all its lineaments and sounds and movements would be so much a part of their life that, conversely, they would almost *cease* to see it, and they would forget this first strange feeling, this first brilliant chilly sunset. Or would this be one of those things they would never forget as long as they lived? The ropes were cast off. Ethan took Jacqueline's hand.

They were away!

U

CHAPTER 34

🌀 *Outward Bound*

Now their little ferry really was bound for Gabriola.

First with the engines off, free-wheeling with the tide, a magic ship, then the engines, starting up again:

> Frère *Jac*ques
> Frère *Jac*ques
> Dormez *vous?*
> Dormez *vous?*
> Sonnez les ma*tines!*
> Sonnez les ma*tines!*

Ethan and Jacqueline stood near the stern watching mountainous Vancouver Island receding. The town of Nanaimo lay in the indigo shadow of the mountains. But far to the left a lumber pile in a railroad yard caught a ray of sunlight so vividly that the timber seemed to be echoing the autumnal gold of a group of maples growing behind it.

Oh God, so this was the moment, the moment he'd never really expected could come to pass. And on its own terms a joyful moment. Yet now too it was as though unimaginably, finally, they really *were* saying good-bye to their cabin, that old, new life on the beach, to Eridanus, and their neighbours there, and now, for an instant, he almost hated Jacqueline for this eagerness and look of hope.

Near them the nuns were also watching Nanaimo falling astern. Like some of the other passengers they had, paradoxically, despite the sea wind blowing colder, and the declining day, been drawn out on deck by the sudden bright sunshine now they were beyond the shadow of the mountains. Ah well, most people's idea of an outing from Gabriola Island would have been to go to the town, not the country, like the nuns, and Ethan smiled with slow grief remembering how Jacqueline and he had, from Eridanus, sometimes done a similar thing. They had picnicked in a sunlit clearing in the forest and then, on returning home, picnicked again on their own beach. But now something in the calm of the nun's gaze touched Ethan to the heart. *In la sua voluntàde è nostra pace.*

So he must try to accept this as the working of a higher will, of God's will? For Eridanus, and the healing peace it had brought him, had come almost like a gift from God, and what that life was, in reality, and in its beauty, could never perhaps be lost: and yet it must be relinquished. And what would the cabin and their life on the beach have been without Jacqueline's love, the love *she* put into it? To remain attached to the place, as property, which in any case it was not (unless a few two-by-fours, and nails, a well—), he thought, looking at the planks askew on the poop, seemed a blasphemy. And in any case what right had he to assume that such happiness was intended for one who, throughout his destiny, had done his best to defend, from human law, those who had transgressed the divine?

Ethan remembered being taught a prayer as a child whose words ran:

"Grant me, Oh Lord, to know that which is worth knowing, to love that which is worth loving, to praise that which pleaseth thee most, to esteem that highly which to Thee is precious, to abhor that which in Thy sight is filthy and unclean."

The childish prayer had been answered, only in middle age, or as middle age approached . . .

Well, let it go. Let it all go. Good-bye! Ethan thought.

The poop, with its yellow-painted lifeboats in their davits, rose and fell, and they stood gazing past its planks standing askew back at the town in the distance Jacqueline had been so impatient to leave; but now she was smiling remotely, her face upheld as though in a dream, or as though the town appeared to her like some town in a dream, under a sort of Gothic spell of enchantment, the post office with its clock-tower and far galloping flag waving farewell, like a turreted castle, even their big beer parlour had to Ethan an air of brooding mystery, as if it were the eternal waterfront tavern. Their happy day!

And indeed in memory it might seem to have been an entirely happy day, and so in time actually become one . . .

Good-bye! And good-bye meant God be with you.

There was a waterfall with an echo they knew, where, to your Good-bye! an echo always seemed to answer "Abye!" and abye was an Anglo-Saxon word meaning "to atone for." But it also meant "to endure."

The ferry tolled, and shipped a spray, the nuns, giggling, ran for the anteroom, while Ethan grabbed Jacqueline who had momentarily lost her footing.

"Shall we go amidships and see if that door leads up on the bridge?"

The door in the anteroom opened from behind just as they reached it, and someone on the threshold stood aside as, tripping everywhere, their steps everywhere overhastened or inhibited by the sea, Ethan still holding Jacqueline's arm, they found in the sudden thunderous gloom, an interior companionway, with a glimmer of windy light on top, and whose rails rose slowly, meeting their grasp. Ethan helped her up the companion to the upper deck, where for a few seconds it seemed all the wind and spray of the Gulf of Georgia caught them in the teeth.

The deck encircled the little glassed-in wheelhouse looking out over the bridge, and there at the wheel stood Jacqueline's obliging skipper of the morning. They smiled and exchanged glances. And smiling too, remembering the bastion, Ethan felt a slight stab of shame as they battled their way forward toward the bridge. Man's conscience was supposed to be an internalization of outward authority, he had read, but what if it were, on the contrary, a kind of externalization of inward authority, but with whom that authority was hardly in touch, barely within one's range of perception, almost outside one's consciousness altogether, a perfect stranger in fact, yet shadowily glimpsed from time to time, a word, just like somebody twirling a wheel in a wheelhouse of his own, coolly smoking a cigar, and exchanging knowing glances with one's wife? Meantime, however that might be, the young couple were also up here, huddling in the lee of the funnel, and the good little priest, in his big shabby boots, his cassock flapping, and standing with his ear inclined to a windward ventilator, as if listening to an imaginary confession. A single ladder at the port side they hadn't seen led down to the black-piled foredeck where, indifferent to the spray blowing over the bows, a hunchback in a sou'wester and oilskins was coiling a long thick rope beside the windlass. So nothing was very mysterious after all. "Brrr it's cold—" said Jacqueline. And there was even apparent up here on the lee side, as they reached it, and looked through the window a sort of lounge, circular, with basket chairs, and a stove, and which connected with the wheelhouse: it looked cosy in there as a tiny back room in an English pub, certainly much warmer than the anteroom downstairs, but its amenities were soured for Jacqueline by its being the theatre at this moment, of a loud altercation, evidently between a new passenger, by no means sober, who had come on board with the cars, and a crew member, a difference of opinion in which seemed mingled in equal parts patience, ferocity, and complete futility, if not actual hebephrenic dilapidation:

"I've fought for all you buzzards for five years in the air force and I'm not going to take any back talk from you. I'm going to Shaughnessy Hospital and as for you, you can drop ezzackly dead!"

"You're not going to O'Shaughnessy Hospital, mac."

It was true he was not. O'Shaughnessy Hospital was on the mainland in Vancouver. But then he might have meant the nursing home.

But the tremendous sight from the bridge! The ferry rolled and worked in the cobalt sea with its blinding causeway of sunlight, while all the magnificent scene before and around them, of deep-forested mountains with the sunset fire lingering on their murderous peaks, and far in the distance, the lone snowy peak of Mount Baker, or old Mount Ararat, seesawed up and down before their eyes violently, as if it were taking place in an adventure film on the screen: there wasn't much to be seen at the moment of Gabriola itself—which, a long thin precipitous island, or as it appeared two islands, it was half hidden at this moment too by a pall of smoke—had changed its shape, as a ship in the distance first seen broadside on seems to have changed shape when now you view it almost from astern, so that you don't know whether it's coming or going; the ferry was shipping seas over her bows, the seaman working on the foredeck was called aft, and this seemed the signal for Jacqueline, who was feeling colder than ever, to go aft too, and she waved her hand at the head of the companionway, before descending to the waist again. Ethan remained alone in the bridge.

And some old mariner's ferment in his blood, perhaps, sustained him to consider that he really *was* standing on a bridge, on the bridge of his own life, of their lives, at one of those moments when lack of continued resolution could wreck them both. Disaster might not come today or tomorrow, but should he revoke the act of will he'd made just now, the act of *his* casting off, this moment would—

Ah God damn it . . . For now a little accident of geography, of direction (the same had disarmed him several times before today) served to confound the courage he imagined he'd just thrown into himself. The ship at present, to avoid a network of shoals, was heading, between lighthouses, not directly at Gabriola, but almost (and almost as it seemed to him secretly) due east, and straight at Eridanus inlet itself. But as if this were not enough, the very elements seemed to have conspired (as before in the bus there had been the trick of geography) in a derisive trick to torment him. For while Gabriola was all but invisible under that pall of smoke (at first this fire had seemed to come from a steamer but now it looked reasonably enough as though it came from an accumulation of autumn leaf fires, or people burning rotten tree stumps off their lands), the mainland, by some sudden shift of dislimning clouds and sunset light now all at once seemed to have drawn very much closer; more diabolical still, mountains that had been far in the background were now, in wild island loveliness, suddenly thrown into bitter bold cold relief, while the nearer mountains seemed vague: Ixtaccihuatelian mysteries of perpetual snows, formerly hidden among the farthest folds of the great mountain chain, enchanted fjords now appeared, though a hundred miles distant, almost before his eyes, and among the former he seemed to see Mount Garibaldi, the sunrise view from their own dear house. And now, there could be no mistake, though some fifty miles distant, minute, yet clear—clear and irrevocably lost perhaps as are those visions of the dead who remembering some aspect of beauty in their old life are drawn to it, and being drawn to it, thereafter haunt it, though perhaps too they can never really find it—

Whatever point they were heading on, every revolution of the engines, every stroke of the propeller, was taking him nearer his beloved and lost home. We live there!

Good-bye! And the echo comes Abye! . . . Was the word in a dictionary? If so, some part of his documental mind informed him, it must be found next to the word "abyss." God help me! But now he didn't want to be helped.

He thought of the last time he'd seen their little house, their last day, that day of moving, only about a month ago, but it seemed five centuries, that day after Labor Day, with no one on the beach any longer save a few fishermen, and some of them not returned yet, but a day far wilder and more autumnal than was this. They'd risen late to find the sky scalloped in Van Gogh-like fierce waves, but remote and silver, one thin dark cloud formed with the top of the mountains a sort of frame for a different, darker movement of the same things into which the paler scallops wildly swirled, and against which the mountains showed an almost shocking serge blue, as in Labrador; a little later, moving the bags out, leaving the boat, the planks askew on the porch—the well!—above them the same sky was even more sensational, great whirlpools and whorls like seashells, suggestive of tremendous wind, and great forces, and much brighter, almost white-silver, with already, low in the west, at midday, a primrose-like brightness, telling of sunset. And later, while they took their last look, these same curdling clouds were dark blue, blue clouds, and an airplane slow as a 1918 Handly Page training plane struggling against the wind, and the sea gulls soaring, and an old gasoline can banging under the cabin in the choppy sea of high tide.

The wind wailed in the rigging. And now Ethan, finding a spot on the bridge where he was hidden from the wheelhouse, near a coil of rope, felt all the fear coming back with redoubled force; fear of the future, fear of himself—how could he fight it? It was as though his whole soul were shivering as great waves of cold fright rushed through it. He felt inwardly like a man who freezes halfway up the rigging, or on a mountain pinnacle, petrified by his own tremors. It was like one of those times when one had wakened up in the morning saying: Ah, I am refreshed, myself at last. Yes, I am renewed and about to jump out of bed to greet the day with courage. But a little later one had not jumped out of bed. And the familiar clothespin tightened on the nose, the ice boiled in the heart and it was only the bed that had taken on a new and terrible significance. For worse than the fear it was this hopelessness that seemed the enemy. Well, he had the mickey of gin, cassia from China, fragrant coriander from Czechoslovakia, spicy juniper from Italy, Valencia peel from Spain—what did he want?—who could resist it? But the screwcap still resisted *him*. He couldn't budge the damned thing, try as he would. It seemed held in a vise.

Try harder. He had bought the gin bottle, hadn't he? Presumably they meant to drink it, or didn't he? He couldn't say he'd resisted the temptation because he couldn't open the bloody bottle. Ethan was half tempted to throw the bottle overboard. No, Jacqueline would like a drink when they got to the Lodge. And so might he. And so why not now. And what had opening a gin bottle got to do with his will anyway, false or true? The gauge was worthless but the metal was priceless: or was it vice versa? But if he couldn't open the gin bottle and have a drink, how was he going to fight this fear, this hopelessness. Ashamed now simply of failure to open the thing he placed the bottle wearily back in his overcoat pocket.

How to fight this fear. Defiance . . . But standing on the bridge again his defiance seemed to blow back on him like ashes flung to windward. Nonetheless he continued to stand on the bridge, facing into the wind with something intended to be a defiant look. Then he walked to leeward and watched the bow wave foaming up to meet him.

Ethan looked toward the mainland again. Yes, it would have been easy. What was not easy was to realize that he'd just evaluated himself as of less worth than a bottle of gin, that the impulse to the act, the abandonment of Jacqueline and his son, and life itself, had not been a velleity, but a genuine impulse, of which he still even could feel the sickening and desperate volition. Great God, had he no courage at all? What of the courage showed every day, every instant, by fishermen, by real pioneers, by soldiers, by sailors, by the shipwrecked, by Jacqueline, by everyone else in the world except him? Well, he had been shipwrecked himself once in a storm on Lake Ontario, on a yachting trip with a couple of partners in his law firm. He had acquitted himself well. He had saved a young couple from drowning in the Niagara River. He possessed a Humane Society medal for it. There had been plenty of opportunities for showing courage just in living at Eridanus, where he had been forced to deal with hazards that were unfamiliar. The great majority of people were courageous on occasion, even out of habit, since they took their lives in their hands every day. But this? What was this? What different kind of courage was required here, in this invisible struggle of which he did not know the real nature.

"You're not going to O'Shaughnessy Hospital, mac."

"Yeah, I am too . . . And you can drop *ezzackly* dead!"

The ludicrous argument still proceeded. And perhaps at last here lay the trouble, that he was as directionless as that unwitting, or unwitted, passenger. Worse: for their passenger at least *thought* he was going somewhere. Or rather, all his aspiration seemed to draw him back to a place he had not only already left, but on the acceptance of whose loss, and its transcending, his very sanity appeared to depend—

Had one of those appalling things happened to him that one read of in ancient manuscripts of the Rosicrucians, but never really believed, whereby he had actually been deprived of his soul? Parted company with it, left it behind? which was to say, right ahead, forever in the realm of the forgotten sunrise! Had Jacqueline and he betrayed the mysterious trust by leaving simply because they were *going* to be evicted? Man faced the possibility of eviction from earth itself, but still went on living without making such a fuss about it. Surely his attachment was not sentimental, however pathological. And if pathological, why was it that now his loss seemed to connect with another loss, with something humanity had lost—that he felt at one too with the homeless and evicted everywhere, yet at the same time as if he were fighting some sort of spiritual battle for them, even without the right weapons to fight it, and even without apparently fighting—with something dark, tragic, overwhelming, inexplicable.

And still Gabriola drew nearer, though not much nearer. Baffling heavy seas, and a head wind, the ferry had not traversed a quarter of the distance yet. And still Eridanus and the little cabin drew nearer, though ever farther away.

—"Pray for me, Father."

On a sudden impulse Ethan had gone to the priest whom he'd caught sight of again and they were standing together in the lee of a ventilator.

"Will you pray for me?—Excuse my speaking to you like this."

"Why yes, my child . . . Gladly . . ."

Ethan was so nervous he could not meet the priest's eyes. But one thing astonished him. The priest was not wearing a cassock at all, just a black overcoat. He had simply imagined the priest was wearing a cassock when, in fact, there was only one place in all Canada where priests wore cassocks, which was in Quebec. Once Ethan had attended a hanging in Quebec, a Hungarian whose few words of French were mostly obscenities, a confessed and unrepentant murderer for whom there had been no adequate defense. Nevertheless Ethan had attended at the request of the murderer's mother to give him what comfort he could: the Hungarian had declined all religious solace. Yet a priest had insisted, despite all insults, upon being present and ready to administer such solace, even if at the last moment on the scaffold—when the Hungarian had suddenly clasped the priest's hand with the words "I believe, Father." One tended to be skeptical of such last-moment repentance and one had heard of similar things before. But to see it happen before your eyes was another matter. The memory was ineradicable in its dramatic mystery, the horror of what was to follow almost obliterated by the inerrarable sense of the miraculous. And it must have been of that priest Ethan was thinking, for though he'd been French-Canadian and was nothing like this priest, Ethan almost felt he was standing on that scaffold again beside him.

"But you are going to Gabriola, you are going to live there?" the priest went on, without waiting for an answer. "With us on Gabriola?"

Ethan kept his eyes cast down; his gaze was now wholly inward, he was terribly ill at ease, moreover he was already beginning to feel slightly ridiculous. They started to pace up and down the deck.

"I don't know, Father," he said at length. "I'm not sure I really want you to pray for me. It's for others. Many others."

"God will know who they are."

"But that's my trouble. I don't think I believe in God. Nor does my wife."

"But if you are truly seeking—? Then you're not a Catholic." The priest smiled.

"Scarcely. And I don't think that I am truly seeking. I feel I've failed in both my duty to God and man," Ethan stammered. "I can't explain even now why I spoke to you . . . I feel like a hypocrite. All I know is I want passionately to *want* not to be a hypocrite!"

"You can come and see me any time on the island, you know, if you're going to stay there for a while, and speak your mind freely."

"I didn't know a Protestant could. You mean, Father, you would even hear confession from a Protestant?"

"Of course . . . Come and see me, bring your troubles, that's what I'm for. We all have to approach God in our own way. Now Buddhism," mused the priest, "there is a very beautiful religion." The priest was silent for a moment, then he said, "Why look, there's an albatross."

"I don't think I ever saw one so close inshore before."

"It must have strayed down from Cape Flattery."

"Yes, or Juan de Fuca Straits."

The albatross was following the now outward bound steamer by whose wash the ferry had just been redundantly caught and which, a cable's length away, seemingly unvexed by the sea, was steaming beneath a gigantic column of smoke. Ethan wanted to go and call Jacqueline but it didn't seem good manners. Moreover he now felt comforted by the priest's presence and by this conversation which he might not have the courage to resume should he break the thread. They watched the beautiful flight of the bird that was not really following the freighter. The albatross had already, without moving a wing tip, far outdistanced it, and now returned sweeping across the Greek freighter's bows with its tremendous sabre wings, like some embodied symbolic fusion of angel with its sword, and now recrossed them, banking, rigidly skimming ahead, buoyantly gliding, toward Gabriola. While the *Aristotle,* high out of the water with thrashing propeller visible, plodded and thudded and thundered after it. They watched until the bird was almost out of sight.

"I'm not sure I know what my deepest troubles are, Father," Ethan said.

"Nor do any of us, my son . . . But God knows."

"I want to *want* to have faith. It sounds childish, doesn't it?"

"Why not?" The priest was silent again, pausing in their resumed walk, then said: "Why not childish? . . . You could repeat the Apostle's Creed, my son, like a child."

"I'm not sure I know what the Apostle's Creed is. Anyhow, if I didn't believe it, what would be the good of repeating it?"

"That's what I meant. Children repeat it, without even understanding it, let alone believing it." The priest looked at him quizzically. "But it's possible that you're one of those to whom dogma in any form is so inimical it would have the wrong effect. Well, you can't be damned for that."

Ethan told him he'd been brought up a Swedenborgian and was perhaps more likely to be damned according to the other's tenets than the priest thought.

"Now *he,*" said the priest benignly with a smile, "was really an expert. You can't say *he* didn't have faith. He'd actually been places and done things, as the Americans say. He had a pretty rugged line of damnation himself, too." Ethan laughed. "But," the understanding and humble old priest went on, "a belief in the supernatural— even based on experience—is not necessarily faith. How shall I say it? For I am well aware that I should probably not say it. It *is* faith—and nearly all faiths should be respected—and can lead to true faith, but it's not the kind of faith you mean. Even though true faith can bring abiding proof of the supernatural."

"Then what is faith?"

"You might try thinking of it as a messenger. Yes, a kind of messenger."

"I thank you from my heart for talking to me, Father."

"You must pray to the Holy Spirit to help you, my son . . . Everything involves self-sacrifice too. You find that out, sooner or later . . . If you and your wife remain on the island, come and see me any time," said the priest, his voice almost lost in the wind, "I have a pretty little chapel on Gabriola, but not many parishioners . . . In fact, at one time I was almost alone there . . . Some people even think that the Spaniards . . . In fact they even believe . . . It's quite a dangerous spot too, perched up there on the cliffs, but people climb up to it. They climb up to it."

Ethan, having failed immediately to find Jacqueline, stood leaning against the bulwarks on the lower deck again watching the bow wave foaming sternward, and a few sea gulls, steadily following the ferry, crying. But for some reason now their cries aroused no answering melancholy within him. It was true that if you suffered long enough and died enough and defied any event completely to cut you down, in the end everything could change very suddenly. Then, just as he'd seemed on the brink of complete despair, the priest had supplied him with a measure of reassurance, indeed a kind of goal. Should they establish themselves on Gabriola, Ethan *would* visit him, *would* visit his chapel, would discuss his problems, and Jacqueline's problems, and their problems. Never had Ethan felt more in need of advice from an older man, be he priest or no. And with this reassurance the priest had given him Ethan found he had attained too, on the sudden, a measure of acceptance. One had to take what might come. And life's very uncertainty was exciting. It was exciting to see what was going to happen next, just as William James had pointed out . . . And with this realization, this acceptance, while with one part of his mind he may have been half congratulating himself that the priest was indeed praying for him, in effect he forgot the priest altogether. No, in a word, he was in a mood of strange self-congratulation. He began to walk up and down the deck with his hands in his pockets and even managed to inject a certain jauntiness into his stride. He began to whistle. Ethan had an impression of self-mastery, though upon what, precisely, it was founded, was none too clear. Positively, or almost positively, and for the first time in a long while he felt in tune with his destiny and that of the universe. The feeling was not unlike one of triumph.

Ouch!

"Hail to the sea gull, in the empyrean!
Who man's head useth, as a spare latrine."

"Returned man?" The old-timer in the mackinaw and the velour hat, which he bravely had not removed, was standing beside Ethan, who, startled, once more tried to incline his ear to the rich nostalgic breath that was suddenly like that of the old pensioner who had directed them to the bastion, and no doubt very much the same as his own.

"Been in the cavalry, may I ask?"

"No, I'm in the lavatory at the moment . . . That is, I mean one of those sea gulls apparently thought I was one."

"There's only two kinds of people walk like you do, with that swagger. I just said to Mrs. Rountree, you were either a cavalry officer or a sailor."

"You can tell Mrs. Rountree I shall be damned careful not to swagger again when a sea gull's looking at me."

"So you're a sailor, eh mac?"

"I'm a lawyer . . . Turned would-be carpenter," Ethan added, smiling and rubbing his head with his handkerchief.

"Carpenter. Ah, that's something more in my line. And you're going——"

Ethan turned: some incident was taking place behind them in the anteroom. "Excuse me, half a moment, sir," he said to the old man.

In the anteroom the pale woman in black with the scarf sat on one of the benches. But the scarf, though still wrapped around her head, was no longer wrapped over her mouth. In its place the woman was holding a handkerchief pressed to her mouth—the handkerchief was stained with bright blood. The woman's dark frightened eyes were turned up to her husband who bent over her, his arm about her shoulder, his face, under his soiled drooping hat, strained with tenderness and anxiety.

The two shirt-sleeved crew members stood by, there was a low-voiced discussion, then one disappeared through the door that opened on the companion to the upper deck. Other passengers—but where still was Jacqueline? where the nuns? (and the good priest, wasting his time praying for him on the upper deck!)—even the youngsters wanting to help, the lady with the bandaged eye and *La Chartreuse de Parme* under her shiny coat sleeve, stood, hesitant to embarrass, but perhaps also from grim common sense, and experience, in the background, like compassionate figures in a Greek chorus waiting for their cue, so that Ethan had time to be impressed by the touching tragic dignity of the scene, even while it dawned on him he might be called upon to act as choragus himself.

"What's wrong here, mister," he whispered, knowing the worst, to the remaining crew member.

"It's poor Mrs. Neiman, buddy. She's had all her teeth out this afternoon."

This did not alter the tragic dignity of the scene, though just for the moment it had seemed to: there was nothing funny about having all your teeth out.

Ethan now approached the husband.

"Can I help, Mr. Neiman?"

"Trouble is, too, I forgot to bring a sedative . . . She's hemorrhaging pretty badly."

"There isn't a doctor on board?"

"Not that I know of—the other sailor's gone to speak to the captain."

"What sort of anesthetic did she have?"

"A.C.E."

"What's that?"

"Alcohol, chloroform and ether . . . She just won't take gas."

"Gas. I thought they blocked off—didn't she have a local?"

"She won't take nothing but this here A.C.E. No injections. She had a wisdom tooth out in 1933 on her birthday, very successful operation and she sticks by it. The same treatment, I mean. And the same dentist. Sticks by him too, even though, to tell the truth, he hasn't got no certificate. He was up north with Wiley Post. Very nice fellow when you get to know him, though."

"Wiley *Post?*"

"Yes, Wiley Post and Will Rogers too."

"What's Will Rogers got to do with it?"

"It's like this. She just won't bow to any of these new-fangled specifics. No persuading her."

"Then a little more alcohol won't hurt her, would it, on top of the anesthetic? What about a slug of gin?"

"If she can get it down." Mrs. Neiman shook her head, then nodded it. She even attempted a smile of sorts.

"Thanks a lot," said Mr. Neiman.

"It won't stop the bleeding but it'll ease the pain." Ethan had produced his bottle of rare cordials (rarified by tangy cassia from China, fragrant coriander from Czechoslovakia, spicy juniper from Italy, Valencia peel from Spain) and unscrewed the cap in an instant, surprisingly, though it was true his former efforts had probably loosened it, while the other sailor disappeared through the door (from which Jacqueline now emerged with a look of slow bewilderment) to fetch a tumbler. Ethan poured a quartern of gin

x

into the tumbler and handed it to Mr. Neiman. "I'll leave you and Mrs. Neiman the bottle, if you like."

"No, that's fine and dandy."

"Tell me if you want any more. Have one yourself."

"No thanks. This is more than enough. The bleeding'll probably stop in a minute."

Jacqueline and Ethan stood by the rail carefully staring the other way.

"You're sure there's nothing more we can do," Ethan whispered, and Jacqueline shook her head, though gravely: she looked unnaturally worried, even slightly antagonistic.

"Poor thing. No, the nuns came in again just as we left, and they can help her better than we can, if there's anything to do." Her voice trailed off despondently.

"What a damn shame. Let's hope she'll be all right. Oughtn't she to be in the lounge where it's warmer?"

"She'd better not move, the way she is."

"I'm not sure the nuns will approve my treatment."

"I wouldn't be surprised."

CHAPTER 36 🌿 *Not the Point of No Return*

Shortly they became aware that the mountains and forests were sweeping past them in a wide arc. The ferry was going about. No doubt of it. Standing now out of earshot of the Neimans they watched, dismayed, their ferry with helm hard over still swinging steadily round.

Compassionate and appalling, and in Ethan's experience, quite unprecedented act, as heartening in its respect for the individual as it was totally if ambiguously discouraging at this moment to the Llewelyns—the skipper was putting back to Nanaimo for the woman in black.

"Never mind, Jacqueline, sweetheart."

"But we'll be too late! It'll be dark!" cried Jacqueline. "We might just as well get off ourselves and stay in Nanaimo."

"Hold on. Remember success or failure of all human effort is influenced if not actually controlled by planetarium."

"But——"

"Don't cry, my truelove—Remember mysticism is produced by a conbustion of the grey vascular matter in the sensorium."

"But darling, I can't——"

"Not forgetting also that it may be combined with intellectual action, in which case the grey matter in the cerebral hemisphere undergoes oxidation as well."

"Oh God . . . you idiot . . . Where are you going?"

"I was going to see if the gin had killed Mrs. Neiman . . . No," he said, returning, "she seems distinctly better."

"Clown."

Frère *Jac*ques
Frère *Jac*ques

It was a sad Frère Jacques.

And, drowning it, sombre, funereal, majestic, and with clacking needle, Aunt Hagar strode forth once more in Ethan's brain. And now he thought he knew what Gwyn might have been trying to say to him in the C.P.R. building which, incidentally, they were now once more approaching (and at which, the evening boat from Vancouver—another prisoner in the dock—could be seen distantly but distinctly and meekly, lying much as the afternoon boat had been lying this morning). When he'd seen his young brother off that last time, drinking beer with him in the Exchange Station Restaurant in Liverpool, it hadn't been the first time he'd seen him off on that fatal trip, as it happened, but the second. And it was that *hyrkontrakt* that was the trouble! Ethan had seen him off from the same station the day before, impressed enough by his brother's guts (for it can require the strength of a healthy will sometimes to make even a fatal mistake) in taking the job at all, and the parting had been a wrench for them both. Gwyn (who must have been frightened half to death—Archangel, the White Sea, the very words were enough to put the fear of God into you) had then traveled by train—and by slow train it can be one of the longest hours of all God's journeys—to Preston, joined his ship, which was to sail the next day, only to discover in the morning, with a gigantic hangover, the ship having meantime warped over to the coal pits, that as a foreigner, from the Norse standpoint, he could not sign on with the captain, who had not been aboard the previous night, *in* Preston, as he had been told, but must return to Liverpool where there was a Norwegian consulate, a point on which Ethan might have advised him. In Liverpool again, having settled matters somehow with the Norsk Konsulat, he ran, quite by accident, into Ethan himself, which produced the second and last occasion of their drinking beer together and getting their good-byes over. Yet how much added desperation of will—for Ethan had offered his brother every inducement to stay—was needed now to take that second train, and on arrival once more in Preston (a town scarcely less black for being the birthplace of Francis Thompson, and which was besides deserted for the wakes), to force his steps down through the rain a second time to the dreary Ribble docks where his ship was on the very point of sailing without him. How much more it must have required of him then to walk, at the last moment, that impossible tenuous plank from the coal tips. And the vessel bound for Archangel of all places; where most likely he would never have been able to get ashore, even had one wanted to. For it must have been as if his original impulse to go were drained already of all its romance and adventure, and nothing remained but the horrible anger, the platitudinous reality, the bitter nonego, the ordeal that was to end in his even more bitter death. But this recollection did not come to Ethan like a warning. On the contrary there was something almost jocular and encouraging about it in its dismal way. Gwyn too had a sense of humor. And Ethan began to laugh.

"Oh God, I knew when I saw that woman in black—" Jacqueline was saying.

"Come now, less evil omens, my love. She's no more an evil omen than you are . . . I was going to say that all we needed now was to see an albatross, but I've gone one better than that, I've just *seen* an albatross while talking to a priest. Moreover it's Edgar Allan Poe's birthday."

"I thought he died a hundred years ago today."

"That's true too."

"You *didn't* really see an albatross?" Jacqueline brightened for a moment, raising her eyes.

"I did."

"Why didn't you *call* me?"

"I told you, I was talking to this priest. The priest has invited us to visit his chapel situated on the side of a cliff . . . I hoped you'd see the albatross. Then I was afraid you'd think it was another bad omen."

"I wish I'd never heard of these Gulf Islands. I think there's something sinister about them. Daddy used to tell me there was a black magician called Brother Twelve who lived on one with his disciples, practicing evil rites. Gabriola will probably turn out to be a leper colony, with only five inhabitants . . . *If* we ever get there."

"No, that's another Gulf Island." The poor lepers had gone away or died, their dwellings fallen, yet fishermen still told tales Ethan had heard in Eridanus of seeing them, on moonlit nights, wandering among the ruins and silver driftwood. "You've overlooked the one that used to be a prison island," he said. "How do you mean *if* we ever get there?"

"Look at the sea."

"You seriously think—?"

"You don't suppose I'm so mean as to make such a fuss about going back if I thought the skipper was doing it simply for that poor woman. With that nursing home and all, she could get treatment on Gabriola."

"We only have to ask to find out."

"What I need is a drink."

And it was true, Ethan did not want to ask either. And it was also true that the weather was getting much worse. There was a tearing wind. On this reverse trip the ferry was pitching into a rough crossflowing current with a sort of abandoned bounding corkscrew motion. One moment it felt as though she were being borne up and along the swells like a surf rider, the surf travelling in the wrong direction. The next moment she seemed sinking deeply in the trough making no headway.

"Well, I've got the bottle open."

"Then hand it over."

Ethan, handing her the bottle, glanced at her laughing with amusement and astonishment. But the amusement was shortly replaced by a sharp sense of self-rebuke. Clown! she had called him. The fact was, though, that while he had very rarely seen Jacqueline take a neat drink before out of a bottle he had never before seen her so quietly ferocious. It was as if he had seen her for the first time, almost as if he had just met her, and the implications were not obvious. Whether she perceived it or not, the drink—and now, coughing, she was taking another one—was a criticism of him. And well was it justified! If his concern for Mrs. Neiman had been genuine, his compassion spontaneous, Ethan now thought, hadn't his action in offering the poor woman the gin as much hypocrisy in it as charity? Odd though it was the screw cap turned so easily, hadn't it really been the excuse his conscience needed to open the bottle so that he could have a drink himself? And the point was too that even that was, as it were, an act of public charity. Public compassion. More histrionics. Everyone would see what a decent magnanimous fellow Ethan Llewelyn was. And was not this a clue to his whole nature? Even, obscurely, his whole life? Was his new attitude, if he had a new attitude, if he had really arrived at a decision, to the Chambers case essentially any different? Charity should begin at home, even if one were homeless. And though two people could not apparently be any closer than they were nowadays, how had he neglected her, Jacqueline, and that not just during the last years but all their married life? What did he know essentially of her hidden troubles, hopes, despairs, frustrations? How much did he help? How much was he helping sympathizing now? And how much did he care? Ah, he cared! But she was not getting any younger either. And what might he not drive her to by this neglect? Far from a decent magnanimous fellow he was becoming as a husband a monstrosity of selfishness, childishness, and self-pity. And on top of that he spoiled everything with his flippancy. Did he cherish Jacqueline as tenderly as Mr. Neiman so obviously cherished his wife? Alas, that had perhaps occurred to Jacqueline too. He was becoming downright irresponsible. He had better change himself and that starting right this moment. That was more important than whether they got the skipper's house or he built a house or whatever the hell they did. He would do what *she* wanted, in future. His own will was no good. It was sick. *He* was sick. Self-sacrifice! The priest was right. He would sacrifice himself for his wife, starting at this instant . . . Easier said than done. And more complicated it was already turning out even than that.

"Thank you," Jacqueline said, returning the bottle with a rather sarcastic and dangerous smile. "But won't you?"

"No, I don't think I care to have one . . . Not straight."

"Do you mean you *didn't* take one?"

"No."

"Not after you got it open and gave a drink to Mrs. Neiman? You want to know why I'm so anxious. All right I'll tell you. Because—And do you know what can happen to *us?*" Jacqueline said, turning up the collar of her fur coat and her head sideways, putting her nose into the collar to keep it warm, and peering out at him one dark, long-lashed eye, "we may have to spend the night in Nanaimo. We won't be able to get in touch with the Anderson Lodge. We can't reach Angela. We might lose the opportunity of a house altogether. If the storm keeps up we might be stuck in that sinkhole for days."

Ethan was silent for a moment. Then he said: "I can find out for sure what the skipper's up to."

"No you don't. You've got the gin. You stay where you are, Ethan Llewelyn. And you *can't* find out anyhow."

"What are you being so confoundedly unreasonable about? Why can't I find out?"

"Because the skipper doesn't know."

"How do *you* know that?"

"I asked him. That's why. Just before the sailor came in to tell him about Mrs. Neiman, I suppose, though I didn't hear what the sailor said . . . I've got it figured out now . . . It's sure he's turning back for Mrs. Neiman but that's partly because he doesn't want to take the risk of having to turn back much later with her aboard . . . There's a much more dangerous stretch of sea farther out in the Gulf and nearer Gabriola and you never can tell what the weather's going to do from one moment to the next. So he said . . . So what are *you* thinking about?"

"If you want to know I was thinking that that doesn't mean we're *not* going to Gabriola, and that it still remains a sporting action . . . and I was also thinking about my younger brother Gwyn that time he had to go back to Liverpool and sign on the ship he'd already joined the day before in Preston."

"You mean you're only too glad to be going back to Nanaimo, don't you? And do you know what I'm thinking? You don't have to be so bloody goddam superciliously noble."

"No."

"So what will happen will be precisely this . . . by the way, tell me what did you decide just now?"

"I decided not to have a drink. It is an obscure feeling, as your father would say, resembling the fantastic passions of the dead in Elysian Field."

"Never again? Not even now?"

"Not until something really wonderful happens to us. Then I'll celebrate with you."

"So what will happen will be precisely this . . . We'll arrive in Nanaimo and you won't have a drink."

"No."

"But where can we put up save the Ocean Spray? What are we going to *do!*"

"We could go to a cinema. They're showing a double bill: *Mr. Blanding's Dream House* and *The Long Voyage Home.*"

Ethan thought of the albatross again, heeling over in the wind and then sweeping forward, with its sabre wings, beyond the S.S. *Aristotle*. A messenger?

"And is this hair shirt and joyless prohibition technique to persist even if we *do* get to Gabriola," inquired Jacqueline timidly, putting her hand on Ethan's arm.

Ethan smiled. "If you honestly think that's in the category of the wonderful I'll relax a bit. But not before we get there. You can take over then. God, don't I sound sententious."

"Not a bit. I've no idea why I behaved like that. It must have been an attack of the vapours or something."

"Hooray, the harbor's near, lo the red light," Ethan sang out.

But the outlook, as the harbor was nearing, appeared less than hopeful, though he hadn't the heart to say so, not to say the prospect of a drinkless evening in Nanaimo ghastly beyond words. The ferry, even closer inshore, as they were now, seemed shipping too many seas to be altogether secure with the deck cargo they had on her. Great dollops of spray, cold as snow, fell on the deck, in the motorcars, even on the washing machine, sousing it thoroughly. The screw kicked out, shuddering, and from down below came a noise like a furious motorcycle with a knocking engine. The stern with its chain and its unfinished pseudo-poop, behind which the sea gulls were steadily and faithfully rowing back to Nanaimo with them, circled and dropped down against the sky, in a manner suggesting they were in a sou'westerly in mid-Atlantic, instead of two miles offshore in the Gulf of Georgia. While the lifeboats, rising and circling and falling in concert wore, with their fresh paint, an altogether new air of potential usefulness.

But as Nanaimo Harbor grew closer still it suddenly became much calmer. And then warmer. Though the flag still galloped aloft on the post office there was scarcely a cat's-paw of wind on the water. They made out some drinkers drinking in the Ocean Spray, where somebody—could it be Henry Knight himself?—was watching the approaching ferry through a window. There was the almost dear old bastion: and there their very bus of this morning perhaps, bereaved of them, or a similar one, beginning its return journey to Victoria, prowling very slowly through the steep streets, bugling, now hidden behind a house, now crawling down a hill, now going musically round a corner, now down another hill, its panting clearly audible.

And now Nanaimo did not seem so bad, even if you couldn't have a drink there. It was even like an old friend who will have a drink anyway, even if you don't. And now, suddenly, Nanaimo seemed more than familiar for a moment, like a town they had known all their lives, heavy with memories of hopes, frustrations, departures and reunions, news of births and deaths, despairs, joys—

> —Have you ever seen a bald sheep?
> Chicken n' the nest.
> Jumboburger.

The engines were switched off.

—There are some feelings so complicated that though they seem indefinably, yet surely, to concern some mysterious order beyond this life, which just as surely, we feel, affects our life, they rarely find conscious expression. And were we to try and express all this in terms of our belief in some supernatural concern for ourselves at such moments, a concern which seems to be leading us on to our design, or purposely hindering us from executing it, we would sound ridiculous, even a little insane. In fact, a step further, into obsession, and insanity, as William James has pointed out, is exactly what the belief may turn into. And, no doubt, as has also been said, it involves a primitive method of thinking the consciousness of civilized man has, or is reputed to have, largely discarded. There is nothing like a series of misfortunes, however, Ethan thought, to make us forget our hard-won battles against the irrational and start us thinking that way again. The Llewelyns had thought that way for so long indeed that they no longer saw anything unusual, let alone uncivilized, about the sheer multiplicity of the signs and portents and circumstances that hurtled—or which they perceived as hurtling—about their destinies, or lurked, observing them, from appropriate coigns of vantage. Certain stupid omens were of course in a different category; at best they made a joke of them, at worst a single crow could spoil a whole afternoon. They only took them with half-seriousness, or none at all, and that depending on their mood. The casual notation of omens was a form of pastime, and at that, of all pastimes, probably the most unrewarding. But what of the serious, the desperately serious, the uncanny, the inexplicable aspect of certain coincidences. The Llewelyns used to refer to a particularly coincidence-ridden day as a sign they were "in the current." Today they had certainly been "in the current" and had scarcely bothered even to mention it. What if—Ethan now reflected —setting apart those that seemed to come about through some correspondence between the subnormal world and the abnormally suspicious—certain coincidences were really brought into being to remind us that a divine supernatural order exists?

Could it be that it was rather as if, on our journey through life, some guardian spirit causes our attention to be drawn, at such moments, to certain combinations, whether of events, or persons or things, but which we recognize, as speaking to us in a secret language, to remind us that we are not altogether unwatched, and so encourage us to our highest endeavor, and especially is this true when we most need help, which is almost the same as saying when we most need assurance that our lives are not valueless? At worst, it is true, we fear it might be the devil. But if beneficent, if not diabolic, then what is it, if it is not God, or of God, this eye that hears, this voice that thinks, this heart that speaks, this embodied hallucination that foresees, with more than crystal clarity, and divine speech. Like light, but quicker than light, this spirit must be, and able to be in a thousand places at once in a thousand disguises, most of them, as befits our intelligence, absurd, this spirit that terrifies without terror, but that endeavors, above all to communicate, to say no more than perhaps, "Hold on, I am here!"

So it was now, as they approached Nanaimo again, gliding, free-wheeling over the calm water back to Nanaimo, Ethan had, suddenly, the most extraordinary sense of being watched, a sense, too, as if he were about to encounter, not merely a coincidence, but the most important thing that had happened in his entire life: at the same time, all of a sudden, all that occurred to them during their day, seemed, not merely suffused with a significance, and interrelated, as if part of some unknown system of logic, but leading up to this very moment: the lumber train at the level-crossing, his thoughts and the stranger's conversation at the level-crossing itself, the difficulties in finding out about getting to Gabriola, the bastion, the bastion itself, the seemingly irrelevant, or perhaps not so seemingly irrelevant, fact that there was a real estate agency in the bastion, the wonderful window at the Ocean Spray, the horrendous Men's parlour—Henry Knight—the difficulties in getting in touch with Gabriola, and then the further delays, at the auto ferry, the conversation with the priest, the albatross, the poor woman's hemorrhage—even Edgar Allan Poe's centenary and now their return—in a way he couldn't have explained, all of these things seemed leading up to this moment, which was of all moments the most unexpected, their return to Nanaimo itself—*why* had they returned, and would they—?

Have you ever seen a bald sheep? Mother Gettle's Kettle-Simmered Soup, M'mm Good!

But the moment was already over.

"Thank you, Tim."

"Thank you, Bill."

No dogs on Newcastle Island Resort . . . Smout Ferry Company. Produce of China.

But the bulwarks of the ferry were flush with the landing stage which no longer skreeked or plunged but was as motionless in the dead calm water as if it had been built on piles and Mr. Neiman had guided Mrs. Neiman onto it, the veteran lumbering after them, happily one hoped just in time to catch the evening boat to Vancouver at the C.P.R. wharf where he had made his mistake, in just the time too that it took a newsboy who must have seen the returning ferry to hurl aboard a bundle of newspapers tied with a string that must have come by the same boat. Seeing he was carrying in his bag some extra copies of the *Vancouver Messenger* Ethan shouted and tossed him a dime, which he dexterously caught with one hand, while he slipped out a paper, folded it and tossed it to Ethan with the other.

The next moment the mountains and forests were sweeping past them again on the same wide arc as before, though in a contrary direction. Beginning: beginning again: beginning yet again. Off we go! Once more they were bound for Gabriola.

CHAPTER 37

🕲 *Uberimae Fides*

*F*rère *Jacques* . . .

"So you see—" Ethan turned to Jacqueline with an almost delighted laugh. They leaned on the rail, smiling at each other, half glancing at the newspaper, Ethan taking the first section, and Jacqueline the second, as was their habit. He hated to read the paper, with its possible evening threat of doom every day, but just the same, that did not prevent him from buying it, whenever he had the opportunity.

"Ethan, my God!—" Jacqueline cried out.

She folded her paper, which was now flapping in a small breeze, and seemed trying to point, though her fingers were suddenly trembling so wildly STONED BABY DYING. PROBE ORDERED INTO SEX BOOKS. JUVENILE DELINQUENCY ON THE he couldn't make out to begin with at or what at this moment he thought it INCREASE. GET TOUGH SAYS MAGISTRATE CHIEF CHARGE AUTHORITARIAN GROSS INSULT was at, no doubt what he feared more than death, at a small sub-headline UN-CANADIAN ATTITUDE CITIZENS ORDERED INFORM ON ALL ECCENTRICS SACRED DUTY at the bottom of the page. THE MIGHTY NECHAKO RIVER IS NO MORE! *"To see the beavers, on a sandbar.* The Llewelyns held each other at arm's length, they stared into *crying like babies because all the water has gone is enough to make many* one another's eyes endlessly, then they flung their arms around each *people cry."* HALF A COCKER SPANIEL FOUND ON DOORSTEP. WHOLESALE SLAUGHTER other in bewilderment. ERIDANUS SQUATTERS REPRIEVED . . . As if he were an angel, or a sea gull hovering over it Ethan saw the inlet in the clear October evening light, the carved mountains with their splashes of fresh white snow, the deep forest with just the tops of the tallest trees catching the sunlight, the row of little cabins beneath reflected in the water, now at high slack. He saw their own cabin, the tame sea gulls still circling over it and now alighting on the porch, wings outspread, and then furled with a little shake, as the great white birds settled down like doves. Down the beach old Mauger would be reading his evening paper, under his oil lamp. Ethan saw him reading thus, and felt his hope and brave joy as he too read this article. Far across the water in Port Boden a lonely bell was ringing, and now a fishing boat with tall white masts swept downstream as the tide turned.

> The Eridanus squatters, among whom are only a handful of year-round residents, mostly fishermen, the rest being the owners of summer cottages or weekend cottages there, and who have been recently a subject of controversy and under the edict of eviction have been reprieved. Certain factions had accused them of holding up the development of the district, but the acting mayor said that after investigation he was convinced they were doing no harm. Plans for a park site have now been abandoned due to a dispute regarding back taxes. "The land these squatters occupy is government land," he said. "They're a clean decent bunch of people and they're not breaking any law by living there. Of course, if someone buys the land that's different. But so far as I'm concerned they can stay where they are until some definite plan for the property is put into action."

"The well!"
"The boat!"
"The ducks!"
"The forest!"
"Jimmy!"
"Mauger!"
"How glad they'll be!"

"Can't you see their faces?"

"Ethan," Jacqueline said uncertainly, after a moment. "But we don't *need* to find a house on Gabriola now. We can go back."

Ethan gazed down at her, he smiled and shook his head. "No," he said. "We need to find a house more than ever now."

"But—"

"Darling, it's only a reprieve, the same thing will happen all over again next spring, or next fall, or the next. We couldn't live there the rest of our lives anyhow."

"But we could stay there until they *do* throw us out."

"Jacky dearest, it wouldn't work. You know, I got so I felt I owned that whole forty acres, I felt just like an English squire. And the more I thought I owned it the more selfish I got about it, and the more I anguished over losing it. And the point is, we *couldn't* own it. I mean, we couldn't own it as it is, and if it ever got so we could, we wouldn't want it, it would be so different. Oh dear, that's not very clear I'm afraid, but what I'm trying to say is something like this: part of what's so wonderful there is that it isn't properly speaking anywhere at all, it's like living right out of the world altogether. In Paradise, sort of. In a way . . . But it wasn't fair to you in many ways."

"Oh Ethan, you know I loved it, You know I did, I do."

"Yes. It wouldn't have been good if you hadn't. But that isn't quite the point either. Perhaps it's something like a sunrise: when it's at its very best you say, oh, if it would just stay like that forever, but if it did you'd never know what full noon was like, or midnight either. No, it was time to leave, however much it hurts. Time to——"

"Mrs. Neiman, poor soul," the old-timer spoke again at Ethan's elbow. "Well, she had all her teeth out today, you know . . . Strangers here, aren't you? I reckon you folks were afraid we were going to tie up for the night in Nanaimo. But the wind's dropped now, we'll make it all right."

Frère *Jacques*

Frère *Jacques*

Y

"Strangers?" Ethan quickly, rather suspiciously took him up. "But we may not be."

"Don't harass yourself, darling," Jacqueline said. "Let's just wait and see what happens. And meanwhile, what about the inner man—?"

"Would I say that this was in the category of something wonderful that had happened to us," Ethan burst out with a roar of laughter. "Yes, I certainly would. But I'd rather like to share my drink with someone. I feel almost too good to——"

"Ask the old man."

The crushed-down velour and the mackinaw had turned away slightly but in response to their invitation the old man replied smiling, raising his hat, and every bit as though he'd been expecting it:

"Does a duck swim?"

"We've just got good news." Ethan stopped, catching Jacqueline's eyes that plainly said, "Don't let's go into that at the moment."

"—But we're thinking of buying a house or building on Gabriola."

"I'll take a symbolic one," Ethan said to Jacqueline. But he took a single generous swallow—downing it, drinking the old man's health, and then Jacqueline's—and rarely had the throat-smarting fire tasted so good. And as the gin bottle went round, Ethan declining the next, the old man's faded but still sharp and twinkling eyes regarded Jacqueline with friendliness, hostility and curiosity. For Ethan himself he had no eyes at all and Ethan had the feeling that he himself had already been summed up, somewhat to his discredit.

"Eh?" the old man now squinted directly up at Ethan, cupping his hand round his ear, and tilting his head. It was an impish trick Ethan felt to be directed toward their mutual strangeness or apparent over-correctitude or accent, their enunciation, its *Englishness* though neither had really an "English" accent, nor yet quite a Scottish or a Welsh one: at the same time to him, no doubt, it was not a generic Canadian accent, he missed that rasping burring derivative American tone, and since it was not a Manx-Gaelic accent either, he disliked it on principle as something pretending to a supposed superiority of some kind toward which he preserved both an innate hostility and a tendency to suspect the ulterior motives of its owners, even though he was most clearly and embarrassingly won over by Jacqueline: yes, he accepted it in her, her title to it, and not his, so by that squint Ethan felt himself doubly set aside once more and created outcast.

"Do you know Captain Duquesne's place?" Jacqueline asked.

"Lived on Gabriola Island for twenty years, and know every inch of it," the old man said proudly, and no, he did not seem to be really deaf.

> Frère *Jac*ques
> Frère *Jac*ques
> Dormez *vous?*
> Dormez *vous?*
> Sonnez les ma*tine*s!

"Oh, then you'll know Captain Duquesne's place?"

"Sandstone is all right, yes," said the old man cautiously, after a while.

Ethan and Jacqueline exchanged a covert glance and Jacqueline was now inquiring, nobly as it seemed to Ethan: "Is there a sawmill on Gabriola?"

"Mill? Oh, sometimes these mills, you know . . . cut so many thousand, then they take two hundred and fifty feet for their share of their cutting it. Regular barter business, little mills on the coast, or in the interior, come to that, in Nanaimo . . . they even have arbutus growing, beautiful it is, on some of the rocks and the bluffs you see it, arbutus growing up to the Seymour Narrows . . ."

"*Duquesne,*" carefully pronounced Jacqueline, "we were thinking of buying Captain *Duquesne's* place."

"Aye. Wood's better felled in the winter, for the sap is down. Get it sawn up and stack it in the wind. Some fellow's here'll cut fir for planking leave it a couple years, to air dry." He turned to Jacqueline with again a sort of stubborn impishness. "Well . . . he could put the frame up, it would dry anyway. If he felled it in October, this month, or November, he could build it in the spring and stack it of course, he *could*—even though he didn't get the best results. Aye, wood'll rot quicker if it's used when it's green. Seasoned lumber isn't so much because of the shrinkage but because it won't rot so soon. When you paint unseasoned lumber you just lock up the moisture in it."

"Yes, my husband—" And then, "Do you know anything about the Lovell lot that was for sale?" Jacqueline asked, avoiding Ethan's eye.

The old man chuckled. "Bring a shovel, lad, he told me, I remember that time, t'was in—no matter—bring a shovel, lad, and we'll go and get some oak. Dig here, that's where it is. What the plague was the matter with the man?" He chuckled gleefully. "Starting to dig in the ground. Dig it up—what's the idea, 'fraid of somebody stealing it? I said. No, Lloyd's said it had to be buried for seven years. Aye. T'was good too. Sap, spunky-like, ivory-colored, you know. Rest of the wood nice, firm. You couldn't put any sap into the construction of the boat. The wood, well . . . darker-looking color, but just like a green tree, nice for the adze . . . Pieces of oak ribs, condemned. Yes, missus," he added abruptly.

"But you must know Mrs. Angela d'Arrivee then. She's lived on Gabriola for fifteen years," interposed Ethan quickly, thinking: *The thin oak plank that separates the mariner from death.*

"Invariably fir. Oh yes." The old-timer nodded. "Cedar's soft, the nails go in—but it doesn't stand any working! Nails pull. Aye, fir's ten times stronger for the frame, lad. But cedar for the two-by-twelves instead of four. Doesn't rot so quickly in the damp. You take hemlock now . . . has to be kept wet or dry. Wet will last forever, as witness my old flume, the wood's good after eighteen years. But fir's stronger than cedar . . ."

"Captain Duquesne———?"

"Very nice that way. I had a preemption at Hyacinth Bay and I never could attend to it. You'd love to have the time and fell some of those trees, so perfectly matched, carrying the thickness of the butt way up into the top branches." He lifted his hand, fingers loosely curled, and gazed upward, smiling. "A definite taper in them you know." He looked from Ethan to Jacqueline, and back to Ethan again, shaking his head a little, almost dreamily, then suddenly he was very brisk and businesslike. "Well, take some good, straight-grained cedar—make a good club out of a hemlock branch, you can—and split some shakes. When you come to splitting cedar you find such a different nature from one tree to another! Good night, all." He walked off swiftly, head down, muttering to himself.

Then he returned. "Good luck," he turned back toward the lounge (the door of which they held, staggeringly, open) waving at them. "If you ever want my help . . . I'll be seeing you."

"Good-bye for the present."

"Good-bye for the present."

Well, time and heart enough to find out about everything now . . . The Llewelyns were battling out on deck themselves. The little yellow ferry boat was going at a fine speed now. They were already right out of Nanaimo Harbor again, and past the lighthouse on the point—was that Hangman's Point?—they'd just seen from the window of the Ocean Spray, and were plunging joyfully through the long deep swells. The *Aristotle* was a scribble of smoke on the horizon. The freighter bound for Newcastle, N.S.W., stood out to sea, outward bound. A fishing boat with tall white masts was running and dashing along behind them, just astern. And mysteriously, there was a little toy boat too, adrift, bobbing there. Lost. There was a boundless sense of space, cleanliness, speed, light, and rocketing white gulls.

Ethan turned round, leaning his shoulders against the rail, staring at the deck. He saw the rain falling in Eridanus with the sound of muted ghostly sleigh bells, and the raindrops looking like little balls, then the sun breaking through and two rainbows forming slowly, then it was raining harder than ever and the rain no longer sounded like bells; it was seething, rustling, whispering. Then the sunlight hit the rain again and the sea was covered with silver and diamond sequins, as it rained harder and harder and the sun became brighter and brighter, through a low rift in the clouds, and now it looked as if the sea were smoking, fuming. Then the ecstacies of swallows against the black storm clouds, a white boat sailing into the rainbow, and a far, far white gull, like a disembodied animated whiteness moving . . .

Ethan turned straight round, looking ahead. There was another point ahead, with yet another lighthouse on it and beyond that lay Gabriola still in sunlight. It was too far to distinguish any details, but there appeared to be two high hills, with a valley between in the center. And all the hope of his heart flowed out to it. Ah, that he might find a home there, for Jacqueline and his son! . . . From the left-hand hill, not far across the water, a column of deep blue smoke rose straight into the sky, then caught the wind and swept off sideways, like a great hand, beckoning. Someone was probably burning tree stumps to clear their land.

"Ethan," Jacqueline said, looking up from her paper. "What do you know! There's going to be a great shower of meteors tonight! Is that a good omen?"

"I don't know what The McCandless would say, but I'm sure it is."

Jacqueline chuckled. "Dad'd make *some*thing of it, you can be sure of that . . . Leonids, it says here, whatever that is. And they'll start about ten o'clock and go on till after midnight."

"Well, we'll do this, then." Ethan put his arm around her shoulders. "We'll get to the Lodge, have a drink and some dinner, and then go down to Angela's, if it's not too far away, and find out where the skipper's house is. We can't very well look at it tonight, but if there's no one in it we might watch the meteors from the porch, or the shore in front. That would give us a feeling of home already."

"No, let's don't go to Angela's tonight at all. Let's just be together. We can probably find out from the Lodge where the Lovell's lot is and we might walk over to there, if it's not too far."

"Whatever would make you happy, sweetheart."

"It probably comes down to whichever is near enough," Jacqueline said practically. And then, with a lightning change of mood, she cried, "Oh Ethan, it's going to be so exciting. There's a full moon, so it doesn't matter at all that we forgot the flashlight. We'll walk along the shore, I can see it all, already—"

Standing at the rail, with his arm around his wife, gazing toward Gabriola, Ethan could see it too, the moonlit, meteor-bright night before them. They would walk along the shore, or the road, arm in arm, it didn't matter whether they saw the house, or the lot tonight, they'd see them in the morning anyhow. Now he saw their two figures, small, detached, standing on the lonely shore, with the burning tree stumps red and sullen behind them, among the black trees, and the sky blazing with silver moonlight and gold meteors. They would watch until the shower was nearly over, and then they would walk back, with the October night wind rising and the night full of the rushing noises of surf, now he saw clotted clouds of silver, and a wild black sea with silver breakers rushing and roaring against the rocky shore. The burning tree was flaming in the rising wind, sparks were blowing, spouting, rising and spiralling into the black forest; the small fires around the stump that had been only glowing dully were flaring and blazing like red lightning, red smoke blew, stinging the nostrils, boiling up through the trees from little fires running along the ground and hot underfoot. Now they left the fires and walked along the beach in the stinging cold salt air and shifting, changing moonlight under the blowing clouds. There were a few lights, far out to sea, that disappeared as the dark waves mounted and dropped, a lonely lighthouse light blinking, and one far freighter. They passed a few dark houses where people slept, unconscious of the night and this beauty and the dark north wind, and now the fires and the bittersweet cedar smoke smell were left behind and there was only the wild beach, with driftwood white and huge as the lashed bones of dinosaurs, a last burst of meteors, stars were falling all through the sky, a bird was calling in this wind, through this silver midnight of driftwood and burning trees, and the wind and the wind and the wind—

The shadow of the mountains had lengthened across the sea, already overpowering the ferryboat, enveloping the Llewelyns as they stood alone at the rail, and reaching out ahead toward Gabriola. Beneath them the sea looked greenish black, then black as India ink, the white bow wave breaking and foaming sternward along its edge then, aft, flattening out like marble.

They were passing the other lighthouse—and this too, he thought again, could be someone's dream of home—another whitewashed cylindrical red-topped structure resting on a rocky point, and already sending forth its regular beam of hope and warning and invitation.

"There," Ethan said suddenly. "Now you can see it all. There's Gabriola for you."

The island lay before them in the last of the sunset light, a long dark shape, spiked with pines against the fading sky. There was no splendor of gold and scarlet maples, it was a splendor of blackness, of darkness. And as they approached, there seemed no beach, just the high, foolhardy cliffs dropping straight into the sea. Behind Nanaimo the sky turned a sullen smouldering red: the mountains on the mainland melted into the twilight. Then the last light was gone and Gabriola too lay in the immense shadow. The wind blew sharp and salt and cold.

Gabriola . . . Ah, how wild and lonely and primeval and forbidding it looked! Not a light glimmered, not a house shone through the trees, there was nothing but the cliffs, so high the trees on the top seemed dwarfed, mere broken bottles guarding the rim, the cliffs, and the uproar of the black sea at their base.

Ethan and Jacqueline stood close together, staring at Gabriola.

Abruptly the little ferry rounded the jutting headland: at the same moment there burst forth a shattering din and everyone clapped their hands to their ears. It was the ferry, blasting on its siren with a deep, protracted chord of mournful triumph. In the sky some stars came out. Capella, Fomalhaut, in the south, low over the sea, then Algol and Mira.

And now through the twilight as the echoes died away Jacqueline and Ethan distinguished the outlines of a sheltered valley that sloped down to a silent, calm harbor. Deep in the dark forest behind was the glow of a fire with red sparks ascending like a fiery fountain; yes, someone *was* burning tree stumps to clear his land. The sound of lowing cattle was borne to them and they could see a lantern swinging along close to the ground. A voice called out, clear, across the water. And now they saw the dock, with silhouetted figures moving against a few lights that gleamed in the dusk . . .

Editor's Note

In October of 1946 Malcolm and I took the boat from Vancouver to Victoria, the bus from Victoria to Nanaimo, and the Ferry to Gabriola Island, British Columbia. As always we took notes, and when we returned we decided we had a short story, which we wrote together. But we decided it wasn't really first rate and it was put aside.

In 1951, Malcolm wrote from Dollarton, British Columbia, to his agent Harold Matson: *"October Ferry to Gabriola,* another novella, a first version of which we wrote in collaboration for you though it didn't come off. This I've completely redrafted and largely rewritten, and it deals with the theme of eviction, which is related to man's dispossession, but this theme is universalized. This I believe to be a hell of a fine thing."

In January of 1953 Malcolm wrote from Vancouver, British Columbia, to Harold Matson: ". . . with a rewritten (and I hope terrific) *October Ferry to Gabriola* as the current and besetting problem that has engrossed and forestalled, obsessed and delighted me for months and is still a problem child, for it grew to a novel on its own and is still not quite subdued and cut to size."

Malcolm later wrote a long letter to Albert Erskine from Dollarton, British Columbia, in October of 1953, which dealt entirely with *October Ferry to Gabriola* and his struggles to get it into the right form.

On April 29, 1957, he wrote from The White Cottage, Sussex, England, to Ralph Gustafson: ". . . that makes me set a touchstone impossibly high, as a result of which I am now writing a huge and sad novel about Burrard Inlet called *October Ferry to Gabriola.*"

Malcolm died in June of 1957.

In 1961 I published a volume of Malcolm's short stories, *Hear Us O Lord from Heaven Thy Dwelling Place,* and subsequently in collaboration with Dr. Earle Birney, the *Selected Poems* (City Lights, San Francisco) and "Lunar Caustic" in the *Paris Review,* Winter–Spring 1963.

By about 1962 or '63 I had started work on *October Ferry* and was sorting out the various versions of chapters, paragraphs, and even sentences. In March 1964, *Show* magazine published *The Element Follows You Around, Sir!,* which comprises three long chapters of the book.

The editing of the *Selected Letters,* with Harvey Breit, delayed further work on *October Ferry* for awhile, and the editing of *Dark as the Grave Wherein My Friend Is Laid,* with Dr. Douglas Day, took some time. But about a year ago I started the final editing of this book. Within months I had a working copy, and soon after the edition as it now stands.

And, finally, there are two themes unfinished in the book that I could not include without some writing myself, which I felt I should not do; every word must be Malcolm's. First, the character of The McCandless, introduced in the early chapters, was meant to be enlarged upon and follow through the book. Second, and perhaps even more vital, the actual reason for Ethan's retreat to the beach was because when he was practicing law in Vancouver, after he and Jacqueline left Niagara-on-the-Lake, he defended a man whom he believed innocent, only to discover he was guilty of a monstrous and hideous murder. It was this experience that scarred Ethan and made him, for the time being, sickened with the law as practiced; hence, his retreat. This is never brought out in the book but it was his intention. We discussed it many, many times and never decided on which way would be the best to bring it out, so there are not even any notes covering it.

Margerie Lowry